THIS IS THE WAY IT W

He had lost a lot of good friends in '88, and the United States had been defeated on the battlefield, obviously, finally, in a way that could not be denied, explained away, or glossed over, the first war in her 212-year history.

They'd fought a determined, well-trained, well-armed and well-equipped enemy, and they had left enormous stacks of dead Arabs and Russians, but they were, of course, still retreating. So they lost a lot of men. . . .

It was odd that he thought of it now in such dispassionate terms. But then, of course, it wouldn't do to let oneself think of it in passionate terms, because they would be very passionate terms indeed; so he deadened his feelings about the matter and survived.

He was still surviving in a very different America. And still fighting a very different enemy. . . .

SPURLOCK: SHERIFF OF PURGATORY

JIM MORRIS

SPURLOCK: SHERIFF OF PURGATORY

TOR

A TOM DOHERTY ASSOCIATES BOOK

SPURLOCK: SHERIFF OF PURGATORY

Copyright © 1987 by Jim Morris

First printing: April 1987

A TOR Book

Published by Tom Doherty Associates, Inc.
49 West 24 Street
New York, N.Y. 10010

Cover art by Royo

ISBN: 0-812-50683-9
CAN. ED.: 0-812-50684-7

Printed in the United States of America

0   9   8   7   6   5   4   3   2   1

This book is dedicated to
the late Foster Harris and
Dwight V. Swain
Teachers and Friends

CHAPTER ONE

NUDE, THE sheriff of Purgatory County, Arkansas, stood in a yoga headstand, balanced precariously on a mat above the uneven dirt beside his marijuana patch. It was an old mat, one that had come to him as a gift a number of years before when he first took up the practice of yoga, long before he became sheriff. One by one the heartbeats ticked off as blood left his feet, oozing brainward. The headstand was one of his favorite exercises, and frequently when he became tired he would do one on top of his desk, down at the courthouse.

Harley Simrod, his deputy, and Clara, the clerk-secretary, had been amused, but the sheriff paid them no mind and they got used to it, as they got used to so many of his odd ways. He was a good sheriff, though unorthodox.

In his headstand the sheriff enjoyed the rush of blood to the upper extremities of his body, and the rest and relaxation afforded the feet and ankles. He also appreciated the mild breeze that tickled the hairs on his body. It made him feel wild and good and close to God, and that was a feeling he sought whenever possible. His position as sher-

iff did not afford many opportunities, even in a quiet place
like Purgatory.

In the past the sheriff had tried to keep the county quiet
by draconian measures, but now he had mellowed in the
job and learned new techniques. He had not carried a
weapon in three years.

When the time ran out on the headstand, the sheriff
came down slowly and sort of melted into a position in
which he was seated on his heels, knees also on the mat. It
was a difficult posture for him, which was one of the
reasons he kept it up. After a few moments his leg muscles
loosened and he began to feel comfortable. Still in that
kneeling position, he went into an *asana*, or posture,
known as the Lion. It is the most ridiculous-looking of all
yoga postures, requiring the yogi to bug out his eyes as far
as possible and stick out his tongue, also as far as possible.

When he opened his eyes to go into the Lion, he noticed
Harley leaning against a tree, off to one side. Harley was
hand rolling a tobacco cigarette. He would have probably
preferred to roll a joint, but the sheriff was dead set against
smoking weed or drinking on duty.

The sheriff ignored Harley and continued his exercises,
knowing that Harley would not have come out if it were
not important but that had it been an emergency, he would
already have interrupted.

Harley fired up the nail in his mouth and inhaled deeply.
He favored Prince Albert, brought in by convoy from
Nashville and disseminated thence from Fayetteville by
drummers who traveled in heavily armed pairs throughout
northwest Arkansas. It was expensive, but as Harley pointed
out, the locally grown tobacco was unsmokable.

The sheriff didn't know about that. All he smoked was
grass, and that only socially. He grew his own and it was
dynamite.

It was another half hour before he came out of his

meditation and stood up to put on his clothes, neatly folded beside the mat.

"Okay, Harley," he said, pulling on an old pair of jeans, "what's the story?"

As the sheriff completed his costume of western shirt, jeans jacket, rough-out shitkickers, and a straw western hat, Harley leaned back against the tree and drew on his cigarette. "That Senigliero fella's comin' in this afternoon, Shurf. Clara taken a message off the radio. He's comin' in from Fayetteville by convoy, motorcycle escort, gun jeep, and the whole nine yards."

The sheriff smiled sardonically. Mostly that crap was for show. Senigliero was some sort of big-time bad-ass with the Maf, down from New York to inspect the Hot Springs operation. He had fended off the Hot Springs guys successfully, but now the big man was coming in from New York on an inspection tour, and apparently he was going to throw in a trip to Purgatory to show the locals how it was done.

The sheriff was not especially eager to make Senigliero's acquaintance. He was a third-generation Mafia don with a Harvard education and a reputation for ferocity that had reached all the way to Arkansas. He was said to have two nicknames in the organization: Porky Pig, because he was short, fat, and stuttered, and the Disintegrator, because people who opposed him tended to disappear without a trace. The sheriff was not completely sure, but he was concerned he might be overmatched this time.

He was bringing all those guns for status. You didn't need all that to go from Purgatory to Fayetteville. It was only fifty miles and the drummers traveled in pairs with maybe a couple of Thompsons. The sheriff could never understand the attraction of a Thompson. They were heavy and so was the ammo. He himself usually made the run to Fayetteville on a motorcycle, with a couple of grenades and a CAR-15 assault rifle. And, of course, a radio. He had only been bothered once, and he supposed the word had got around after that.

The sheriff got up from pulling on his boots, rolled up the mat, and slid it under a strap behind his horse's saddle. Harley got up and walked to where his own horse was grazing next to the sheriff's. They mounted and rode away from the marijuana patch, down a quiet country lane which led toward Highway 51 and back to Purgatory.

"Shurf," Harley said, "you ain't goin' to let them Maf move into Purgatory, are you?"

The sheriff looked at Harley and grinned. "Well, yes and no," he replied carefully. Harley shook his head and looked reproachfully at the sheriff.

"Shurf, we cain't do it. Them bastards come in here and they'll brang in skag and high-roller gamblin' and whores and all that and first thang ya know Purgatory's gonna be a sufferin' hellhole, just like almost ever'place else in the United States of Amurka in nineteen and ninety-six."

Nineteen and ninety-six. Sometimes Harley overdid the goat roper routine. The sheriff smiled, feeling his horse move under him and admiring the light through the trees in the country lane. "By God, you're right, Harley." He gave Harley a look of feigned surprise. "Tell you what. Soon's we get back to town, you and me, we'll get us a couple of M-60 machine guns each, out of the arms room. Then we'll go up on the roof of the courthouse with those and maybe an eighty-one-millimeter mortar, and when Senigliero's convoy comes in, we'll open up on 'em and kill 'em all. That's all we have to do. We'll just kill 'em."

Harley's eyes widened in horror. "Shurf!" he exclaimed, and his inflection went higher at the end and his face went white. "We cain't do that. If we kill all them guys, the Maf'll send a hundred guns down here, kill us all, and burn the town to the ground."

Laughing inside, the sheriff turned his head aside, pursed

his lips, and snapped his fingers. The horse did a little skip. "Darn!" the sheriff said. "You're right, Harley. We can't do that. Seemed so simple, too."

Realizing he'd been taken for a ride, Harley shook his head and looked to his boss for leadership. "What're we gonna do, Shurf?"

The sheriff shrugged and looked into Harley's eyes. "We're gonna do what everybody always does, Harley. We're gonna do the best we can with what we've got and trust in God that our cause is just."

Harley snickered cynically. "That's what we done in eighty-eight and look what it got us."

"Yeah," the sheriff nodded, remembering '88 with a particular pang. He had lost a lot of good friends in '88, and the United States had been defeated on the battlefield, obviously, finally, in a way that could not be denied, explained away, or glossed over, the first war in her 212-year history.

They'd fought a determined, well-trained, well-armed, and well-equipped enemy. In the sheriff's battalion they had fought them well, and consequently they had been the last out in every retreat, and they had left enormous stacks of dead Arabs and dead Russians, but they were, of course, still retreating. Some of the other battalions, the ones not fighting rearguard actions, had lost upwards of 50 and 75 percent of their men. They had lost them to raids and ambushes and air attack. But mostly they had lost them because they couldn't soldier their way out of a damp paper bag.

They had lost them because the mothers of America and the Congress of the United States had complained every time one of the kids bitched about extra KP or because they had to march twenty miles and their feet hurt or the nasty old sergeants talked bad to them. The kids screamed and the parents trembled, the parents screamed and Congress trembled, Congress screamed and the generals trembled, and the generals screamed and . . . oh, well, you get the idea.

So the kids had a pretty good deal until it was time to ship out and they looked at each other and realized they'd come into the army not knowing what to do or how to do it and now they were going into combat the same way. Some of them tried very hard to catch up, but by then it was too late. And of course their officers were the sort who would tolerate such a situation.

The sheriff's battalion had not been like that. As a paratroop unit it had been composed entirely of volunteers. When he thought back on it, the sheriff realized that there had never been assembled in one place, at one time, at least in his experience, a more neurotic or bitter group of young men. They had arrived at their bitterness and neuroses in the usual ways. Their parents didn't understand them, or they had been royally screwed in some way.

The mentally healthy and well-adjusted draftees in the other battalions had been well scrubbed, happy, earnest children, out to do their best as long as it was neither difficult nor dangerous. The ones in the sheriff's battalion had only wanted to kill somebody to get even for all the wrongs, real or imaginary, they'd been done; or maybe just because they had a different metabolic setup than the rest of them. Anyway, they'd all volunteered to be jumpers and been placed under the command of a madman who had them out for bayonet training every afternoon, the troops screaming, "*Kill! Kill! Kill!*" while their commander stood off to the side, laughing like an idiot.

If those kids were crazy, the commander was utterly mad, and the rest of the officers and NCOs were worse. They'd all got killed, of course, but they'd seemed to be having a good time until then and the sheriff had gotten into the swing of it, too.

It got to be a drag after a while, though. All you had to do to kill them in droves was pull a trigger. It was no test of skill or talent. It was just a test of your ability to keep pulling a trigger long after the novelty wore off.

Incoming fire had been a negative factor, too. For eight solid months he had survived in a matrix of flying steel.

It was odd that he thought of it now in such dispassionate terms. But then, of course, it wouldn't do to let oneself think of it in passionate terms, because they would be very passionate terms indeed; so he deadened his feelings about the matter and survived.

They had lost a lot of people. They'd started out with over seven hundred and the sheriff had been a buck-ass private, owing largely to the matter of a hash deal in Rabat. When the war was over and the surrender signed, the sheriff was the executive officer and they were down to fewer than a hundred men, only thirty-six of them from the original seven hundred.

So the sheriff had reason to remember the war with bitterness, but he only said, "We got what we deserved, Harley. That's all anybody ever gets, so let's hope we don't deserve what Mr. Senigliero wants to give us."

CHAPTER TWO

THEY RODE in silence until they reached the outskirts of town. The highway was badly pockmarked by mortar rounds and poorly patched with rough gravel and bad asphalt. There was an old guard tower, left over from when they'd maintained a guerrilla watch, before the sheriff had made his peace with the guerrillas.

They passed Ed Taylor's old Texaco station. There wasn't any gas now. There was only gas for a couple of days a month, when the convoy came through from Fayetteville, or sometimes Joplin, Missouri, which was about the same distance the other way. But Ed made a fair living selling kerosene for lamps and cordwood for stoves, for the townsfolk who didn't cut their own wood. He sat back in an old cane-backed chair in front of the store, wearing bib overalls and an orange hunting cap, whittling. He looked up as the sheriff and Harley rode by.

The sheriff touched the brim of his hat and nodded. "Mornin', Mr. Taylor," he said. He and Ed Taylor had been more than acquaintances and less than friends for over twenty years, with time out for the war; but he still

14

maintained a kind of formality with most of the people in
the town when he was on duty. He wanted them to know
that the law was impartial.

"Mornin', Mr. Spurlock," Taylor responded to the sheriff's salutation. It had taken a long time for Ed Taylor to
start calling him Mister. He had been running that station
when the sheriff hitchhiked into Purgatory twenty-three
years before, a scared, skinny kid running from a corpora-
tion lawyer father who had wanted to make him a corpora-
tion lawyer, too.

All he wanted to do then was stay high and get balled.
He'd heard there was a commune outside Purgatory that
would accept strays if you were willing to work. He hadn't
been so sure about the work part, but if it wasn't corpora-
tion law, it was worth a try, so here he came.

He had become a communard farmer and taken up with
a girl from New York who drifted in. The only things
they had in common were that they were the only two
people there who had ever been east of the Mississippi,
and they were good in bed together. Then they had her
pregnancy in common and got married. Another kid later
and he got drafted and she went back to New York. After
the war he came home and took the first job he was
offered, deputy sheriff.

She came with him and stood it for a while, but she
missed the excitement of the city, and you could travel
then, so she had, with the kids. He had a couple of
pictures of the kids. They were six and eight when the
pictures were taken, and would be fourteen and sixteen
now. They were cute kids, and that's all he knew about
them. He wished it was different and he could be a father
to them, but it wasn't and he couldn't. He sometimes
thought it would be good to go get the kids, but there was
no way to do it. He'd have to fight his way across fifteen
hundred miles of guerrillas and feudal police, like himself,
only in most cases not so nice.

On the outskirts of town they rode past Delcey's Café, run by Delcey Creech and her husband, Elroy. The food wasn't much, but they sold homemade beer and moonshine hooch, and for that matter, grass by the joint or the lid, and organic mescaline and psilocybin. They ran a few girls in the back. The sheriff had a deal with the Creeches. They could do anything they wanted, but they had to make sure it didn't become a problem for him and it didn't get in the way of the good church folks. Delcey's was on the outskirts of town and it had a lot of open land between it and the next building.

It was warm and there were tables outside. Riding by, he noted a few guerrillas in their raggedy uniforms, hoisting a glass in the afternoon. He glanced over and saw no weapons, so he rode on.

One of them lurched to his feet and walked out to the dirt street to meet the sheriff and Harley.

The sheriff reined up to let the guerrilla come out and talk. He recognized the man. In fact, he had fought him before in one of the battles for the town, and unless he was mistaken, he had shot him. He was a squad leader in the remnant of a ranger company that had deserted rather than accept their defeat and a discharge. They had sworn to fight to the finish and would not accept that the finish was sixteen years before.

Now they were really just bandits. God knows they were nothing like a revolutionary force. There was no support for a revolution. The government was not oppressive here. It wasn't organized well enough to be repressive, so the people were left alone and they treated the "guerrillas" like bandits and the Gs treated them like victims when they caught them on the roads. But in town the guerrillas were tourists.

A few of them were still believers in the revolution, though. Their captain was like that, still lost in his revolutionary dream.

But not in Purgatory.

That was the nature of the truce the sheriff had worked out with them eight years before. When they came into town, they checked their guns at the sheriff's office and they were free to do as they liked. They bought a few supplies, but no weapons and no ammo. Technically the arrangement was illegal, but it kept the town free from attack, attacks that had killed a lot of people for no good reason. Mostly the Gs came into town and bought their stuff and went over to Delcey's and got laid and drunk or stoned, usually drunk, and headed on back out for the hills on horseback.

The sheriff felt kind of sorry for them. Many of them had started out really believing the countryside would rise up and support them. Now they were wanted for treason and they were stuck out there. He wasn't sorry for the one staggering out in the road now, though. The man was a killer and if the sheriff ever caught him in the woods, he would be in a lot of trouble.

He lurched out in his old jungle fatigues and his beat-up old boots and waved his hand at the sheriff. "Hey, Spurlock!" he called.

The sheriff reined up and nodded. "Hello, Martinez," he said quietly. "What can we do for you?"

Martinez let out a dry cackle, his eyes boring wildly into the sheriff's, and he groped quickly under the grimy uniform jacket. The sheriff was off the horse and onto Martinez before the hand with the pistol came back out. He grabbed the barrel of the pistol and bent back quickly, breaking Martinez's trigger finger. He screamed in pain and amazement.

Leaving him there on the ground, the sheriff walked over and picked up the weapon, an old Smith & Wesson .38. Some poor devil on the highway patrol must have been caught in an ambush. He checked that the hammer was on an empty chamber and put it in his hip pocket.

Then he walked back over to Martinez. The rest of the guerrillas at the outside tables were on their feet, but old Harley held a shotgun on them and they did nothing.

Martinez glared at him with hatred as he walked back through the dust and stood in front of him. Then the sheriff clapped a hand on Martinez's shoulder and said, "Now, Marty. I've told you boys several times that you have to turn in your weapons when you come to town. I appreciate your trying to give it to me now, but you have to do it when you get here. I'm going to have to confiscate this one, and I'm going to have to ask you all to leave now."

"Fuck you!" Martinez grated between his teeth. He spat on the ground.

The sheriff just laughed. "Give my best to Captain Frazier," he said.

Martinez shook his head again. "You asshole," he muttered.

The grin on the sheriff's face broadened. "Sorry about the finger," he said, "but I don't want you to stay in town long enough to get it fixed. You'll just have to have your medic set it for you."

"We ain't got no medic," Martinez whined.

Unheeding, the sheriff went on. "And I'd like you to ask Captain Frazier to call on me before any of the rest of you come back to town. This business of the weapon is quite serious and we need to discuss it."

"And the horse you rode to town on," Martinez called over his shoulder as he walked back to his friends. The sheriff ignored it.

"Be sure to give that message to Frazier. If anybody comes to town before him, they'll remain as my guests until he comes for them."

The sheriff mounted his horse again and he and Harley watched as the guerrillas mounted and rode off toward the sheriff's office to get their weapons, other than the pistol, of course.

Harley looked at the sheriff in some wonderment. "My God, Shurf. One of these days one o' them bastards is gonna get lucky. Why didn't you throw that'n in jail?"

The sheriff grinned. "No point, Harley, and it would have caused trouble. My deal with Frazier is not to interfere with guerrilla justice. If I'd thrown him in the slam, Frazier's just crazy enough to have rode in here with his whole bunch to get him out. In fact, he'd have had to do that to keep control of his men. But this way Marty's going to be back out there this afternoon minus one valuable weapon and with a broken finger. God only knows what Frazier's going to do to him, but I pity the poor guy. Frazier's likely enough to break the rest of his fingers for him. For sure he won't be a squad leader in the morning."

Harley went "Hummph!" and they rode off toward the courthouse.

The five guerrillas passed them on their skinny nags as they rode up to the hitching post outside. Usually they spurred their horses when they left town and let out a whoop at the city limits, but this time they left quietly.

The sheriff dismounted and sighed at the thought of the matter of Senigliero. He wished that was going to be as easy to handle as the guerrillas. When you dealt with the Mafia, you dealt with real power: military, political, and economic power. The sheriff was small potatoes indeed compared with the Maf, and the only counter he had was his brain. If he could show them it was in their interest to leave the town alone, he might have a chance to salvage something of the quiet life he and the people of Purgatory had managed to make for themselves in the midst of this chaos.

He pushed through the swinging door on the railing inside his office. Clara was typing the daily arrest log as he entered. She was a pretty young blonde. She reminded him of a slightly wacky swan. She had a degree in general fine arts from the University of Oklahoma, and as a consequence was deeply involved in the Purgatory Players.

She actually was what you could call beautiful if you were so inclined. The sheriff was not so inclined, at least not out loud. An efficient clerk was a lot harder to find than romance. With Clara the sheriff was friendly but impersonal.

She looked up from her typing and said, "Morning, Mr. Spurlock. Morning, Harley."

Harley leaned on the railing and rested his hand on his gun, reaching with the other hand for his cigarette makings in his shirt pocket. "Hiya, beautiful," he said. He had none of the sheriff's scruples about hustling the hired help, but that was okay, since he wasn't the boss.

Clara looked at Harley with exasperated fondness and tossed her head.

"Hi, Miss Clara," the sheriff said as he walked past her desk.

She looked at him with a slightly gaga expression.

"Hon," he went on, touching her lightly on the shoulder, "could you brew up a pot of that coffee you got hid? We got an important guest comin' in a while and we want to be hospitable."

He went over to the old coatrack in the corner and took his .45, hanging in its Marine Corps shoulder holster, and draped it over his frame like a pullover sweater.

"Hospitable, huh?" she said, eyeing the pistol, which he hadn't worn for three years except for target practice. She got up and went to the safe to get the coffee. It was the last can of coffee in Purgatory, and it was half empty.

The sheriff grinned. "This pistol's just for show. I don't want the bastard to think he's got us intimidated."

She looked over her shoulder, kneeling by the open door of the safe. "Does he?"

The sheriff nodded. "Does he what, have us intimidated? Yes, I'm afraid he does. But maybe we can deal with him anyway. Worth a try."

Her face formed a question, but she didn't ask it. The sheriff never revealed his plans in advance. They were always only half formed anyway and they depended on an awful lot of last-minute corrections for the situation. He had found it futile to form a hard-and-fast plan that depended on other people acting in a certain way. They never did.

The sheriff went on into his office and unlocked the gun rack, getting out his scope-sighted CAR-15 and a shotgun. He threw the twelve-gauge to Harley, leaning in his door, and said, "Okay, let's go up on the roof."

Worried, Harley asked, "Are you goin' to start somethin', Shurf? I thought you wasn't."

The sheriff shook his head. "Huh-uh!" he said. "I just want them to know they aren't dealing with a bunch of patsies. They know we don't have the power to fight them and win, but if they think we're crazy enough to fight them anyway, they'll have to consider whether it's worth it or not."

Harley nodded.

The sheriff walked outside to the fire escape. He and Harley rattled up the old steel stairs to the top of the ancient stone courthouse that had been there for over 130 years. There had been a move afoot in the late sixties to tear it down and replace it with a more "modern," which is to say cramped and ugly, substitute. The city council had voted it down, not on grounds of aesthetics, but on grounds of economy, and instead had placated their contractor patrons with a remodeling job, which had turned out fairly well.

The sheriff took the ladder over the top and walked over the tar and gravel roof, gravel sticking to the soles of his shitkickers as he walked. He sat down on the ancient ledge that looked out over the courthouse lawn, the Civil War statue and the plaques in honor of the Spanish-American, World War I, World War II, Korean, Vietnam, Central American, and Middle Eastern dead. We get any more of them plaques, he thought, and there ain't going to be any grass left. He pushed the straw hat down over his eyes, reached in his pocket and rolled a toothpick into the corner of his mouth, then extended the stock on the CAR-15 so he could fire aimed shots, or look like he intended to.

Opening the stock didn't make much noise, but when Harley sat down and jacked back the pump on the twelve-gauge, the two old duffers whittling on the bench in front of the courthouse looked over their shoulders, got up, and strolled casually down to the pool hall a block down the street. It was well out of the line of fire, but had a good view of the courthouse lawn. A few minutes later they came back out front with a pair of heavy wooden chairs and sat down in front of the pool hall, took out their case knives, and started whittling. One of them spat a stream of tobacco juice past the gutter and into the street. Then a crowd of younger men drifted out of the pool hall. Some of them brought chairs to sit in, but most of them were leaners. They stood with their weight on one hip and folded their arms or put their hands on their hips and every so often they shifted their weight. None of them was armed. Nobody went armed in Purgatory, except Harley sometimes. The sheriff could have, but he thought it was a nuisance.

The last man out of the pool hall was Theron Himes, the proprietor, burly and glowering because there wasn't going to be any business until this thing was over.

He looked up at the sheriff on the roof. "Hey, Spurlock!" he bellowed, "you want us to go get our guns?"

The sheriff grinned. "Not unless the shootin' starts," he called back as nonchalantly as he could under the circumstances. He appreciated the offer, though. These were

good people and they'd fight without thought for the consequences to keep their lives like they wanted them.

"Damn," Theron called back. "By the time we could
get back you and Harley'd be dead."

The sheriff laughed. "Yeah," he yelled again, "that's
why we get paid so much."

The whole gang in front of the pool hall laughed at that.
They weren't worried anymore, at least not too much. If
Spurlock had it under control, that was good enough for
them.

He wished to Christ it was good enough for him. He
didn't have it under that good a control. It wasn't that he
was just worried about his personal survival or keeping his
job. He could live off the commune again, if it came to
that, and be happy doing it. No, if the Maf came to
Purgatory, the town wouldn't be fit to live in and it was
the last place he knew of that was.

One end of his toothpick was pretty well chewed by
then. He switched ends.

It was hot up there on the roof and they had to wait for
quite a while, but finally he felt a tingle along his spine
that told him it wouldn't be much longer. He knew there
was some sensory input somewhere that told him Senigliero
was coming, because although he believed in telepathy and
clairvoyance and all of that, he was pretty sure he didn't
have any of it. Not enough to count anyway; but he knew
something was coming.

If the road to Fayetteville had been dirt, he could have
told by the column of dust a long way off, but it was paved,
though badly pockmarked. Maybe there was a sound, but
he was pretty sure he couldn't hear the sound of an auto-
mobile engine a couple of miles off. The best answer he
was finally able to come up with was that although he
himself couldn't pick anything up, the animals could.

There was not much vehicular traffic around here these

days. It had been over a week since some trucks and an
armored car had come through. He figured the birds and
the squirrels were picking up on each other's excitement,
and maybe he could subconsciously pick up a difference in
their twitterings and chatterings. Anyway he knew for sure
that something was coming and he straightened his spine
and looked down the street with more alertness. Harley
picked up his tension and he too became more alert.

Then around the bend on the edge of town came an
escort of four motorcycles, the riders all with Thompsons
slung over their shoulders like guitars. The sheriff snorted.
They had them slung over their left shoulders so they
could fire and continue to work the throttle at the same
time. If they ever opened up, they'd be damned lucky if
they didn't kill each other, let alone their enemy, whoever
it might be.

Behind them was a slick, fairly new jeep with a pedestal-
mount .30-caliber machine gun manned by either the brav-
est or most stupid, or both, man the sheriff had ever seen.

Behind that was an '84 Cadillac, well tuned and shined
to a fare-thee-well. Behind that were four more bikes, all
Harley 74 choppers rigged in the Hell's Angels manner.

The riders were even dressed like those antebellum motorcycle greasers, only considerably spiffed up. Their jeans
and jackets were clean and they all wore shiny black
helmets. The design of the colors on the back of their
jackets was a black hand with the word "Mafia" in old
English script above, "M.C." below, and "Hot Springs,
Ark." under that. They were all clean-shaven and looked
like somebody's palace guard, which in fact they were.

The little convoy roared up in front of the courthouse
going about thirty-five. There was a quick beep on the
horn from the Cadillac and the whole shebang stopped in
front of the Civil War statue.

The bikers had their kickstands down and took up their

Thompsons, switched back to the right hand for something approximating an aimed shot, in about ten seconds. The four guys in the gun jeep were out and on the ground, and the clown behind the .30 looked around as though for a target.

The gang down at the pool hall took all of this in with stoic calm, glaring at the hoods as though they were an interesting brand of new fauna for the zoo.

All four doors on the Cadillac exploded simultaneously, and four hoods in black uniforms with black boots, high-collared tunics, and Sam Browne belts got out. They wore brand-new, clean high-top butch haircuts and not hats, and three of them were armed with Thompsons. The one who got out of the right front seat seemed to have a little better idea of what he was about. He looked older and a little heavier and moved a little slower, but more alertly. And as he got out, instead of glaring up the streets and down the streets like the others, he began checking out the rooftops. Like the sheriff, he carried a scope-mounted rifle. Only his was an M-14 instead of the truncated model the sheriff had. Doing his job, that's what Spurlock would have carried, too. The guy picked out the sheriff and Harley immediately, and sighted in on Spurlock with the scope on the rifle.

Spurlock repressed a momentary shudder. It would be simplicity itself for the fellow to pull the trigger and you could scratch one rural sheriff. But as he had assessed the situation, they would not do that. The fact that the guy looked at him through the scope told him two things: that he had no particular regard for another man's life or feelings and that he felt pretty damn sure of himself. The sheriff would have liked to have that feeling, too. He grinned around the toothpick clenched in his teeth and the AR was lowered, the gunman favoring him with a wry smile.

Then the great man himself dismounted from the Cadillac. He wore a uniform similar to that of the gunman, similar to the Russian model with its high-necked tunic. The don's uniform was gray and a snazzy-looking dagger dangled from his Sam Browne belt. He too wore the high-topped butch haircut that was all the rage in the cities now that the goddamned Russians were in the saddle. The sheriff shook his head and his brown mane whipped back and forth across his back. It felt good. He was an old-fashioned kind of guy.

Senigliero looked to be about fifty years old. He looked like an old gray shark. He looked up at the roof and threw the sheriff a harsh glance. "S-spurlock?" he called up.

"That's right!" the sheriff called back, repressing a smile.

"I want to s-s-see you!" It was a command and it brooked no resistance, in spite of the stutter.

The sheriff smiled. It was important not to lose face, but it was important that Senigliero not lose any either. If that happened they would take the town and there would be nothing he could do because in fact he would be dead. This was a very delicate balancing act indeed. "Meet me in my office," Spurlock called down. "We can sit and talk, and I've got the last pot of coffee in Purgatory." Hospitable, but not conciliatory, that was the ticket.

Senigliero glared for a second, then whipped his head toward the courthouse and started up the steps. Spurlock and Harley went over to the ladder and started down.

All the guards but the older fellow remained in place. The one with the scoped M-14 followed Senigliero up the walk, about ten feet behind. His eyes searched everywhere.

By the time Senigliero had got up the steps and into the hall, Spurlock and Harley were back inside. The sheriff handed Harley his CAR-15 and said, "How about puttin' these back up, Harley. Then you can go and get that bunch at the pool hall to go back inside and shoot some pool."

Senigliero glared, then softened and said, "N-never expected to find a c-c-cup of coffee this far out in the sticks."

"Been savin' it," the sheriff explained.

As they went into the office, he slipped out of the shoulder holster and hung it on the old coatrack. Then he led the way into his inner office.

It was surprisingly luxurious for a rustic county sheriff, quite spacious with large windows, and the sheriff's desk was flanked by two well-stocked bookshelves, some of the books on the law or criminology, but many of them social and political analyses and some novels and not a few works on mysticism and religion.

The sheriff watched Senigliero to see if he was the sort of person who judged a man by what he read. He did not appear to be such a person. His eyes did not flicker toward the books. He still looked grim and businesslike.

There was a long couch along one wall, one that the sheriff had slept on many nights when he stayed on duty in case of guerrilla raids, and two comfortable chairs in front of the sheriff's desk.

"Sit down, gentlemen," the sheriff said, "sit down."

Senigliero sat down heavily in one of the chairs, and the bodyguard took up a post to the rear of the chair.

The sheriff went to the desk and sat leaned up against it. He didn't want to go back there and sit behind it. That would be a little like an emperor holding an audience. He did not want to give the impression that he was condescending to the Maf, nor did he want to give the opposite impression. He wanted it to seem as though it were a meeting of equals in every respect. "What can we do for you?" he inquired quietly.

At that moment the door behind them opened and Clara came in with a tray with a pot of coffee and three cups. The guard whirled and leveled on her with the M-14. She gasped, halted, but did not step back or drop the tray.

Good girl, Spurlock thought. "Come on in, honey," he said as the bodyguard lowered his weapon. She walked to the desk and put the coffee tray down.

"Would you care for cream and sugar, gentlemen?"

Senigliero, his face twisted into a perpetual tough-guy sneer, eyed her up and down with grim interest. "C-c-cream, no s-sugar," he said.

"And you, sir," she said to the guard. "Would you care for coffee?"

"No," he replied in a flat, emotionless tone.

She nodded and handed Senigliero his cup.

The sheriff had quit taking coffee a long time before it had run out, just as he had quit smoking and drinking. He wished he could cut out grass, but it was a sort of tribal rite, and a certain amount was protocol. Nonetheless he took a heavily creamed and honeyed cup from Clara, just to be sociable.

Senigliero took a sip and nodded, cocking his head to one side. "This is quite good," he said.

Spurlock nodded, pleased that he seemed to be loosening up a little, took a sip of his own, set the cup down, and said, "Weed?"

Senigliero looked up to see the sheriff extending a silver cigarette case with a row of rolled reefers in it. He considered for a moment, then took one. The sheriff ripped a kitchen match across the sole of his boot and lit the joint.

Senigliero took a deep hit and held the smoke. He sat attentively for a moment, then his eyes bulged slightly as the first rush hit him. He let the smoke out in a gasp and said, "Th-this is good shit."

"Thanks. I grew it myself." The sheriff took a shallow hit and held the smoke for a long moment. It was, in fact, very good shit, but he had to deal with this man, and didn't want to be wrecked because he was going to have to do some good analytical thinking if they were going to survive this day.

Senigliero too was smoking more cautiously now, because he had got off on the first hit and he knew if he wasn't careful not only would the sheriff not surrender the town but Senigliero would leave without his boots, and perhaps without his store teeth.

Spurlock was mildly pleased with the way things were going at this point. Senigliero had come in here ready to break his spine, and while they weren't exactly old buddies they weren't snarling at each other either.

Suddenly Senigliero seemed to wake out of a dream he had fallen into, stubbed out the reefer, and sat up in his chair, frowning. "I'll come straight to the p-point, S-spurlock. I sent for you in Hot Springs and you didn't show. We had business to discuss. You don't seem to appreciate the kind of t-trouble you're in. The Maf doesn't like to be kept waiting. And it doesn't like to have to come down to see little county sh-sh-sh-sheriffs in hick towns." He leaned back in his chair, his deep eyes boring into the sheriff's. His mouth was hard.

Spurlock put a toe to the opposite heel and one at a time pushed his boots off. Then he assumed the lotus position on top of his desk and took a small sip of coffee. He considered for a moment whether it would demonstrate weakness to apologize. He decided it would.

Senigliero, for his part, continued to glare, and scowled at having one of his threatenees nonchalantly bend himself up like a pretzel. It certainly followed no scenario with which he was familiar.

Or was that just Spurlock's imagination?

"It's seldom that I'm able to be very far from town," the sheriff said. "And then not for very long. We are ringed by hostile guerrillas here and the town depends on me to organize its defense. Also, as I explained in my reply, the people of Purgatory are not interested in any way in any of the services offered by your organization." He cocked his head, narrowing an eyebrow.

"We lead a quiet life here. Nobody could afford a skag habit. What gambling there is consists of four or five guys who get together to play poker on a Saturday night. As for women, we have women. Most everybody has a relationship, either as part of a pair or group marriage, and for them as don't and want something else there's three whores over at Creech's café, though why anybody would want to jump one of them is beyond me. We don't object to any of that as long as the people aren't bothered. Such dope as is done we grow our own. We don't object to any part of the Maf's business. What we object to is the size of it. We have no big business here of any sort. We don't want any, nor any big government either. The Maf is a big business, and we all live here just to avoid that sort of thing. I don't think you people could take enough out of this town to make back what you put into it. I really don't understand why you want to mess with Purgatory at all." He lowered his eyebrows to half-mast and waited for a reply.

Senigliero reached into his breast pocket for an honest-to-God tailor-made tobacco cigarette and lit it with a gold lighter. "B-b-because it's about th-th-the only place left we don't run. This and f-five or six other p-places. W-we intend to c-consolidate our control b-before th-the wave starts r-rolling back the other w-way." He took a deep drag off his cigarette.

"W-we don't usually listen to a bunch of j-jive from p-p-people like you, Spurlock. W-we usually break them," he said. "N-now, I could have Cl-Clarence"—he inclined his head toward the guard—"hammer your bones to jelly, and there's nobody in this town who could stop him. B-b-but I don't want to make threats. I came to talk business. You don't seem the sort who threatens easily anyway."

Spurlock smiled at the oil Senigliero had poured on the steel and gave Clarence a level glance, which Clarence returned. He had a little reach on Clarence, and Clarence had a little weight on him; the sheriff was maybe five years younger. They were fairly evenly matched. Undoubtedly Clarence had a big rep in Hot Springs, but he wasn't in Hot Springs now. The sheriff smiled a little at Senigliero's threat. Whatever the outcome, Clarence wasn't going to hammer his bones to jelly. He might win, but by the time he did it, he wouldn't be in shape to hammer anything.

He had known this moment would come, and he had hoped to avoid it. Conciliation was one thing, but the appearance of weakness was quite another. This man had threatened his life and his duty and he had to reply in kind. And make it sound like he believed it. There was a brief skip in his thinking.

Of course everything he said was true, so he did believe it, but he could not think of a more disastrous course of action to follow than the one he was about to describe to Senigliero.

The sheriff had tried to calm the rages in his soul. He had tried to make himself into a good, kind, and religious man. In the main he had succeeded. But he knew that none of these aspects of himself would have any effect on Senigliero. If Senigliero thought he was a pushover, then the sheriff's bargaining position was blown, so he dredged back into his past to a time of complete and overpowering rage and let some of that creep into his face. His eyes narrowed.

He inhaled, let his eyes and mouth go a little crazy, and gradually he started to shake all over. He fixed Senigliero's eyes with his own.

The impassive Clarence looked at him with something like respect as he grated, "You'll break nothing. It would take me exactly thirty seconds to put this cretin"—he inclined his head toward Clarence—"in traction for a month. Your men downstairs will do nothing because they're covered by guns from half the second- and third-story win-

dows in this town, and if you want to start a war like that,
Jack, then we'll start it right by sending your bleeding
body back to Hot Springs in a Christmas package."

Senigliero sank back into his chair a little. Clarence
fidgeted behind him.

Spurlock had spoken very quietly, still in the lotus,
somewhat embarrassed by using the position he had assumed to gain calm to loose such a tirade.

"So let's not make threats, huh?" he stormed on. "I
don't threaten and neither do the people in this town. We
will fight for our freedom, and if we lose, so be it. But
what you win won't be worth keeping, and you"—he shot
out his finger and pointed it at Senigliero—"will not be
around to enjoy the fruits of your victory. You can bet I
will see to that."

Senigliero shook off the tirade. He couldn't take this
kind of hassling without a response.

As Senigliero opened his mouth to speak, the sheriff
finished in a calm, smooth manner. "Sorry, I seem to
have lost my cool there for a moment. We are business-
men after all. We are here to discuss business. I just don't
want you to think you already hold every card in the
deck."

Senigliero sneered at him. "M-my old man used to
blow up like that. Y-you may b-be tougher than w-we
thought."

The sheriff smiled slightly. "Well, I have to take threats
into consideration, just like every other factor, but it's a
point of pride with me to do my job the best I can, so I
don't cave in too easy."

Senigliero nodded coolly. He didn't cave in easily either.
"That's just my point. You want to do the best you can.
Now, I grant that you p-p-p-people have a very nice setup.
But you aren't going to have it much longer. P-p-people
are leaving the cities, man. Industry is moving into the

c-country and so is communications and g-government. The cities are jungles now and we've finally c-caught on to the fact that most office work can be done either through wire or wireless communications. M-men won't go to work in an office. They h-have an office in their h-homes and if their staffs live nearby they come there." He spoke urgently, jabbing his finger at the sheriff.

"Of course the c-closer you are, the less it c-costs, but the point is that people aren't tied to the c-cities anymore and they aren't really t-tied to the suburbs either. The people left in the inner cities and the suburbs are g-guerrillas and t-t-terrorists, j-j-junkies and petty criminals. Ev-every so often the g-g-goddamn Russians have to g-g-go in and clean out a n-n-neighborhood that the t-terrorists have taken over. That's what's h-h-happening in the cities. P-p-people have to get out."

The sheriff shuddered. That's where his kids lived.

"What's the matter?" Senigliero sneered. "You look kinda green around the gills."

Spurlock couldn't see any reason to keep it secret. "My ex-wife and kids live in New York," he said.

Senigliero grinned at him. "Old lady took off on you, huh?"

Spurlock nodded. "That's right."

"M-my old lady took off on me one time," Senigliero said. "R-ran off with a s-singer in a rock 'n' roll band."

He paused for a moment and smiled. "It took me five months to find them. When I did I made her watch while I had that bastard cut into one-inch cubes with a chainsaw." His stutter went completely away when he said it, and a weird gleam came into his eyes. He smiled. "We started with his shlang. That alone took seven cuts. Maybe that's why she left with him."

"Jesus," Spurlock said, "what did you do to her?"

"Let her go," Senigliero said. "I f-figured I'd given her something to think about. B-before she left, though, I told her that no matter how long she lived I'd live longer, because if it w-was the last thing I ever did I w-was going to piss on her grave. I d-did, too. She died in a mental hospital about eh-eight years later.

"It's a failing, I guess, but I tend to hold a grudge. Y-you ought to r-remember that."

Spurlock nodded. He didn't think he would forget it.

For a moment Senigliero looked wistful. "I d-don't think the bitch ever loved me," he said. "B-but she thought she d-did for about a year, until she found out what I was r-really like."

Spurlock found himself feeling sad for Senigliero and for his ex.

Senigliero went on as though what he had said was of no consequence.

"W-what you say about Purgatory m-may be true now, but we have to p-plan for the future. In five or t-t-ten years this little town here is going to be a haven for p-people from as far away as D-dallas and K-kansas City. It's going to fill up with a w-wealthy middle and upper class, and they're going to want the kind of s-s-services they're used to in the cities, to include c-casinos and high-class dope and high-class women." He jabbed a finger at Spurlock.

"Your little p-paradise is doomed, Spurlock, and th-there's money to be made from that kind of social up-heaval. Y-you might as well m-make some yourself." He nodded for emphasis.

So there it was, the reason he had been waiting for. It hadn't made sense before, but it did now. They wanted into Purgatory for the same reason everybody in Purgatory wanted to be there, to get away from everything the Maf represented. It was a paradox. He grimaced.

Spurlock creakily unwound himself from the lotus and walked to the window to look out on his town. He looked out on the courthouse lawn and at Senigliero's Cadillac, with the doors still open and the motor running. He grinned at that. Conspicuous consumption, show the rubes that power can do anything it wants. It was just a stupid waste, and to him it signified a decadence in the organization, rather than overwhelming power.

He reached into his shirt pocket and took out another toothpick, rolled it into the corner of his mouth, and commenced to chew. He wondered if, as he had read somewhere, the little particles of wood were bad for his throat. Jesus, you couldn't smoke, drink, screw, or cuss without doing some damage to yourself. In fact, if you did nothing at all, you died eventually anyway, so maybe there was no use to worry about it. He rolled the toothpick to the other side of his mouth.

Then there was this other thing, the thing about the cities. He could discount about 50 percent of that because Senigliero would exaggerate, but 50 percent was pretty bad. Spurlock had two kids in New York and he didn't want either of them involved in urban warfare. He had seen Beirut and he didn't want his kids in any place like that. He waggled the toothpick in his mouth.

He knew he should have gone to get them a long time ago. But the odds were that he would be killed in the process, pretty strongly that he would be, and so he had never gone to get them on the grounds that dead he would be no good to them, but sometime later he might be. He shifted his weight to the other hip.

It had obviously got to the point that there wasn't going to be any sometime later. Now was the time. He knew that once the problem at hand had been dealt with, this one would consume his entire being, and a jolt of fear ran through him when he thought about it. He scratched the back of his head, thinking it was work he could not turn down, no way. But it was almost surely going to come to a bad end. He couldn't even imagine what New York would be like with all the city services broken down and 10 million people jammed together like that, living in anarchy. He put his fist under his jaw and leaned back, propping up his elbow on the other hand and resting his jaw on his fist.

He put that thought aside and turned to the problem at hand.

From the standpoint of dealing with the Maf, that business of the cities was one of the luckiest breaks imaginable. If everybody else was leaving the cities, the Maf would be, too. And whatever else they'd mark for other places, they wouldn't want *their* kids growing up around skag and whores. If the Maf dons lived around Purgatory, they themselves would keep it clean, but at a cost of diminished freedom to the townspeople. They wanted their kids to grow up clean just like everybody else, Spurlock included. It was time to tell them about the houses.

He walked back over and sat down in the chair opposite Senigliero, since Clarence didn't seem to be using it. He flopped one leg over the arm of the chair and reversed the toothpick in his mouth. Senigliero looked at him as though he were an interesting entomological specimen.

The sheriff pursed his lips ruminatively, then sighed. "Mr. Senigliero," he said, "do you know anything about the history of this region?"

Senigliero shook his head. "N-n-not really," he said. He smiled his shark's smile.

The sheriff nodded. "It's among the most beautiful and unproductive areas in America. The land isn't fit to grow much, just subsistence farming. There is no mining or anything like that. A lot of folks around here grow chickens and sell them, and the eggs, and oh, back thirty years or so ago there used to be a mobile-home factory, but we don't have that now, not since the war."

Senigliero tapped his knee with an irritated finger, beginning to be bored with all this.

"People wanted to live here because of the beauty of the

hills," Spurlock went on, "but not many could afford to move here because there was no way to make money in the Ozarks. That's even more true today than it was twenty years ago. But there were a few people who moved here and built retirement homes. One fellow was a millionaire Ford dealer from Dallas, and there were a few others, elderly people of great wealth and nothing to do with it but move out in the hills and build these goddamned palaces for themselves to occupy while they lived out the last ten or fifteen years of their lives."

Senigliero looked at him with interest now. The sheriff nodded. "The thing about these homes is that there is no one you can sell them to. Most of the damn things required about four thousand dollars a month just to run, even back then. They required full staffs of servants and all that goes with it. You have to see them to believe them—marble hallways, crystal chandeliers, the whole works. There is literally no way they could be reproduced now at any cost. The workmanship doesn't exist anymore." He shrugged.

A tiny quirk of a smile was playing at the corners of Senigliero's mouth. "Are they st-st-still there?"

Spurlock nodded. "Yeah! Once they were built, there was no way to unload them. Nobody could keep them up but millionaires and nobody could live in them but the unproductive. Now, if you were a retired millionaire, you wouldn't want to live in somebody else's dream house, would you?"

Senigliero shook his head.

"So there they are, out there in the woods. When the old folks died off, they were mostly closed up. The guerrillas hang out there sometimes, but they can't stay too long because the army and the state police are always checking for their bases. A lot of the marble and crystal and stuff has been hauled off, but not all of it, and the basic structures are still mostly intact. It would take maybe a couple months and a few thousand dollars to put them in business again.''

Senigliero favored him with a suspicious grin. "I th-thought you were trying to keep the M-m-maf out of here.''

The sheriff grinned back. "Huh-uh. I'm trying to keep your business out of here. The only sure way I know of to keep the Maf business out of town is to have your top people come here to live, or to vacation. You don't want *your* kid to become a junkie, do you?''

Senigliero's face flushed angrily for a moment, then crumpled. He visibly forced himself to be calm.

The sheriff pursed his lips and nodded. "Well," he said quietly, "if you people move in here . . .'' He paused and arched his eyebrows. "I don't allow any addictive dope in this county and I don't think you folks want any in your own backyard.''

Senigliero glared back at him. "And wh-what do you get out of all this?''

Spurlock glared at him. "I guess I have my price like everybody else, but it's already been met. I want to live a decent life in a decent place and I'm willing to compromise with you folks to keep it that way. All I want out of it is for the Maf who live here to be good citizens.''

Senigliero smiled oddly at him. "Oh, we're always g-g-good citizens where we live. But wh-wh-what's to k-k-keep us from taking over the town and throwing you out of office and running the p-place ourselves?''

Spurlock shrugged. "Nothing. I was a dirt farmer before the war, and then they made me sheriff, and I was a field hippie before that, and I can still be any of those things or I can be nothing. It's all the same to me. But I don't think you'll throw me out of office''

Senigliero's glance was truly penetrating. "Well, mister—''

The office door slammed open violently and Clara was halfway in the door saying, "Sheriff, he won't—'' and she was brushed aside as a man who looked like a cross between Attila the Hun and George S. Patton, Jr., strode into the room. His eyes were burning sparks and the long hair shot straight out from his head and flowed down around the U.S. Army field jacket, bleached almost white from repeated washings, with the captain's bars on the epaulets and the rest of the old, patched, but still sharp uniform. His ancient, cleaned and oiled AK-74 pointed directly at Clarence, and when he said, "Drop it!" with all the calm and detachment one might expect from a clerk at the bank, Clarence dropped it with dispatch. He sighed as his weapon hit the floor.

CHAPTER THREE

"NOW LET'S see what else ya got?" the apparition grated through his teeth. He favored Spurlock with a wild grin, a wild acid-freak grin. "These clowns always got four or five weapons stashed on them." He was a bouncy little joker, his face grinning and emaciated under the cavalryman's mustache.

Slowly Clarence divested himself of his belt and his jacket. Senigliero looked at him with undisguised contempt. The threat was unspoken, but there nonetheless. He swung his glance back to the sheriff. "Y-you won't get away with this, you know. When New York hears about this, there'll be more guns down here than you ever saw before in your life. There won't be enough left of this town to build a chicken coop."

The apparition with the AK laughed wildly. "Who ya gonna bring? Some more o' them ying-yangs like you got outside?"

· Grinning, Spurlock got up and went back over to the window as the last of Clarence's visible knives and pistols clattered to the floor. The Maf heroes lay facedown in the dirt outside, and about twenty grimy, long-haired soldiers held guns on them. He turned from the window and said soothingly to Senigliero, "Don't be dismayed. This is just Captain Frazier's way of saying hello."

He turned to Frazier. "Hello, Frazier!"

Frazier favored him with a cold grin. "Hello, Spurlock. What's the idea breakin' my man's finger?"

Senigliero glared around. "Wh-who is this, anyway?"

Spurlock held his hands out, palms up. "Sorry about this interruption. This is Captain Frazier, commander of the guerrilla company here in the hills. He's a little upset because I had to chastise one of his men this afternoon." He turned to Frazier.

Frazier gestured toward a large picture of Meher Baba on the wall, one of the ones taken when he was younger and looked like a benign Frank Zappa. "Picture's crooked."

"You tripping again, Frazier?" Spurlock demanded.

Frazier grinned a little sheepishly and nodded. "Want some? It's peyote. I get it from them Indians over in Oklahoma."

Spurlock examined the picture closely. The right side was a little higher than the left, but you'd never notice it if you weren't tripping. He started to feel the effects of Frazier's trip as he thought about how it must look to Frazier, with all the colors brighter and sort of like it was through a fish-eye lens and all the irregularities emphasized. It had been a long time and would probably be longer before Spurlock did it again.

You got all sorts of insights tripping and the insight he got the last three times he had done it was that he ought to quit, and he had. But he was getting a contact high off of Frazier, who was almost glowing. Spurlock felt the beginnings of a screwy grin creeping across his own face.

Back when he was a kid they had thought that psychedelics made you peaceful because you got into the oneness of it all, but it didn't actually. The Mescalero Apaches took their name from the same root word as mescaline and they weren't exactly a bunch of pacifists.

Frazier had been a ranger company commander in an armored cavalry unit and he wore the cavalry mustache and the long hair favored by the rangers, perversely, since it got tangled in the woods, but it was a part of their Wild Bill Hickok image. And he had done a lot of acid, which was also a ranger thing, since it made them extra sensitive to signs in the jungle. If you got yourself psyched up right, it made you pretty dangerous, too.

Frazier was dangerous now, looking out through his burning eyes, wild long gray hair raining down around his shoulders. The safety was off on the AK and Frazier's finger was on the trigger and the weapon was pointed at Senigliero, and if Senigliero died, so would almost everybody in Purgatory, except the ones who made it to the woods and the tender mercies of the guerrillas.

Spurlock took two or three deep breaths and made a strong effort to keep his voice calm. In fact it was. Danger always cooled him out. He didn't know why it did, but it did. Most of the time he was a little nervous and jittery, but when the shit hit the fan, he took two or three deep breaths and felt fine. He would court danger all the time for that effect alone, except that danger was, after all, dangerous and the law of averages would get you if you kept at it long enough.

His voice was very calm as he said, "Captain Frazier, may I present Mr. Senigliero of New York."

It was apparently the wrong thing to say, because as he said it Frazier's face changed to a mask of hate and his voice became high and shrill. "You goddamn collaborator. I oughta blow your head off."

Senigliero's face had gone through a lifetime's worth of changes in that office, from arrogance to reasonableness to rage to fear, and now he was just puzzled. He turned to the sheriff and said, "What is this n-nut talking about?"

The sheriff sighed. It looked like the only way he could take the heat off Senigliero was to turn it on himself. "Frazier!" he barked, and stamped his foot. The sudden movement drew the barrel of the weapon away from Senigliero and toward the sheriff, but wasn't threatening enough to make Frazier pull the trigger. Calmly he went on. "Now, dammit, whatever you may think of the Maf's role in the late war, which, by the way, is over, Mr. Senigliero is a guest in my office and I have your word that there won't be any fighting in my town, so just put the gun away and sit down." He got up and indicated the chair to the guerrilla captain.

Frazier's face broke out into a screwy grin and he said, "Aw, fuck, Spurlock. I was just funnin' him a little." He swaggered over and sat in the chair.

The look on Senigliero's face was one of sublime relief. Then, as he realized the moment of greatest danger had passed, a little of his old arrogance came back. "N-now, listen," he said.

Spurlock cut him off with a glance and he lapsed into silence again. The unfortunate Clarence stood behind him, looking as though he wished he were somewhere else.

The sheriff turned his attention back to the guerrilla captain again. He was really fond of Frazier, even though he thought him a dangerous nut. For instance, his dream of uniting all the guerrilla bands and taking over the country was totally screwy.

No question about it, Frazier didn't know when to quit. On the other hand, if Spurlock's unit hadn't been captured he would have probably become a guerrilla, too, and it was quite possible that had he and Frazier been in each other's outfits their roles would have been reversed.

Idly, Spurlock wondered what kind of sheriff an acid freak would make. He turned to face Senigliero. "Look, maybe if I can talk about what Frazier wants to talk about we can get him off our backs and get down to business."

Senigliero just shook his head slowly. "Y-you run a weird t-town here, Spurlock."

Spurlock nodded and turned his attention back to the little captain, putting his hands on his hips. "Look, Frazier, the clown drew down on me. What'd you expect me to do, kiss him? He's lucky I only broke his finger instead of his goddamn neck."

Frazier paused and looked speculatively at the sheriff. "Drew down on you, did he?" He tapped his mouth with his finger and nodded once, definitely. "Why, that boy's in a peck of trouble."

Spurlock turned to Senigliero and explained carefully. "See, me and Frazier got a deal. He doesn't bother me in town and I don't bother him in the woods. It works out pretty good for both of us."

Senigliero's eyes widened perceptibly. Then he smirked, "Th-th-that's illegal."

Spurlock sighed cynically and shrugged. "He's got a hundred of the best light infantry in the world and I've got me and Harley and maybe twenty or thirty shopkeepers and dirt farmers and a bunch of kids. What do you want, man, the Alamo?"

Senigliero glared with righteous indignation. "If-if necessary," he snorted.

Spurlock laughed outright. "If I was going to do an Alamo," he said, "I'd do it on you before I'd do it on him. He's nothing but a nuisance. You're poison." He turned back to Frazier. "Anyhow that's the story on Martinez. Now, why don't you and your merry men hit the road so Mr. Senigliero and I can conclude our business."

A suspicious gleam came into Frazier's eye. "No. Now that I got the drop on you people anyway I think I'll hang around and see what that business is."

Spurlock looked at Senigliero. "I don't see any reason to keep it secret, do you?"

Senigliero grimaced and shrugged.

Turning back to Frazier, Spurlock nodded. "Okay, Senigliero wants to open the rackets up in Purgatory, preparatory to a big influx of the middle class that he thinks is coming in here to escape the cities. I'm trying to convince him that he oughta move his Maf biggies here and into those old mansions out there in the middle of the woods, and keep the middle class and the rackets out."

Frazier directed a furious glare at Senigliero. "You ain't going to have no fucking middle class in my woods," he said. "I got a truce with Shithead here. But it don't apply if you bring in the middle class. I could give a shit about the rackets"—and here his voice rose to a piercing, penetrating scream—"but no fucking middle class."

Senigliero held up his hands. "You mean I gotta fight this g-gink to take over the town?"

Spurlock shrugged. "Beats me!" He turned to Frazier. "Whadaya think about maybe five or ten Maf hotshots and their households move in here. You think you could live with that?"

Frazier thought a minute. "Yeah, maybe," but again his glance was furious, suspicious, "but no fucking middle class."

Shaking his head and striding about the room, Senigliero said, "Aw right, aw right, already. I get the picture. If I wanta run rackets in here I gotta fight a hundred guerrillas and all I got on my side is these h-hicks here."

Spurlock grimaced slightly. "Well, maybe and maybe not," he said. "We already know we can't beat him because we tried. And we know that he can't beat you, 'cause there's too many of you. But we don't know that you and us could beat him any more than we know that him and us can beat you." He shrugged. "We already know we can live with him, but we don't know that we could live with you, so we might just join up with him and see if together we can beat you. See, we'll probably lose, but even if you win you lose, too, because there ain't gonna be enough of this place left to bring the middle class to.'' He jabbed his finger at Senigliero. ''Ya dig?''

Senigliero brought the palms of his hands to his cheeks and shot them straight up into the air. ''J-jesus!'' he exploded.

''On the other hand,'' Spurlock went on, ''if you decide to come here and live and be good neighbors, I don't think there's going to be any problem.''

Senigliero nodded toward Frazier. ''What about dum-dum here? He starts to do a bandit number on us and I'm going after his ass.''

Spurlock nodded carefully. ''Frankly,'' he said, ''I don't think you'd have much luck trying to find him. The Fort Chaffee garrison sent a battalion down here a couple of years ago and did a search-and-destroy on him. They lost about thirty men. How many'd you lose, Frazier?''

Frazier shrugged. ''My clerk got a paper cut making out the morning report, and I myself developed a terrible blister on my left big toe.''

Spurlock nodded again. ''So there you have it. I recommend you hire Captain Frazier's company as guards to defend you.''

Glowering, Senigliero snarled, ''W-we already got guards.''

Spurlock thought it would be tactless to mention that the guards he already had were prostrate in the dirt in front of the courthouse. ''You got city guards,'' he said. ''Look at it this way. You have networks of informants who keep you posted on what threats are coming your way in the city. But the countryside around here is very largely open.

''There are a few farmers, but those guys have deals with the guerrillas and they aren't going to be any help to you. If you keep Frazier paid off he'll be your early warning system. You'll be his defense against the influx of population, which would bring the army and a more sophisticated brand of law enforcement, and he'll be your outer defense against any assault by the government''—he shrugged here, because there was very little likelihood of the ineffectual government of the United States, or for that matter the state government of Arkansas, bothering anybody—"or a rival family. Frazier is hell to be against, but he might be a lot of help on your side.''

Senigliero paced the room, mulling all of this over.

"As I see it," Spurlock interjected gently, "you got three choices. You can start operating here, in which case you got a war that you'll win, but you'll have to destroy the town. Or you can go ahead and destroy it anyway, just because we jacked you around here today. But if you do that, the word'll get around why you did it and you'll look pretty silly." Spurlock smiled slightly. "Or you can check up on buying some of these old homes and make yourselves comfortable here with the rest of us.''

"I'll think about it," Senigliero muttered sullenly. The whole thing had come as a rather unpleasant shock to him. He had come down here to dictate terms or start a war. He was totally unprepared to deal with the contingencies with which he had been presented, and it would take thought.

Senigliero paused in his pacing and looked at Spurlock for a moment. "F-from a business point of v-view your proposition makes s-sense, Sp-spurlock, but I got other c-considerations. S-see, when you're the boss's son, th-th-the old guys think you're a patsy. Especially when you st-st-st-." He got completely stuck on the word *stutter*, stopped and spoke clearly and distinctly, with a pause between each word.

"When . . . you . . . can't . . . s-s-,"—he made himself bear down on the words carefully—"speak . . . well, so you have to do a lotta rough st-stuff you wouldn't ordinarily d-do. I m-may have to make an ex-example of y-you people." He passed a hand over his forehead. Such a long speech was apparently difficult for him. "T-tell you the truth I-I just l-like to hurt p-p-people.

"M-my shrink h-h-has helped me to c-come to terms with it. M-my old m-man used to sh-shi-shit on me because I was a l-little f-f-fat k-kid, and n-now I'm in a p-p-position to take it out on the world."

A look of real pain crossed Senigliero's face. "When I was five he threw me in the deep end of the p-p-pool. He said I'd swim, but I couldn't. I almost d-d-drowned. Nobody would save me because they were afraid of him. Finally my mother pulled me out and he b-b-beat her for it. Now when I kill somebody I think of him.

"I used to f-feel g-g-guilty, but the sh-sh-shrink says go with it, s-so I do." He put his hand on Spurlock's forearm and looked him square in the eyes and said, "M-make no mistake about it, Sp-spurlock. I'm a m-malevolent f-f-force." He said it with pride.

Spurlock nodded, concluding the interview. He turned back to Frazier. "Captain Frazier, whaddaya say you give Clarence his hardware back, just as a good will gesture?"

Frazier shook his head. "That stuff's hard to come by," he said. "You know how long it's been since I got a new sniper rifle?"

It was a rhetorical question. Spurlock went right along with his persuasive line. "Frazier, damn it, we're going to have to live with these people from now on. For God's sake, I'm trying to get Senigliero to give you clowns work. If you're working for the Maf, then you can forget about hassling with the army from now on. You'll have the freedom of the woods, man. You'll be able to stay in one place more than three days and set yourself up a nice little deal out there. And you'll have money in your pocket. You can quit hassling traveling salesmen and things will be better around here for us all."

Frazier stood with the AK dangling from his shoulder, lost in thought. This wasn't what he'd come expecting to find either. "Son of a bitch," he said. He looked at the M-14 with almost naked longing. Then he looked back at Senigliero.

Senigliero glowered back. He wasn't happy. The only happy man in the room was Spurlock, because he was in charge of the proceedings again. If he could run this shuck out, he might save the town, or part of it. But if he flopped, things would be very bad indeed, and the fight was a long way from won. He didn't push Frazier any harder. He didn't want his back up.

Frazier finally nodded. "Aw right, hell with it!" he said. "Keep it!" he said. He gestured with the AK at Clarence's little pile of weapons.

Clarence started picking the stuff up and putting it back in his jacket. Frazier strode to the window and raised it.

"Let them goons up," he bellowed out the window. His back was contemptuously turned toward Clarence.

Clarence saw his chance and raised a small pistol to shoot Frazier in the back. Spurlock was just about to launch himself into a tackle when Senigliero held up his hand to Clarence, who lowered the pistol. That was a very good sign indeed.

Frazier turned without having seen any of this byplay, but there was a slight smile around the corners of his mouth that told Spurlock that he knew.

"Frazier, would you please get out of my town for a while," Spurlock said.

Frazier just grinned. "Adiós," he said, and strode from the room, his long gray hair bouncing and blowing behind his back.

There was a long pause in the room after Frazier left. "J-jesus Christ!" Senigliero exhaled.

Spurlock smiled and walked to the window in time to see the guerrillas riding out of town. There was a rattle of gunfire as they passed the city-limits sign, and a long burst from an automatic weapon. Stupid bastard, Spurlock thought. He's short of ammunition now. He shrugged. Maybe not.

Senigliero and Clarence were ready to depart. Spurlock turned to see them looking toward him and sort of leaning toward the door. He turned and ushered them out of the room. "Y-you often have visitors like that?" Senigliero asked as they went down the stairs.

Spurlock smiled. "Not often. He was only miffed because I broke Martinez's trigger finger, until I told him how it happened."

Senigliero looked at him questioningly as they strolled down the courthouse steps. "He'll take your word over that of his own man?"

"Sure," Spurlock nodded. "He'll take my word over Martinez's because Marty is a liar and I'm not."

As he stepped to his car Senigliero said, "M-maybe we oughta get rid of that g-guy Frazier."

Spurlock shook his head. "I don't think it can be done. Once he gets off in those woods there's no catching him, and he can get food from the farmers out there because he keeps them supplied with stuff he rips off from traveling salesmen, just trades it at one third of what it's worth. Nope, it's better to have him inside the tent pissing out than outside pissing in."

Senigliero paused in the door to his car. "W-well, Sheriff, th-things haven't gone according to my p-plan here. Usually wh-when that happens I start killing people. I may buy your idea and I may n-not. You've been very enterprising in getting your own w-way. Y-you're an interesting p-person. It would be a p-pity to w-wax your ass. Either way you'll h-h-hear from m-my representatives in the near f-f-future."

Senigliero was stepping into the car, Clarence holding the door. As he did so, one of the bikers came up and did a kind of nodding salute. It wasn't a full military salute, but it was a gesture of the same kind of respect. All the other guards had taken their places. There was a kind of expectancy, but they weren't saying anything, except for this one guy who reported to Senigliero. "Sir," he said, "we ain't got no ammo."

The storm clouds gathered on Senigliero's face again. He had been tried sorely in the past two hours and he was near the point of killing somebody, anybody, just to relieve the tension. "And pray t-tell, what happened to it?" he grated.

The biker gulped. "Them guerrillas took it," he said.

Spurlock looked carefully to see how Senigliero was going to react. There were a lot of people in positions of authority who responded by holding the bearer responsible for bad tidings. Senigliero glared at the biker for a long time. "You," he said. "W-who told you to tell me this?"

"Nobody, sir," the biker said. "But I didn't want to make a run into Hot Springs without no ammo. Them Gs won't bother us here in town because of him"—he gestured toward the sheriff—"but they just might hack us once we get past the county line."

"Take off those colors," Senigliero snarled, without a trace of a stammer.

Quaking, the biker did what he was told.

"Clarence," Senigliero commanded.

The gunman ran around the car, seeing his chance to switch some of the heat off himself and onto the biker. "Yessir?"

"What do you think we should do with this man?" he asked gently. There was tension running all over him, but he smiled.

Standing idly at attention, Clarence answered without hesitation. "Shoot him, sir."

Senigliero nodded and reached inside the flap of his jacket, withdrawing a small flat automatic pistol. "Shoot him," he muttered, while the biker in front of him turned white and Clarence started to relax. There was a suggestion of a smile on Senigliero's lips.

If Spurlock had it figured right, Clarence thought that once Senigliero had taken cathartic action by shooting somebody else, his own punishment for letting Frazier get the drop on him would be minor.

Himself, Spurlock didn't think Clarence was giving Senigliero enough credit.

Sneering, Senigliero jacked back the slide on his little automatic and shot Clarence square in the temple, causing a small hole on one side of his head and a larger one on the other, from which flew little bits of bone and some blood and a whitish gray substance. Then he laughed. "Sh-shoot h-him," he said.

The biker almost fainted, but he continued standing at attention.

Senigliero addressed him. "Y-you are the only one of these g-goons who had enough sense and enough b-balls to tell me we didn't have any am-ammo," he said to the biker. "You are now my chief guard. If you d-don't do a better job than him"—he gestured toward Clarence—"y-you'll end up like he d-did."

"Yessir," the biker said.

Senigliero turned to Spurlock and motioned toward the body beside the car. "S-sorry to l-litter your street like that."

Spurlock shrugged. "Think nothing of it," he replied. "We'll plant him for you. No sense getting your car all bloody."

The biker turned to Sheriff Spurlock. "Sir," he said, "can we score some ammo off you? I don't want to make that run to Hot Springs without it."

Spurlock nodded. "Ain't got a whole lot," he said, "but you're welcome to enough for the run." He turned to the courthouse. "Harley," he called.

From a second-story window a voice answered, "Yeah!"

"Bring down a couple boxes of forty-five ammo and a belt of thirty cal."

Spurlock stood and waited while the ammo was brought, then watched as Senigliero, the biker, and the other three guards climbed into the car. As soon as he was in the car Senigliero punched a cassette into a video rig. The convoy cranked up and tore out of town, leaving a Harley 74 chopper and a bloody corpse behind, the strains of *Aïda* trailing behind the car.

Spurlock turned and went inside the courthouse, sighing as he walked up the steps. It hadn't gone as he expected; in some ways it had been better, and in others worse. Frazier's appearance had been a help in a way. He stopped in the outer office and left instructions for cleaning up the body, and told Harley he could have the bike, until or if the Maf showed up to claim it.

Then he went into his office. He paused in the door when he saw Frazier sitting at his desk, his muddy boots on the top, all over the previous day's police blotter. His heels were together, feet turned out equally at a forty-five-degree angle, forming a notch for the barrel of the AK that was propped so it pointed exactly at the sheriff.

Spurlock grimaced. "Well," he said, "if it isn't the Robin Hood of Modern Crime."

Frazier favored him with a long piercing glare. "Why are you bringing that shithead into Purgatory? We got a pretty nice little deal here without him." He took the AK off his feet and leaned it against the wall.

Spurlock walked into the room and stopped to fish Senigliero's discarded joint from the ashtray. "You wanta finish this number?" he asked Frazier. "Usually I wouldn't, but it's been a long hard day."

Frazier shrugged. "Might as well," he said. "I'm coming down anyway."

Spurlock lit the number and took a deep hit, sitting on the corner of the desk and passing the joint to Frazier. He felt the first rush hit him even as he held the smoke down. Lord, he didn't think he and Frazier were going to be able to finish it either. He exhaled the smoke through his nostrils and said, "I'm not bringing him in. But I can't keep them out with just me and Harley and the guys down at the pool hall."

"You kept us out," Frazier snapped, grinning bitterly.

Spurlock nodded. "Sure, but you guys are lightly armed and there's only a few of you. With them it's just the town against the world. They couldn't get you because you can dodge around in the woods and pick them to pieces. But us, we're fixed. The town is our life, and we got women and kids here and all that sort of shit. So we try to accommodate." He shrugged. "We got a few things going for us that Senigliero hasn't figured on."

"Such as?" Frazier's expression was truculent.

Spurlock took another hit and nodded. He held the smoke for a long time and then graveled out the response, in order not to lose the smoke. "Well, for one thing they ain't gonna come down here at all until New York decides whether they're gonna try to operate here or live here. I think Senigliero's gonna decide to take some of those old mansions for country retreats, which means that we'll have maybe a hundred new people in here, tops. And most of them are gonna have kids, so they're gonna want to keep their operations out of here."

Frazier shook his head. "I still don't like it. All them high-powered guns come in here and they're gonna take over. Those people are used to being in charge, wherever they are."

Spurlock grinned at the grizzled little captain. "Maybe, maybe not," he said. "They're used to dealing with people who are venal, stupid, and cowardly. The folks in this town aren't any of those things. They are people who are able to live pretty good in a bad time. They don't bother anybody and they don't want anything except to be left alone. You never can tell. The Maf might not do anything at all. They might deliberate for years before making a decision, and then decide to forget the whole thing."

He jabbed his finger at Frazier. "But if they do come down here, you are gonna be their early-warning system, and some of the servants and workmen for these houses are gonna come from the town here. They're not gonna fly in everything they buy, because there's no airport and the ground isn't flat enough to build one without a hell of a lot of work, so they're gonna buy their stuff from us. So if we're venal, cowardly, and stupid, like they expect, then they'll have us. But if we're not, then it's a question of do they have us or do we have them."

Frazier looked at the sheriff, still mulling. "Got it all figured out, huh?"

Spurlock shrugged. "Maybe, maybe not," he said.

"I'll tell you one thing," Frazier said, reaching for his AK and laying it across his lap. "I wish I had that bastard's organization. I'd take control of every guerrilla band in the country, weed out them mobsters, and put this country back like it used to be."

Spurlock looked at him, incredulous as usual at Frazier's fantasy. "Like it was when?" he inquired. "Seventeen seventy-six, eighteen sixty-five, or maybe nineteen sixty-seven?"

Frazier grinned square in his face. "Sixty-seven," he said. "I really liked sixty-seven. That was the year I dropped my first acid and waxed my first gook. Best year of my life."

CHAPTER FOUR

IT WAS dark and the wind sighed in the breeze as one very stoned sheriff rode out the old road toward the farm. He always enjoyed the ride and being stoned kept his mind off troubles as he rode. Almost off his mind anyway.

Every few minutes he thought of his kids in New York and lost his cool again. They would be fourteen and sixteen now, and in the picture he had from when they were five and six they were blond and beautiful like their mother, slender and clear-skinned, blue-eyed and the eyes bright with intelligence. He couldn't tell exactly how his feelings were for them. It's very difficult to say that you love someone you haven't seen for eight years, and it's equally difficult to deny love for your own children.

What he felt was not so much anything you could describe as love, but a kind of nameless longing. The sheriff didn't suppose he was exactly what you could call a family type of man. He had run away from his parents' home, and when his wife left him, it almost killed him, but he couldn't deny that she had reason. He wasn't an easy person to live with. He supposed he was considered a cold man by many, but he didn't feel that about himself, and he was very curious about his children, and worried about them.

He had no conception of what New York was like now. Senigliero had said it was bad, and he supposed it was, but every place was bad now. Still, New York had always been the worst place, garbage piled in the streets, people having to lock themselves in at night, muggers and rapists accosting people in broad daylight, and never anything the cops could do about it.

Here in Purgatory, for all practical purposes, he was the law. There was seldom anything that got to court in Purgatory. Spurlock's method was to make thieves make restitution and fine traffic violators. There were no laws in Purgatory against anything anybody might do that didn't bother anybody, and that included sexual intercourse between consenting adults in private, drug use, and gambling at home. Those cases that came to his attention did so because they were public nuisances and they were handled as public nuisances. An overnight stay in the slam and a fine usually handled it.

Aside from guerrilla battles, there had been one murder in Purgatory, and Spurlock had been dreading the ordeal of holding the guy until trial and having to testify. Besides, he was pretty sure the evidence was insufficient. The guy had stabbed his wife, presumably in a fit of jealousy.

Anyhow, when Spurlock and Harley rode out to talk to the man he had come out of the house waving a 30.06 and yelling that old saw about "You'll never take me alive!"

Spurlock and Harley had just ridden out to investigate. There was no evidence that he was the killer.

The house was on a slight rise over the road and there were woods behind the house the man could have run to. He could have taken a horse and left the county, in which case there was very little likelihood that anyone would have ever caught him.

But instead he had come storming out of the house bellowing, "You'll never take me alive," and zinging a couple of rounds down toward the road. He was too far away to hit anything.

When the first round snapped over his head, Spurlock swung down off the horse, the animal still walking, hit her on the rump, and barreled into the ditch. He didn't have to tell Harley what to do. Harley was right with him.

Once in the ditch he extended the stock on the CAR-15 and carefully sighted the scope on the man in his front yard. "Son of a bitch!" he muttered, and sighted with the left eye. He had forgotten a bruise on his right eye socket.

Harley looked at him with wide eyes. "You wanta try and take him, Shurf?"

Spurlock shook his head. "No!" That would be very difficult and very dangerous and this seemed to be the way the fellow wanted it. He carefully emptied his mind for the total concentration of firing a well-aimed shot, and put the scope right down on the man, right on his right eye, took in a breath, and let it out halfway. The wobble in his rifle settled down to a tiny circle around the man's eye. Spurlock caught a feeling of almost total evil coming from the man, and the thought that it must be canceled came to his mind. He squeezed the trigger slowly, but before his rifle fired, the man's expression changed to one of sheer terror and he dropped out of sight, never to rise again.

"Oh, hell!" Spurlock muttered, thinking his shot had been spoiled. When there was no more action from the house, they rose and cautiously approached. They found the man already dead. Neither of them could explain it, but Spurlock was glad. Ammunition was already hard to get.

Harley looked down at the body in awe. "How'd you do that?" he asked.

"I didn't do it," Spurlock said. "He just dropped dead. Maybe he had a heart attack."

"Yeah, prob'ly so," Harley muttered, but it didn't sound right and neither one of them quite believed it. Spurlock never got over the feeling that he had something to do with it, but he had no idea what that something might be. He filed it away as one of those unexplained incidents, but sometimes, like now, he remembered and wondered.

He could see the light from the farmhouse flickering through the trees up ahead. It was a cheering thing to see, especially in his condition. A few minutes later he was in the farmyard. He rode to the corral and took the saddle off his horse, checked to see if there was feed in the feeder, and strolled on into the house.

He could hear music coming out of the windows as he approached. Randy and Bob must be at it again. And Miriam. Randy was on guitar and Bob on harmonica. Both sang. There was a piano also, so Miriam was sitting in with them. The old screen door squeaked as he strode through the front door and paused to hang his jacket on the coatrack in the hall.

The music was blues, one of Randy's. He sat all folded up in a chair, wearing no shirt or shoes, only a pair of jeans, his curly brown hair all down in his eyes, and his mustache rambling all over his face. Bob had on bib overalls and clodhopper shoes, but he also wore no shirt. Miriam was a big, redheaded girl, freckled, and she wore a green-checked cotton dress, a long one that came all the way to the floor. She was very pregnant, but didn't seem to have slowed down much.

Clancy stood in the door, toweling herself dry from the shower and listening to the music. Her long blond hair had knotted itself into curls in the shower. The towel was more or less in front of her body, which was no big deal since the people at the farm went nude whenever they felt like it. That had pretty well resolved itself to sunbathing, bathing, swimming, and sleeping.

Nonetheless, Spurlock ran his eyes over Clancy's body. Little too heavy, nice tits, not bad. Clancy's main claim to fame was her smile anyway, which could light up any room she flashed it in. Spurlock and Clancy had done a little thing a couple of years before that hadn't maintained itself for long, and now they were close friends.

He waved at the people in the room. Clancy waved back silently so as not to interrupt the music. He walked into the kitchen to see what smelled so good.

Megan stood at the stove, dancing a little to the music and stirring the stew. She grinned slyly at Spurlock when he walked through the door and over to the stove to give her a kiss. It was a very warm and wet one. In fact, she let go of the spoon and they made a production of it. "Hello, Sheriff," she said.

"Hiya, sorceress. That stew smells terrific."

She touched his elbow, inhaled, and said, "You don't."

He smiled and nodded. "Been a kind of heavy day," he said. "How long before dinner?"

She shrugged and looked into the pot, her heavy black curly hair falling across her face as she did so. She was a big woman, graceful with a big-eyed, sullen beauty. "Maybe twenty minutes," she said.

"Oh, well," he replied. "I'll shower after supper. Lemme wash up and I'll set the table."

"Good boy," she approved, and went on stirring the stew.

The relationship between Spurlock and Megan was an undefined one; they had no arrangement. They each had separate rooms and slept in them about half the time. She was a teacher at Purgatory High School. She taught Spanish and math, and her son, Jon, who was fifteen, lived at the farm also. Jon and Spurlock were good friends, and Spurlock supposed he was as close to a father as the boy had. He had taught him to ride and shoot and a little about carpentry, although Spurlock himself wasn't what you could call a red-hot carpenter.

Spurlock and Megan had no intention of formalizing their relationship. They had a good family life with the people at the farm, and they had both been hurt too many times to place the fragile remains of their egos in the hands of any one person for an extended period of time.

He went into the bathroom and washed his hands and face, then came out to set the table.

By the time he did that, Clancy was in the kitchen preparing a salad and Jon came in the kitchen door, tall and blond, with fashionably short hair, although not as short as the kids in the cities wore theirs. The kid was really one of the most handsome young men Spurlock had ever seen, and he looked at him fondly. "Hello, tiger," he said.

Jon nodded a greeting. "Evening, Spurlock," he said. "Been hoein' and fencin' all day, you?"

"Organized crime and the guerrilla menace." Spurlock smiled.

The kid threw him a sock on the arm. "Trade you," he said eagerly.

Spurlock smiled. "Not yet."

"Never," Megan threw over her shoulder.

The boy gave his mother a pained look, but said nothing.

It had been a standing joke since the boy was twelve that he would become a deputy when he was old enough. Spurlock had simply assumed he would grow out of it and want to be a farmer, or a jet pilot, or a history professor, or any sensible thing. But so far he was hanging right in there wanting to be sheriff.

For that matter he was a lot smarter than Harley.

"Wash up and help me set the table," Spurlock said.

"Roger," the kid replied. That was guerrilla slang. Spurlock wondered whom the kid had been talking to in the woods. He grabbed eight plates and took them into the dining room.

Spurlock said very little during dinner, which wasn't unusual. He was thinking about his kids in New York City. Sometimes he thought the old-fashioned monogamous marriage was a good idea. At least if the families stayed together they got to see their kids. Jon's father was a chiropractor somewhere in Florida and the kid hadn't seen him since he was ten, when Megan left her job there to come here to teach. The airlines were for the rich and for those with official government business. Surface transportation was by charter convoy and very expensive also. Once people moved, they stayed moved, and almost nobody went for a visit to anyone farther away than one day's horseback ride.

Spurlock sat very quietly there in the midst of the dinner table conversation, occasionally passing the sweet potatoes or the salt, but taking no part in the talk.

Sometimes he felt alienated from the farm people because of his job. Even Megan, who was dedicated to teaching, could afford not to take it totally seriously every day. But being the sheriff you took it easy when you were spoiling for action, and then there were days like today where all he'd wanted was to lie out in the field and contemplate the infinite, and he'd had to hassle with the Maf and Frazier both on the same day. Jesus!

Dessert was Clancy's apple cobbler in sweet cream. That got his attention for a while. "This's great!" he told her.

She did her whole sunshine lady smile thing for him. He did appreciate that smile.

After dinner he wandered in a preoccupied way to the shower, still thinking about the events of the day, wondering when he could get away. He would have to leave Harley in charge, which would probably be okay as long as nothing too hot came up. The Maf would be cool for maybe another three months before they started to make their big move. So the best thing would be to leave right away, maybe day after tomorrow, or the day after that. He soaped vigorously, his face screwed up in thought.

He tried to picture what the kids would be like now, and he couldn't do that either. All he could see when he thought about New York was gutted buildings, dried maroon blood in gutters filled with cigarette wrappers and vomit. What could his kids be into at sixteen? Would they be junkies like Senigliero's kid? Could he get them out here and . . . aw, hell, it was just too much. He didn't even know for sure that there was anything wrong. He just had Senigliero's remarks and a general feeling of unease. He squinted hard under the shower and turned, rinsing the soap off his body. He didn't know whether he was trying to talk himself into it or out of it.

He turned off the water and got out of the shower, scowling. It was one thing to be heading into a good adventure, and another to be going into something like this. He dried off and knotted a towel around his waist, then brushed his teeth, grimacing at his already scowling face. He really looked grim.

Anyway, he would leave in two or three days. He wanted a gas-powered vehicle, maybe a trail bike, and a lot of ammo. In fact, to go more than fifteen hundred miles he maybe better take a four-wheel-drive vehicle and a couple of automatic weapons. Be good to have somebody else along, too; but this was his personal hassle, and the only person he could ask was Harley, who would have to stay here and watch the store.

Tightening the towel, he went down the hall to his room, then threw the towel on the bed. It was already fairly dark outside and he looked into the dim tangle of trees out past the yard. He loved this country, wild and mean as it was. It was beautiful and it let a man be a human being, not some insane robot, like in the cities.

Fatigue crawled along Spurlock's back and in his shoulders. He flopped his head over to one side, and it snapped twice like a dried twig. He repeated the process the other way. There was a tightness at the base of his skull and his feet hurt. He'd be forty in another two or three months, and even though he was in fine shape he felt the days. When he was young, he had simply been healthy and never thought about it, ran around day and night, lived on Coca-Cola and peanuts, smoked dope and chased pretty little women, put in a full day the next day, and the night after did it all again and never thought a thing about it.

He went into a yoga warm-up posture and felt the muscles all along his spine go *pop-pop-pop*. He grinned at that. Anyhow, he'd got in really bad shape by the time he was thirty-four, been your typical fat pig cop and been surly and hard to get along with, sluggish and highly unalert.

That's how the guy had shot him in the gut, coming out of the liquor store with the day's receipts in a blue canvas bag. Old Spurlock had been stomping down the street, fat, dumb, and happy, and this dude took one look at him, badge and all, and started whanging away with an old Tokarev pistol.

The clown was scared and couldn't hit a bull in the ass with a bass fiddle, but just on the law of averages the fifth round hit Spurlock in the gut. By that time, of course, he had his S & W .357 magnum highway patrol model out and blew a large hole in the robber's chest, but Lord, five rounds late. He could have been killed easy.

So he had a lot of time in the hospital to think it over and he mentioned to the doc that he wanted to start an exercise program, because his reflexes were shot and he was fat. The doc had turned him on to yoga, and from there it was a short jump to the philosophy that went with it, and when that happened he found his entire attitude changing. He was looser and easier to get along with. He lost interest in making a bust just for the sake of making a bust, and before long they asked him to run for sheriff.

By that time he was more interested in becoming a good person than in career advancement, but sure, why not?

He ran through the postures deadpan. But inside he was grinning, feeling all those tense little muscles he was unaware of, even when they were tense, come loose. He wrapped himself into a lotus for meditation, hoping to perform the same service for his mind.

Something the doc told him popped into his mind.

A year after getting out of the hospital Spurlock was back in the doctor's office for his annual checkup. Once again he was struck by the fact that the doctor was well over fifty, but his body moved like a twenty-five-year-old's, and his eyes were ageless.

When the doctor entered the room, Spurlock was sitting on the examining table. The doc gave him a quick once-over, then went and adjusted the venetian blinds, flooding the room with light. He paused and looked out the window for a long time, then turned and gave Spurlock a rather perfunctory examination, looked at his eyes with a scope, peered in his ears, listened to his chest, tapped his patella tendon. "Hmmmmmmmmmmm!" he said.

Then he went back to his desk and sat down slumped, with his chin propped up in his hands, for the longest time. His expression was so grave that for a moment Spurlock thought he was about to be told he was dying. That seemed a little strange, since he felt great.

The doctor shot him a glance out of the corner of his eye. "Been doin' your yoga?"

Spurlock nodded. "Just like Patton read the Bible, every goddamn day."

The doc nodded. "Meditation?"

"Sure."

The doc nodded again. "Most people aren't that disciplined."

Spurlock shrugged. "It's free, it feels good to do, and when it's over I feel great. Where's the discipline in that?"

The doctor rose and went back to the window, looking out again. "Spurlock, you're a big surprise to me," he said. "I should've known better, but when you came into the hospital I saw nothing but an overweight cop. You're a different man, and you're still changing."

Spurlock nodded. "Sounds good to me," he said.

The doctor turned around and leaned back against the window. "Yeah, but now that it looks like you're going to stay with it I need to prepare you for the rest of it."

Spurlock cocked an ear at that.

"I've been at this yoga stuff for twenty-five years," the doctor said, "and I know I can do some things that most people can't do. I keep the jibber-jabber in my brain to a minimum, and as a consequence I see more of what's going on around me than most folks. That's going to start happening to you, too."

Spurlock shrugged.

"Frank, I'm not saying this right," said the doctor. "Look, about five years ago I had a patient on the operating table, a woman, and she died; clinically dead, medically dead.

"Happens all the time, right? You can't save them all. Only I *knew* somehow that I could bring her back and I went on working and prayed under my breath while I was working, and that woman is not only alive but has two more kids now than she had then. And I've done that seven times since.

"Or rather, I haven't done it, but it has been done through me, understand?"

Spurlock shook his head negatively.

"Okay, lemme see if I can put it another way. Your feeling, my feeling, everybody's feeling of being a separate entity is only an illusion. The universe is all one thing, and we can only be a part of it. This notion of separateness is language-induced, because in naming things language separates them. Normally we think in words and that gives us the illusion of separateness. In meditation we still the verbal mind and train ourselves to experience the world more directly. Sometimes in a desperate situation we are shocked right out of our verbal thinking and become consciously one with the universe. At such times we can do anything, absolutely anything at all, if that's what we're supposed to do.''

Spurlock pondered that for a moment. It was all kind of new to him. He had not expected to become a saint. All he had been looking for was a way to lose some weight and get the crick out of his back. "How do you know what to do?" he asked.

"But you don't *know* it, you *are* it.''

Spurlock squinched his face up into a mask of apprehension. "You expect something like that to happen to me?''

"It will if you keep goin' like you are," the doc said. "Look at your body now, man. Do you have any idea how much better your reflexes are than they were just a year ago?''

Spurlock nodded. "When do you expect this stuff to start happening?'' he asked.

The doctor shrugged. "Took a long time for me,'' he said, "but it's more a matter of faith than time. It just took me that long to see that my scientific objectivity would only take me so far, and from there on out I needed my trained intuition. It happened to me in the operating room.'' He looked at Spurlock for a long moment. "My guess is that it'll happen to you about the time you have enough faith to get rid of your guns.''

Spurlock started. At that time he thought of his guns as parts of himself. In fact, if the truth be known, he thought of himself as part of his guns. They were the essential element, he was only their director. "Be a cold day in hell when I give up my guns, Doc,'' he snarled.

The doctor smiled ruminatively. "That may be,'' he said. "These things have a way of coming about regardless of climate.''

That was a good thought, a useful thought, but he let it slide by, to be recollected when he could use it.

Once in a great while he had something that approached a mystical experience while meditating, but mostly it was just like getting all the crud cleaned out of your head so it could be aired out. When that was over, he usually felt better than he had when he started in the morning.

When he was through, Spurlock put on a clean pair of jeans and a sweatshirt, slipped his feet into some sandals he'd made, and started back down toward the living room to see what was going on. Randy, Bob, and Miriam were playing again.

Clancy had changed into a full-length blue cotton dress and wound her hair into knots over her ears. She sat on the sofa, crocheting a scarf or something. He couldn't tell knitting from tatting from macramé. It was all screwing around with string to him. He looked around the room, smiling warmly at his people. Jon sat over in a corner, cross-legged, singing quietly and reading a paperback science fiction novel at the same time.

Megan leaned over the upright, singing along for all she was worth, voice cast to the heavens. She was the most out-front woman he had ever met, this imperious woman he had got himself connected to. He thanked God he didn't have to live alone with her to be her lover. She was just too much.

Curiously enough, she said the same thing about him.

He went over and leaned against the other side of the piano, looking over at her. She was just as beautiful in jeans and a work shirt, with an old red bandanna in her hair, as she was in those gorgeous purple velvet gowns she was apt to wear.

She smiled at him. He smiled back at her. Now they were singing "The Old Rugged Cross."

He looked around the room. It was her room for certain. Before Megan came it had been a pretty standard farm living room, except for the stereo set they only ran when the generator was on, Saturdays and holidays. When she moved in, the entire character of the place changed. First she re-covered the couch in red velvet. She had an entire roll of the stuff in the back of her VW van. Then she started putting in the really weird things. The walls were decorated with animal pelts and the gutted bodies of partridges. The feathers were extremely beautiful, and the effect was not macabre, but simply strange. She put shingles all around the top of the fireplace and all down the front, leaving only enough of the old front so that the shingles wouldn't catch fire.

One day she dragged in a couple of huge rocks, or rather Jon and Randy hauled them in while Megan told them where to put them, all the while gesturing like a cross between an empress and a top sergeant.

The rocks had formed the base for their coffee table, and if the rocks weren't on the same level, it didn't matter because the top was a dried-out chunk of a very thin limb from a tree that had been struck by lightning and left out to weather for about five years. There was a red candle dripping down one end of it.

That and the plants all over the room gave it the air of being the lair, or den, of a particularly benign witch.

It was a peculiar talent Megan had, that of turning whatever her environment was into a *Megan Carney Production, Inc. Tah-dah!!!* He'd seen her pull that little number with sunsets, for Christ's sake, whip back the curtain and gesture at the sunset like it was a little thing she'd spent an hour or so arranging that afternoon.

He'd seen her do it in her bedroom unconsciously one afternoon; like some people would sit and doodle, she'd reached out and grabbed a swatch of velvet and some silk, red silk and purple satin. She'd surrounded herself with this stuff, reached out and grabbed a handful of costume jewelry that she had stashed in an old chamber pot under her print of El Greco's "Toledo," fake rubies as big as eggs and pearls and emeralds, many-faceted, that you could look through and see many images, a cartoon Oz. She'd thrown in seashells dragged all the way from Florida, and Oklahoma rose rocks, and marble eggs. When she was finished, she had fabricated, all unawares, the nest to end all nests. She sat in it like the Blue Jay's gypsy princess.

She was really something, this woman.

She really was a witch, too. That had come as something of a shock to Spurlock. They'd been lying in bed sometime after that first week they'd been together, lying in her big bedroom upstairs in the afternoon. It had been some sort of school holiday and he'd turned the sheriff's office over to Harley and come out to the farm and there'd been a big picnic going on, games for the kiddies and so on, and he'd gone back up to the house to wash up after pitching three innings of softball and found Megan in the living room, hanging a picture. He'd given her a hug and they'd wound up in bed.

After making love he told her how much she reminded him of a witch queen.

"I am, you know," she informed him, and took a big hit off the joint he'd rolled them.

"A queen?"

She shook her hair, lying so softly there on the pillow, her wild beautiful hair spread out around her, tumbling down over her breasts and on the pillow. "A witch," she said.

He leaned up on his elbow and looked at her carefully. She was obviously serious about it, but he couldn't imagine her in one of those witches' covens, a dozen or so naked, acne-ridden wretches chanting, the candlelight reflecting off their glasses. "How so?" he inquired.

She'd smiled up at him, a shy, sly, imperious smile. "When Jon was in the fifth grade they wanted a witch for

a Halloween assembly program in his school. I volunteered and made myself up for the part and was a big hit,
but in the process I started reading up on it and found I
could really cast spells, and things did come out the way I
wanted them to.''

"Really?'' he murmured, impressed. "Like what?''

She shrugged; the hair falling all over her shoulders
brushed her breasts as she moved. "Oh, the usual stuff,''
she said carelessly. "Love potions and little hexy things.
There was a kid down there in Florida who wouldn't take a
test at the university without coming to see me first.''

He took the joint from her hand and took a deep hit.
"Y'ever do any of that stickin' pins in people or conjurin'
up the devil or any of that?''

She shook her head again. "Nope.''

He grinned and lay back down beside her. "I think
you're shuckin' me.''

"Try me,'' she suggested.

He reached out, took her nipple between his thumb and
forefinger, and squeezed gently. It hardened immediately.
"I intend to,'' he said. "Not once, but many times.''

She leaned up and kissed him, a very warm and good
kiss. "That, too,'' she said, "but right then I was talking
about witchcraft.''

"Okay.'' He thought a minute. "Clara lost one of her
contact lenses today, and there's no way she can replace it.
Get her to find it.''

She nodded. "Done!'' she said. Then she reached up
and kissed him again, and they made love.

When he walked into the office the next day, Clara
wasn't wearing her glasses and she wasn't squinting at the
typewriter.

"Find your contact?'' he asked, striding through the
office.

She looked up and grinned at him. "It was right beside

the bed, down in the rug. I saw it first thing when I got up this morning.''

"She found it," he told Megan when he got home that evening.

"Who found what?" Megan asked, a light smile on the corner of her mouth.

"Clara found her contact."

Megan nodded and went on with her dinner preparations. Neither of them had ever said any more about it since then.

Witching was the sort of thing she'd take up. She was always sudden like that, presumptuous. That was how they'd met, as a matter of fact.

She said the first time she saw him he was storming down the middle of the street with his hat jammed over his nose, a toothpick sticking straight out the middle of his mouth, clenched between two angry rows of teeth. He didn't remember seeing her then, and he didn't remember storming down the street like that either, for a long time. Then he remembered there had been a couple of old boys got loaded up on beer down at the pool hall and he'd been on his way down there to break up the resulting fight.

After breaking up the fight he'd taken the police cruiser and headed out down the highway toward Fayetteville, figuring to set up a little speed trap and see if he couldn't nail a couple of the college kids who'd been racking through Purgatory for the last couple of weeks. Gas was more plentiful then.

Tooling out along in the hills, he noticed this little VW microbus, sort of dun-colored and badly in need of a paint job, pulling up behind him. He was going plenty slow enough for her to pass him legally, but she didn't. Lots of people are like that, scared to pass a cop even if he's going slower than the speed limit. So he slowed down a little more to signal that it was okay for the VW to pass, but it didn't.

He speeded back up to about ten miles an hour faster than he'd been doing. At least that way he'd get that VW off his ass. Then the driver of the VW started honking the horn and giving a right-hand turn signal. He couldn't figure out what the hell was happening, so he pulled over to the side of the road, and the VW pulled in behind him.

He was damned if he was going to walk back to the VW so he got out of the car and stood leaning, half on the car, half on the door, one cowboy-booted heel hooked over the edge near the seat, still chewing on his toothpick, his hat down over his nose and the dark glasses he wore in the summertime. He was in jeans and a jeans jacket and he wasn't wearing a gun.

She got out of the VW and stood there with the door open, a big woman, like nobody he'd ever seen before. She wore wine-colored pants and a blue velvet top and black gloves. Her hair tumbled down her back and over her breasts in great waves to her waist. She stood by the door of the van, with a sort of blank expression, as though she were thinking.

Then he noticed the way she looked at him, as though she hadn't eaten for three days and he was an entire steak dinner. It caused a very strange sensation in him because he could tell, looking at this lady, that she was something special, and had been something special to a lot of people. This woman had obviously set out to experience all of life she could find and so far was still at it.

Did he actually know all that in advance? He thought he really did. That it was implicit in that first glance, and even though he couldn't have described the thing to anyone who asked about it, he wasn't surprised when it happened.

He held out his arms to her and she ran and jumped into them. He kissed her. It was fine.

She broke away from him for a moment, after the kiss

had gone on for a long time, and said, cocking her head, "Haven't I met you somewhere before?"

He shook his head, laughing. "No, I don't think so." His mind was aswarm with the possibilities of the moment. He had never seen her before, and he knew everyone in the county. Therefore she was a traveler. The question was, was she going to keep traveling? They were very close at the moment, as close as lovers of long standing. There was someone else moving around in the van. A closer look revealed a scared-looking boy, about ten or eleven, with a pugnacious expression overriding his fear, ready to defend his mother.

He supposed all this business about Megan was running through his mind because he was thinking about maybe leaving tomorrow or the next day and he'd miss her.

She walked around the piano and took his arm, leading him down the hall to her room. They went in and sat down on the rug at the foot of her bed. "You're awfully quiet tonight, Spurlock. What's the trouble?"

The sheriff leaned back against the heavily padded frame of the water bed and pushed off his boots with his toes. Then he proceeded to describe the events of the day, finishing by telling her of his thinking of going to New York.

She sat up and wrapped her arms around her knees, resting her head on her shoulder. As she did so, her wild hair tumbled down across her shoulders and he thought again how beautiful she was. Not because she was born beautiful, but because she had made herself that way.

"That's going to be very hard to do," she said, "getting across the continent that way. Isn't there some way you could fly?"

He chuckled grimly. "That would mean coming up with some official reason why I was going to New York. You think I could tell the government that I want to go get my kids because they can't maintain order? I don't think the government is going to buy that, because they can't afford to admit they don't govern.'' He shrugged. '' 'Fraid I'll have to go overland.''

"How?" she inquired.

"I dunno," he replied truthfully. "The only transportation I own is my horse. Figure I could go maybe thirty miles a day on the horse. It'd take me about two months to get to New York, allowing for washed-out bridges and setbacks. That's a long time, but the roads are so bad that maybe the horse is the best and safest transportation."

"What about the police car?"

He shook his head. "That belongs to the county; besides, it would just be a target for every Hunyak I met along the way. I'm afraid the horse is all I've got. If I had the money, I might buy a trail bike and make it a lot quicker, but I don't. Besides, there'd be the gas hassle, and I don't think there's a trail bike to buy in Purgatory anyway. There might be one in Joplin." He thought about taking the Maf's chopper, but it wasn't a trail bike, and he was no biker.

She looked at him gently. "You could take my bus."

He shook his head. "Naw, I couldn't do that. You need it and besides it'll be hard to get gas, and the bus won't go over very rough terrain. If it was a Land-Rover or something like that, I might consider it."

She shrugged. "It's up to you," she said. "But if you want it you're welcome to it."

"Thanks," he said, smiling.

His mind was aswarm with details. He was going on a journey that would take months, and he was packing alone over dangerous terrain. Food—easily portable food, most of it dried—groundsheet, tent, sleeping bag. He was figuring how to strap the stuff to a packhorse.

He knew he should go armed, but it stuck in his craw somehow. It was a real moral dilemma. He had things squared away in Purgatory so he could function as a law officer without killing or threatening to kill people, but it wouldn't be that way on the road. It wouldn't even be that way outside the town of Purgatory itself. He frowned and started chewing on his lower lip.

Spurlock was worried that if he went armed he would put the entire structure of spiritual progress he'd gained over the past ten years in jeopardy. Some holy man, he couldn't remember which one, Meher Baba maybe, said that when your spiritual development reached a certain point you simply did not encounter situations in which you had to kill people. And Spurlock hadn't encountered such a situation in about three years, which was just about the amount of time since he'd progressed past doing yoga simply because it was good for his selfish, dope-soaked body, and started pursuing it further because he wanted to be a better person. But that might be a coincidence.

Sometimes he wondered if the whole structure of Vedantic thought he'd become embroiled in could be nothing more than a delusion brought about by fasting and abstinence. And other times he didn't think it mattered at all whether that was true or not, since those people who had sacrificed their lives for spiritual peace were obviously so much happier than those who had not, and had better relations with their neighbors.

By this time he was squinting, gnawing on his lower lip, and drumming on the floor with his knuckles.

Megan reached out and put her hand on his arm. "Easy," she said.

He shrugged and came out of his deep thought trance to explain what he was thinking.

Now she too had a frown. "You really think you can make it to New York without a weapon?"

He shook his head. "Hard to say," he replied. "The damn thing just might get me in trouble. But it might save my life. You know there were a lot of holy men who felt you had to fight sometimes. The one-hundred-percent pacifists among them are the exceptions rather than the rule. Like, maybe they're right and if I've gone far enough I just won't have to do any final-type stuff. God knows I don't want anybody else's death on my karma. It's bad enough as it is. You know everybody I ever killed I did it in ignorance of the psychic consequences of the act. If I kill somebody now, a vital part of me will die with him.

"And it might screw up my life to the point that I'll have to come back as somebody really loathsome, like old Martinez, and have to work that out."

He looked at her very carefully. "But I have to weigh all these other factors. See, for one thing, I'm not going to grease some other joker unless he's trying to do me in. What's the moral weight of letting him absorb all that bad karma when I can stop him? Besides, what's the moral weight of letting myself be diverted from my mission, and maybe having my kids get stuck in New York City and become a pair of junkie cannibals? You see? And maybe I'm well enough developed spiritually that I can do it without guns, and maybe I'm not, and do I dare take the chance? 'Cause I'm pretty good with a weapon."

She shook her head. "I think you're thinking too hard. That's a fine rational analysis of a situation that's not susceptible to rational analysis. It's an intuitive, not a mental, decision."

He squinted and grimaced as though in agony. "Yeah, that's right," he said rather lamely. He sat quietly for a moment, then went on. "But the thing is . . . yeah!" He held his hands out, palms up. Then he stood on his long lanky legs and shoved them into his cowboy boots. It was all too much for him. For a moment he thought it might help to get stoned and think about it with the aspects of his mind that were opened in that state, but he decided not to. The best thing would be meditation to clear his mind entirely, and then in the morning when he started doing it, he would be doing the right thing, whatever it was. "I'm going to my room to meditate, Megan. It seems to be the appropriate thing to do now.''

She looked at him and her face held a question. It was his last night in Purgatory, maybe forever, and maybe she had visions of a passionate leave-taking. But he was too messed up in the head right now for that, and maybe a little renunciation would be in order to get this thing started on the right foot. He knelt and kissed her on the forehead. ''See ya!''

She nodded and gave him a rueful wave. ''Yes, indeed,'' she said.

He walked down the hall to his room. Inside, it was the same barren place it had always been except for a few odds and ends he had picked up since knowing Megan, mostly things she had given him. There was a huge rug on the wall, an Oriental rug with a mandala pattern, a huge but lovely red rock by the door, and a piece of driftwood by the bed.

He lit one of her fat red candles and put it on top of the dresser. His mind was still churning with a million details, none of which he could take care of right now and all of which, taken together, had his mind so occupied that he couldn't get to an area where he could think rationally. His mind was a maelstrom of disembodied facts, each crying for attention. The only sensible thing to do was to clear it completely and start over from scratch. He went to the closet and dragged out his yoga mat, placing it in front of the mandala rug. Then he kicked off his boots and the rest of his clothes, threw them on the floor of his closet, and shut the door so he wouldn't have to look at a pile of dirty clothes. Slowly and deliberately he went through a complete yoga set. It was difficult at first because his mind was in such flight that it seemed incredibly boring to be going through these exercises. And his muscles were still tensing as he was trying to relax them.

By the third exercise his mind had calmed sufficiently

that he took a pure sensual pleasure in feeling the angry knotted muscles smooth out and start to sing again. By the end of the set he was positively loose.

Once the hatha-yoga, the physical portion, of this ritual was complete, he sat in the lotus position and directed his gaze at the mandala and shortly was lost in the point at the middle where all the patterns met and disappeared into the other side.

That's what it did if you thought of the circular pattern as a tunnel. And that's how he thought of it, sitting there in the lotus position, all the muscles in his body relaxed now. His face was dead. No longer did his cheeks his mouth, and his eyebrows, jerk and grimace like everybody else's when he thought. No, he was inside now, and inside there was this whole other outside, because he wasn't using his body at all. It was dormant, and he stared down that long tunnel of mandala to the point where the pattern disappeared at the center and saw a glimpse of what was on the other side of where the pattern disappeared, which was . . . something else.

Thoughts tried to come up and make themselves felt, but he blew them off. Spurlock . . . no, Spurlock was a label. He was . . . this, this calm being at the center of his essence. Children . . . yes, but not now. Now was the time to smooth and pamper his mind and soul so it would be ready. One by one the thoughts came and then they went away and soon he was left with, not nothing, because it was something, but he was in the part of his mind where the words don't go and there is nothing physical or tangible to describe. It is sufficient to say he was happy.

A half hour or so later Spurlock opened his eyes and slowly unpretzeled his body from the lotus. He was left feeling very peaceful and content. Once again he knew that what he needed would be there when he needed it. If that need called for the termination of his corporeal existence, he could handle that. But mainly he was going to keep his shit together and try to stay alive and do what he thought he should be doing.

Totally relaxed, he lay quietly on his mattress on the floor, rolled under the sheet and blanket, and fell immediately to sleep.

The next morning he went down to the office and checked out his CAR-15 and a thousand rounds of ammunition, three baseball-type hand grenades, a couple of hand-held flares, and an old AN/PRC-25 walkie-talkie radio, set on the common law enforcement frequency. If he got in trouble and there was any law within fifteen miles or so, he would be able to reach help—and his .357 magnum.

He was not sufficiently pure and it had come up guns.

He said good-bye to Harley and Clara, told Harley he would be back before the Maf tried anything and to keep it clean until he got back. Then he lugged his arsenal out to the horse, loaded it on the animal, and started back toward the farm.

He enjoyed the ride, and when he got back, Megan was out front, packing stuff into the VW microbus. She was in jeans and a work shirt and had her feet tucked into suede hiking boots. Jon was handing her boxes, which she carefully stowed in the back of the bus. He knew bloody good and well what she was doing, but nonetheless he rode to where she was loading the bus, dropped the reins, dismounted, and strode casually to her. "Goin' campin'?" he inquired.

She looked over her shoulder and replied calmly, "Going with you."

He didn't say anything for a moment. He looked at the stuff she was packing. There was a lot of food, and it was more and better than he could have taken. She had kept her talismans and objets d'art to a minimum, pretty practical for Megan. He had not really considered taking her along. She was in dismal physical condition for any kind of rough trek. But mentally she was equal to just about anybody in the world. Megan had her shit together in ways he did not, and maybe she would provide some essential element that would make it work. All questions of chivalry aside, he considered whether she would be more help than hindrance. There was no way to tell for sure, but on the whole he thought he'd be better off on this kind of deal without her. He shook his head. "Don't figure you ought to go," he said quietly.

She turned and put her hands on her hips. "No, I didn't think you would. But there are some things I know that you don't. Your awareness is still too much in your head, and not enough in the gut. So I'm going."

Spurlock shook his head. This was exactly the kind of crap he didn't want to have to put up with. There had to be only one boss on this kind of deal. That was the only way anything ever got done. That was why he and Megan couldn't live together, because she was the star of her show and he was the star of his. Neither would be able to stand playing second fiddle to the other. Now she was trying to pull this crap, and already it was impossible for him to plan what to do. He had to deal with this situation instead of getting his packhorse saddled up like he wanted. Well, this one he could deal with in a hurry.

"Woman," he said, "in about forty-five minutes I'm going to ride out of here on that horse, with another horse behind it. I don't tell you what to do and you don't tell me. I am going to New York by myself and as far as I'm concerned you can take that VW microbus and shove it."

She moved closer to him and put her hands on her hips, her face close to his, and he felt like an umpire in an argument with Leo Durocher. "You stupid moron," she began, "even with all that yoga you have the spiritual awareness of a mad bull. You need me."

"Bullshit!" he bellowed. "I am a cop and it is my job to move around the country, dealing with baddies. This is the biggest challenge I've faced since Frazier and his cretins were shooting up the town, and I can't afford to be saddled with a Spanish and math teacher while I do it. I'm going by myself and that's that.''

"Bravo!" said a voice behind him. He turned around to see Jon standing beside the microbus, clapping his hands together. "You two sure know how to put on a show," the kid said.

"Shuddup, kid," Spurlock snarled, turning to stalk away into the house to get his saddlebags.

When he returned a few minutes later she was still packing the microbus. Stubborn, stubborn, stubborn, he thought. He went to the stable and led out his packhorse, loading her down with two thirds of the ammo, almost all the food, and his bedroll. He kept enough ammo and food on the saddle horse to function if he lost the pack animal. In the clear light of day his worries about karma the night before seemed silly. The karma would take care of itself. He was going to do the best he could and if that wasn't good enough, then there was nothing he could do about it.

When the horses were ready, he went inside and made himself a sandwich, took a bowl of salad out of the icebox and ate it. That good bread and the salad were things he was going to miss on the trail. Then he got some canned peaches that Clancy had put up last summer and threw them on top of one of Megan's cakes. It was some kind of swell cake, an orange cake with chocolate icing. He added a big gob of cream, thick as mayonnaise, on top of that, and sat down and gorged himself.

Normally he didn't allow himself to stuff like that, but he was pretty sure it would be four or five months before he had any of this good stuff again, and he was going to get awfully tired of jerky, hardtack, and dried fruit.

At the end of his meal he gave an appreciative burp and got up, strapped the .357 magnum in a cowboy rig under his temporarily bulging belly, and set his hat low on his nose.

He wasn't thinking about spiritual advancement now. He was thinking about the best route through the mountains. He was going to try to make about twenty miles today, camp in the undergrowth, and get into Joplin tomorrow. With any sort of luck at all he could score a hot bath and a hot meal in Joplin. They'd probably let him crash at the jail free.

That was a fairly important consideration. Sure, he could camp out all the time. But there was no sense in being miserable when it wasn't necessary. He'd be miserable enough without working at it.

He went outside, feeling the lump in his belly, a little drowsy from lunch. He walked over to where Megan was standing beside the VW. She regarded him with a serene expression which he took to mean that she had accepted his decision. "Look," he said, "I'm sorry I can't take you, but this is something I can do better alone."

She nodded. "Sure," she replied, "I know how you feel."

He was gratified that she was taking it so easy, but a little surprised. It wasn't like her to be so accommodating when she wanted something else.

He kissed her. She returned it without fervor. He had expected a more passionate leave-taking, but . . . He shrugged. "So long," he said.

"See you," she replied with a sly grin.

"Where's Jon?"

"Over by the stable," she said. She appeared slightly perturbed when she said it. "He said he was going to curry his horse."

Spurlock nodded and walked to the stable, breathing in the smell of hay and horse and horse manure, feeling the shade as he walked in. It was dark inside. Hay was piled in the corners, and assorted tack hung from the pegs on the wall. He went to where Jon knelt, running a currycomb down his horse's leg.

"So long, kid," he said. "I got to be gettin' on."

Jon stood and extended his hand. Spurlock took it and shook it. "Be good," Spurlock nodded. "Take care of things for me."

Jon grinned slightly conspiratorially and said, "Yeah, I'll do my best."

Spurlock turned and went back out. He repressed a pang at seeing the last of these good friends, but there was also the thrill of adventure ahead and he looked forward to it. He mounted and checked the knot where the packhorse lead was tied off on his saddle horn. Then he waved at Megan and started riding down toward the highway to Joplin. When he reached the road, he looked back to see the VW following him. He supposed Megan was going to town to get something. He gave another slight wave and dimly, through the windshield, she returned it.

Down at the highway he turned right and rode on, expecting her to turn toward town. Instead she followed him. Could she be . . . ? Naw, she couldn't be . . . ! He stopped and thought for a moment. Yep! She not only could be, she was. He turned and rode back to the microbus. He stared down at her face through the window. "You mind tellin' me what you think you're doin'?" he demanded.

She grinned up at him. "I thought I might take a little trip, since you're going to be out of town and school's out for the summer."

He nodded. "Little vacation, huh?"

"Yeah!"

"You mind tellin' me where you're going on this little vacation?" He put one hand on his hip and reached for a toothpick with the other. He put it in his mouth, bit it in half, spat it out, and reached for another. He could feel all the good effects of this morning's yoga vanishing as tension prickled along his spine and a headache began at the base of his skull.

"Well," she said, smiling innocently. "I haven't been to the big city for a while. I thought I might go to New York."

He nodded. "You're driving awful slow for somebody going to New York."

She shrugged. "I'm in no hurry. Besides, if I pass you it might frighten your horse."

He inhaled deeply and then sighed. "Frighten my horse."

"Yes!"

"What you're going to do, woman, is you're going to get us both killed. You're road-bound in that truck and you're going to be hit going that slow."

She grinned happily at him. "Well, I've got plenty of room. Why don't you put your stuff on the bus and send the horses back to the farm? Then we could make some good time."

He shook his head. "Goddammit! Can't you get it through your head that I don't need you and I don't want you. You are a menace to you and me both."

Very seriously she looked him in the eye and said, "No, you don't want me because you don't know what you're facing and you don't know if you can handle it at all, and you're afraid I'll get hurt or killed or something. But let me tell you something, buster. There are things out there that neither you nor I can imagine. More things than bandits and bomb craters. There are unimaginable forces and powers afoot in the air and you will never deal with them with that straight-ahead mentality of yours. But I can deal with them. They are my natural element." She gestured with her hand to indicate the eagle's claw hanging from her rearview mirror, the faded rose in the ashtray, and the driftwood on the dash.

He shook his head again and repeated one of the stock insults of his childhood. "You're as full of shit as a Christmas turkey."

"Precisely!" she exclaimed. "Exactly what you need."

He hit his forehead with the heel of his hand. "Oh, hell! Where's Jon? This is just crazy enough for him to want a piece of it, too."

A flicker of fear flashed across her face. "No!" she exclaimed. "He wanted to come, but I wouldn't let him. It was too dangerous."

Spurlock nodded. "Too dangerous," he repeated.

"Yes," she said. "He's just a baby."

Spurlock shook his head mockingly. "Just a baby, huh? Well, listen here, honeybunch. Him I could use, but you, you'd just get in the way, so you'll have to turn back."

She shook her head. "No way," she replied.

He nodded. "Have it your own way. It's a free country, sort of. Anyway, don't expect me to help when your truck is hijacked and you're raped and thrown into the ditch to be shot."

She shuddered, then said, "I can handle myself."

He nodded, scowling, turned his horse away from the van and angrily spurred it, jerking the reins for the packhorse to follow. It was a stupid thing to do, and very hard to coordinate, but with the VW following he galloped on. As they rounded the first left turn, Spurlock turned and went up the hill and into the woods, hoping that when she lost him Megan would lose heart and turn back. It didn't seem like the thing she'd do easily, but if she couldn't find him she wouldn't have a hell of a lot of choice.

It presented him with a tricky problem, because he would have to shadow her from the woods until she did. He didn't want anything to happen to her.

Fortunately he was far enough back in the timber that she couldn't see him by the time she rounded the turn. Also fortunately she continued to go at the same pace once she realized she'd lost him. She was looking anxiously up into the woods, trying to locate him.

But he had gone into the woods on the right, and there was a blind spot to her right rear, and up, which was where he was, and she couldn't see him.

But she didn't stop and he had to ride through the woods, limbs crackling under his horse's feet, branches sweeping at his face and slowing him down as he struggled to keep up with her.

It gave him time to reflect on the perversity of women. He hoped that she would realize she had no chance of finding him before she got far enough out from town for it to be dangerous.

Unfortunately that was not as far as either of them figured. Spurlock had tracked her for about half an hour when the silence was shattered by an ear-splitting whoop and half a dozen guerrillas on horseback swooped down on the van, firing short bursts from their weapons.

At the sound of the first shout Megan floorboarded the van, but it failed to respond with much vigor. She was slowly picking up speed when one of the guerrillas shot out her left front tire.

Screw the tire, screw the rim, Spurlock thought. Drive out of there, baby.

But the van slowed to a stop and the horsemen dragged Megan from it. What she had accomplished with her brief burst of so-called speed was to get too far away for Spurlock to open fire without running the risk of hitting her.

The guerrillas were off their horses and two of them started ransacking the VW, dragging out bedding, clothes, and food. Two of the others held Megan and one big one examined her with interest.

Spurlock untied the reins on the packhorse and tied them to a nearby tree. He had all the ammo he would need for this job on him. Unencumbered by the packhorse, he made much better time through the trees. For a moment he considered dismounting and trying to get in on the guerrillas on foot, but abandoned this idea. If they rode off while he came forward, he would have to go back for his horse and would run a big risk of losing them. He decided to play it safe.

He hadn't been concerned about being silent when he was tracking Megan because she couldn't hear him over the sound of her engine, and he had made comparatively good time. But now he moved very carefully through the brush. As he got closer to the guerrillas, he dismounted and led his horse forward, being careful to pick up any big dry sticks the horse might step on. He slung the CAR-15 over his neck and it clattered and rattled around in front of him as he crunched through the brush.

As he got closer he could make out the guerrillas. The big one who seemed to be in charge was Martinez.

That figures, he thought sourly.

He could just barely make out Marty saying, "Ah, Spurlock's woman. Hunh! Hunh! Hunh!" he chortled. He stepped forward and slapped her.

She looked at him with undisguised loathing and suddenly unleashed a ferocious kick at his groin. He easily sidestepped it and slapped her again, laughing. He did it left-handed, though. His right was still in a splint and filthy bandage.

Spurlock wondered what their game was. Frazier was not likely to work this close to town. Nor was he likely to pick on a lone citizen in a van. Traveling salesmen and goods convoys were more Frazier's meat, but then he had more men to work with. A little band like Marty's couldn't expect to get much.

Spurlock could only surmise that Martinez had taken his loyal followers and broken away from Frazier before the little captain could deal with him. Frazier would probably have killed him without a thought, for the loss of a weapon and the hassle with the sheriff. Martinez was now probably trying to get some supplies and get far out of Frazier's way.

Spurlock's immediate problem was how to confront six armed guerrillas and get the drop on them before they could do Megan any harm, and split. If he opened up now, Martinez would simply shoot her and ride away.

As soon as they loaded up all they wanted, they scattered the rest and left the truck. Megan was mounted behind Martinez and they rode off through the woods.

Spurlock got one lucky break in that they entered the woods on his side of the road, and he was able to follow them more easily.

He let them move entirely out of sight through the woods and then started after them, listening for the sounds of horses and the curses of the men as they moved branches out of their way. He continued to lead the horse and track on the ground. It wasn't hard. Six mounted men leave quite a trail through virgin timber.

The way led over one ridgeline and down another. Actually it wouldn't have been too hard to find them even if they hadn't left such a trail. He was sure they wouldn't set their ambush far from their camp, maybe a couple of miles, no more. And they would go over at least one ridgeline and they would camp near water, and with good overhead cover. The rat-ass army of the alleged government was known to go out with helicopters sometimes. And while they would never do anything so bold as to launch an attack, they had been known to spray the woods with machine-gun fire when they found a suspected guerrilla position.

Spurlock had been summoned several times to escort the bodies of farmers who had been caught fishing that way and shot from the air. He often wondered if the army was so stupid it really believed a guerrilla would sit on the bank of a river and fish when he heard a chopper coming, or if they were so vicious that they didn't care.

He plunged on through the woods until the ground started sloping down. He knew he was moving toward water, and therefore was closer to their camp, at least probably closer, and he moved more cautiously.

Finally he heard the sound of rushing water ahead and the sound of voices, so he tied the horse to a tree and took

an old ragged olive-green canvas ammo belt off from
behind the saddle. It was an old army pistol belt hung with
big ammo pouches crammed with four magazines of M-16
ammo each. He had loaded the pouches himself. The
ammo in the left-hand pouches was all ball ammo, which
is what the army euphemistically calls antipersonnel ammunition, after the old musket balls of the Civil War. One
pouch on the right was loaded with every third round
tracer. These were handy at night when you couldn't aim
very well. The other pouch contained armor-piercing ammo,
which could be useful against people in automobiles should
such an eventuality arise.

He left his radio back there on the saddle. Martinez
wasn't stupid. The ambush was conducted just out of radio
range of Purgatory.

He went forward toward the sound of the voices and
stopped about twenty yards through the woods from a little
camp where Martinez and his people had put up their
grubby hammocks and little tents made from old ponchos.
There was a small fire on a flat rock down near the river,
carefully made so as to minimize the smoke.

The men clustered around Martinez, standing near Megan,
who was tied to a tree, her arms racked back around the
trunk. From the expression on her face Spurlock could tell
that the tying had been none too gentle. The men gestured
heatedly. He crept closer to hear what they were saying.

As near as he could make out, Martinez had culled the
six slimiest of the men who made up Frazier's guerrilla
band. And none of Frazier's people were what you could
call solid citizens.

Martinez brandished his wounded hand and snarled,
"Now, I'm the guy whose hand her old man broke, and I
say I fuck her first."

A stoop-shouldered specimen with green teeth, who
was, if possible, even more foul-looking than Marty, whined,
"Now, that ain't fair, Marty. We all taken the chance you
done. I says we draw straws for it."

There was a chorus of Yeahs and You-betchas from the others. Spurlock had never seen such expressions of open, ugly, naked longing in his life. It was kind of hard to figure. They had all been at Creech's yesterday. Presumably if they'd just wanted to have their ashes hauled, they could have taken care of it there. No, this was something else. These men wanted to use sex as an instrument of hatred. This was an open appetite for rape and murder. For there was no likelihood that they would leave Megan alive after they were through.

They might, though. Martinez would get a lot of pleasure out of leaving her to walk home on the road and tell him about it. Spurlock thought about it for a moment. He wondered if Martinez had the balls to throw down that kind of a challenge to him. He decided not. Martinez had no way of knowing he was leaving town, and he was quite capable of deducing that Spurlock would track him to the ends of the earth if he pulled such a stunt. Quite correctly, too, karma or no karma.

Spurlock looked at Megan. There was no fear on her face, just open loathing.

The sheriff put the sight to his eye and put the cross hairs on the base of Martinez's shaggy, lice-ridden skull. He eased the safety off and put the weapon on single shot. It would be so simple to squeeze off a round and see the small red dot appear on the back of Martinez's head and watch the off-white goo of his brains explode out the other side like a poorly digested lunch. But he didn't want to do it. He had seen that too many times to think there was any fun attached to it, even for a creep like Martinez.

And there were other factors to consider. There were six of those bastards, all of them armed in some way, and some of them standing directly between him and Megan. It wouldn't be such a hot idea to fire on them. He was a good shot, but there was no guarantee that he would miss her. He would rather have her alive and raped than dead and "pure." She had lived quite a while and thrown herself headlong into life the whole time. In the course of that she had been balled enough times under disagreeable circumstances that she could handle it once more if necessary.

God knows, though, that it would be hard to find any circumstances more disagreeable than these.

It would help, he observed sourly, if these slimy creeps just jumped in the river for a moment with a bar of soap.

Helpless in the face of unswerving opposition from his five heroes, Martinez agreed to draw lots for the privilege of gouging Megan's body. There was hearty laughter as they drew coins from their pockets and commenced to odd-man.

That gave Spurlock a little more time and he decided on a plan. There was a five-gallon gas can near the fire and he had a silencer for the CAR-15 tucked away somewhere in his saddlebags. He had never used it in all the time he'd had it. But, still and all, he'd thought when he started out, you never know. Quickly and silently he moved back to the horse and took the heavy metal cylinder out of the saddlebags and fitted it over the flash supressor of his weapon. Then he moved back to his position, replacing the magazine with one with tracer ammo.

The silencer would sharply reduce the muzzle velocity of the weapon, which meant that his aim would be all wrong. The rounds would drop sharply. Fortunately the range was so short that they wouldn't drop too far, and with tracer ammo and the weapon on full auto he could adjust quickly.

As luck would have it Martinez won the toss. Lucky you, Spurlock thought, and set the cross hairs just over the top of the can, figuring on just enough drop to set the can off. If there was no sound and the gas just exploded, there would be enough confusion that he had a good chance to pick them off before they knew what was going on.

Martinez snorted when he won the toss and stepped up to Megan, shambling obscenely and smirking, winking at his cohorts. He was making a game of being the slimy rapist he was. He stepped up to Megan and she spat full in his face. Looking through the telescopic sight, Spurlock could see the spittle oozing through Martinez's oily beard. Martinez just laughed, slapped Megan full across the face, once, twice, three times, very hard across, back, and across again. Then he leaned forward and rubbed his spit-soaked beard on her cheek. He laughed again. He was enjoying this very much.

For that you die, Spurlock thought, and switched his aim back to the gas can. He thought it with a sort of queasy twist to his guts, because he had hoped very much to get through the rest of his life without ever having to kill another man. It hadn't seemed too much to ask.

His finger was on the trigger and squeezing slowly when one of the guerrillas stepped between him and the gas can. He eased off.

With the time provided by this respite Martinez started ripping Megan's clothes off. The shirt was easy, but the jeans he could only unbutton and pull off. He tried to pull off both legs at once and she lost her footing, causing both arms to be abraded badly on the tree trunk. "Here, you stupid asshole," she said, and stepped out of them casually.

All of the guerrillas gawked obscenely.

Martinez dropped his pants and waddled toward Megan, erect penis sticking out the front of his shirttails. He grasped it with his dirty left hand and sneered, "You know what that is, you bitch?"

Megan laughed out loud. "Looks like a penis to me," she said, a sort of stricken grin on her face, "only smaller."

"You whore," Martinez grated as the other guerrillas exploded into laughter and the one who was blocking Spurlock's line of fire stamped his foot and moved aside.

Spurlock squeezed the trigger and the weapon went

bapbapbapbap softly. The first two rounds kicked up dirt
in front of the can and he raised his aim slightly. The first
tracer went squarely through the center of the can. The can
exploded with a loud *Whoooom!* and an orange and black
fireball showered burning gasoline over three of the other
guerrillas, catching their clothes on fire. Martinez caught a
lot of it right on his naked hairy ass and at that point there
was a lot of screaming.

Two of the guerrillas took flat running dives into the
river. Martinez took two steps forward and fell flat on his
face, his clothes burning. He screamed loudly and rolled
over and over in the dirt, trying to put the fire out. All he
succeeded in doing was catching the bandage on his right
hand on fire.

Spurlock took a quick look at Megan to see if she was
all right. She was laughing.

Spurlock had delayed his move because he was waiting
for the perfect moment to stop all this bullshit without, if
possible, killing anybody. The way Martinez looked rolling around on the ground like that he'd have been a lot
better off if Spurlock had blown his head off. But that was
Martinez's bad karma, not Spurlock's. Intent was what
counted here. Martinez was rolling in the dirt, trying to put
out his fire. Two of the Gs were in the water, putting out
their fires, but when they came up for air they didn't seem
to be interested in coming back up on the bank and fighting it out. They went back under the water and swam
downstream.

That left three of them. One was beating out a small fire
on his shirt and the two others were going for their rifles.
Spurlock figured this was the crunch. It was time for him
to start killing, much as he wanted not to.

He raised his sight to his eye and started his trigger
squeeze.

There was the sound of another automatic weapon, not
Spurlock's, and one of the men came all apart in a bloody

mass in front of the sheriff's eyes. The other two simply dropped their weapons and put their hands in the air.

Spurlock wondered who the invisible sniper might be. It might be help and it might be hindrance, but in any case he elected to wait until the fellow showed his hand. It was probably Frazier or one of his men, and he couldn't gauge at this point what their reaction might be, so he sat tight. This was scary as hell, but he enjoyed the adrenaline rush that went with it.

He waited only a few minutes and a swaggering form came down out of the woods. Tall, slender, and blond, the kid looked positively heroic. It was Jon.

Spurlock grinned and shook his head. The kid was making all kinds of mistakes, but for a kid he really had it together. He should have waited until he knew for sure who blew up the gas can, but still and all he was doing a pretty good job.

The faces on the two remaining Gs, one of whom was the one who had his shirt on fire, fell when they saw who their assailant was. The one who had gone for his rifle shook his head. "A kid," he said, "a goddamn kid."

Martinez said nothing. He was moaning and shivering on the ground. Spurlock figured that if they could get him into a chopper and evacuated to a first-rate burn hospital he might have a chance to survive. Only there was no burn hospital within six hundred miles. Martinez would have to die, and although there was no joy in it, there was no guilt either.

"Hi, Mom!" Jon said.

Megan smiled wanly. "How about getting me off this tree," she said. "I'd like to get dressed.

Jon nodded. "Cut my mother loose," he said to the ace gunner, who winced at the sound of the word "mother." He cut Megan loose quickly.

Spurlock could have got up and gone down there then, but he wanted to watch and see how the kid did, and also he wanted to cover him, which he could do better from his concealed firing position than he could walking down the hill through the woods.

Besides, this had been a day of surprises, and if there were any more he wanted the last one to be his.

As soon as she was loose, Megan started putting on her clothes. "You're too old to see me in this position," she said to Jon, "or maybe not old enough."

Jon herded the Gs back together, the better to keep an eye on them.

"What're you doing here anyway?" his mother demanded.

"Well," he replied, grinning, "I figured if you could follow Spurlock, I could follow you."

Good kid, Spurlock thought, smiling.

Megan's face clouded over and she glared at him angrily. She opened her mouth to speak, but said nothing.

"Don't chew me out," the kid said. "I just saved your life."

She shrugged and nodded. "That was pretty clever, blowing up the gas can."

A slightly surprised look came into Jon's face.

"What! If you didn't, who did?"

"It was probably one of my people," said a voice from the edge of the clearing. Frazier and three of his men stepped out of the treeline. "And the fucker fired without authorization. I'm gonna have his ass. Drop the rifle, kid."

Jon did as he was told.

Hiding in the woods, Spurlock nodded and grinned wryly. Martinez had never had a chance. Frazier had undoubtedly been looking for him the minute he took off. The only thing he could have done was get out of Frazier's territory as quickly as possible, but the fool had to hang around long enough to knock over Megan's truck, and it had cost him a lot of pain, and finally it would cost him his life. He'd be a lot better off dead than moaning on the ground like that.

Frazier walked over and looked at the scorched guerrilla, said, "Hmmmmmmmmm!" and fired a four-round burst into his head. The body twitched once and was still.

He turned to a big soldier less ragged than the rest and said, "Top, I want you to get the entire company here, and I want to know who fired the round into the gas can. We could have got all of these bastards if it wasn't for him, and the son of a bitch is going to be suitably punished."

"How about us?" Megan inquired.

Frazier shrugged. "Kinda hard to say," he said. "You two were an unexpected bonus. For sure it won't be anything as spectacular as old Marty here"—he pointed to the corpse on the ground—"had planned for you. Spurlock's kind of a hard dude, but he's played fair with me and I'll play fair with him. But I'll let him sweat a little, and maybe make him let us take our guns to town, something like that."

Bullshit, take your guns to town, Spurlock thought from his concealed position.

The clearing was beginning to fill up with guerrillas. The first sergeant dispatched a couple into the woodline in each direction to take up security positions, and the rest flopped down under the trees. Spurlock noted that they were not just crashing where they were, though. Relaxed as they were, they were staying in definite groups, each under the command of its own sergeant. It was a loose force, but still disciplined. As far as Spurlock was concerned, though, Frazier relied too much on discipline after the fact, and not enough on training before. But then maybe not. It wasn't one of Frazier's men who had fired on the gas can after all. It was Spurlock. And as soon as Frazier had his force all in one place, Spurlock could run a little bluff on them and see what he could get away with.

In addition he'd get to see Frazier's company all in one place at one time, which would give him an item of intelligence he'd been trying to get for years.

When they were all in, there seemed to be about sixty of them, which was maybe twenty less than Spurlock had thought, and that was counting the eight he'd seen the first sergeant send off into the woods. In actuality Frazier's company was nothing more than a reinforced platoon. Spurlock repressed a grin.

Frazier stepped into the middle of the clearing. "Aw right, which one of you clowns fired that tracer into the gas can?"

The men looked at each other, but no one said anything.

"You might as well speak up now," Frazier went on, "because I'll find out who it was and it'll be a lot harder if I have to wait. As it is now nobody goes to town until I find out who it was."

There was a low moan from the soldiers.

Frazier waited a long moment, then said, "Aw right, goddammit, I'm gettin' mad."

Spurlock laughed out loud, and it sounded vaguely supernatural in the woods. "Forget it, Frazier," he called out. "None of these idiots has the sense or the aim to shoot out that gas can. It was one of my men and all you cretins can drop your weapons and let Jon and Megan go, or we'll open up on you."

Frazier jumped at the sound of Spurlock's voice. Then he let his AK drop to the ground and all the guerrillas did likewise. "Fortunes of war, eh, Spurlock, you fuckhead!" he called out.

"Fortunes of war, Frazier," Spurlock called back. "Now, send those two up to me."

Frazier nodded and Jon and Megan started running toward the sound of his voice. As soon as they got to him he whispered, "Take my horse, get back to the VW, and change the tire. Do it!" He slapped Jon on the rump, gave Megan a quick hug, and sent them on their way.

"Have your first sergeant call in your outposts," he called down to Frazier. "I want all of you in one place before we move in."

Frazier gave the order. Spurlock figured it would take about five minutes for the outposts to move in and he wanted to be as far away as possible when they did. He and Frazier had a pretty good relationship for enemies, but he didn't think that would prevent Frazier from killing him if he found him in the woods.

With Spurlock gone forever it would only be a matter of time until the Gs moved in on the town again. He was pretty sure he couldn't be gone more than six months. Harley could hold them off for that long, but he wasn't slick enough to keep the whole thing going longer than that. Frazier would figure out a way and the town would be his. Pretty much his anyway. The army would throw him out if he tried to occupy it, but he could control it from the woods through intimidation if Spurlock wasn't there.

Spurlock was up and moving quietly through the woods, back up the hill. Once over the crest of the hill he ran like a gazelle toward the truck. Happy to have got what he wanted without personally killing anybody. True, Martinez was dead, but that had been Martinez's doing, not Spurlock's. It wasn't even Frazier's. Frazier had just killed him because he was dying anyway. But Spurlock didn't doubt that Frazier had enjoyed it.

It took him about twenty minutes to get back to the truck. He figured Frazier and the Gs were maybe ten minutes behind. It would have taken them a little over five to find out that they weren't surrounded and never had been. Then there would be a brief session of Frazier cursing and hopping up and down and they would be hot on his trail.

Good old Jon had the tire on when he got there. Spurlock came over the crest of the last hill and looked down through the greenery to see Jon slapping the hubcap onto the wheel. Megan stood beside him, watching. Most of the scattered stuff had been picked up and apparently thrown into the truck. The saddle horse was behind the truck, reins tied to the rear bumper.

Panting a little bit, but not badly, because he was in damned good shape, Spurlock charged down the hill, his CAR-15 dangling in his right hand. He laughed as he jumped off the edge of the hill and slid down the dirt cut in the hillside that had been 'dozed off to make the road. He got about halfway down, skidding like a skier on a steep slope, and then slipped and went the last twenty feet bumping along on his ass, grinning and laughing, pulling his shirttail out and getting a large dirt stain on his jeans, like a kid at recess. He hadn't had that much fun since the war with the Gs ended.

The guerrillas were probably right behind him and he wanted to be gone when they got there. With the truck it wouldn't be any problem. He was going to have to take Megan.

Jon stood up beside the truck as Spurlock ran up. "Kid," Spurlock panted, taking the ammo and supplies off the horse, "where's the packhorse?"

Jon smiled. "Off-loaded it into the van and sent it back to the farm."

Spurlock nodded. "Okay," he said. "I want you to take the saddle horse back to the farm. Frazier's going to be hopping mad and he's going to come around tonight and zing a few rounds into the house. The folks will have to be warned."

Spurlock had no idea whether this was true or not, but it was going to be hell with Megan along anyway, and if she was mother-henning Jon it was going to be impossible.

Disappointment clouded Jon's face. "I wanna go with you guys."

Spurlock shook his head. He reached out and clasped Jon's shoulder. "I'd like to have you, kid," he said. "You did a fine job here today. You're a good troop." Jon's face lit up at the praise. "But you're needed back at the farm. Those folks need to be warned, and then they might need every gun they've got.''

Jon nodded, his face becoming firm with resolve. He had been praised and given a mission. Spurlock punched him on the arm and said, "Do it!"

The kid vaulted to the back of his horse. The horse reared up on its hind legs and the kid waved like the Lone Ranger, turned, and galloped back toward town.

Grinning, Spurlock waved back.

Spurlock sighed and threw the rest of his stuff in the van. "Okay, baby," he said, "let's hit the road."

He vaulted for the driver's seat and Megan went around the van to get in on the shotgun side. Spurlock quickly accelerated to the van's full forty-five miles per hour and checked the road to the rear in the mirror with the eagle's claw hanging from it on a small gold chain. They were halfway to Joplin before either one of them said anything.

Megan broke the silence when she said, "See, I told you you'd need me. We'd never have got away from those guerrillas without the van."

Spurlock sighed and rolled a toothpick into his mouth. From there until they got to Joplin he reflected on the perversity of women.

CHAPTER FIVE

SOON AFTER, it got dark and Spurlock had to consider whether to try to drive through or hang it up for the night and make camp. In a way it would make better sense to keep driving, since nobody in his right mind would do such a thing. Since the woods were crawling with guerrillas, nobody traveled at night and the guerrillas slept like everybody else. So Spurlock and Megan kept going. Even at forty-five miles an hour they made it to Joplin in a couple of hours and stopped for a cup of coffee at an all-night diner.

It hadn't been kept up and the orange plastic upholstery on the booths was ripped in spots and the fake wood Formica top was split and ripped. The orange plastic in the light globes was broken, sending weird splashes of light into odd corners of the room. Spurlock eased himself into a booth and Megan sat across from him.

It was odd. They hadn't been on the road that long, but the road tiredness was already creeping over them. Two hours behind the wheel, with the little engine going *rrrrhhhhuuuummmmmm*, and the joint they'd done just after leaving Frazier's guerrillas behind had left him a little spaced. Megan had the same look.

The muscles in the back of his neck were stiff from being held in the same position for two hours, and the VW hadn't been made for somebody with long legs. His right ankle cramped from holding the accelerator. He would have given a lot right then to have had a place to go and spread out his yoga mat and ease the strain out of those muscles.

The dangers of the road were one thing, to be hounded by hostile guerrillas and shot at by bandits, have your identity papers checked by all kinds of weird cops, some of whom could be counted on to react favorably to his being a cop, and others who would react just as adversely. He never got it quite straight why that was, but cops were, by and large, an obstreperous breed.

The waitress, a forty-year-old slattern in jeans and a work shirt, came over, chewing gum, and demanded, ''Whadaya want?''

Spurlock leaned back with both of his arms dangling over the back of the booth, looked her up and down, and sighed, ''Got any pie?''

She nodded. ''Yeah, apple.''

He glanced at Megan and she nodded.

''Two pies with ice cream and two coffees.''

The waitress wrote it down and minced back to the kitchen to give the order to the counterman, an oily geek with long hair and a harelip.

Yeah, being in danger on the road was one thing, but what really chapped his ass on the road was the fact that you couldn't get a decent meal. Spurlock was thirty-nine years old and in extremely good physical condition. He looked twenty-nine and felt about twenty-three. His only concession to age was carrying in his head all the collected memories of all the people he had been. Some of it gave him a modicum of wisdom, but the rest was just obsolete information which cluttered his thoughts and made him have to be careful about launching long, boring digressions.

But he knew that by the time this trip was completed he would look his thirty-nine years and more besides. The wrinkles on his face would be deep creases that would take a week of steady yoga to smooth out. His digestive system would be thoroughly screwed and his energy level would be way down because he hadn't had a balanced diet. Basic good physical condition would carry him through, and he was really into the adventure of it, but he wished there were some way to travel without destroying your health.

It seemed strange to him that now he was into it he wasn't worried about his kids at all. They were the end result of what he was trying to do, and he was doing it. He threw all his worry into the worry of the moment. When he got to the kids, he would worry about them, but probably not very much until then. He did wonder what they looked like now, though. They'd been cute little buggers before.

He and Megan sat there, stared at each other, and engaged in semipolite conversation until the waitress brought the pie and coffee.

"Do you want to try and drive all night?" Megan asked.

He thought for a moment, then nodded. "Yeah, I think maybe so. It might be a good idea to make time while we can."

She nodded in agreement.

He threw some money on the counter as they left and they got back in the VW and headed out to the interstate.

Looking down the road like this, it was easy to visualize how it had been back before the war, when he was a kid and the interstates were clean, sweeping curves from coast to coast. So many times he'd hitched all the way across the country and back, out on the highway with a rucksack.

It was so clean and easy then, because he was young.

They were all young and didn't give a damn. A couple of nights he slept under a picnic table in a roadside park. Most of the rides he got were with freaks in vans which looked about like this one, and a lot of them had good music systems. They'd get out on the interstate and smoke a couple of numbers and watch the road movie.

In his memory it didn't seem that he had ever got tired, or sick, or wet, but he knew that wasn't true. He had a cold most of the time and his nose ran. Some nights under picnic tables his sleeping bag got wet as he curled into a tighter and tighter ball, trying to fit himself into the dry spots left in the bag. Finally the bag got as wet as it was going to and he got some sleep, and then had to pass up three good rides the next day while it dried.

The difference between an adventure at sixteen and an adventure at thirty-nine was that an adventure was a damned nuisance when you're middle-aged.

It was hard to drive on I-44 in this year of our Lord 1996. The son of a bitch was all over chuckholes, badly patched with asphalt until a couple of years ago, and now filled only by mud and rocks by the so-called Highway Department, which was nothing but a chain gang for captured guerrillas. Somehow these guys didn't seem to have their hearts in road repair. The guards had orders to shoot them immediately should the other guerrillas try to bust them loose.

Of course it didn't make much sense for the guards to do that, because if they did and the guerrillas won the fight, then the guards could expect to be shot out of hand. Conversely, if they didn't kill the prisoners and then tried to go back after the fight, they would find themselves on the chain gang. It was sort of an awkward situation all around. Normally the Gs didn't try to bust their people loose. It was too sticky for everybody.

He slewed the VW around a big chuckhole and looked at the scenery, what he could see of it at night. It was low rolling hills here, although they were getting back into the Missouri Ozarks. Maybe that was Arkansas chauvinism, though. Arkies prided themselves on living rough.

He reached up on the dash for Megan's stash box. She herself had crashed in the back shortly after they left Joplin. She said she'd take over driving as soon as he got too tired. He was expecting that maybe he could make it to a hundred miles this side of St. Louis, another festering pesthole. The way it was now any city with a population of over a million was almost unlivable. But for some weird reason people continued to cling to them. They lived mostly on canned food. The electricity never worked long enough for fresh food to stay fresh.

But there was still lots of manufacturing in the cities. It was done with antiquated equipment and it was dangerous as hell, but the city folk were afraid of guerrillas and the great open spaces away from . . . what? It used to be that they were afraid to be away from their traffic noises and their sirens. What kind of weird scenes were they habituated to now?

Spurlock hadn't been in a city larger than Joplin in eight years.

He fished a number out of the stash, rolled it into his mouth, and lit it. Never in his life had he tried driving cross-country without smoking. He had gone a couple of hundred miles like that once and the boredom got to him so bad he'd almost gone crazy. He took a deep hit off the number. It was his own dynamite grass, Arkansas sinsemilla tops, "donkey dicks" in the trade, and he felt the first boredom-numbing hit curl around in his brain, soothing his anxieties. He finished the number and stared off down the road at the lights that seemed suddenly brighter. It was very pleasant to drive like this, winging down the road in this beat-up old van, slewing around the chuckholes, watching to see if the overpasses had been blown by guerrillas. In a moment he was humming happily and singing:

Goin' to New York City, all the way from Arkansas
Goin' to New York City, all the way from Arkansas
Where I'm goin' I ain't nothin'
Where I come from I'm the law.

Got a stone mean woman and a beat-up
   Vee-Dubya van
Got a stone mean woman and a beat-up
   Vee-Dubya van
Interstate blues take a-holt of a drivin' man.

It wasn't much, but it was the best he could do, just pulling them off the top of his head like that. He couldn't sing and he couldn't play, but sometimes out on the road these eight-bar blues kept popping into his head, and when they did he kept singing to see how they'd come out. Sometimes he didn't think they were half bad, but the next day he could never remember them.

He got stopped at a checkpoint on the first Springfield exit. The only guard awake came to the window, a scared kid in a shoddy army uniform, badly tailored by the local laundry, with a bad spit-shine on his boots and the shag haircut favored by the MPs. His armband and baton would help him very little if the Gs raided his checkpoint, and there wasn't more than a squad in the tent next to the checkpoint, stuck out on the interstate like that. They'd be all right if they could get a couple of helicopters out in under maybe five minutes. Otherwise if any Gs hit, they were fucked.

The kid got his fear together and said, "Don't you know enough to keep off the highways at night, citizen?" They made them call all civilians "citizen" for some reason.

Stoned, Spurlock got his head together, grinned at the MP, and reached into his pocket. The kid flinched and raised his carbine, but didn't clutch so badly that he started shooting. Spurlock flipped out his wallet and showed his badge. "Official police business, son," he said in his most authoritative manner.

The kid came to attention and saluted, for by custom sheriffs were honorary colonels, or some such. "Sorry, sir, I didn't know," the kid blurted.

Spurlock nodded. "That's all right, kid. You're just doin' your job. Doin' all right, too." It sounded like something from a John Wayne movie.

"Thank you, sir," the kid said.

Spurlock engaged the gears and eased forward into the night, singing.

> The army's bad news and the navy is a fake
> The army sucks and the navy is a fake
> But you can sleep well,
> Your national guard's awake

There was next to no traffic on the road at night. For an hour after he passed Springfield there was none. There was about half a moon way over the truck somewhere but he couldn't see it, and there were dark clouds overhead. Scattered but dark. When he was a kid, there'd have been cars and trucks on the highway all night long, and he and his lady would have played leapfrog with the passing semis, lit up like Christmas trees as they roared by in the night, making the truck slew in the wake of their passing. He missed those semis.

He wasn't especially worried about getting ambushed. It takes a while to organize an ambush, and nobody was expecting traffic at night. So he drove along, happily stoned, and watched the clouds overhead, also checking for chuckholes.

The overpass was blown out on the Branson exit so he had to take the VW off the exit ramp, across the highway, and back up on the entrance on the other side. It was only a momentary delay, since there was no cross traffic, but it made him a little sad to look up and see the jagged edge of what had been a really fine highway, with steel reinforcing rods sticking out, bent and rusted. The clouds whipped aside for a moment and the moon shone down on these ruins of what had been a mighty civilization and was now only this rat-shit empire.

He saw a series of headlights coming up from the rear. From the regularly spaced intervals he recognized it as an army convoy, probably the only thing apt to be out at this time of night anyway. His guess was that it was a battalion of infantry which had been out on a G-sweep and their commander hadn't wanted to keep them out an extra night when his mission was over.

Under normal conditions a convoy wouldn't travel more than thirty-five miles an hour, but these clowns were pushing it for all it was worth, trying to get back to Fort Leonard Wood before some long-haired greaser who wore an older version of the same uniform opened up on them. He didn't blame them. They were all draftees and none of them cared.

The fifteen-vehicle convoy burned past, whipping the little microbus in its wake. As the last vehicle roared by, the VW slewed wildly to the right and it was all Spurlock could do to hold it on the road. Then the wind died and he roared through the night, after shaking his fist at the retreating column of tail lights and muttering, "Hang it in yer ear, scumbucket." From the back of his mind a voice said, Easy bud, give them good for evil, so he sent a thought of sympathy after them, feeling slightly hypocritical at the same time. He tried to work up a genuine feeling of love for his fellowmen, but it wasn't easy.

Megan stirred from where she was sleeping in the back. She sat up and looked at him, bleary-eyed, her beautiful black hair tumbling down around her soft face. "Whazzat?" she asked.

"I said, 'Hang it in your ear, scumbucket,' " he replied.

She shook her head. "I din' do nothin'."

He shook his head, grinning. "I was talking to the army."

"The army," she repeated. "What you talkin' to the army for? They're nothin' but a bunch of scumbuckets."

"Go back to sleep."

Her head disappeared and again he was alone. He lit another number. The tank was getting empty and there was no such thing as an all-night gas station. There'd been a five-gallon can of gas strapped to the outside of the vehicle, but Martinez and his crew had taken that off and they'd been in such haste to leave they hadn't retrieved it. He pulled off at the exit to Fort Leonard Wood and drove down a corridor of lights to the main gate.

This time he had his badge out to show the gate MP before he got nervous. "Anyplace I can get some gas this time of night?" he asked the guard.

This one was an older version of the kid at the checkpoint outside Springfield. He was a corporal and he seemed to have his stuff pretty well in order. He leaned forward and looked into the VW, seeming to size Spurlock up. "Got any dope?" he asked.

Spurlock was startled, it was so blatant. But the MP was no fool. It was his word against the civilian's and it was very unlikely that any civilian would voluntarily hassle the army. Spurlock quickly ran through his inventory. He had a couple of keys of his homegrown grass tucked away back there in what was left of the baggage somewhere, and that was all, as far as he knew. Who knew what Megan had? But it was still better to ask questions than to give answers. "What kind of dope?" he asked.

The MP leaned against the VW and grinned. "Well, we got a battalion of them Russians runnin' exercises here, and them suckers'll give up to five bucks for a hit of good acid. Man, the Russian army's discovered LSD. It's flower power all over again."

Spurlock grinned. "Their commanders must love that."
He paused a minute. "Sorry," he said. "All I got's some
grass. It's good, though."

A slow smile spread over the MP's face. "Jesus," he
said, "this fuckin' place's so dry it's pathetic. You really
got grass?"

Without hesitation Spurlock reached up on the dash and
grabbed a number from the stash box. He stuffed it in the
MP's mouth and lit it, all in one smooth motion. Just like
the MP, he didn't feel he was taking much of a chance. If
he got busted, he could always claim he had impounded it
and hadn't got around to turning it in yet. Nobody would
believe him, but nobody could prove differently.

"Got any more?" the MP asked, a calculating smile
lurking around the corners of his mouth.

Spurlock nodded. "About a pound," he said.

There was a brief spark of wonderment in the MP's
eyes, and then a crafty look replaced the awe. "What you
want for it?" he asked suspiciously.

Spurlock shrugged. "I'll give you a full pound for a full
tank of gas and six five-gallon cans."

The MP shook his head in wonder. "That's all?" he
asked, eyes wide.

"Okay, a pound and a half," Spurlock grinned. "But
that's my last and final offer."

The MP grabbed his hand and shook it. "I'll take it! I'll
take it! Jesus, that isn't what I meant, is that all you want
for a pound. Jesus, this shit is dynamite."

Spurlock nodded proudly. "It ain't bad," he said. "Just
a minute."

Carefully he crawled over Megan's sleeping form and
into the back where the grass was. There was about a key
each in two gunnysacks and he needed another container to
put the MP's stuff in. Finally he found a paper bag full of
oranges and dumped the oranges into a cardboard box of
M-16 ammo. Then he split one of the keys and put half

into the paper bag. It was only an approximate measurement anyway. There was between two and three pounds of grass in each gunnysack, and somewhere between a pound and a pound and a half went into the paper bag. It was a goodly bunch of grass and it hadn't cost him anything. He crawled back to the front and handed it to the MP.

The MP, who gave the impression of being more than somewhat zonked, nodded thanks. "You got an Oklahoma credit card?" he asked.

Spurlock shook his head no.

The MP went inside his little guard shack and came back a moment later with a siphon hose. He handed it to Spurlock. "Your card, sir." He waved his hand toward a row of three-quarter-ton trucks parked inside the gate. They were mostly MP vehicles and a few troop carriers. "There's your gas, friend. Fill up your tank and rip off all the five-gallon cans you want. The motor sergeant's a friend of mine. He won't say anything if I lay a couple of lids on him."

Spurlock took the hose and put the VW in gear, to drive over by the trucks.

"Keep the hose," the MP said. "You can never tell when one of them things will come in handy."

Spurlock nodded with a conspiratorial smile. He drove to the line of trucks and got out. Pretty soon he was spitting the vile gasoline taste out of his mouth. He supposed there was some possibility of getting caught, but the MP seemed cool, and if something did come up, he could probably handle it.

He had the tank half filled when a staff car drove by, the driver giving him a hard look. Spurlock glanced out of the corner of his eye. He couldn't see the driver's rank, but from his youth and exaggerated air of importance he was probably a second lieutenant. He drove on to the guard shack and got out to hassle with the MP. There was a few minutes of conversation, starting with the lieutenant talking in an agitated manner and waving his arms a lot. The MP talked in a low and soothing voice the whole time.

A few minutes later the second lieutenant drove away again, giving Spurlock a sort of puzzled wave of his hand, friendly but confused.

When the tank was full and the cans strapped on, Spurlock drove back to the guard shack. The MP was just trying to relight the number he'd put out when the lieutenant drove up. He was grinning like a Cheshire cat.

So was Spurlock. "What'd you tell that joker?" he asked. "He sure changed his tone in a hurry."

The MP shook his head, smugly complacent. "Naw, for a minute I thought I'd have to lay some dope on him. But the little sucker's so stupid he wouldn't know what to do with it if I did. I told him you were a law officer from Arkansas in hot pursuit of a fugitive and couldn't get gas this time of night. I was pretty sure if he called you on it, you could get through it with that phony badge and your rap."

Spurlock nodded and grinned. "Yeah, I could have, but the badge isn't phony."

The MP grinned and lightly rested one hand on the club hanging on his black leather Sam Browne belt. "No lie! Are you in hot pursuit of a fugitive, too?"

Spurlock shook his head. "Not exactly, but that's close enough for government work."

The MP shook his head and cocked it to one side. "How about that?" he said. "Say, you got any papers?"

Spurlock only had two packs of rolling papers in the truck. It was his most serious supply deficiency. He shook his head sadly. It would be a pleasure to meet this splendid fellow's every request with a flourish and a blare of trumpets. Then a thought occurred to him and he reached in the glove box and pulled out an old corncob pipe that he'd whittled out a long time ago and almost forgotten about.

He handed it to the MP. "Smoke out of this," he said. "You'll look just like General MacArthur."

The MP smiled and posed with the pipe in his mouth, hands on hips, jaw jutted forward. "How's that?" he asked.

"Perfect," Spurlock said. "Smoke it in good health." He put the van in gear and drove off toward the interstate.

Feeling fat and comfortable with all the good gas, Spurlock ran the little VW down to the interchange and headed out toward St. Louis and the Mississippi. The hills around were beginning to get lower. He couldn't remember if the bridge was still in or not. They might have to take a ferry.

He was getting really tired and Megan was going to have to drive pretty soon.

He was also developing a bad crick in his neck. He tried cocking his head quickly to the side, and then back the other way. His neck popped both times and it felt a little better, but when he tried to do neck rolls, rolling his head around as far as it would go, his perspective changed and he almost ran the VW off the road.

There was a bag of munchie food just behind the right-hand seat, apples and some cheese and dried and salted soybeans. He reached for an apple and a chunk of cheese and found, wonder of wonders, a bottle of white wine. Yeah, this was going to be all right.

It was a little hard to drive with a big hunk of mild cheddar in the left hand and an apple in the right. Still, though, he was only going forty-five. Goddamn eyes getting like sandpaper. He batted them to stimulate some tears to make them feel better. Maybe he'd be a little less sleepy when he got some food in his belly. If he did another number now, he'd probably go to sleep at the wheel. 'Nother bite of cheese, sure went good with the apple.

Light up ahead. Seemed to be some sort of roadblock. Looked like a regular army roadblock, sort of like the one at Springfield. But he didn't see any vehicles beside the road, just a couple of sawhorses, a fire off to the side, and some soldiers with rifles slung over their backs, pacing beside the sawhorses. Under normal circumstances he'd have dimmed his lights approaching a military roadblock. But something wasn't right here. There should be at least a three-quarter-ton truck beside the roadblock and probably a jeep, too. He couldn't see any horses either. Sometimes it's kind of hard to tell the difference between a regular soldier and a guerrilla anyway. They both claim to be the legitimate representatives of the same army. Only in most cases the Gs didn't have access to laundry and barber facilities.

And sometimes the regular army, which had access to them, didn't use them. There had been a move afoot to change the uniform for years, so the Gs wouldn't look so much like the regular army. But it had always been shelved because of the expense.

He eased the VW toward the roadblock, slowing down easily.

Somebody yelled, "Dim ya lights, ya dumb bastard," and he hit the light switch, turning them off altogether and at the same time floorboarded the accelerator, running right through the sawhorses and past the shouting and shooting soldiers. Whoever they were they didn't sound too friendly and he wasn't waiting around to find out. He cringed at the thought of one of those rounds hitting a gas can. He could feel his sphincter pucker.

He heard a thumping to his left and looked to see a dirty, bearded uniformed person hanging onto the window and the rearview mirror, and apparently kicking the side of the van as he held on. He heard a *p-snap-p* over his head and checked the rearview mirror in time to see a neat hole and a spiderweb of crinkled glass around it appear in the back window, and feel a tiny rush of air as the same round went out the roof.

It was hard to tell over the road noise, but he could swear he heard a shout, ". . . get you, Spurlock!" but that couldn't be right. He shrugged it off.

The VW had accelerated to its full forty-five miles an hour and no more rounds were coming in the back window, but there was still the matter of the fellow hanging on to the truck. He reached out and rapped his knuckles smartly and the guy yelled, "Stop, goddammit!" But he didn't let go.

Actually that struck Spurlock as an excellent idea and he smiled at the G clinging to the side of the truck. "Okay, sweetheart," he said. "You want it, you got it." He hit the brakes hard and the machine squealed and slid sideways on the road as it skidded to a stop. The guerrilla, barely clinging to the side of the truck, swung forward and yelled "Gaaaaaaahhhhh!!!" as he flew off into the night.

In the back Megan and the entire cargo shifted forward and she woke and came up out of the back, screaming, "What? What? What the hell's . . ." just as Spurlock turned his lights back on to avoid running over the G, who was as likely as not to be in the middle of the road, and accelerated again, so that the whole load shifted to the rear as Megan went over backward and yelled, "Ooooohnooooo!"

Spurlock twisted the wheel just in time to avoid running over the G, who apparently appreciated the sheriff's consideration so little that he fired a burst of whatever number of round he had in his magazine, about seventeen, none of which seemed to come anywhere near the van.

Spurlock snapped the lights off again and roared on down the road, steering by the light of the half moon as it slid through the clouds, the machine jarring horribly as it hit all the chuckholes in the road.

Goddammit, he had to turn the lights on again. If those holes kept up, he'd break off a wheel. He hit the lights and then they went around a turn and he couldn't see the roadblock behind them anymore.

Megan crawled into the right front seat, her great soft eyes wide and staring, but her face calm. The bandanna headband she'd been wearing since Joplin was loose and hanging from one side. "You wanna tell me what happened back there?" she asked. "That was pretty exciting, especially when you don't know what's going on."

Now that the moment was over and he didn't need that charge of adrenaline to get through the roadblock, he felt as if his head were going to come off. His palms perspired so badly he had to grip the wheel doubly hard just to maintain control of the bus, and his hands were shaking. "Yeah," he gulped, his throat dry. "Just a minute. I'm going to stop the bus."

Slowly he braked to a halt, not pulling to the shoulder, since there was no guarantee there would be a shoulder, stopping in the middle of the road. He sat for just a minute, his hands still shaking on the wheel. Then he started to laugh. The laughter rolled from him, peal after peal. It wasn't laughter at any humor in the situation. It was just a cathartic release of tension. He laughed so hard that it was difficult to sit in the driver's seat, so he opened the door and rolled out onto the roadway, still laughing, lying out full length on the pavement. He laughed and laughed and laughed.

Finally, running down but still chuckling, he noticed that Megan sat on the edge of the driver's seat, facing out onto the road, chin in her hand, her head kerchief rearranged. She regarded him glumly. When he finally ran down, she asked, "I don't suppose with your busy schedule you could find time to tell me what happened?"

He sat up shaking his head and told her. When he got to the part about the G hanging on the window when he hit the brakes, he started laughing again, this time not so hysterically. Megan laughed, too.

"My God," she exclaimed. "You can imagine how I felt when you started to slow down. That kind of woke me up, then you accelerated and a bunch of apples fell over me and I sat up and then you hit the brakes and I went over on my ass and no sooner was I back up from that than you hit the accelerator again and down I went. I couldn't imagine what was going on."

He decided to say nothing about the shout. He wasn't that sure.

He shrugged and grinned. " 'Atsa way it goes in the big time."

She made a face at him.

Suddenly it washed over Spurlock just how tired he was. He had been driving for what, it was maybe four o'clock in the morning and he had been driving for eight hours, not to mention the hour or so horseback before that and the shoot-out at the creek. It had been a very tiring day. If he had to drive much farther, he would go to sleep at the wheel and that would be all she wrote. "You reckon you could drive?" he asked.

She smiled. "Well, I'm awake. That's for sure."

He nodded. "Aw right, I'm gonna climb in the back of this thing and crash." He opened the side door and crawled over the overturned boxes and dumped-out fruit and vegetable containers, and about a key of marijuana that was just scattered all into the sleeping bags. He didn't care. He just crawled into the bag and lay there for three minutes while his metabolism ran down and he slid off to sleep.

The tossing and turning of the van kept him from sleeping well, and he was tortured by weird dreams, full of fire and gunshots down strange long green hallways and woods full of Gs behind every tree. He saw Megan with her clothing torn away and the whole scene there by the creek in close detail. He didn't sleep very well at all.

The van shuddered, then shuddered again and again and again as a roaring noise rose and fell and rose again and he realized they were being passed by another convoy. Then Megan screamed and there was a ripping noise and a squeal of metal as the bus turned over on its side and all the glass in the windows on the bottom imploded, just as Spurlock was thrown on top of it. "Aw unh!" he said, feeling himself for broken bones, of which there didn't seem to be any. There were some minor cuts and his neck seemed stiff, but he figured that would work its way out. "You okay?" he yelled at Megan, who was picking herself up off the passenger side, which had come up on the bottom.

"Seem to be," she said. "I don't have any broken bones. Couple of small cuts and maybe a sprained leg. We were really lucky that time."

Spurlock started to drag himself out of the sleeping bag, feeling his way around in the dark. "See if that interior light will come on," he told Megan. She tried it and sure enough. In the dim light he could see that the van was a ghastly mess. "What happened?" he asked.

She gave him a contrite look over the seat as though she were afraid that he would think it was her fault. That was the last thing he had to worry about, who was at fault for this ludicrous situation. He'd have to deal with it first, and worry about fault later, if ever.

"A convoy went by," she explained, "and I was having a hard time fighting for control, but I'd swear one of the drivers sideswiped me, just in time to run me into a really big chuckhole, about as big as a bushel basket. I know he did it on purpose."

Spurlock nodded in agreement. "Yeah, there's some of them will do that to a civilian. I don't know why, but wherever the army takes charge in a country all sorts of these little minor functionaries, down to and including truck drivers, take it upon themselves to start jacking the citizenry around. Aw, well, here we are. By the way, where are we?"

"Illinois," she said. "Somewhere across the river in Illinois. What do you want to do?"

He looked at his watch. It was five-thirty. "Take this sleeping bag and a couple of weapons and some ammo off in the bushes and sleep until it's light and we're awake enough to cope with this situation," he said. "We need rest and we need to take a little time to come up with a plan."

Spurlock was too tired to roll the sleeping bag up tight like he should have or carry the weapon in an alert position, as habit had taught him; besides, there didn't seem to be anything around to be afraid of. He just threw the big double sleeping bag over his shoulder, at least half of it dragging behind him in the dirt, the CAR-15 sort of jammed in under his arm and a couple of pouches of clipped-up magazines on an old army pistol.

He couldn't tell whether it was a precaution, or whether she just wanted to do something useful, but Megan picked up a paper bag full of food and a water jug, and they dragged themselves through the sandy soil by the side of the road to some bushes and a slight depression in the ground, spread the sleeping bag, and crawled in. Spurlock started unzipping his side of the bag.

"What're you doing?" she mumbled.

"Unzipping the bag," he said. "If anybody hassles us tonight, we can't afford to get caught in this sleeping bag. We're going to have to be up and moving almost immediately. I don't want to get caught and I don't want to have to use this weapon unless I have to."

Megan nodded and went almost immediately to sleep. She didn't unzip her side of the bag, probably because she thought he was worried about nothing, but that was okay. If they did get moving, it was only necessary to have one side of the bag unzipped. She'd be able to roll out plenty fast once he was out of her way.

There was a line of cold down his right side, which he found very uncomfortable, but it didn't keep him from going back to sleep.

He woke, stiff and sore, about four hours later, only to find the sun fairly high in the sky. It was a good morning, the clouds of the night before having been burned or drifted off. Spurlock got up and stretched. His body was tight, every muscle taut, and since he wasn't used to that, and knew exactly what to do to get rid of it, he found it almost unendurably miserable. But still, body tensions aside, it was a lovely morning. There was a swirl of birds drifting lazily in the air over them, too high to tell what they were, and Spurlock wasn't exactly what you'd call a naturalist. Sometimes he felt his life would be a lot happier if he knew less about weapons and more about birds and trees.

He looked down at Megan still sleeping in the bag and decided not to disturb her yet. She could sleep while he went and looked over the van. It wasn't likely to be usable, but maybe.

He strapped on the pistol belt, slung the CAR-15, and walked back to where the VW lay on its side.

The van wasn't in unrepairable condition. The only major thing wrong was that the front wheel was broken off.

But they were in central Illinois, somewhere where they didn't know a soul, and they had to be moving on soon. He was going to have to ponder the possibility of abandoning Megan's bus. She would be less than overjoyed at that, but that's what she got for coming along uninvited. He shrugged. Maybe . . . ah, well. He wasn't thinking too clearly yet. He decided to take advantage of their disaster to do a complete yoga set and maybe Megan could rustle up some grub and by the time that was done maybe, just maybe, he could think out what to do next.

Actually that was a bunch of crap. He could tell he wasn't thinking right when he started thinking like that. If he had been doing meditation for the last couple of days, his head would be all smoothed out and he would know, and accept without question that the proper course of action would present itself to him when the time came. He would be very calmly going about the next step rather than worrying about decisions he had insufficient data to make and wouldn't have to make for another two or three hours anyway.

"Spurlock! Hey, Spurlock!" he heard Megan call. He looked over toward the bushes they'd slept behind to conceal them from the road and saw her rise from behind them, not exactly like Venus from the waves. She was far too bleary-eyed and chagrined for that.

"Yeah, babe, I'm over here by the truck," he called back.

She looked at him, shook her hair, which was wild and tangled beyond description, shook out the sleeping bag and started dragging it back toward the road. She had a sort of worried frown on her face. "Can we use the van?" she asked.

He shook his head. "Not like it is now," he said.

She put her hand on her hips and cocked her head, regarding the van irritably. "Oh, hell!" she said, and then gently, "Well, Mr. Sheriff, what do we do now?"

He paced back and forth on the macadam, feeling it get hot under his cowboy boots as the sun warmed the road. "Dunno for sure," he muttered, fingering his chin. "We got a few chores we have to do, and that'll give us a while to think it over. Myself, I am thoroughly uptight in mind and body, and unless you have some objection I'm going over behind the truck and do some yoga to loosen myself up. I'll think better and work better and not be so god-damned irritable. I'm so tired of all this now I could eat nails. Religion or no religion, I'd almost welcome the chance to shoot somebody."

She nodded. "Yep, when you get like that, it's time to

yoga, for sure. Maybe we'll do a number when you get through.''

He shook his head. "I don't think so. Marijuana doesn't seem to be the thing to lubricate the parts of your mind that make little nit-picky decisions. And as far as this trip is concerned we're kind of past the philosophical stage.''

She struck a ballet pose and pirouetted down the highway. "How mundane,'' she said.

Without replying, Spurlock reached over and picked up the sleeping bag, and wished he had a real yoga mat. The bag seemed always to bunch up under him. He spread the bag out beside the overturned van and looked at it for a moment, then sighed and started methodically taking off his clothes.

He considered doing what exercises he could in his jeans, and decided that he would be shortchanging himself, and he considered going to the truck and rummaging around for a pair of shorts and decided that was too much trouble, and in his present mood what he wanted was to get started and do it right. If the sight of a nude man standing on his head beside a wrecked VW microbus was too much for any passerby, that was going to be just tough. There wasn't much traffic on this road anyway, and he was in no mood to be conciliatory toward the sort of moron to whom the sight of a nude human body was repellent. He commenced the salutation to the sun, bending slowly and feeling the muscles in his back start to go Ahhhhhh!

In twenty minutes his body was fairly loose and free again, although not so much so as when the exercises were done in the security of his own place. His mind was still going jigga-jigga-jigga, though, all his problems and complaints competing with one another for space in his consciousness, and he remembered what he had learned, which was that if he neglected his meditation for very long he turned into a nervous wreck. And after so long a time probably into a homicidal maniac. Spurlock was no ordinary dude after all. There had been a time in his life when he *liked* to kill people.

He curled into the lotus, legs crossed and feet resting on his thighs. He touched his thumbs and forefingers together, rested them on his knees, shut his eyes, and waited for the competing thoughts to get tired of jockeying for position.

The red swirlies on the back of his eyelids sorted themselves out and it all became black as the blazing sun which seemed to bloom in his head at the start of meditation grew like a great red ball in his mind and the crickets down and at the back of his hearing chirped and chirped and drowned out all of the thoughts that were trying to drive him mad and the sun grew closer and he passed through that into the place that words can't describe.

Om mane padme hum Om mane padme hum Om mane padme hum. Spurlock came back out through the ancient mantra and looked at the world with eyes very like that of a new baby. He got up and started putting on his clothes, humming little snatches of "Just a Closer Walk with Thee," which, upon reflection, he judged too somber for his present situation, so he followed that with:

> See that spider, climbin' up the wall
> See that spider, climbin' up the wall
> He goin' up there for to get his ashes hauled

He wandered back to find Megan sitting disconsolately beside the truck, a few of their pitifully wrecked belongings arrayed beside her. She looked at him and said, "Isn't this just the worst you ever saw?"

He looked at the mess and said, "Yeah, there have been better times." He saw that she was just as messed in mind and body as he had been, and since she had never expressed any interest in yoga, he had decided not to shove it down her throat. But there was something he could do for her before they got to the business of sorting their gear, taking what they could in rucksacks, and starting off toward the next town, which was what they would have to do. It didn't require any decision at all, since that was the only choice available. It had just taken clearing his mind to see it.

He reached out and took her hand, drew her to her feet, kissed her warmly, enjoyed the fact that she returned it, and took her by the hand back toward the sleeping bag spread inelegantly across the northbound lane of I-44. "Take off your clothes and lie down," he commanded.

She cocked her head to one side and grinned. "Oh, no," she said. "We're in the middle of an interstate highway."

He spread his hands expansively. "We can see for miles in any direction," he said, indicating the dead flatness of the landscape. "If we go back behind that bush, you'll get sand all over you and that will be so uncomfortable you'll lose the effect of the massage."

She shook her head. "Massage, huh? That's a relief. For a minute I thought you wanted to ball right in the middle of the highway."

He shook his head. "I just wanted you relaxed for whatever we have to do next. It's really hard to react fast and make sound decisions when you're tired and tense like we have been. Everything we have is damaged beyond repair and the only thing we have is time and ourselves. I want to use that time to get ourselves in good shape, and then we'll worry about the rest."

She looked around at the expanse of flat grassland. Sure enough, you could see for miles. She still looked a little apprehensive, then shrugged, grinned, and began to take off her clothes.

Spurlock admired her body as it came out of the old work shirt and jeans. Megan was about thirty-five, and she was a big woman, with swelling hips and big, soft, pendulous breasts, but she was not fat and she was not wrinkled. She was just a hell of a woman, who had her shit together as a woman and as a person.

Spurlock never ceased to marvel that this excellent person had chosen to go with him. Of course he had hoped she wouldn't go this far down this particular road, but she had, and once she had, he accepted it and thought about it no more. It was a recent discovery of his that everything that happened in his life happened for a purpose and that no matter how bad it seemed at the time, it fit into the overall pattern of his life perfectly when he could look at it in perspective, usually some years after the event. He did not know why this was so, except to ascribe it to the plan of God, and that was kind of begging the question, since it left both God and the plan undefined. But still, ever since he had made this discovery he worried less about things when they didn't go according to his plan. He was sure that they were going according to some plan, and a better one than his, even though he didn't have access to it.

It hadn't changed the way he did things so much as it changed how much he worried about them.

Even if he and/or Megan got greased on this job, he could still go out content, if not overjoyed, in the knowledge that this was part of the plan. In fact, he had read the reports of people who had been close to certain death and knew it, and somehow survived, and they had reported being filled with a sort of ecstasy which none had felt before. So maybe he'd even be overjoyed. But not too soon if he could help it.

He found these thoughts in no way morbid as his lady undressed and stretched out on the sleeping bag. In fact, he found them quite the opposite. He was filled with awe at the beauty of a life that had brought him to the middle of this highway with a hot sun beating down and this lovely lady spreading herself on a moth-eaten and battered old sleeping bag before him. God, she was beautiful.

He tore his shirt off over his head and kicked off the rough-out boots, then knelt over her back and began to smooth the knotted muscles.

She stirred lightly under him, as he knelt on her ass with his knees on each side of her. The sleeping bag wasn't exactly the best surface to do this on, and with the road under it he wouldn't be able to apply much pressure. On the other hand, small beads of sweat appeared immediately on her back and ran together to form a light lubricant which made her skin flow under his gentle hands like the finest oil. She would be pretty funky by nightfall, but right now this couldn't be much better.

When the worst of the knots had been smoothed out of her back, he began to work on her neck. The back, the neck, and the feet were the key to an excellent massage. The rest was only to make it perfect, and Spurlock was no slouch at the massage game. He smoothed her earlobes and her eyelids and all the other parts of her body.

And when he was through she was still there on the sleeping bag, nude, with the sated and excited look of a well-rubbed cat.

He lay down beside her and she moved to kiss him, which seemed to be a reasonable thing to do at the time, and all the fear of interlopers seemed to have left her.

She looked around at the open skies and the miles and miles of flat open country around them. "Jesus Christ, this is exciting," she said. "Take off your pants. I want to feel all of you next to me."

Spurlock did as he was told, because he had been fairly sure it would turn out like this from the start. Neither one of them was the sort who would miss the chance to do something interesting for the first, and probably only, time.

He had just spent forty-five minutes smoothing out all

the tense muscles of her body. He kicked off his jeans and spent the next forty-five nuzzling into all the secret parts of that body which could awaken it to excitement. He did it until they had reached, and passed, the point of insupportable longing and then he did it some more, and by and by the thing she had feared came to pass.

It was lovely and they rested awhile and started to do it again, then Spurlock saw the horseman on the horizon.

CHAPTER SIX

THEY WERE sliding smoothly on the warm sweat between them and it was so, so . . . close, but it's one thing to do it out in front of God and everybody when everybody consists of a few ground squirrels, and quite another when folks start riding over the horizon on horseback.

Spurlock couldn't say for sure what it was that made him spot the horseman. Just a flicker of movement on the horizon maybe. Anyway he said, "Darlin', I think we better table this for the time being. It seems we're going to have a visitor."

She lurched up and following his gaze, saw the horseman. But by this time she was relaxed and all the tension had gone from her body. He was dealing with a fairly happy lady rather than the uptight person she had been before. They were both in control of their entire selves and were ready to deal with whatever came up.

The horseman didn't seem to be looking at them or to have spotted them, so they moved into their clothes without much haste. Spurlock knew from his army training that a quick, jerky movement was apt to be spotted more quickly than a smooth, natural one, and Megan followed his lead.

When they were dressed, she asked, "Okay, coach, now what?"

He grinned as he stood up. "Well, it's like this. We're going to have to get out of here and we got no wheels to move with. So we got to scrounge around and load what we can into a couple of rucksacks and abandon the rest."

She looked at him aghast. "We can't do that."

He looked at her very seriously. "The alternative is to sit here either until help comes or some guerrillas arrive, kill us, and take everything. The guerrillas are about ten times as likely as the help. That horseman on the horizon is probably the point for a guerrilla unit, and I want to have my ruck loaded and be off in that field there with a basic load of ammo before they arrive. That guy doesn't look like he's spotted us yet, and when he does, it'll take him some time to get back to his men and some more time for them to come up here. I figure we got between fifteen and twenty minutes to do what we're going to do. Maybe less. Let's get to it."

All her objections to losing her van and the precious objects she had collected all these years melted as she realized that they were in terrible danger all the time.

"If we were in such danger," she said, irritated, "what the hell were we doing balling in the middle of the road?"

He grinned. How could you explain a thing like that? All Spurlock knew was that he followed his hunches before everything else, and sometimes they were very illogical. But they were almost always right. Right now he had no hunch, except that it was time to get ready to go. He didn't feel in serious danger from the horseman on the hill, although logically he should have. He had simply fed Megan a little scare propaganda to get her functioning. He wanted to get their stuff together and he wanted her to accept the fact that she was going to have to give up the van.

But how do you tell somebody that you have found it pays to follow your hunches without sounding like an Old Testament prophet shouting that God has told him what to do? And maybe that's what it actually was. Maybe God had told him, but he wasn't going to put himself in the position of claiming divine inspiration. Nor was he going to insist that he knew everything. There wasn't really anything he could say. He slapped her on the rump and said, "This is no time for conversation. Move!" And hoped that it would never come up again.

She nodded and set off at a lope for the van. Spurlock ran along beside her, dragging the two sleeping bags. He was lucky in that his rucksack was already packed. All he had to do was roll up the sleeping bag and strap it under the bag on his ruck. He snapped suspenders onto the pistol belt and put two more ammo pouches on it, strapped that on, and put the ruck on over it. Then he slung the CAR-15 over his shoulder and checked to see how Megan was doing. She wasn't as familiar with the gear as he was, and she wasn't sure what she would need. She had too much food, and too much of what she had was nice-to-have stuff like bread instead of necessities like canned goods and jerky.

She was also unable to restrain herself from taking a few little glittery objects, some costume jewelry and the eagle's claw that hung from the mirror.

Shit, Spurlock thought, but he kept it to himself. Megan's priorities were different from his, but it had never been demonstrated to him that they were inferior, and he wasn't going to take it on himself to tell her what to do.

He checked his watch. She could take whatever she wanted, but she was going to have to take it fast.

He glanced at the horizon. The horseman was gone.

Now was the time to leave. "Finish that and let's get out of here," he said.

She looked up and nodded. She started doing the strap on her rucksack, and he knelt and strapped the other one, then rose and grabbed her hand, leading her out into the dry grass. The best cover for several hundred feet seemed to be the bush they'd slept behind the night before, and there was no woodline to head for, no hill to get on, no creek bed to lie in. The bush would have to do. He glanced behind. They had left nothing readily identifiable as footprints in the sandy soil.

They skidded in behind the bush and he took the weapon off his back, jacked a round into the chamber and set the selector on auto. If he had to defend them, he was going to accrue such a load of bad karma that it would take ten lifetimes to work it off. If self-defense counted.

He didn't want to kill anybody, but he would do it no matter what. That was just the way it was, so why worry about it?

Megan was moving around to his right. "What are you doing?" he demanded.

"Sand in my shoe," she said.

"Leave it," he said. "Lie still and keep low."

She glared at him evilly.

He looked at her. "This is my work," he said. "I know how to do this and you don't. If you don't want to take my orders, you can start walking back toward Purgatory now. I cannot do this if you don't cooperate."

She gave him an irritated look and did as she was told. But it put Spurlock in a black mood. It had been only with the greatest difficulty that he had restrained from slapping her. This was not the time to start giving recruit training.

They lay quietly in the dirt behind the bush, and the sun, which had seemed so sensual when they lay naked in it, was hot and uncomfortable in their sweaty clothes.

But Spurlock still felt good. His pack was tight and his

weapon was clean. He had managed to go this far without killing anybody, and he had every expectation that he might finish this mission without it. By keeping ready. He really couldn't have told you why, but the old adventurous adrenaline flow was running through him, a feeling of mingled expectation and fear, the fear part being kept rigidly under control. It was the most exciting feeling he had ever had and he found it one of the most pleasurable.

He had found, however, that it was best to ration it, since the feeling only came in times of extreme danger. It was the way the body got itself ready to deal with those times, and the difficulty with facing too many times of extreme danger is that eventually the law of averages will catch up with you.

In his youth Spurlock had sought that feeling like a promiscuous lover, but now that he was older he avoided it when possible. When it was unavoidable, though, he enjoyed it.

The rider on the hill appeared again. He stood in perfect silhouette. Spurlock estimated the distance at maybe 350 yards. He did it by imagining a football field in front of him. Then on the far end of the football field he put another football field and then another and part of another. The rider was on the hill about three and a half football fields away.

"Spurlock!" Megan whispered.

He looked at her, irritated. Was she going to come up with some more of her crap at a time like this?

"There's another one behind us!"

Slowly he turned his head. High on the horizon there was another rider. They were maybe a hundred yards off into the bush and this guy was out maybe two hundred more. Then he knew what they were. They were flank guard. They were flank guards and they were moving ahead of whatever it was they were guarding, a combination of flank guard and point. And whatever they were guarding was probably moving on the road.

He couldn't imagine what it could be. The army would be vehicular-mounted and wouldn't be moving on the road. A standard commercial convoy would also probably be in motor vehicles.

There was no category of personnel he could imagine that would be coming down the road exactly like whoever this was. He watched down the highway with interest. If it wasn't guerrillas, they would probably be fairly safe.

But whoever they were he wasn't so confident that he came out from behind his bush. He wasn't too worried about the rider behind them. They were low to the ground and in the shadow of the bush, and there was no reason for him to expect to see something out there. Abandoned wrecks on the highway weren't all that rare, although new ones were something of an oddity. But from three hundred yards away the horsemen would have difficulty in guessing the age of the wreck.

He saw them before he heard them, five dots moving a long way away on the highway. He could tell there were five wagons, each pulled by a team of horses. Three of them seemed to have two-horse teams and the two larger wagons had four-horse teams. Slowly Spurlock shook his head in disbelief. He had never seen anything like it in his life.

As they got closer, he could hear the clink of the harness and an occasional whinny from the horses and the bray of a mule. He couldn't tell that they were mules by sight yet, but that bray carried a long way across the plains.

"What in the world is that?" Megan whispered.

He shook his head again. "Beats me. I been to two goat ropin's and a county fair and I ain't never seen nothin' like it before." They both stared at the oncoming column.

As the wagons got closer, they could see that they were painted gaily, apparently all the colors of the rainbow, and they were all painted in stripes. There was some writing on the sides of the wagons, but Spurlock couldn't make out what it was.

The wagons were a hundred yards away now and the letters were beginning to take shape, but he still couldn't make them out. They seemed to be some kind of old-time letters, painted in red and gold over the rainbow paint job on the wagons. Dogs scurried around through the wagon train, and occasionally people would dismount and walk along for a while, then get back on again. Children ran from one wagon to another and there were mounted horsemen visible, two to the side and two to the rear. Whoever these people were they were not about to be surprised by any Gs.

A woman in a long calico dress got off the lead wagon and stood beside the road for a while to let the next two wagons run past her. Then she started walking between them. She had a full-length, commanding stride.

Swinging along in the long calico dress like that, she kind of reminded Spurlock of the statue of the Pioneer Woman in Ponca City, Oklahoma, which he had seen as a boy. Except that lady had a sunbonnet on and this one had long blond hair, shimmering in the sun, running halfway down her back and chopped off square, and a pair of enormous sunglasses to do the same job the bonnet would have done. As soon as she started walking, three big dogs fell in behind her and followed along in her tracks.

Two young boys chased each other off into the brush, apparently improvising a game of tag.

"Junior! Willie!" she called. "Y'all getcha ace back in here."

The dogs barked at the boys, as though echoing her command. Her voice, a deep contralto, carried clearly over the dry soil. "And yew dawgs shut up!" There was no rancor in her voice. She was just hassling to keep everything straight.

They were close enough now that Spurlock could make out the printing on the side of the wagons clearly. It said:

RAINBOW KATHY'S
ROCK 'N' ROLL MEDICINE SHOW

Spurlock stood up from behind his bush. "I think we can go in now," he said.

Megan stood up beside him and they both stepped out from behind the bush and waited for the folk from the show caravan to spot them.

Directly Spurlock heard a shout from the driver of the second wagon, who pointed to them. The woman walking behind the wagon waved, a huge circular motion, starting with the hand straight over her head and going all the way down to her side and back up again.

Spurlock and Megan returned it as nearly to those specifications as possible. Then they started tramping in toward the caravan, walking directly to the figure of the large blond woman.

She stood in the middle of the highway surrounded by her caravan, which had stopped, waiting for them to come in. Her hands were on her hips and she stared at them with a quizzical expression.

When they came up to her, Spurlock saw that she had strong but beautiful features. She was, all in all, a hell of a woman, maybe, oh, he couldn't tell. She could have been anywhere from twenty-five years old to forty. Around her neck she wore a finely wrought golden crucifix on an elaborate gold chain. Spurlock admired the workmanship.

"That your VW?" she asked, indicating the van with a broad gesture. Spurlock nodded. He introduced himself and Megan, and the woman introduced herself as Kathy Meshevsky.

"How'd the van get broke up?" she inquired.

Megan told her.

She nodded. "Well, let's take a look at her and see if anything can be done." She turned to face away from them and called out, "Ed! DeWitt! Let's take a look at this here van here."

One of the drivers climbed down from the wagon and another fellow dismounted from his horse. They reminded Spurlock of gauchos the way they sat their mounts, bell-bottom jeans blousing down around the stirrups, flat-topped cowboy hats on their heads. DeWitt, the one who got off the horse, had a sort of lance or guidon mounted with a rainbow pennant on it. The whole convoy was patched and ragged, but clean and shipshape, with an air of irrepressible gaiety and bravery combined, to keep up with this dangerous and foolhardy enterprise in the face of all common sense, and have a good time in the bargain.

They all clustered around the overturned van. DeWitt squatted down and gave it a close look. He was a blond man, his handsome face totally devoid of expression. "Ain't nothin' we can do with it here," he said. "I reckon we can put a team on her, drag it into Hyattston, and have Mike Dale look at it."

Kathy nodded. "That okay with you folks?"

Spurlock allowed as how that was a lot more than they had any right to expect.

It took about a half hour to get the VW shoved upright and two mules detached from each of the four mule teams and hooked to it.

"How's about lettin' DeWitt steer the van and ya'll ride with me?" Kathy asked. "I don't get to talk to strangers much on the road."

They nodded agreement.

Slowed by pulling the van and having lighter teams on the two heaviest wagons, it took the little caravan another five hours to get to Hyattston. Spurlock hadn't seen one of these plains towns in years, although he had hitched through this country many times as a boy. It was interesting to him,

the patterns they took. In Arkansas the towns were smaller
and closer together, as though people settled on any available plot of flat land. Purgatory had a cramped look about
it, tucked away in the mountains like it was. The town was
only a convenience; the mountains were the significant
reality for the people of Purgatory.

Hyattston, on the other hand, was spread out over several
miles, with wide streets and low boxy buildings. As they
approached the town, it loomed like a collection of saltine
cracker boxes on the horizon, an ugly, plain town, a
suitable ornament to the flat ugliness surrounding it; a
landscape of dun plains, all flats and straight lines, with
the flat straight lines of the highway converging on these
flat, straight cracker boxes.

There was the usual assortment of shops on the main
street, featuring a drugstore, hardware store, and movie
house. The movie was showing *Beach Blanket Blowjob*
and *The Fornicators*.

He and Megan enjoyed swapping yarns with Kathy on
the way into town. She was some fine lady. He had always
wondered how Megan would get along with another volu-
ble, expansive woman like this. They seemed to be getting
along fine. He supposed as long as there was no conflict
they would continue to get along fine.

Dale's garage was closed when they got there, but they
unhitched the van and attached the horses back to the
wagon, and continued on to the fairgrounds, where the
show was to be set up.

Kathy showed them where her tent was going up and
said, "Ya'll stay here tonight, with me and DeWitt."

"DeWitt your old man?" Spurlock asked.

Kathy laughed an infectious laugh and slapped her thigh.
"Yeah," she crowed. "Old DeWitt, he's a pistol."

Spurlock was thoroughly captivated by Kathy and quite
willing to let her tell him anything. Megan, he noticed,

was watching his reaction to Kathy with interest, but with nothing like jealousy, at least not yet.

He and Megan offered to help the show set up, but Kathy declined, pointing out that they could set up about an hour quicker without inexperienced help than with it. So he and Megan spent the next couple of hours wandering around the fairgrounds while the show was set up.

They were an island of calm, walking around slowly, sweaty and tired, surrounded by an ocean of activity, as tent ropes were staked in with heavy wooden mallets, canvas stretched, and booths set up. DeWitt seemed to be the straw boss of the outfit.

Spurlock related to him as the type of dude who'd make a really good first sergeant. DeWitt stood quietly on the edge of all the activity, arms folded across his chest, feet sunk in engineer boots and an old pair of patched jeans. He wore a kind of Mexican peasant shirt of coarse white cotton, with little patterns embroidered on it in gold, and wore his long blond hair tied back in a ponytail. He had been and still was a very handsome man, but his face had been of the pretty-boy variety, and the character lines around his eyes and mouth had hardened in such a way that the man seemed a very different fellow from the boy. The men around him swung their hammers in a pattern set up through long usage. There had been a brief conversation at the start as to where to set up and then they had gone to work.

DeWitt stood and let it all happen until it became obvious that a correction was necessary. Then he'd yell, "Hey, George! How about takin' up the slack on that rope there?" He carefully kept any note of command out of his voice. It was simply the voice of the guy whose job it was to watch and make sure that nothing went wrong overall, speaking to the guy whose job it was to pull a rope or swing a hammer.

When DeWitt could do something manual without losing track of everything that was happening, he did so, leaping in with a hammer or pulling a rope when necessary. When he bent over swinging a sledge, a crucifix identical to Kathy's fell out of the front of his shirt and swung on its gold chain. He did his job very well. Nobody resented him and everything got done.

When it seemed as though things were well started and they could ask questions without interrupting, Spurlock and Megan went over to him and asked him if he had time to talk.

He shook his head. "Sure, I don't mind if the interruptions don't bother you. I gotta get this show on the road." He grinned.

"What kind of show do you put on?" Spurlock asked.

DeWitt pulled on his chin meditatively for a while. "Well," he said finally. "We got a rock 'n' roll band. I'm the drummer, Kathy sings and plays keyboards. Her dad's on lead guitar and Ed plays bass. All that's for free and it draws a fair crowd. For money we run a couple massage parlors, a few games, a little carny kind of deal, you know, and we sell patent medicines and run a little girlie show. Kathy and some of the chicks do a dance."

Spurlock pushed his hat back, standing there in the hot sun. "I wouldn't have thought there'd be much market for a girlie show these days," he said. "Who's gonna pay to see a naked woman when they can go down to the swimmin' hole and see all the naked girls they want?"

DeWitt laughed and bellowed. "Herb, goddammit! Run that line about ten feet to the left there." He watched for a moment to see that this had been done, then he said, "Naw, this ain't like that at all. Them chicks down at the swimmin' hole don't have any clothes on at all, or maybe just some of them screwy dee-cals like they're wearin' now. It's all just so much meat on the hoof. These girls in our girlie show aren't naked at all. They wear these little tantalizin' outfits that sort of tease you with it; now you see it, now you don't, or did you ever. They dancin' to some slow sweet music and it just drives the boys wild. Birth rate takes a twenty percent jump in any town we go through nine months later. I guarantee it."

That sounded like carny folklore to Spurlock, but De-Witt said it with absolute conviction.

Spurlock laughed. Megan smiled and asked, "What kinds of medicines do you sell?"

DeWitt nodded. "Oh, well," he said, "we got several kinds. There's an all-purpose tonic for folks that's feelin' poorly. Then there's a laxative that's absolutely the best on the market, and a whole bunch of different vitamin tonics and a painkiller that works real good."

Megan, interested in potions, cocked her head and asked, "What's in them?"

DeWitt gave her a close look, as though determining whether to give her an honest answer or not. Then he nodded. "Well, lessee. The all-purpose tonic's about fifty percent alcohol and fifty percent water, flavoring, and color. The vitamins are plain vitamins we buy at discount in bulk and sell at a markup. The painkiller's mostly laudanum, but we don't sell anybody enough to get hung up on it. And the laxative's just untreated water, with coloring and flavoring. Gives diarrhea for about three days. Works real good. Cleans out the whole system."

Megan nodded and smiled. "Sounds good to me," she said.

DeWitt nodded agreement, his mind obviously on the work to be done. Spurlock waved and said, "We'll just walk around for a while and see what's going on. See you later."

DeWitt waved back. "Don't play any of the games," he said, "unless you can afford to lose."

They smiled and continued walking around, watching the show go up.

A few local people were starting to gather around and

watch also. There were a lot of older folks in jeans and longer hair, and a few of the young ones in their close-cropped butch haircuts and the Russian peasant outfits the kids were affecting nowadays. They were very aggressive-looking, these Russian-costumed kids. Spurlock noted that the girls dressed exactly the same way as the boys, down to the same haircuts and baggy pants, boots, and tight-necked collars. He didn't like it much. It was hard not to take it as a personal affront.

"Megan, look at these kids," he said, aware that his face showed a disapproving scowl.

She did and grinned. "They're not all like that," she said.

Spurlock looked around and noticed that she was right. There were a lot of kids in jeans, but they all had shorter hair than he did. There was something else he noticed about them, too. The kids in jeans and longer hair had a kind of smarmy, sanctimonious look. When he was a kid, they'd called kids with that look "suck-asses." Only the suck-asses then had worn short hair and shirts with button-down collars and stuff like that.

"Goddamn," he said. "I don't like them either."

Megan laughed and punched him in the ribs. "Spurlock, you're incorrigible," she said. "I think you're getting old."

"No faster than anybody else," he answered defensively.

She just grinned impishly at him and said, "I don't want to get into a philosophical rap about it. My point is that every generation of kids has to find its own way."

Spurlock pushed his hat back and then put his hands on his hips, thinking about it. He supposed she was right, and to be sure he liked these Russian-looking kids better than he did the ones who were just trying to imitate their elders, but dammit, if they were going to be different, why couldn't they be different in a way that was more the same . . . or something. Hunh!

Since the crowd had started to gather, some of the games were opening up already. He and Megan sidled up to a contest of skill and science, i.e., to knock over a pyramid of wooden milk bottles with a baseball and win a Kewpie doll.

Spurlock moved in until he stood next to an adenoidal youth with a big Adam's apple and a butch haircut. The kid had flaming red hair, which Spurlock thought would look great if he'd let it grow down to his ass, and a yellow peasant shirt. He looked to be about sixteen and was studiously rolling up little rolls of dirt in the palm of one hand with the middle finger of the other. He looked up suspiciously at Spurlock.

Spurlock nodded and smiled and the kid gave him a suspicious smile in return. "Boom-boom, tovarich," the kid said.

Spurlock nodded again. "Hiya, kid," he said. "Likin' the show?"

"It's okay," the boy replied. Spurlock and the kid stood with their feet planted in the dry, dusty grass and watched as another kid in a Russian peasant shirt tried to knock down a stack of bottles. Finally he did it and won himself an old Kewpie doll dressed to resemble Paul McCartney.

"Goin' to the rock 'n' roll show tonight?" Spurlock inquired, awkwardly bouncing on the balls of his feet, hands behind his back, still trying to make conversation and establish some sort of rapport with the younger generation.

The kid shook his head disdainfully. "I don't much like that kind of old-timey music," he replied.

To Spurlock the idea of rock 'n' roll as "old-timey" was startling and a little hard to take. He had listened to rock all his life and loved it. To be sure the music had evolved and changed a great deal over the years, but to brand the entire genre as "old-timey" was ridiculous. He himself had never cared much for the Alice Cooper deco-

slezoid school of rock 'n' roll, nor even the Johnny Winter
dude act kind of rock, but then there were the Beatles and
the Airplane and then later Fleetwood Mac and the Kill
Thang. He had really loved those people.

"Well, what kind of music do you like?" he inquired,
somewhat testily.

The kid gave him a smug look, like, you poor fool,
you'll never understand. "Martial music," he said. "My
favorite is the Soviet Army Marching Band and Chorus."

"Nice talkin' to you, kid." Spurlock shuddered, spun
on his heel, and strode off toward the main tent.

It was getting along toward suppertime anyway, and
Kathy had told them to show up for supper and meet the
folks in the show. She said they'd have something special
in honor of their guests and they'd like it.

They walked in a leisurely fashion back to the cook tent,
stepped carefully over the ropes and tent pegs and inside.
It was dark inside the tent at first, even though the sides
were rolled up to let the air in. And the air seemed
somewhat musty. Rolled canvas always gives that kind of
mustiness to the air. About twenty show people were
inside the tent. They had changed their grubby jeans and
work shirts for something a little more up-to-date and
flashy.

Kathy greeted them at the entrance in a paisley satin
peasant shirt and green tights with the same kind of boots
that the kid had worn. DeWitt too was in Russian peasant
garb, but much flashier. He had tied his long hair back
into a ponytail and dropped the tail down the back of his
shirt so it wouldn't appear unfashionably long.

"Hah! How yew?" Kathy whooped, and grabbed them
both in a smothering embrace. Spurlock wasn't used to
that kind of treatment from strangers, but from this chick
he liked it a lot.

He and Megan muttered assurances that they had been
having a good time.

"Goin' Russki on us, hey, kid?" Spurlock said, and prodded her lightly in the middle of her peasant shirt.

"Got to keep up with the times, hon," she said. "Keep the customers happy. We're the show folks from out of town. We gotta be the firstest with the latest."

Spurlock shook his head. "Yeah, I reckon so," he said. "Kinda makes me glad I'm not in show business. Next thing you'll be cuttin' out the rock show and put in a fancy marching band."

Kathy shook her head and pursed her lips. "I don't hardly think so," she said. "C'mon over here and meet the folks." She turned and announced loudly to the show people who were gathered around the supper table passing a couple of joints and talking over the events of the day: "Folks, this here's old Frank Spurlock, the sheriff of Purgatory County, Arkansas, and his lady, Megan the Witch. They're the folks from that wrecked van we picked up out yonder."

The show folks gathered around and Spurlock shook hands with more people than he could possibly remember. He wished he could get to know each of them individually. They all seemed like good folks, but he would never get them sorted out like this.

He glanced at Megan and she gave him a smile. She was feeling a lot of the same thing. Maybe they'd have time to sort it all out later.

He noticed that the young kids in the show all wore the same short ugly haircuts as the kids in town, maybe even shorter, the show kids considering themselves hipper, or whatever they called it now, than the town kids.

One girl, who Spurlock thought would have been absolutely lovely with long hair, had it all shaved off, all of it, not so much as a little stubble remaining. She was in the act of setting the table when Spurlock spotted her. As soon as that chore was done and a couple of the other kids finished putting food on the table, they all sat down to eat.

Once they were seated, Kathy introduced Spurlock and Megan to her father. Spurlock liked him immediately. He was definitely of the old school. His long gray hair hung down to his waist in back, and his beard hung to his navel in front. He wore jeans and a yellow silk Errol Flynn dueling shirt. His hair was tied back with a paisley scarf. He was a magnificent figure of a man, and Spurlock estimated he was maybe fifty-five years old, no older. He was apparently in good health, but his face was deeply lined and he seemed to have recovered his health after many years of dissipation. His face was very thin, and he had full, sensual lips and deep burning eyes. Spurlock didn't get the name.

As Kathy's father handed Spurlock the mashed potatoes, he asked, "You into rock 'n' roll, Spurlock?"

"Yessir," Spurlock replied. "But it's kind of hard to come by these days. There's no more rock 'n' roll recording going on, and there's not many live bands get to Arkansas. We got plenty of people who play good acoustic there, but we can't get enough electricity for amps and stuff, so we can't play any good old hard-assed rock 'n' roll."

Kathy's father snickered. "Ya'll oughta get some o' them Coleman guitars," he said.

Spurlock shook his head. "I'm afraid I never heard of a Coleman guitar," he replied.

Spurlock caught the shaven-haired girl giving a pained look out of the corner of her eye.

"It's just like an electric guitar, except you gotta fill it full of kerosene and pump it up," the old man replied.

Spurlock took this in all seriousness for a moment, then grinned when he realized he'd been had. "Y'know you got a fat mouth for such an old fart," Spurlock said, smiling.

The old man laughed and wheezed until tears ran from his eyes.

Kathy guffawed and slapped her thigh, pumping her leg

up and down. "Gawdamn, Spurlock, you really bit on that one," she said. "I didn't know there was anybody left in the world that hadn't heard that one at least once."

Spurlock laughed. He had no cause for complaint. After all, he'd pulled a practical joke or two in his time. He'd once put a Jesus Saves sign in front of a bank, and in the army he'd once kept a kid running all over Fort Chaffee looking for a shot-group tightener. "Sounds like an inside joke to me," he said. "My guess is that you've got more than a passing acquaintance with the rock guitar."

The old man's head bobbed up and down a couple of times. "I fool around a little with a Fender Stratocaster," he said. "Probably got one of the few left in working order. Wa-wa pedal still works, too, but my echoplex broke down a couple of years ago."

The bald-headed girl sitting a couple of places down looked up in irritation. "Oh, Grandpa, you're not going to go on about that old echoplex again, are you?"

The old man looked at her peevishly, but also with considerable fondness. "Goddamn younger generation," he muttered. "Got no appreciation for the finer things." He looked back at Spurlock and Megan. "That echoplex was great," he went on. "Useta get to playin' and I'd get a thing goin' with the echoplex, and it never did the same stuff twice. Get that old dude goin'," and he went into a fair imitation of an echoplex unit, whining and howling off what had been played, howling repetitive moans that filled the room. It struck a responsive chord with Spurlock. The echoplex is a mechanical device that sets up a tape loop, amplifies, distorts, and repeats the sounds, and the old man was piling sound on sound and sending weird ululations throughout the tent. It was getting dark and a couple of Coleman lanterns hung from the tent poles, sending weird shadows throughout the room, and the ululations gave a genuinely bizarre effect: eerie, but familiar.

The old man stopped his howling and said, "Echoplex

never did nothing over. That's why records never did it justice. On record you kept hearin' the same song the same way over and over, but live it never did do that. It's more of a challenge to play good without it, but I sure like the effects you got off it.''

The kids looked at the old man in open irritation now. It was obvious they'd heard this subject discussed more often than they wanted by a factor of about eighteen.

The old man shook his head, completely lost in remembrance. ''Man, that was fun, stand up there with all those amps glowing red around you, hummin' and the stage lights so hot, but you didn't care, just so high and gone on the music and maybe fifty thousand people gettin' off on it, and you gettin' off on their gettin' off, and the whole thing just building and building and building like that, till ever'body in sound of it was goin' crazy except for the very cops theirselves, and a couple times I caught the younger ones tappin' their feet when they didn't think nobody was lookin'. Like, I never played Woodstock. I was still in college when that happened, but I played at a few festivals, and there was this bleedin' sea of people just goin' out of their gourds, and it was great.''

The bald-headed girl looked down the table in irritation again. ''Oh, Grandpa, these folks don't want to hear all those old stories. Fifty thousand people, really. We can't even get two hundred to come and hear you guys play. Where you going to get fifty thousand people to come and hear a rock band?''

Spurlock looked down the table at her. ''It used to happen . . . not all the time, and not every band got to play for them. But it happened. Once when I was fifteen I hitched five hundred miles to a rock festival at Heavener, Oklahoma. Honey, it was fantastic. They always used to block them in Oklahoma, but this time it happened for some reason, and we all stayed stoned for the entire three days. The music was great and it was just like your grandpa said. It was fantastic. We just boogied for three solid days." Spurlock got excited all over again, just thinking about it.

An expression of doubt, as though she weren't quite as sure of herself as she had been, came over the girl's face. The old man looked pleased.

"When was that you was at Heavener?" he asked.

Spurlock had to think for a moment. "Early seventies," he said. "Somewhere along in there. I was fifteen at the time."

"Wonder if that's the one I played at?" the old man asked, bemused.

"Musta been," Spurlock said, nodding. "Far as I know they never had another one there. This governor they had let just the one come off, and he got such a bad press that he announced there'd never be another, and sure enough there never was. What'd you say your name was again?"

"Jack Flashman," the old man said. He said it sort of hesitantly, as though he were pretty sure what was going to happen, and sure enough it did.

Spurlock came halfway out of his chair and clapped the old man on the shoulders. "Have mercy, baby," he exclaimed excitedly. "You're Jumpin' Jack Flashman himself. You played lead guitar with the Rill Thang. That was one of the best goddamn rock 'n' roll bands I ever heard. Man, you are a guitar player. You are the guitar player."

A look of pleased modesty came over the old man. "I ain't all that hot," he said, "but I'm glad you think so."

Spurlock shook his head and sat down. "Jumpin' Jack Flashman," he said, turning to Megan as if to see if she caught the import of it.

She looked at Spurlock as though he were being excessive again. Then she turned back to the old man. "I remember your playing very well, Mr. Flashman," she said. "I used to have a couple of your albums, as a matter of fact. I had *Music Hath Charms* and *Night of the Rock Monster.''*

She stopped and thought a moment. ''I wish I knew what happened to those albums. They were really good and they'd be collector's items today.''

The old man smiled broadly and turned to the fifteen-year-old girl as if to say, ''See!''

The girl had her hands on her hips, head cocked, mouth open. She had never seen anybody as impressed as these folks were with her old grandpa. ''Gee!'' she said. ''I never knew anybody was that interested in just old rock 'n' roll before.''

Spurlock smiled at her, trying and not succeeding in keeping any trace of condescension out of his voice. ''It was our way of life, darlin','' he said. ''It was a way of life for our entire generation, and it made us happy.''

She gave him an angry look. ''And while you were listening to your old rock 'n' roll the Russians took over the entire world. America used to be in charge of the world until you and your dope and your old rock 'n' roll.''

Spurlock shook his head again. So that was where their heads were at. It was a charge he had heard before, and he didn't think it was valid. ''No, honey,'' he said. ''It wasn't like that at all. America became a world power in spite of herself and then our leaders became addicted to it. It's not dope addiction and rock 'n' roll music that ruined America. It was the stupidity and venality of our leaders. It was fighting wars just so munitions manufacturers could sell explosives and it was 'pragmatism' in politics, rather than simple adherence to what was right.

''I was in the army and I can tell you that we fought to maintain American business ventures abroad, when they operated with business practices we wouldn't allow here. We fought because we supported every little scummy country that advertised itself as anticommunist until the term anticommunist became synonymous with fascist. The communists were able to back revolts in those places because we had nothing to sell the people. The fact that they treated the people in those countries worse than we did once the revolution was accomplished was beside the point. It was too late then.

"But that's why my generation turned to dope and rock 'n' roll. It was because there was nothing decent we could do otherwise. The choice was to be a pothead rock 'n' roll freak or some sort of international brigand. Some of them tried to do both, of course, but the two didn't mix."

She didn't look particularly convinced, and Spurlock decided not to worry much about it. He could remember leveling similar charges at his own father, about the horrible mess his father's generation had left the world in. Spurlock's father, having lost an eye in Vietnam and having donated half of his legal practice to the defense of indigents who seldom appreciated it, hadn't been in the mood to accept the guilt either. Spurlock had finally caught on that the world wasn't supposed to be perfect, and he guessed this young lady would do likewise in about twenty years. The human race was venal, stupid, horny, and wretched, and it was only fear, necessity, and religion that had brought civilization to the alleged level it had so far achieved.

Kathy gave her daughter a glance that managed to incorporate fondness and a glare and said, "Sugar, you leave old Spurlock alone. He's been truckin' halfway across the country in that little old microbus, and hassled by guerrillas and the dumb army and who knows what all else, and he's gotta start doin' it all again tomorrow, and tonight he's gonna have a good time. We're all gonna have a good time, ain't we, DeWitt?"

DeWitt grinned around a mouthful of mashed potatoes and said, "I don't know about the rest of you, but I'm gonna have a good time. I always have a good time."

Their daughter gave them a look of righteous indigna-

tion. "And while you're having a good time the Russians
are taking over the country. I oughta leave you people and
go join the guerrillas."

Kathy glared hard at her daughter. "I don't want to hear
any more of that kind of talk. Them guerrillas are shame-
less killers. They're not heroes, they're just a bunch of
damn bandits. Spurlock knows. He fights them all the
time. Ain't that right, Spurlock?"

Spurlock regarded Kathy seriously. "Most of them are,"
he said. "Old Frazier, the guerrilla chief near Purgatory, is
just as mean and ornery as they come, but he's sincere, I'll
give him that. He really wants to turn this country back
into what it was before. That's his mistake. You can't go
back. I'd like to see it just turned into a decent place where
people can go about their business unhassled. If old Frazier
could get into that, he and I would get along just fine."

The daughter decided that anything less than condemna-
tion was approval and gave Kathy a look like, "See there!"
and Kathy gave Spurlock a look like, "You traitor!" A lot
of heavy glaring going on all around.

Spurlock smiled defensively and said, "Kathy, there's a
lot of young folks in the country going to join the guerrillas. I don't see that as necessarily a bad thing, as long as
they don't lose the ideals that led them to do it in the first
place. The country's stagnant now, and it's not fit for folks
to live here."

He turned back to the girl. "But for you I would
recommend against it. There's no harder or more dangerous life, and the likelihood that you'd accomplish anything
with it is extremely remote. What is more likely to happen
is that you'd turn into a bandit and die at the age of about
twenty-three, shot in the woods by the same people you
started out to help. If you really want to make this a decent
country, then try and be a decent person, and convince
your friends to do likewise."

The girl gave Spurlock a look that would have wilted

lettuce, and he decided to abandon the entire project. "Oh, hell, I quit," he said. "Pass the peas."

Megan had watched this conversation with growing un-happiness. Spurlock could tell that she didn't want him put in the position he'd been put in, but he hadn't known how to get out of it. She turned to the old man and asked, "Whatever happened to the rest of that band? That was really a fine rock 'n' roll band."

The old man grinned. He had watched the hassle be-tween Spurlock, Kathy, and the girl unhappily, Spurlock judged, because he didn't like arguments and he didn't want his daughter upset, and because he didn't like losing the spotlight after all these years. Jumpin' Jack Flashman had never been what you might call modest. He grinned and launched into an explanation of what happened to the other four members of the Rill Thang with considerable relish. And that's how they finished the meal.

CHAPTER SEVEN

HYATTSTON WAS a fairly large town and the show had been able to hook on to the municipal power supply instead of its own generators. For that reason the midway was ablaze with lights and the crowds of people moved, grinning, from booth to booth as they cheerfully lost money to this most ancient of hustles. Everybody had always known that these shows were a little crooked, but the crookedness was good-natured and the color and flash were real. So was the good nature of the show people.

Spurlock and Megan moved contentedly with the crowd, lining up outside the big tent before the rock 'n' roll portion of the evening. It was an older crowd than had come to the shows when Spurlock was a kid, but then so was Spurlock, and so was Megan. They began to realize that most of the rock 'n' roll fans were people their own age, a few younger and a few older. Most of the young people, the Baldies, as Spurlock was beginning to think of them, were with their parents and didn't look exactly overjoyed to be there. "Mindless drool," he heard one of them mutter.

He thought, And that's the story, kid. Tonight me and my lady are going to get right out of our heads, and I guess that's mindless, and from the look of you, you could use a little of it yourself. Aloud he muttered, "You little rodent."

Megan grimaced and gripped his arm. "Oh, c'mon, Spurlock. You're supposed to be here to have a good time."

He grinned back at her, a little surprised at the vehemence of his reaction. "You're right," he said. "I guess nobody likes to see something he loves rejected by the people he thought he was going to pass it on to."

She nodded at him. "I suppose that explains your devotion to big band jazz."

He shook his head, remembering his father's collection of Benny Goodman records, and how he'd never really been able to get into them, although, even at the time, he'd realized that it was very good music. It just didn't speak to him for some reason. He couldn't identify with the musicians and their bow ties and all that. "Okay, you win," he said.

The crowd squeezed down toward the door and then fanned out again as it moved inside. It seemed funny to be going to a rock concert inside a tent, and it seemed funny to be sitting on wooden bleachers instead of theater seats, but he was still filled with a suppressed excitement he hadn't felt since before the war. "Hot damn," he said, "it's been fifteen years since I've been to one of these things. I didn't know there was such a thing anymore."

She grinned back at him. "I'm sure glad there is." She looked around and shot him a glimpse from under furrowed eyebrows, feigning paranoia. "You got the joints?" she asked in a hoarse whisper.

He laughed at her. "Why? You're so bleedin' stoned now you don't know you arse from your elbow."

Still wearing the same idiot grin, she asked, "Did you

say I don't know my arse from a rainbow? I could swear you said I don't know my arse from a rainbow.''

From somewhere in the crowd he could smell marijuana. This was going to be a congenial group. He and Megan crowded down toward the front. They were early enough not to have too much trouble getting good seats. There was no curtain, just a bunch of amps and speakers on a small stage, the drum kit in the middle and a guitar and bass leaning against their amps. There was a microphone in front and over to the side a small synthesizer. There were a bunch of small-town cops standing in the aisles and Spurlock bummed a light from one, to fire up a joint. It was funny how those kinds of rules varied from town to town. After things had been so dry back there at Fort Leonard Wood, he had been surprised to find that there was no city ordinance against grass in Hyattston and that nobody would hassle him for smoking as long as he didn't run over anybody with a truck or something. "You wanna hit?" he asked the cop.

The cop shook his head. "Better not while I'm on duty.''

Spurlock grinned at him. "This's gonna be a really good show,'' he said. "You oughta get ripped for it.''

The cop shook his head again. "Know what you mean,'' he said. "But I'd be in bad trouble if I got wasted on duty. It ain't that big a concession anyway. I get off pretty good on the music.''

Spurlock nodded and passed the number to Megan, who took a hit and passed it back.

DeWitt came out on stage, grabbed the old rusty microphone, and said, "Ladies and gentlemen, Rainbow Kathy's Rock 'n' Roll Show.''

The crowd applauded loudly as DeWitt took his place behind the drums. Kathy came out and sat down behind the organ. The old man, Jack Flashman, strode onto the stage, knees jerking, head held high, long gray hair down to his waist in back, big studded vest over his jeans, and a red, yellow, blue, and green shirt in some weird paisley pattern.

Spurlock applauded loudly. It was the first time he had seen a man stride on stage with that air of arrogant authority since he'd been a teenager. That air seemed to say, "I'm gonna pick up this guitar and knock all you people on your collective ass and there is nothing you or I can do about it. It is set. It is in the stars. It is a thing so certain that it might as well be past, except that you still have it to look forward to."

He and Megan stood and beat their palms together. The crowd around them picked it up. They were no fools. They knew class when they saw it.

The old man grinned at the audience like a shark at smaller fish and slipped the guitar over his shoulder with a familiar gesture, immediately beginning to check its tuning.

Kathy ran a couple of trills on the keyboard and DeWitt went *ba-dump*, *ba-dump* on the drums, followed by a *ba-da-da-da-DA-DA—rump*, as he ran around all the drums to check their tune.

One of the other guys in the show came out and put on the bass. He looked a little reticent, but absolutely solid. The kind of guy you'd want with you in a pinch, but not the main man. Good bass players always look like that.

There was a little more *zunga-zunga*ing on the bass, and a few more guitar runs while the old man finished checking his tune and Kathy made a couple of runs and then there was rock 'n' roll.

One minute there was just of bunch of people up there on stage messing around and another bunch watching them do it and then the music crashed in on them with a high whining feedback squeal as the old man jammed his instrument into the amp and they leaped right into the old Stones song "Jumpin' Jack Flash."

Instantaneously, the band and the audience were welded

into a solid unit. The audience was on its feet and down the aisles surrounding the cop, who shook his fist at the band and bellowed.

Spurlock took an appallingly deep hit off the number, feeling his head go *wwwwaaaaaooooooiiiiinnnnnnggggg!!!!* as everything else left him but the music and he and his lady stood there beside this small-town cop, all three of them crouched, bent-kneed and jumping up and down in time to the music like a trio of chimpanzees on the jungle floor. Spurlock was off.

They stayed like that for a solid four and one-half hours. Sweat poured off the old man, who didn't look like he had it to lose. DeWitt took his shirt off halfway during the first set, slick sweat running off his nose and in great streaming rivulets from under his armpits.

Kathy was the only one who kept her cool. She sat at the keyboard like the great lady she was, smiling to the audience, rocking back and forth, obviously having a hell of a good time, but not forgetting who she was, or where she was, or what she was doing at any time during the performance. Spurlock supposed that if he were she, he wouldn't want to forget it either. She looked so cool and beautiful sitting there at the keyboard, making that wonderful music. He loved her and knew Megan didn't mind because Megan loved her, too. It was a good time for Spurlock, the best he'd had in a long time, and he supposed the best he would have for a long time to come. They ran through all the old numbers that he loved, a lot of Stones, a lot of Dylan, a lot of old Moody Blues, and a lot of their own stuff that they'd written about life on the highways, and encounters with guerrillas and small-town cops who'd hassled them, and encounters with nice people and with small-town preachers who thought they were sinful people and preached that and then came back around when they thought nobody was looking.

Small-town preacher, lookin' for a piece of tail
We wouldn'ta give him none,
   and there wasn't none for sale.

God, how he loved these people, and he wondered if
there was any way he could get them to bring their show to
Purgatory. He'd love to see them again. He was going to
have to ask DeWitt if there was any chance. All this was
perking through his brain at the same time he was leaping
and screaming to the music. He looked at Megan there
beside him and grinned at her.

It was like the good times of their youth except that in
some ways it was better, because he'd been deviled by so
many worries then, about who he was and what he was
going to be, and by now he'd learned that you didn't have
to worry about any of that stuff, not that he knew any
more now than he had then, but he had learned that you
couldn't define yourself consciously, that if you let go,
your subconscious would define you for you, and that you
would be who you were, but never know who you had
been until it was past, and maybe not even then.

The old man went crazy on the guitar. He sent burst
after burst of rippling notes out to the audience, swaying
his body and grinning at Spurlock and Megan. He was an
old man, but a good man. Spurlock yelled at him. He had
no idea what, just yelled, probably some inchoate gargle
of appreciation, and the entire audience of scroungy, grizzled old freaks thronged down the aisles.

Spurlock saw the cop reach out and grab a joint from the
fingers of some kid with short hair and take a big hit and
pass it back. The sheriff lit one and just laid it on the cop,
who sucked in on it until his eyes bugged out and his face
turned purple. When he handed it back to Spurlock, his
eyes had glazed over and he was screaming and leaping,
"Far out! Far . . . out!"

An hour later, completely wrung out, they groped out of

the tent, to find the rest of the show still going on.
Spurlock and Megan roamed around for a while with silly
grins on their faces, winding down, and finally found
themselves at Kathy and DeWitt's tent, where they had
been directed to come for the night.

Kathy and DeWitt were drying each other after a shower
when they got back. They both stood nude in the middle of
the tent, their bodies lit by the pale orange light of a
kerosene lantern.

Kathy turned to them and smiled. "Y'all wanna take a
shar? It's right out there." She pointed to the rear flap of
the tent, where two fifty-five-gallon drums had been set up
on a platform over their heads, one with a mermite heating
unit in it.

Spurlock didn't say anything. He simply advanced to
Kathy and gave her a big hug. There was a strong feeling
of love and understanding that was flowing among the four
of them. He didn't feel awkward about hugging DeWitt's
nude wife in front of DeWitt or in front of Megan. In fact,
he didn't feel awkward about kissing her, which he proceeded to do.

"What's that for?" Kathy demanded when they came
up for air. She didn't look displeased.

Spurlock touched his cheek to hers and said, "It's for
the concert. It was Fannnnnn-tastic. I haven't seen anything like that for years."

Megan disrobed for the shower, stowing her gear over by
the rucksacks piled in the corner. Spurlock started unbut-
toning his own shirt.

Kathy put on a robe and DeWitt climbed into a pair of
cutoffs, then reached into a cabinet for one of the biggest
hookahs that Spurlock had ever seen. He sat down cross-
legged on a large fur at the foot of the giant water bed
they'd filled in the tent. The bed had no frame, since there
really wasn't any floor to flood, and the bed was drained
and refilled every five days or so. Spurlock wrapped a

towel around his waist, from a stack on a table Kathy had set up. Megan swathed one around her middle, covering her breasts and leaving her legs bare.

Looking up from his labors, DeWitt said, "Watch out for that water, it's really hot."

"Right!" Spurlock said, nodding, but not really listening too closely. That was a mistake. He stepped into the shower, turned on the hot water, and immediately jumped back out again as the scalding water touched his shoulder. He moved too quickly to get burned, but had the devil's own time reaching back in to turn the hot water off. Then he turned on the cold, which was icy, and gradually got the water to a steaming but bearable temperature.

"Okay, baby, let's do it," he said. He and Megan got under the shower and soaped each other, running their hands over each other's bodies gently and carefully, enjoying all of it.

Spurlock would have made love to her then, right there in the shower, but Megan found that awkward, she was so much shorter, and so they finished their shower and went back into the tent to dry themselves.

The drying was constantly interrupted by DeWitt's stuffing the mouthpiece of the hookah in their mouths. By the time they were dry they were also wasted.

Wrapped back up in the towel, Spurlock sank down on the fur beside Kathy, while Megan sat next to him. They continued smoking for quite a while. DeWitt got up and turned on an ancient battery-operated cassette recorder, playing some soft, slow blues.

After a while Spurlock asked, "Where do you want us to throw our sleeping bags?"

The next morning, when they got up to dress, Kathy and DeWitt instead of putting on their crucifixes placed them over the heads of Megan and Spurlock. "What's this?" Spurlock inquired, astonished.

Kathy smiled and kissed him. "We got these from

someone we loved very much,'' she said. ''And we feel
that you guys need them now. By and by you won't need
them anymore, and you can pass them on to someone you
love. You'll know who when the time comes.''

The gift made Spurlock feel wonderful, but he didn't
know what to say. He just kissed her back.

CHAPTER EIGHT

AFTER BREAKFAST DeWitt and Spurlock saddled a couple of horses and rode back through town to Dale's garage. They reined up outside and tied their horses to a small hitching post.

DeWitt led the way inside. It was dark and everywhere was equipment, covered with dark grease. The van was hoisted up on a grease rack and the front wheel was off. "Hey, Mike Dale!" DeWitt called.

"Hey, man," came a voice from behind the grease rack. A deceptively slender black man in jeans and a sweatshirt came out wiping his hands on a rag. His smile contrived to be open, friendly, and shrewd at the same time. He moved with the controlled grace of a dancer and athlete. So much so that Spurlock felt awkward just watching him. "DeWitt, what's happenin'?"

DeWitt grabbed his hand, shook it. "This here's Frank Spurlock," he said. "He belongs to that van there."

Dale looked at Spurlock with a tense, puzzled smile. "Hit a big chuckhole, eh?" he said, but it came out awkwardly.

There was something wrong here. This guy was tense about something, and it had all come on when Spurlock was introduced. The sheriff looked at DeWitt. He got the same glance back; no question about it. "When you reckon you'll have it ready?" Spurlock asked.

Dale cocked his head and grimaced. "Maybe tonight, maybe tomorrow morning," he said. Then he shut up. His gaze went steadily over Spurlock's left shoulder.

DeWitt put his hands on his hips and narrowed his eyes. "What's goin' on here, Mike? What are you bent out of shape about?"

Dale's eyes automatically went over his shoulder. He stood for a long moment and did not reply. Then he said, "Nothin', nothin'," quite loudly. There was another long unnatural pause. Dale walked over to an old desk with a clipboard and several pens and pencils covered with dirty grease. "I'll go ahead and figure up your bill, long's you're here." He sat down and picked up a pencil and the clipboard, turning the sheaf of work orders upside down as he did so. This left blank paper exposed.

Dale wrote, "May be bugged. Two guys looking for Spurlock yesterday. Said not to tell." He made a throat-cutting gesture with his finger.

DeWitt looked at Spurlock with something like panic in his eyes. This was way out of his line.

"Hmmm!" Spurlock muttered. "That's kinda steep." He picked up the clipboard and wrote on it: "How look?"

Dale took it back and said, "Parts and labor, man. Everything goin' up." On the order form he wrote, "Both dark, long hair, beard, one short-fat, one tall-thin."

Spurlock nodded. "Okay, thanks a lot. I'll be back to pick her up tomorrow morning."

Dale tore the sheet off the clipboard and very carefully set a match to it and dropped it in the wastebasket. No question that he was badly frightened. It had taken considerable balls for him to do what he had done in warning them. The Maf, for that was who it had to be, doesn't take kindly to interference in its operations. Old Senigliero really had it in for him for some reason. He must have also been behind that roadblock. But the roadblockers had not been Maf gunsels. They'd been guerrillas.

Spurlock and DeWitt turned and, with Spurlock in the lead this time, left the garage.

For the first time Spurlock questioned his wisdom in leaving Purgatory now. Nothing in his dealings with bureaucracies had led him to believe that one could make a decision about anything in less than three months, and a bureaucracy is what the Maf had become. But he had never considered how fast a bureaucracy might be disposed to move when the top man was pissed about something. The only feasible explanation to what was going on was that Senigliero was after him. Probably because Spurlock had made him lose face.

That meant he had contacts in Purgatory who knew where he was going, and probably why. But it did not necessarily mean that they had made their move in Purgatory yet. In all probability they would wait until Spurlock was safely iced to do that. He was determined that they have a long wait.

P-snap-p!

DeWitt looked startled when Spurlock shoved him to the ground behind a '78 Mercury. He looked even more startled at the sound of the *BLAM* that followed the snap. Not to mention the two more snaps and blams that followed.

"What the hell was that?" DeWitt asked, an immemorial question. DeWitt thought that all bullets passing overhead sounded like a TV ricochet, Spurlock supposed.

Spurlock sat against a tire on the old Merc, with his pistol out, checking the cylinder and wishing to Christ he'd brought the CAR-15. "Sounded kinda like an old thirty-ought-six to me," he said. "Hard to tell, though." But more important than that was where the fuck was it coming from? Sounded like their right rear to him, and cautiously he turned and poked his hat up. Whoever the dude was he didn't rise to the bait. He didn't want to stick his head out too far either. Spurlock stuck his hat on the pistol and put it out a little farther. That didn't work either. Shit!

Grimacing, Spurlock put his hat back on. He was going to have to deliberately draw some fire to find out where they were. There was a collection of buildings to his right rear and an old shopping center across the street. The firing had probably come from the rooftops, but he had to be sure and he had to get out of the dude's sights and find some way up there without being discovered. "You wait here," he said, and was up and moving, running, crouching behind a line of old fifty-five gallon drums and old cars. After the first snap all the rest were lost in a chorus of blams as he ran, cussing the sandy loam at his feet that offered poor traction, himself for leaving the CAR-15 behind, and the son of a bitch who was coming pretty close when you figure he was firing at a moving target from about seventy-five meters.

Spurlock slid behind an old junked Toyota, squeezed off three fast rounds at the rooftop, reloaded quickly, squeezed off two more, and was off and running again, hoping that whoever it was thought he only had one round left in the chamber.

Sand kicked up at his feet in neat little spurts until he hit the street, but the adrenaline was pumping so strong in him by then that he couldn't hear the gunshots coming from the roof.

In a moment he was under the overhang in front of the old grocery store and out of the line of sight of the hit man, or men, whatever. He punched open the door of the grocery, one of the old type that is supposed to open when you step on a rubber mat in front of it. It didn't work, and probably hadn't for years. Two distraught housewives and a grocer put their hands in the air when he came in. He didn't pause to explain but simply charged through the place, through the double swinging doors of the stock-room, past the freezer and out the back door fast, and then pressed up against the brick wall in the alley.

He was breathing heavily, spotted the old rusty iron ladder that hung just low enough that he'd have to jump for it, which he was about to do until he saw two dark figures, one clutching a scope-sighted rifle, cross at the end of the alley. Mike hadn't been fooling. They were both dark, one short-fat, one tall-thin, but that's about all he could see.

He ran down to the end of the alley, but they were gone when he got there. "Shit!" he muttered. There was an-other ladder on the end of the building, apparently the way they got down. He climbed it and walked along the edge of the building until he found what he was looking for, a small pile of bright, shiny .30-caliber cartridges. He picked up a couple and put them in his pocket.

In two minutes he was back across the street. Mike and DeWitt stood outside the garage with their hands in their pockets, waiting, when he got back.

"Git 'em?" DeWitt asked.

"Huh-uh!" Spurlock replied. "But they left their call-ing card." He held up the two cartridges. "Listen, thanks, Mike. If I hadn't been expecting something, I might not have been so fast on my feet." He was speaking freely because they were out away from the garage. They could have been monitored by a shotgun mike, but Spurlock considered that extremely unlikely.

Mike nodded. "You going to leave town in the old van with those two after you?" he inquired. "They oughta be able to run fast enough to catch you."

Spurlock shrugged. His plans, as usual, were not fully formed, and he saw nothing to be gained by sharing them, but Mike's question was well founded. Even if he left by an evasive route, they would find him if he stayed on the main roads. If he went by side roads and county roads, he tripled his risk of being hassled by guerrillas and low-grade desperadoes. Finally he muttered, "There's several things I can do. But they all involve leaving here pretty quick."

"Anything I can do to help you get those guys, all you gotta do is ask," Dale replied. "But it looks to me like you gotta find them first. That's about your only hope."

"Well," Spurlock replied, "the first thing I want to do is check on my lady. Then I'm going to work on what to do next. If I need help, though, I'll know where to come."

Mike nodded emphatically. Spurlock shook hands with him once more, then he and DeWitt mounted up and started riding back toward the show. When they'd rounded the first bend, Spurlock inclined his head back toward the garage. "He seems awful eager to stick his neck out. Any chance he could be working with them some way?"

DeWitt shook his head. "I don't think so. I've known Mike maybe four–five years now. He just hates the Maf because he used to be a big coke dealer in Evanston and they broke him up. He used to be a wealthy man and now he just runs that little garage because he wouldn't play ball with them."

Spurlock nodded. The man had been cool. The man was angry. It all fit. "Interesting fella," he said. "He got any other unusual talents?"

DeWitt nodded. "About three years ago he used to be the champion dirt bike rider of central Illinois."

Spurlock grinned. Then he got to thinking, hard . . . and hoping Mike was everything DeWitt said. He had a plan, but it still had a lot of holes in it. You couldn't really call it a plan, just a notion.

"You in a really big hurry to get back to the show?" DeWitt asked as they entered the downtown section.

Spurlock thought about it for a moment. "Huh-uh. I

don't really figure those two are going to sprint across town to mess with Megan. If anything, she's safer where I'm not. For a day or so anyway. What you got in mind?''

"Just a cup of tea in a little restaurant here downtown. Some pretty nice folks run it. I try and stop there every time I come to town. If you like the menu we could have lunch.''

It had been a while since Spurlock had eaten anything like a balanced meal. And he was used to them, being about half a health food nut. After a couple of days his body started yearning for certain foods. In this case it was greens, salad oil, and fresh fruit in that order. He snapped to DeWitt's suggestion like a trout to a fat fly.

A few minutes later they reined up in front of a row of glass-fronted stores just off the main street of Hyattston. There was a place that sold guitars and banjos, a ladies' dress shop, a pizza joint, a boutique, a football emporium, and a weird little establishment that Spurlock ignored because he couldn't quite make out what it was.

He dismounted and started toward the pizza joint. DeWitt grabbed him and said, "Wrong restaurant," leading Spurlock toward the little establishment. The letters on the sign above the storefront were so misshapen that he hadn't read it at first, but now he followed the looping, elongated golden letters through the word "Illumination." The glass storefront had been painted in what could be interpreted as either a Mideast or an East Indian motif, depending on the predilection of the viewer. It did help to take the curse off the Early Saltine architecture.

DeWitt pushed open the yellow screen door and Spurlock stepped into the dim interior. A dozen or so glossy, bright-colored, handmade tables and chairs were arranged about a room that was really too small for them. Spurlock grinned. Facing him from a large painting on the wall was a Tibetan om symbol. There were other paintings on the wall, of famous religious leaders: Jesus, Buddha, Meher Baba.

Spurlock beamed. It wasn't often he ran into other "bliss ninnies," as Megan called them. The warmth of the place wrapped itself around him like money from home.

A bouncy little man in jeans and a T-shirt that said, "Don't Worry—Be Happy!" approached them from the back of the restaurant. He had a hair and beard combination that looked like a bushel basket of Brillo shot with gray. He bounced along on orange tennis shoes. "Hello, gents, what'll it be?" Then he brightened. "Oh, hi, De-Witt. Saw you play last night. You were dynamite. Who's this guy?"

He held out his hand for an elaborate handshake, announcing his name as Grady.

"Spurlock," the sheriff said, shaking hands.

Spurlock's first impression was that Grady was stoned out of his gourd, and he tended to think that his cooking would not be very together for that reason. They exchanged pleasantries for a few minutes.

"You into meditation?" Spurlock asked, nodding toward the om symbol.

Grady beamed at him and nodded. "Krya-yoga," he replied. "We're a kind of mystical mishmash here. My wife, Anna, and I follow Krya, some of our people are into Meher Baba, some are Hare Krishna people, and some are just your usual dope-sucking weirdos!"

DeWitt pulled out a chair and plopped down in it. Spurlock followed suit. Grady disappeared back into the kitchen. Spurlock hooked a boot heel in a rung of the chair, tried to lean back on the back two legs, and stopped as it creaked alarmingly. Instead he rolled a toothpick into the corner of his mouth.

"I wanna ask you something," he said to DeWitt. "Is that guy stoned or what?"

DeWitt grinned. "Ol' Grady hasn't smoked in four, five years now. He just says his oms or whatever."

"No lie," Spurlock said. He kind of halfway wished he could get off weed. He was pretty sure it was blocking his progress. Still it didn't interfere with his normal day-to-day efficiency, and all the instruction he had read said not to worry about it. When it was time, it would happen.

A pretty lady, also with electric Brillo for hair, came and took their order. DeWitt introduced her as Anna, Grady's wife. She was tall and slender, wore jeans and a Mexican blouse. She had a soft doe-eyed look, which in no way implied weakness. Spurlock took one look at the menu and totally freaked. He wanted everything on it.

There were enough different things that he could have eaten for a week and not repeated himself. It was all natural foods, spinach casseroles, yogurt, honey and fruit, all that type of stuff. He was completely shorted out by the choices. Finally he simply slumped down in his chair, defeated, and said, "Surprise me." DeWitt ordered pan-fried trout and a strawberry smoothie.

Anna laughed at Spurlock's confusion and went away, only to return a second later with a basket of homemade whole-wheat bread, butter, and honey. Spurlock dived for it. "Ahh! Ahh! Ahh! Ahh! Ahh!" he sighed as he sank his teeth into the first mouthful.

DeWitt grinned at him. "Steady, boy. The best is yet to come."

"Oh, I hope not," Spurlock replied. "If it gets any better than this, I may not survive."

Spurlock had automatically placed himself with his back to the wall so when the two dark guys, one short-fat, one tall-thin, came in, he immediately noticed them and registered the possibility that they might be his potential assassins. The tall skinny one in the lead allowed his eyes to widen perceptibly when Spurlock came into his field of vision. That didn't clinch it, of course, but it was another indicator.

They didn't look much like potential assassins to him.

He had never seen a less menacing pair physically. The tall skinny one had a sort of Vandyke beard and longish hair, a large hooked nose, and big soft eyes. He wore a maroon turtleneck sweater and a matching maroon knit beret, a big floppy one. The short fat one obviously hadn't had a shave or haircut since puberty, and probably not a bath since then either. His glossy black beard and hair both hung almost to his waist. He was barefoot and wore jeans cut off just above the knee. He also wore a jeans coat and a broad-brimmed old army jungle hat. Over his shoulder hung an ancient canvas paperboy's bag with "Louisville Courier-Journal" stamped on it. His hand dipped into the bag, easily large enough to accommodate a wide variety of firearms, including an M-1 rifle, which fired the kind of ammo Spurlock had found on the roof, if it were broken down into its three main groups. Spurlock almost went for his .357 right there, but the short fat one came out with an ancient hard-backed copy of *Crime and Punishment* and began to read.

Grady brought their menus and the tall-thin announced, "Hey, dis is a flipped-out menu," in a Brooklyn accent, as he glanced at it. Another indicator. They weren't from here. It was a safe enough thing to play the odds a little. If the plan that was currently working in his head was as good as he thought, it might be worth a try.

Anna brought their order. Spurlock was being treated to the spinach casserole and he did immediate justice to it. After Anna had gone he inquired of DeWitt, in a low voice, just barely audible enough to carry to the table where the two probable assassins sat, "I oughta get out of town by some back road that will connect with the main highway about a hundred miles from here. You know this area. You got any idea where that might be?"

DeWitt pondered a minute, then nodded. "Best thing would be to take the county road north for about twenty miles, then head east till you hit the freeway. You gonna leave at night?"

Spurlock thought awhile. "Huh-uh, I'll leave just before dawn tomorrow morning. That way Megan and I'll get a good night's sleep and be able to travel all day. I want to put as much distance between me and whoever that clown is as I can tomorrow."

DeWitt opened his mouth to express surprise at Spurlock's reference to a lone assassin, but Spurlock went on. "I wanna get my mission accomplished and get back home as quick's I can. If they got some guy trying to wax me here, that probably means they're going to make their move in Purgatory quicker than I figured."

DeWitt looked at Spurlock in a somewhat puzzled way. He wasn't into all the ramifications of Spurlock's business. He shrugged, let it ride, and got back to his trout.

Spurlock demolished his spinach casserole handily, then ordered a cup of yogurt and chopped fruit. "I hope that horse is strong enough to carry me after this meal," he said, laughing.

DeWitt nodded. "Well, it pulls my wagon, but it has another horse to help, so maybe so, maybe not."

Spurlock leaned way back in his chair, which creaked alarmingly again, picked a small piece of apple peel from between his two front teeth with a toothpick, and started working his way around his mouth with it. A few minutes later he and DeWitt arose and strolled to the door, feeling the tall-thin's eyes on him as they left.

Once out the door he turned to DeWitt and said urgently, "Let's get out of here, babe. We got a lot to do and not much time to do it in."

They cantered back to the show, to let Megan and Kathy know what was going on, then back to Dale's garage to explain Spurlock's plan.

Spurlock sat on a corner of Mike's beat-up old wooden desk while DeWitt sat on his haunches hand-rolling a tobacco cigarette. Mike Dale sat leaning in his chair against the wall, his tennis-shod feet tangled up in the rungs, regarding Spurlock with hooded eyes, his grin quiet for once. He reached up and scratched his short, nappy hair. "It's a strange little plan, and it's tricky, but I don't see any big holes in it." They had the radio turned up loud, in case there was a bug, and spoke very low.

Spurlock shook his head. "Tell you the truth, it's entirely too iffy for my taste. I sure as hell wouldn't hold it against you if you don't want to do it."

Mike examined Spurlock closely. "But you intend to go ahead by yourself if I don't come, right?"

"Yeah!"

"That's too risky. That's two to one against, and they're firing from concealed positions. That more than cuts your chances in half, more like by three quarters."

Spurlock shrugged. "I got to get out of here. I got to shake those two permanently. So I have to do it with help or do it by myself."

Dale nodded. "Okay! But either way you need at least one of my bikes. If you screw up I lose a bike. Plus it won't take them long to find out where you got the bike. It looks like I'm gonna have to go along just to protect myself."

Spurlock smiled. That's what he had wanted Mike to say.

"I'm goin', too," DeWitt grunted from the floor. "I don't want Megan drivin' the van."

Spurlock nodded. "Good."

"I got some old rusty boiler plate out back of the garage. We might line the van with that," Mike said, dismounting from the chair. "Then we'll go over to the house and get the bikes."

They rose to follow him.

Spurlock went to work, picking out several pieces of boiler plate that looked like they would fit fairly neatly against the walls of Megan's van. Mike and DeWitt walked over to Mike's house and came back a half hour later, riding two motorcycles. Mike's was a big stripped-down Kawasaki, about a 650, Spurlock estimated, although he actually knew very little about the beasts. He had ridden the farm's 350 Honda to Fayetteville and back a few times and that was about it.

The other bike, the one DeWitt rode, was also a Kawasaki, a 350 Enduro. It looked new, still had the original factory paint job, and was clean.

"You ride one of these dudes before?" Mike inquired.

Spurlock shook his head. "Not one like that."

DeWitt snapped down his kickstand and got off.

"Get on!" Mike Dale commanded. "I'll break you in on some dirt riding."

Spurlock gingerly mounted the machine and kicked it to life. Mike led him out to the open country and they spent a couple of hours churning around the rough sandy plains on the outskirts of Hyattston. It didn't seem to Spurlock that he got significantly better on the bike than he had been before. He busted his nuts a couple of times going over jumps and finally got to where he could turn in the sand without falling down. He also practiced riding with one hand, since it looked like they were going to have to do a lot of that.

"Whatcha think?" he inquired after they had been chasing around in the dunes for a couple of hours.

Mike leaned back in his seat and put his hand on his hip. "Frankly," he said, "I think you're a fool to even try with no more experience on one of these than you got. On the other hand, I be damned if I'm gonna do it by myself."

Spurlock nodded. He didn't feel like making any flip comments. Mike was right. What they were doing was dangerous as hell, even for good riders who were also good shots. As it was, they were both half qualified. He was somewhat subdued as they rode back to the garage.

They could have used a lot more time to practice—a couple of weeks would have been about right—but there was still a lot to do on the van. They still had to cut and fit the ramp, for instance.

After the usual quota of unexpected delays they finally managed, by midnight, to get everything set up like they wanted. It was going to be a hell of a tight squeeze, but if Spurlock had figured correctly, those two goons were going to be in for a huge surprise the following morning.

That night he and Megan racked out in their sleeping bags in a corner of the tent. There was no repetition of the previous evening's fun. Everybody there, all four of them, were far too uptight about the events of the following day.

"Why don't we just sneak out tonight?" Megan inquired.

Spurlock lay with his body rigid, naked except for his toothpick. "Because I want those two clowns off everybody's ass for good and all," he replied.

It was his intention to go to sleep after that, which he was finally able to do after a half hour of meditation to quiet his racing brain and nervous body. He set the clock in his head to go off at four-thirty, which it did.

Getting DeWitt up was another matter. "Jesus, I only been asleep ten minutes," he gasped as Spurlock jostled him, trying to avoid shaking the bed and waking Kathy. "Don't worry about it," Spurlock whispered. "When that first rush of adrenaline hits you, you'll be wide awake."

Very carefully they dressed by the light of a candle, the two sleeping forms of their women not moving. Guess they're not too worried, Spurlock thought, if they can sleep at a time like this. He did not delude himself that they had underestimated the danger, so he deduced that they had great confidence in him and DeWitt. He sincerely hoped their confidence was well founded.

Apparently, though, they weren't quite as confident as he expected because as they went out the tent flap Kathy muttered, "Be careful," and Megan called, "Good luck!" almost simultaneously.

Spurlock turned and grinned into the darkness. "Don't

worry; be happy," he said, and they went to saddle two sleepy horses.

It was five when they got to Dale's garage. They found Mike squatting on his haunches beside the van, placidly smoking a cigarette. "How long before we leave?" he inquired.

"Just before first light," Spurlock muttered. "About twenty minutes."

"I got a thermos of coffee and a pack of Winstons in the garage," he said, rising. "I expect we got time."

"You got a pack of tailor-made cigarettes?" DeWitt exclaimed incredulously.

"I got half a fucking carton," Mike answered proudly. "Put 'em in my freezer five years ago and been takin' 'em out for special occasions, of which this is one."

They went inside to prepare themselves for battle. Spurlock accepted a cup of coffee but declined the cigarette.

Fifteen minutes later DeWitt started the van and eased the heavily laden, low-riding vehicle out of the garage and headed north on the county road.

Even after having taken all of Spurlock's and Megan's gear out, it was still cramped with the two men and the two bikes in the back.

Spurlock squatted down with his back against a piece of rusty boiler plate, nervously rolling a toothpick around in his mouth. Mike and DeWitt were chain-smoking Winstons as they drove, on the grounds that there was no point in saving them if they might be dead within the hour.

Spurlock had all the windows open he could, but still the air was dead and he was claustrophobic. He felt like a frogman waiting to be ejected from a submarine. But he didn't want to spoil their smoke, so he kept quiet.

They drove on and on, heading north on the old road. Soon a gray light filtered into the van and a few minutes later Spurlock began to distinguish color.

"You reckon they're gonna do it?" Mike asked, looking at his watch. They had been on the road for over half an hour. Pretty soon they'd be at their turnoff to head for the interstate.

Spurlock shrugged. "My acting might not have been as good as I thought. We'll go on for a wh—"

P-tiiing BLAM!!

"That's it!" Spurlock bellowed as the first round punctured the skin of the van and ricocheted off the boiler plate just before the sound of the firing reached them.

Spurlock and Mike Dale were both on their feet, kicking their bikes to life as the little van filled with explosions, roars, and noxious smoke.

"Sheeeeeesh!" DeWitt exclaimed as he slewed the van to a stop. They were all coughing from motorcycle exhaust smoke as Dale slammed open the side door of the VW. DeWitt had his window open and was pouring curses and double-ought buckshot from a 12-gauge pump through the driver's window.

Spurlock felt faint until the door was open, revealing sandy hills and the pink-and-gray-rippled sky of a beautiful dawn.

"Let's get this," Dale screamed as he and Spurlock grabbed the plywood ramp they'd made and put it in the door. In a moment it was in place. Thirty-caliber bullets were hitting all around them as the door opened and their boiler-plate shield was removed. Spurlock had hoped that it would come from the other side of the road, but that was not to be. Worse yet, rounds were coming in the side door and ricocheting off the boiler plate inside the van. If they didn't get out of here fast, one would hit a gas tank and explode, or maybe a tire.

But Mike was up on his 650 and gone, coasting down the ramp and accelerating into the sand. He slewed left, righted himself and was away.

Spurlock followed an instant later, almost losing control of his machine as it hit the dirt, but with a twist of his wrist he was up and gone, wind roaring in his ears as he zigzagged toward the firing.

He turned and skidded through the hard sand and morning air, his vision a blur of sand and sky, but he had a clear mental image of his opponents behind a hill to the left.

He and Dale assaulted on line as they dodged and twisted their bikes to present an unpredictable target. Riding with one hand, they poured out suppressive fire from their weapons, Spurlock with short bursts from the CAR-15 and Mike with multiple shots as fast as he could trigger an old M-1 carbine.

Suddenly the firing slacked off and Spurlock heard the sound of an engine starting. He and Mike both reacted by accelerating flat out for the little hillock where the firing had come from. Mike took a dune with a jump and Spurlock went up after him, only he didn't control it right and his bike went nose-down, bounced, crunched, and sent him into the dirt. He landed clear of the bike and rolled so his weapon didn't get clogged by the sand.

An ancient jeep, modified as a dune buggy, sprinted out from behind the hillock. Mike's engine growled louder as he charged forward, firing all but unaimed shots from the carbine. Spurlock laughed a grizzly cackle as he snapped out the stock on his weapon and rolled into a firing position. He fitted the scope to his eye and picked up the jeep, large and fuzzy behind the cross hairs. It wasn't going very fast in the sand so he picked out the left front tire, took a lead on it, and squeezed off a single shot. The sand kicked up a couple of feet behind the tire and he took a longer lead and blew the hell out of it.

The dune buggy slipped to the left front. The roll bar may have protected the machine, but the two prospective assassins came out of their seats as the jeep flipped, having failed to fasten their seat belts in their haste.

That looked like a mistake to Spurlock, because from where he was, it had looked like the buggy was about to fall on them.

He got up and brushed the sand off himself just as Mike Dale rode carefully up to the dune buggy.

"Hold it!" Spurlock bellowed. "Get down! We'll go in together."

Mike nodded and lay down behind a dune.

Spurlock looked at where his bike lay, looked at where the dune buggy lay, and decided to ride. He righted the machine, started it and rode over to where Mike was, dismounted and motioned for Dale to go around to the left while he went around to the right.

The short fat one was on Spurlock's side, dead, neck pinned under the windshield, body angled grotesquely away from the machine. There was the sound of one round fired from Dale's carbine and Spurlock ran around to find Mike standing over the body of the tall-thin, who clutched the scope-sighted M-1 rifle in his hands. Michael had put a third eye in the middle of his forehead.

"This joker wanted to kill somebody bad," he said. "He was dyin' anyway."

Spurlock shrugged. "Let's go home," he said. "I got to repack the van."

"Spurlock!" Mike said, a note of puzzlement in his voice. "How'd you know where those guys were? I couldn't see nothin', and I couldn't tell from the sound either."

Spurlock thought for a moment, then shrugged. "Beats me," he said. "When the lead starts to fly, I always know what to do."

Mike nodded. "That must be handy in your line of work," he said.

CHAPTER NINE

THEY WENT up through the east, into Pennsylvania, hooking up with the tail end of a convoy headed toward New York City. Finally, six days after they started, they got to the ferry slip which stood under one end of where the George Washington Bridge used to be. Spurlock pulled the van in behind a long column of trucks and buses waiting for the ferry. Up ahead in the morning fog he could barely see what had been the entrance to the bridge, and the crumbling blacktop road that had been constructed off the edge of the highway down to the ferry. Rusted steel stuck out from what had been the end of the bridge. The support islands still stood in the channel, with their dropped, jagged-ended spans angled between them.

He stopped the van, and they sat there for a long time. The column of trucks didn't move. Spurlock looked at the truck in front of him, his brow starting to furrow. He began drumming on the steering wheel. "Son of a bitch!" he snarled. "I'm gonna see how long we have to wait for this ferry."

Megan nodded. He got down out of the cab and walked

to the produce truck in front of him. The driver sat there
stolidly, a burly fellow in a cap and a lumberman's jacket,
chewing on the remains of a cigar, staring without emotion
at the long line of vehicles ahead of him.

Spurlock put one foot up on the running board and
leaned on the truck. He pushed his cowboy hat back on
his head and waggled the toothpick in his mouth. "How
long you reckon it's gonna be before we get on that
ferry?"

The driver looked at him, scornfully incredulous, and
burst out with something unintelligible, very fast, like,
"Jeez, wheddayacmfrm?"

"S'cuse me," Spurlock said, "but I didn't catch that."

Shaking his head, the driver repeated, "Wheh . . . da
. . . you . . . come . . . from?" It was slow enough, but
the cadence was very strange to Spurlock, even though he
had been in this city before. He'd get it right in a moment.
He made an effort to smooth the Arkie out of his talk, and
speak basic disc jockey English. "I come from Arkansas,
and I want to know how long we'll have to wait before we
cross this goddammed ferry."

The driver looked at the van and whistled. "You come
from Okkinsawr in *that*? Din' you get shot at?"

Spurlock sighed and nodded. "Sure we got shot at. How
long for the ferry?"

The driver shrugged. "Maybe six hours if it all goes
quick, more if it don't."

Spurlock spun around in the road, beating his hand with
the opposite fist. "Jesus H. Christ," he exploded, eager-
ness to get on with it, to see his kids, making him scream
with impatience. "I thought you Yankees were supposed
to be efficient!"

The driver gave him a shrug. "Whaddayagonnado?"
he said. "If it was upta me, dey'd rebuild da bridge."

Spurlock clenched his fists and ground his teeth in

frustration. "Thanks for the information," he said, and headed back to the van.

"Don't t'ink nuttin' of it," the driver called after him.

Muttering darkly, Spurlock stomped back to the van, ripped open the door, and installed himself behind the steering wheel, gripping the wheel with both hands and glowering out at the truck.

"What's the matter, babe?" Megan inquired.

He glowered at the truck before him and drummed on the steering wheel. "Looks like we're gonna be stuck here for about six hours," he muttered. "These stupid Yankee bastards don't have enough sense to reopen the bridge, and they don't have enough sense to get another boat on this ferry. This kind of bullshit is going to drive me crazy."

She sat and thought for a moment. "Why don't you take the time to do some yoga and get rested? This is going to be something of an ordeal, especially on the other side of the river. At least I expect it is."

He nodded. "Yeah, okay. I'll go do some yoga in the back, but that'll only take an hour at the outside. We'll still be stuck here for another five hours." He waved his arm toward the river, at the barges and tugboats going by. "My kids are over on the other side of this river and I haven't seen them for eight years. This is driving me nuts." He looked at her and grinned crazily.

She smiled. "Well, do your yoga and when you get through, we'll see what we can do."

He wasn't paying much attention to what she was saying. All that got through was that he should do his yoga, and he'd be able to deal with these hassles better, which was true.

It was cramped in the back of the van, though, and he couldn't do a headstand, and he never really got off on the meditation because the tootling horns of the boats on the river kept dragging his mind back again. He hadn't had a decent meditation since they started on this trip. He sat there grumpily and thought about lighting a joint, but he was wired too high and wanted to think about what was coming. How was he going to find the kids?

Could he just start with a phone book? That was the sensible thing to do, if they still had phone books in New York. Purgatory hadn't had a new one for five years, but it was a backwater. New York ought to at least have a current phone book. No, that's not the thing, blank all that out of your mind, Spurlock old boy. *Om mane padme hum. Om mane padme hum.* Where's the sound of crickets way back in the back of your head? Concentrate on that, and on eye center, and you'll see the fire blossoms blooming in your head again. *Om mane padme hum. Om mane padme hum . . .* maybe I could check with the police. They might have access to a current crisscross directory. Hall of Records. Jesus!

Sixteen years old. I wonder if their hair's still blond like their mother's. Fine, fine hair. Soft to the touch. Forget that one, Spurlock. Hall of Records. Crisscross. *Om mane padme toooooooooot!''*

Hell with this! Spurlock exploded out of the back of the van and installed himself in the driver's seat again. He felt a little better, but not much, and he felt a little resentful and cheated that he had got himself set for a good meditation and hadn't had one.

"Feel better, babe?"

He growled what he intended as an affirmative response.

"Not so hot, huh?" She patted him on the arm as he continued to glare at the truck ahead of him. "Excuse me," she said, and climbed over the seat into the back, unhooking the eagle claw from the mirror and taking it with her. She picked up a blanket and started to arrange a curtain between the front and back seats, so he couldn't see what she was doing.

"What's goin' on?" he asked, trying not to be too demanding about it. He knew he came on heavy when he was mad, and he was anxious not to put the burden of it onto Megan.

"I'm going to earn my keep," she said, shutting the curtain with an air of finality.

He shrugged and looked out at the same scene they'd been looking at for forty-five minutes. It wasn't any too scenic. Vile factory smoke billowed up from across the river. Even so, the Manhattan skyline was still imposing from a distance. He glowered. He wanted to smoke, but he didn't want to be stoned, and he didn't smoke tobacco. Jesus, he hadn't been this nervous in years. He felt like getting out of the van and pacing back and forth, anything to dissipate this absurd tension. He cracked his knuckles and started jiggling up and down in his chair.

"Hold still, goddammit!" Megan howled from the back of the van.

All wrapped up in his frustration, he had paid no attention to her muttering and had no idea what it was about.

In a moment she parted the blanket curtain she'd made and sat down in her seat. "Ought to be any minute now," she said, hanging the eagle claw back up.

"What ought?"

"These trucks will start pulling out so you can be the next one on the ferry. We'll be over in about an hour."

Incredulous, he inquired, "Why the hell would they do that?"

"Because I cast a spell on them," she said sweetly.

"Voodoo?" he inquired.

She shook her head. "Diarrhea," she said.

At that moment the first of the big trucks in the line broke ranks and headed back up the road, away from the ferry. In a short time the others started pulling in behind the first one. In ten minutes Spurlock had a clear path down to the ferry slip.

"Good deal!" he said, and started the engine. There were four trucks and maybe fifty people and maybe half a dozen motorcycles already loaded on the flat steel boat. Smoke poured from its exhaust, showering black crud down on everything on board.

A guard in blue uniform pants and a white shirt and tie stepped out from a small shack beside the ferry slip. "Boarding pass!" he demanded.

Spurlock made his voice hard and authoritative and flashed his badge. "Official police business," he announced.

"That's no good. I need an official New York Port Authority boarding pass."

Spurlock considered all the alternatives open to him. He had no pass, and this guard was no kid who could be bluffed that easily. He would either have to convince him that they should be allowed on board or turn around and go back and get a pass. He decided to fess up and see if the guy would help him. "Look, man," he said, "I don't have one, because I never heard of one before. I haven't been to this city for years, and the bridge was in then. I've got to get across the river and into that city. So what do I do?"

The guard shrugged. "You gotta go back to Newark and make a request to the Port Authority. They'll consider your application and if they accept it they'll send you a boarding pass. Take maybe two weeks." The guard favored him with a bland expression.

Spurlock decided to weasel. "Is there, uh, any alternative method which might produce quicker passage?"

The guard looked at him for a long time. "Well, in certain extraordinary cases it's possible to issue a temporary permit which'll get you over and back one time, but that requires a lot of extra work on the part of the administrators, and they don't like to do it very often . . . y'know?"

Spurlock sighed and smiled. "Yeah, I know. That would certainly be very generous of them to help out at a time like this. You don't suppose that the administrators would feel offended if perhaps a small token of gratitude was—"

"Ten thousand bucks," said the guard.

Spurlock nodded. He couldn't afford to give the guy three days pay at this point. They were getting short, and there was no way a New York bank was going to cash a check on an Arkansas bank. He smiled conspiratorially, ready to go all the way. "Give you a pound of homegrown Arkansas weed," he said with a wink. "I guarantee you it'll blow your head off."

A crafty look came into the guard's face. "You got it there in the van?"

Spurlock didn't like the look on the man's face. It was not the expression of an honest person about to take a businesslike bribe. "Yeah, I'll get it," he replied. He reached around to grab the bag of grass, and brought the CAR-15 with it. He kept the gun low and held up the grass. "Right here," he said.

The guard grinned. His hand went to his pistol and he said, "You're under arrest. Just open the door and get out slow. Keep the grass in your hand."

Spurlock nodded. There had always been a chance the guard would bust him and keep the dope. He slowly pushed the door handle down and opened the door. Then when the door was halfway open he kicked it. Surprised, but not so surprised he would shoot, the guard jumped back, only to find himself staring down the barrel of Spurlock's shorty assault rifle. "If you shoot me with that pistol," Spurlock said, "it won't kill me right away, and when I shoot you with this thing, great chunks of your vital organs will go flying all over the landscape. So either we both live or we both die. Why don't you give me the pistol and get in the truck? I'll let you go on the other side of the river. It's the only chance you got."

The guard nodded glumly and threw the pistol up into the truck.

"Now go to the back of the van and lie down," Spurlock ordered. He watched the guard open the back door and climb into the van. He made him lie facedown in the back and told Megan to cover him with his own pistol. Then he put the van in gear and drove onto the ferry.

They sat anxiously quiet, waiting for the ferry to cross. It was some time before it started to move. Megan kept the gun pointed at the guard, who lay with his face mashed down on the side. "You can't get away with this," he mumbled into the mangled sleeping bag. "They'll check your papers again on the other side, and when they do you've had it."

Spurlock nodded, teeth clenched. The old weird trouble feeling was coming back to him, a wild feeling, the highest-stakes-gambling-in-the-world feeling. The tension crept up his back, breaking out in a wild grin. It was exhilarating almost beyond belief. He was in it now. Into this entirely other mode of being.

Finally there was a rumble and a lurch and the ferry started to sputter away from the slip. They slid slowly across the glassy water, the engine rumbling and black soot flaking down around them. Most of the other passengers had gotten out of their vehicles and were chatting, standing on the studded steel deck plates.

Check our papers on the other side, he thought. Well, that might be a lot of trouble.

He turned around in the seat and rummaged in one of the bags until he found a baseball hand grenade. This ought to do very nicely, he thought. He put it in his lap.

He wondered, though, if he might try the official police business hustle again on the other side. If he told them it had been okay in Jersey, they might buy it. But then again they . . . no way to tell unless you try.

The ferry slowly slid into the slip, and the other vehicles started. One by one they drove off onto the ferry dock on the New York side. Each stopped at the guardhouse and handed a stack of papers to a guard. The guards duly inspected each stack and stamped them with about six stamps each. The mark of an ossified administration, Spurlock thought.

Ah, well, nothing for it.

Theirs was the last vehicle in line. Time to start the van and drive to the window. The guard was already eyeing him strangely. They were the only noncommercial vehicle in the line.

He pulled the van up to the window and the guard came out. "Papers, please," he said in a bored, official voice.

"Right!" Spurlock said, grinning. He pulled the pin on the grenade and, very carefully, holding the handle down, put it in the guard's hand.

"Wha'?" the guard exclaimed.

Spurlock held his own hand around the guard's. "Don't let go," he said. "If you let go of the handle, it'll explode. Be seein' ya."

He put the van in gear and carefully drove off the end of the ferry slip, down the street, and around the corner. He stopped the van briefly and turned around. "Okay, bud. This is your get-off. I sure wish you'd just taken the grass and given me a temporary pass. It would have been a lot easier all around."

The guard got up and gently opened the door, pleased and a little surprised at his own survival. "We'll get your ass," he promised.

Spurlock took the pistol from Megan, dumped all the ammunition from the cylinder to the floor, and threw it out to the guard, gave a cheery little wave, and drove around the corner, turning the wrong way down a one-way street and pulling up right in front of a police car.

Holy shit! Spurlock thought. He braked the van and jumped out into the street, as Megan cried, "What the—"

"My goodness, this is luck," Spurlock exclaimed to the policeman, who leered evilly up at him from the seat of the police car.

"Sorry about the wrong-way turn," he blathered on, leaning down into the driver's window, "but I sure am glad to see you." He flipped his wallet out of his pocket and flashed his badge. "Ah'm Sheriff Frank Spurlock of Purgatory County, Arkansas," he added, slipping quickly into his country boy routine. It's something he'd learned from dealing with city people before. They can't relate to you as a human being anyway, so the best you can do is give them the cartoon they expect, and let them cope with that. No point in coming across with any surprises.

"Ah'm involved in a custody fight with mah ex-wife, and I need some he'p locatin' her and the chilern. Ah was a-wonderin' if y'all could call on yer po-lice radio and get aholt of the address for me?"

The cop gave a gimlet-eyed stare of astonishment and turned to his partner. "Is he fa real?" he asked.

At this moment the ferry guard came screaming around the corner with his gun drawn, waving in the air. Without his cap, in blue pants and white shirt, he didn't look at all official. He merely looked like some nut waving a gun and running down the street.

"Get that yimp!" the cop in the shotgun seat screamed. Both were out of the car and into the street in a split second. The one on the driver's side almost knocked Spurlock down as the door opened. Pedestrians dived for cover all up and down the street. The cop driving went into a crouch with a MAC-10 .45-caliber submachine gun and squeezed off three quick four-round bursts, causing pavement and bricks from the buildings to chip off all around the ferry guard.

The other guard squeezed off a round from an M-79 grenade launcher, which went *ponk* as the grenade exited from the mouth of the little short fat shotgun-looking weapon.

Before it landed, however, the ferry guard deduced that the situation was not in his favor and darted off down a side street, presumably to forget the whole business and try to get back to his ferry. The cops took off after him.

From her seat in the van Megan waved to Spurlock to get into the car. "C'mon," she said. "Let's get out of here!"

Spurlock strolled leisurely over to her side of the van and said, "Naw, the worst they can do is give us a ticket for turning the wrong way down a one-way street. It was kind of dangerous while that guard was coming this way. But now that he's going away, it's cool. I'm going to try and get these guys to run an address check on Linda, and we can go over there and see how the kids are. It'll be the quickest way if we can bring it off."

"And what if they're looking for the mad ferry-crosser?"

At that exact moment the police radio, which had been sputtering and squawking along, exploded with, "All cars, all cars! Be alert for a Victor Whiskey microbus, about an '84 or '85, with Arkansas plates, wanted on a 412, 716, and 204. Acknowledge."

" 'Scuse me a minute," Spurlock said, and stepped back over to the police car, glancing at the radio for a call sign as he did so. It was typewritten and taped to the face of the radio with Scotch tape. "Four-six, ten-four, out!" he muttered into the radio, and strolled back to the van. "I think we'll be all right now," he said. "I'll rip off a New York plate from a parked car before another cop spots us."

She looked at him as though he were mad, but said nothing. The two cops came back around the corner, winded and empty-handed. Spurlock gave them an admiring glance. "You guys get that kind of stuff very often?" he asked.

The cop with the M-79 gave him a tough look and stood in a position of exaggerated nonchalance. He two-fingered a cigarette out of his shirt pocket and lit it with a gold lighter. "Lotta nuts runnin' aran in d'streets dese days," he said. "Fuckin' city drives people nuts, man. Dey go crazy and run amok and we gotta hunt 'em down. Ya can't blame d'poor shmucks." He shrugged. "Whadaya gonna do?"

"Whew!" Spurlock said. "My hat's off to you guys. Po-lice work must be a lot rougher here than it is out in Arkansas." He pushed his hat to the back of his head, feeling a slight breeze stir through the concrete canyons.

"T'ings kinda quiet out dere in Okkinsawr?" the cop who was driving asked.

Spurlock gave them a comradely grin. "Aw, we have our days," he said. "But nothin' like this."

"Y'get used to it," the cop driving said smugly.

"I dunno, man," Spurlock said. "That's a lot to have to get used to, running gun battles in the street every day." He shook his head again. "Anyway, I'd sure appreciate it if you guys would help me locate this subject." He took out his notebook and wrote down the name, Linda James Spurlock. Last known address 474 E. 72d.

The cop who was driving took it from him. "Yeah! We'll call it in and if there's any record we'll have it back for you in maybe five minutes." He went to the car and reached for the radio, calling in the name and address.

Spurlock sweated blood while waiting for the information to come back. He was thinking of all the ways he could get caught. If the cop said he was trying to help a sheriff from Arkansas in a VW microbus, he and Megan were done for.

A few minutes later, though, the cop came back and handed him another sheet of paper with the same name and another address on it. "Fuckin' broad's got a record as long as your arm," he said. "What you want her for?"

"She usta be my wife," Spurlock said softly.

The cop looked at him, startled, and said, "Oh!"

"What's the record for?" Spurlock asked, trying to keep the emotion out of his voice, trying to keep professional.

The cop looked at him for a long time, not saying anything. Then he shrugged. "Narcotics and prostitution," he replied.

"I see," Spurlock said as his insides went numb. When the New York City cops said narcotics, they didn't mean grass. They meant junk, and they meant a lot of junk.

He put the emotional aspects of that on ice for a while. "You guys gonna give me a ticket for that one-way street or what?" he asked.

The cop shook his head no.

"Thanks," Spurlock said. "Be seein' you."

The cop snickered. "Ya watch dem one-way streets," he said.

Spurlock waved and got in the van.

"Did you get it?" Megan asked.

"Yep." He put the van in gear, backed it up, and turned around.

Driving to Linda's address was something Spurlock would never forget. New York looked halfway like pictures he had seen of Berlin after World War II. The streets had a few brightly but shoddily dressed people, walking like zombies. All had a hideous yellow pallor and spindly, rickety bodies. The old bustle that had characterized New York was gone. This was like the night of the walking dead. There were very few cars in the street, all official, but there were piles of garbage and trash everywhere. The remains of gutted and burned-out buildings were on every street. He didn't know why they were like that—from riots, or some sort of gang wars, or what. News of them had not reached Arkansas. The government-controlled media only put good news on the air. No riots, no bombings.

Spurlock eased the little van through the silent streets, the address in his left hand, right hand on the wheel. Beside him Megan sat quietly, looking out at New York City. Impressions of New York conflicted in his mind with memories of Linda and the kids. So many emotions were waking up in him, emotions that had been shoved down and down toward the bottom of his consciousness.

One thing for sure, he wasn't having any trouble moving because of the traffic. So far they had passed a few wraiths who seemed to live in this place, and very few cars, one a police car and the other an old sedan, stamped "U.S. Government, Central Motor Pool, For Official Use Only."

There were four occupants in the For Official Use Only car: two couples, the men middle-aged, the women young. They wore the official fashionable uniform, Russian peasant garb, and sleepy grins. The music of Charlie Parker's saxophone came pouring out of the official U.S. Government tape deck. Spurlock knew the type well enough. They were junkies with a good racket, just riding their government shuck as far as it would go.

He wondered where the rest of the people were. The population of New York had shrunk to one-third what it had been, down to about four million people, but even at four million he should have seen more than seven of them.

Four hundred block on 72nd Street. He remembered that as the swinging Upper East Side, but there was no telling what it was like now. He couldn't even remember which way to turn off Lexington Avenue.

With false starts and wrong turns he was getting closer and closer to his goal. Along the way he passed large buildings where business seemed to be going on. These buildings had concrete or sandbag bunkers outside of them, and strings of concertina wire on top of the bunkers.

They appeared to be patrolled by private guards, none in the uniform of the NYPD, but in very snappy, Russian-looking uniforms, Sam Browne belts, Uzi submachine guns, and a lot of M-79s. The private citizens seemed to walk very carefully around these buildings. Then suddenly, as though they had turned a corner into another world, they were in a gutted and pitted neighborhood, blacks and whites warily stepping around each other. It seemed as though the black people were on one side of the street and the white people on the other, and they looked at each other suspiciously as they passed. The storefronts here were gutted, too, but there seemed to be commerce going on inside them, business, not as usual, but business.

He started to turn a final corner. A kid in jeans, sneakers, and a tweed cap ran out and put up his hand to stop them. "You ain't goin' down there," he stated flatly. He held an M-1 carbine in his right hand.

Spurlock leaned out the window, speaking cautiously but with some command in his voice, to the armed, unknown quantity. He didn't want to get shot by a shaky kid. "I was," he said. "Why, what's the matter?"

"There's a war goin' on down there," the kid said. "That's what's the matter. It's the Kings of Spades against the Izods." Spurlock noticed that the kid's green shirt had a little alligator on it.

Spurlock looked at the kid for a long time and then asked, "What are those?"

"Gangs," the kid said with exasperated impatience.

Spurlock put the car in gear. "I'm not going to be stopped by a bunch of kids with chains and zip guns," he said.

The boy looked at him pityingly. "It ain't chains and zip guns no more, mister. When I said war I wasn't kiddin'. Listen!"

Spurlock listened. Sure enough, just down the street he heard the *pop-pop* of small-arms fire.

"Look," Spurlock told the kid, "we've got to get down that street. We came a long way to see some people down there. Is there any way we can arrange a safe conduct or something?"

The kid shook his head. "Mister, the only safe conduct down that street is an automatic weapon. None of those jokers has one, and they're scared shitless of them."

Spurlock nodded. "Okay, I got that. Now, is there any way I can keep this van secure while I go down there?"

The kid nodded. "Yeah, I can put a couple of people on it if the price is right. You do me right and nobody'll mess with it."

Spurlock pursed his lips and looked at the kid speculatively. "Tell you what," he said. "I'll give you three ounces of cleaned weed now, and another three ounces when we get back."

The kid's eyes flew wide. "You got all that?" Then they narrowed fast, and he grinned. "Sure, I'll be glad to watch it for you."

He was a thin, mean-looking kid. And the ammo belt and ancient carbine gave him confidence; also avarice.

Spurlock grinned back at the kid. "And I keep your I.D. card," he told him.

The kid looked at him evilly. "No deal!" he said.

"Look, kid, if you lose your I.D. card in this city, you're done. But if I lose this van in this city, I'm done, too. We both know if I don't have some kind of hold over you this van will be stripped clean, if it's here at all, when we get back. But I *have* to give you your card back. It's no good to me, except as a way to hunt you down and kill you if you steal my van."

The kid shrugged and his shoulders sagged. "Okay, mister, you win." He reached into his pocket and pulled out his wallet and the card.

Too easy. Spurlock reached into his cab for a thumb-print I.D. kit and placed the kid's card in it. He held it out to the kid. "Thumbprint!" he said.

The kid grinned again. "You're really a suspicious bastard, aren't you?"

The thumbprint checked out, but there was one thing more to check. Spurlock got in the van and went back to where there was a small, portable black light plugged in. He drew the curtains and turned on the black light. Sure enough, the lamination on the card had been tampered with. This I.D. had been stolen and altered. The marks of the forcing showed all over the card under the black light.

He got back out of the van to find the kid covering Megan with his carbine. "Okay, mister," he said with a little snarl in his voice that only barely covered his fear. "I got my gun on your old lady, and I want the dope and the automatic weapons, and anything else valuable you got in there. After that you can go. I got no use for this bus."

Spurlock's hands were in the air, and he didn't want to do anything to shake up the already excited boy.

"You just stand right there," the kid said. "I'm going to get a couple people to go through your truck."

"Hey!" he yelled, followed by a loud whistle that he had to try three times, because his mouth was so dry. His eyes flicked down the street for an instant, which was all Spurlock needed. His foot shot out and the kid's carbine went arcing through the air, away from the action.

Spurlock was on the kid in the following instant, rage flaring in him. He had traveled all this way to see his children, and he had not done it to be stopped by no goddamned New York City punk who was out to rip him off. The kid was down and Spurlock was on top of him, had the kid's head in his hands, repeatedly banging his head against the sidewalk, all the repressed hatred for these little shorthair motherfuckers, all the filth and ugliness of this vile and detestable city, all the crap, all the years of waiting and wondering how his kids were, only to be stopped now by this slimy little jerk-off from an Irish Spring soap commercial.

Whap! Something knocked him up beside the head. *Whap!* He looked up and it was Megan, beating him with her fists. "Baby, stop! Baby, stop! Baby, stop!" she called repeatedly. He looked down at the kid, who looked back in sheer terror. He was still conscious, he wasn't hurt badly, but he was hurt, and he was plenty shook up.

Fortunately he had whistled during another outbreak of shooting and no one had come to his aid. Megan had his carbine. He shook himself and looked up. "Jeez!" he said.

Spurlock got off him and extended a hand to pull him up. "Sorry, kid, I sort of lost control there. You oughta be more careful next time you go drawing down on somebody's lady."

"Whew!" the kid said again. He stood, dazed, reached up and touched the back of his head. His hand came away bloody. "Jeez!" he said again. "You din' have no reason to try to beat me to death. I was gonna let you go."

Spurlock was a little shook himself. He hadn't lost control like that in a long time. "I doubt it," he said to the kid's last statement. "I think you'd have killed us and found some way to sell the van." He stopped and thought a minute.

"Okay, kid. I think we're going to use a variation of your plan. I want you to get a couple of your punks to come and watch the van, only instead of using your I.D. card as our insurance, we're going to use you. You're coming with us."

Spurlock got back in the van and put on his ammo vest, pouches loaded with armor-piercing ammo. He also festooned it with concussion grenades. He climbed back out again. "Megan, you keep the kid's carbine." He pointed to the boy. "Okay, kid, get some of your goons to come here and watch my truck."

The kid yelled and whistled again, and a minute later two other kids in more or less the same costume showed up. One had pleated khakis and the other had jeans on, but both wore shirts with little alligators on them, although at least one was a fake; the alligator wasn't made right and it had obviously been sewn on later. Both wore billed caps. One carried an M-1 rifle and the other an old Russian SKS carbine. "Whadaya want?" the kid with the M-1 demanded.

"Don't let anybody mess with this guy's van," the boy said. "He's holding me prisoner, and if anybody messes with it, he's going to kill me."

They looked at Spurlock curiously. He nodded. "That's right," he said.

He gave the paper with Linda's address on it to the kid. "You know where this is?" he asked.

Ratface's eyes widened. "Yeah, I know who lives at that address. Whadaya lookin' for Mako for?"

Spurlock shook his head. "I don't know any Mako. I'm looking for a woman named Linda Spurlock. She's got two teenage kids."

Ratface stood there, dark and snarling. "Yeah, Leslie and Mark. That's Mako. I can take ya to him."

Ratface led them off down the blasted street. They had gone less than half a block when, simultaneously, a shot was fired, the round snapped by Spurlock's right ear, and the stone in the wall by his head exploded into chips. Quickly, Ratface shoved them down the steps leading to a garden-level apartment. "Sniper," he said.

"I noticed," Spurlock replied.

"What now?" Megan asked. "We can't stay behind these stairs forever."

"No problem," Ratface replied. He rattled an iron gate protecting the door to the garden level. "Izods," he barked. "Open up!"

"Whadaya want?" a voice whined.

"Don't gimme no shit. Open up or we'll be back."

The door opened a crack and a fearful eye peered out. The eye widened when it saw them, specifically when it saw Spurlock's CAR-15. It seemed to be a woman, but that was all Spurlock could tell. "Please, please," said a quaking hoarse female voice. It never did say please what.

"Open it now," Ratface barked. "We're taking fire out here."

The door opened and the woman stepped out and unlocked the gate. Her hands trembled. The remains of her old-style punk hairdo, half grown out, looked even more awful than the original had been intended to.

"Don't hurt me," she cringed.

"Fageddabadit!" Ratface commanded as he brushed past. They barged through the darkened cave of the apartment, which in the gloom seemed to be furnished with charred lumps. They swept through as she scurried ahead to undo the locks and bars that led to the back.

Out the back door was a small overgrown garden. Ratface, quickly, with practiced ease, climbed a garbage can and scurried up the iron ladder that dangled from the fire escape. Spurlock pushed Megan up after him and lumbered awkwardly in their wake, needing at least three hands to do it while carrying the slingless carbine.

Once they made the roof it was a breeze. There was considerable climbing up and down as they passed to buildings of different heights, but there were homemade ladders galore up there. Apparently the roofs were used for transportation as often as the street. Spurlock's boot heels scraped on tar and gravel. He looked into the dingy sun hanging half over the skyline to the west and was partially blinded as they went up over a roof. "Boom-boom, comrade," he heard a callow voice say, and he stiffened slightly.

"Hey!" he heard Ratface respond.

Spurlock's eyes adjusted to the light, and he saw that there were four kids, one at each corner of the roof, each in the shirt and cap that seemed to be the insignia of the Izods, each with some sort of weapon, all semi-auto. One of them had a .22 rifle.

CAR-15 or no CAR-15, they were surrounded by armed kids now. Spurlock figured he was going to have to do some fancy talking, because he couldn't shoot them all.

"What's goin' on down there?" Ratface asked.

Breathlessly one of the four turned to him and said,

"We got one of their patrols holed up in the building across the street. The way it is now nobody goes out our front door, but they can't get out of the building either. They're boxed in."

Ratface nodded thoughtfully. "You know how many?"

"Huh-uh."

Ratface turned and without another word headed for the edge of the roof, where he said, "Follow me," and went down the fire escape before anyone had a chance to reply.

Spurlock immediately went after him and the ancient iron ladder creaked and shook with every step as caked black crud flaked off on the insides of his fingers.

The kid got down to the first landing, then disappeared inside a window.

Spurlock clambered down after him and followed inside. There were four or five other teenage kids sitting around on mattresses, rifles and carbines leaned up in the corner. A radio the size of a suitcase played heavy-metal rock 'n' roll next to one of the mattresses.

As they entered the room through the window, the kids inside looked up.

Everybody looked at them and then everybody looked at Ratface, who seized the opportunity to hold center stage for a second. " 'Ey, Mako," he called out, "this guy heah's lookin' fa you."

At a desk that dominated the room a short kid with blond stubble on his head looked up. His face could only be described as handsome, maybe too pretty for masculine tastes, dominated by clear burning eyes. He had incredible shoulders for a kid his size. He glanced up and focused on Spurlock. He blinked as his expression went from surprise through comprehension, evaluation to recognition. "Hi, Pop," he said, "long time no see. Welcome to Beirut-on-the-Hudson."

Spurlock just stood looking at him, not knowing what to do or say. Finally he said, "Hello, kid. I've been worried about you."

"Took a while to build up, did it?" sneered Mark "Mako" Spurlock. Spurlock felt a stab of hurt such as he had not felt for years, such as he had not known he could still feel. He had not been the leaver, he had been the leavee, but still he felt as guilty about his kids as though he had abandoned them.

"Not fair," Megan interjected. "Not fair at all. He had to leave a county under siege in charge of a dimwit, and run through an army of assassins to get here. That run cost three people their lives."

Mark smiled. "And who might you be, my lady?"

"Megan Carney," she replied, and held out her hand.

He took it. "And you were his companion on this journey? Why you and not, say, Gabby Hayes?"

"The lady has hidden resources," Spurlock interjected.

Mark eyed her closely. My God, thought Spurlock, is he bright. The kid was both streetwise and book smart. He's a leader and he's a fighter. Spurlock couldn't wait to get him back to Purgatory.

"I bet she does," Mark replied. He stood up and walked around from behind the desk. No alligator shirt for this kid. He wore jeans, sneaks, a black T-shirt, and a cut-off jeans jacket with an alligator sewn over the left breast pocket. He walked with a swagger that covered the slightest touch of a limp. He was only sixteen, but somewhere in there he'd been hit.

He shook his head. "My old man!" he said. "Now of all times. Unfuckinbelievable!"

A warmth that was one of the most powerful emotions Spurlock had ever felt filled him. He grabbed and held the boy until it would have been unseemly to do so longer. Then he stepped back and held the kid at arm's length by the shoulders. "Why now?" he said. "What's so strange about now?"

"What's so strange," said another young man, stocky, with curly brown hair, moving with a swagger that was almost a carbon copy of Mark's, "is that da Izods have a chance to break into da big time." He held out his hand for a plain old-fashioned handshake. "I'm Marlon Donadio, d'war counselor fa d'Izods." He wore a genuine Izod shirt and the tweed cap that seemed to be a part of the Izod look, and jeans.

Spurlock returned the handshake.

Mark smiled. "That's right. The Russians stayed pretty well out of New York City until two weeks ago. I guess they didn't want to aggravate the world's largest established floating guerrilla war, but now they're here."

He leaned back on his desk and crossed his legs at the ankles. "There's always been anti-Soviet propaganda comin' out of Brighton Beach, in Brooklyn. They never liked that, but lately there's been wholesale desertions from the Russian Army. Russian GIs start gettin' out among the people here, havin' a good time. Bad as times are here, they're better than they are in Russia, and a hell of a lot better than in the Russian Army."

Spurlock crossed his arms and put his weight on one hip. "How does that get you guys into the big time?"

Marlon swaggered to the wall where a subway map of New York City was taped. "The Russkis decided that Brighton Beach had to go. The idea was that they'd just blow it to hell and then send in some troops to kill what was left. They decided to do it with artillery so's they could keep their gunners locked up all the time. No chance for 'em to desert.

"But during the day they shift away from one city block, put in an infantry company, and clean out that block of anybody left alive there. They put in a Spetznaz company, specially trained party members who won't desert. Then after they clear that block they occupy it with U.S. Army guys and the next day they go on to another block."

Spurlock looked at the map for a long time. The Brighton Beach area would be easy to cut off if you had troops you could trust. Just put a patrolled barricade along Neptune Avenue and that would be it. "Who's bottling them up there?" he asked.

"New York cops with KGB supervisors," said Mark.

Spurlock scratched his head and looked at the map. Then put his hands on his hips. "Am I missing something here? Somehow I still don't see this as a golden opportunity for you guys." What he could see was that any hopes he had for a reunion with his son and daughter had to go on hold until this matter was resolved. So best he and Megan help resolve it.

Mark sat up on the desk and crossed a leg over his knee. "It's real simple. Those Russian guys in Brooklyn, the deserters, and the Russians who lived there before, mostly Jews, they're organized into a resistance. They belong to a guerrilla outfit called the Jewish Defense League. They got some weapons, enough that they can take out that Spetznaz company with a little help.

"Aside from them the only armed force that the Russians don't control is the gangs. That's us, and we can deal with the JDL.

"There's one key part of that artillery battalion that if we can knock it out they can stage an uprising. It's called the Fire Direction Center. If that's gone, they're just firing blind. They can't aim or nothin'."

Spurlock grinned. "Right! One trailer full of guys with computers. Knock that out and it's all over."

"Check," said Marlon. "But we gotta do it before some udda gang gets there first, y'know. We gotta move fast."

"So what do you guys get out of it?" Spurlock asked.

"Weapons, man," said Marlon. "We get AK-74 assault rifles and rocket-propelled grenades, y'know, bazookas, and hand grenades. What we get is we become da most powerful gang in Manhattan, and instead of sixteen lousy blocks we run the entire Upper East Side.''

Spurlock thought for a moment. He didn't like the idea of all that power falling into the hands of these vicious little criminals. They were dangerous enough already. ''So what happens if you don't do it?''

Marlon shrugged. ''If a Brooklyn gang does it, nuttin'. If some udda East Side gang does it, they take us over. If it's the Kings of Spades, we all die. Just that simple.''

Spurlock nodded. It looked like somebody was bound to do it, and it probably would be better for his kids if it was the Izods.

Marlon looked at Mark questioningly. Mark nodded and Marlon started laying out their plans. He rooted around until he found a folded piece of butcher paper that had a diagram of the Russian artillery battalion's camp. It was crude, done freehand in felt-tip pen, and he had to tape it to the wall three times because the stickum on the postwar tape didn't work very well.

''This is da Fire Direction Centa,'' he said, pointing out a little square in the middle of a heavily guarded, heavily fortified compound that included eighteen 130-millimeter howitzers, enormous cannon systematically pounding the Brighton Beach area into rubble, and very likely slowly pulverizing the people in it. But it very quickly became obvious to Spurlock that Marlon's plan was too elaborate and that he didn't have the stuff to bring it off with.

''We only got forty guys with guns,'' Marlon said. ''So we gotta get inside wit'out bein' spotted. There's a break in d'wire heah ova this shellhole. If we can knock out this searchlight.'' He pointed at a circle on his not-drawn-to-scale chart. Spurlock let him ramble on, spotting a half-dozen holes in his plan that would doom the mission and the boys running it. He was trying to think of some tactful way to point them out when Megan cut in.

"But it looks like you boys will get killed doing that. Those Russians have a lot of very powerful guns in there."

Mako gave her a cool glance, but Marlon's look and wave of his hand embodied both a kind of withering contempt for female weakness and the stubborn bravado of the kamikaze. "We hate them Soviet mothafuckas bad enough to risk it. You seen what they done ta this city. It usta be a jumpin' place. Now it's a fuckin' graveya'd. We may go down, but we'll take a bunch of dem muthafuckas with us."

Megan smiled ever so sweetly. "It would be a shame to die so young if you don't have to. Why don't you let Frank and me knock out the FDC and you can concentrate on something else?"

Marlon's glance was contemptuous and Mark's . . . Mako's was curious and a little amazed, but they both asked the same question almost simultaneously. "How you gonna do that?"

Spurlock was wondering the very same thing.

"I'll need some things," she said. "I assume they let food contractors and such into the camp on some kind of pass or bumper sticker or something like that."

"That's right," Marlon said, "but they always search da trucks real careful. We can't get no guys in that way."

She shook her head. "We don't need that. All I need is a vehicle with the right credentials and a kitchen. I'm not going to kill them, but if you get me those things, you won't have to worry about the artillery for more than eight hours. Can you do what you need to do in that amount of time?"

Marlon grinned. "Easy," he said.

Mark spun back around on his desk and sat cross-legged. "Marlon, my man. If we don't have to attack the artillery camp, we can attack something else. We got to talk."

He and Marlon left the room for a while. The other gang

members eyed them curiously, but kept their distance. Their lives had made them wary of surprises, and Spurlock and Megan had been an unimaginable surprise. They were very young but they had been around the block more than a couple of times. There was a set to their faces and their eyes that Spurlock found disconcerting. They looked, to a man, ready to get real fatal real fast.

"How the hell are you going to knock out an artillery FDC for eight hours? Can you hex thirty people at one time?"

She smiled slyly. "I'm not going to hex them. I'm going to feed them. They're going to like my cooking so much that they'll be ecstatic . . . for about eight hours. Megan's Pizzeria."

"Mushroom pizzas!" Spurlock exclaimed. "God knows what they'll do when they eat those."

Megan smiled. "No telling. But what they won't do is fire their guns accurately."

Mako and Marlon chose that moment to reenter, grim smiles spread across their faces. "You knock out the FDC and we'll hit that Spetznaz company from the rear. They won't be expecting that, and by the time they know we're there, we'll already have enough AKs to keep workin'," Mark said.

Spurlock shook his head. "You guys might be pretty tough, but the Spetznaz are really good. You've never fought anything like them before."

"Fuck that," said Marlon. "They ain't never fought nuttin' like us before neither. Fuckin' Russians know how to level a city, but they don't know how to clear one. You watch."

"But first we gotta get rid of those Spades across the street," Mark said. "What's the story on them?"

Marlon whirled and led them to another map on the wall. It was crudely drawn and densely notated, and seemed to show about a square mile of Manhattan Island. All the buildings, streets, and alleys were meticulously drawn in, each building had the number of stories written on it, showed all entrances and exits. There were a lot of markings that Spurlock couldn't figure out, but he could see that it was a thorough job, much better than what they had on the Russians.

Marlon took a pencil from his pocket and tapped the map. "Okay," he started. "At approximately three-fifteen this afternoon six niggers from the Kings of Spades came down the street and occupied the building across the street."

"How'd they come in?" Mark demanded.

"They done it slick," Marlon went on. "They split da street, t'ree to a side, firing at anything upstairs on da udda side of da street that might take them out. They leapfrogged down and took that building. We think they thought they was movin' in heah. They ain't doing themselves no good ova there."

Mark nodded. "They aren't doing us any good either. Okay, I want it made clear to those people that they can't play that way in Izod territory. What happened to the civilians in that building?"

"As near as we can tell they all split."

Mark nodded again, and pulled on his lower lip some more. "Good," he said. "I don't want to have to worry about a bunch of civilians. Okay, put two molooka teams on the windows. I want those dudes burned out right now. We got to get out of here."

Marlon nodded. "Check, Chief. It's on the way." Marlon started to leave.

"Lemme know when it's ready," Mark ordered. "I wanna show it off to the old man." Spurlock smiled at the tone of his kid's voice. It was half proud and half sarcastic.

"Y'gonna like the way we burn them niggers out," Marlon said, grinning. Spurlock winced at the sound of that word in his ears. "A 'nigger' saved my life the day before yesterday," he said gratingly. He waited to see what kind of effect that announcement would have.

It was very strange. They both blinked and looked puzzled, as though he had reported seeing a flying giraffe. Since what he said was, to them, clearly impossible, and since they could see no reason for him to have said it, they just blanked it out. Spurlock realized then that he had stumbled into a first-rate little war, right here in New York City, and that, whatever the cause of its beginnings, it was now split on racial grounds.

Not only that, but it had been going on long enough to have reached a level of hatred at which these young men could not regard their opponents as human. No Geneva Convention, none of that stuff. This would be the whole baby-murdering, prisoner-torturing, third-world horror show. All he could think to say was, "What's a molooka?"

Mark grinned. "Marlon made it up. It's a bazooka for Molotov cocktails. Accurate as hell at fairly close range."

Marlon nodded seriously. "I had the basic idea, but Mako figured out the trigger mechanism and dreamed up the best way to use it. Gimme fifteen minutes to set up. You'll see."

Spurlock didn't know what to think. What Mark was involved in made him sick.

On the other hand, he had to admit that the kid had class. He didn't know for sure, but he thought the map had been Mark's idea, and he was quite impressed with the way he had tried to give Marlon all the credit for inventing the molooka. The kid had exhibited a number of first-rate leadership characteristics.

As Marlon and some of the others disappeared, Mark sighed and collapsed against the ancient wooden desk. All the bravado drained out of him when he no longer had to keep up a front. He looked at his father and Megan. "I useta dream about you," he said to Spurlock. "Mom said you were a sheriff out west, and I looked at your old pictures a lot, tried to be like the sheriffs in the movies. You know Marlon's a year older than me. There's some

Izods two years older than me." His chest seemed to fill. "I dunno why, but I know things they don't. Most guys don't know how to think for themselves, but I know how to think for a whole mob." He sighed. "But sometimes I don't think I can think for myself either, just for other people."

He stopped and looked at Spurlock with a strange combination of emotions, but love was prominent among them. The kid loved him and he loved the kid. It didn't have to be said. They both knew it. Spurlock felt that no moment would top this one for as long as he lived. He had done nothing to deserve it, but it seemed to be some sort of natural law that children loved their parents and vice versa.

Marlon swaggered back into the room and came up to them. "All set, man," he said.

Mark nodded. "Right!" he said. "Let's go!"

Marlon led Spurlock and Mark out into the hall and down two flights of rotting stairs to the third floor. They went into another apartment. It was empty. Two boys in the Russian costumes knelt in front of the window. Beside them on the floor was an eight-foot-long cardboard tube, with what appeared to be a handle on it, three feet from one end.

"How's it goin'?" Mark demanded of one of them.

The kids looked up. The face of one of them was covered with several cuts, apparently where rifle fire had knocked the windows out. "Not so hot, Mako," one said. "Every time we get close to the window they put about three bullets through it."

Mark looked to Marlon for an explanation.

"There's another molooka team in the bedroom," Marlon said, indicating a door to Spurlock's right, "and I got four gunners comin' down to get 'em away from them windows while the molooka's set up."

Mark nodded. "How you gonna take 'em out?"

Marlon put his hands on his hips. "Hold 'em down with rifles and burn 'em out with molookas."

Mark was pulling on his lower lip again. "Two things," he said. "First, call the fire department. I don't wanna burn down a whole block."

Marlon nodded, pointing at one of the kids lounging against the wall. "Do it!" he said.

The boy disappeared.

Mark nodded his head again. "Start a fire on the stair-well above them first," he said. "I want 'em coming out in the street, not going up on the roof."

Marlon's eyes brightened as he realized that Mark had caught the one essential element of the plan that he had missed. Spurlock smiled at Marlon's reaction. He couldn't tell if Marlon was pleased or jealous, but it was obvious he knew who was boss.

There was a knock at the door. "Yeah," Marlon demanded.

"Fire team, Marlon," was the reply.

Marlon called them in and explained what windows the Spades were in, and that they were to keep them away from the windows while the molooka teams set up.

"Check," the fire team leader said. He sent two of them into the bedroom and waited for word that they were in place.

"Yeah!" came the reply from both the bedroom and the kids in the living room.

It seemed so odd to Spurlock. They had the bodies of children and faces more ravaged than all but the worst of Frazier's guerrillas. These kids were fighting without hope or cause, just fighting for survival from day to day.

"Do it!" Mark commanded. His voice was controlled, and it carried well.

In the living room the two gunners swung into the window, popped off three rounds apiece, quickly, to star-tle the Spades, then settled down to firing well-aimed shots.

"Molookas!" Mark commanded.

Two boys with the cardboard tube moved into the center of the window, under the covering fire of the rifles. One boy reached into a cardboard box and withdrew a prepacked Molotov cocktail, a wine bottle with a cloth wick stuck in the tip. He pulled a leather ring attached to two long strips of surgical tubing hooked to the inside of the cardboard cylinder. Spurlock grinned. Now he understood. The molooka was a slingshot for Molotov cocktails. It was not a half-bad idea, if you were into that system of thought. "You use soap flakes in your gas?" he inquired of his son.

Mark favored him with a smirk. "We aren't amateurs," he replied.

The kid hooked his bottle into the leather ring and angled the tube to let it slide as far back as it would go. The other kid reached his arm inside the tube and dragged it back until the neck of the bottle stuck out the back. The first kid threw the tube up on his shoulder and sighted through the crude sight affixed to the side of the tube.

The two riflemen continued firing all the while. It was not quite like anything Spurlock had ever seen before, but he had to admit that they seemed very professional.

"The stairwell first," Mark commanded.

"Check, Mako. Ready!"

The second kid stuck a lighter into the wick and released the bottle. It scraped quickly down the tube and arced across the street.

"We bring this Brooklyn deal off and the next time we'll have rocket-propelled grenades," Mako said.

The first cocktail hit the bricks to the left and down from the window about four feet. The gasoline, turned into napalm by the addition of soap flakes, burst into orange and black flame that stuck to the side of the building, burning harmlessly. The kid who held the tube bent to grab another one as soon as the first one hit, but he had not seen where it hit.

"Right, four feet. Up, four feet," the kid intoned as he reached for the neck of the next bottle.

"Check!" said the gunner as he adjusted his tube, then, quite quickly, "Ready!"

Sssssssss-WHOOOOOM!!!

Dead center, inside the window. The stairwell burst into flames, the trash and garbage piled in the hallways catching quickly.

The molooka team didn't pause to check the results of their work. The team in the bedroom had already put two cocktails into the right-hand window of the two from which fire was coming, and this team quickly put two more into the left-hand window. Both rooms were in flames, black smoke pouring out.

"Okay!" Mark yelled. "They gotta leave those rooms and they got no place to go but the hallway downstairs." Then he looked pained. "Oh, shit! They'll try the back door first."

Marlon grinned. "They won't try it twice," he said. "I got a good fire team down there." He was delighted. This time he was one ahead on Mark.

"Good!" Mark said, pacing the floor. He picked up a wooden ruler from the table and beat his thigh with it, like a general with a swagger stick. "Give 'em a minute or so to find that out, then put a couple of mollies into the hallway. Either way they come out, we pick 'em off. Now get this," he said, raising his voice so everybody could hear him. "I want them all dead but the last one. I want that one terrified Spade to go back there and tell those black motherfuckers they don't wanna come down here ever again."

Spurlock was of two minds about all that was going on. He hated it on one level, but as a former soldier and as a cop, he had to admire his kid's leadership abilities and his sure tactical sense.

"Okay," Mark said. "Put some fire in that downstairs hallway."

Both molooka teams quickly put two mollies apiece

through the window in the front door of the building across the street. Flames burst out. There was some more firing, and shortly thereafter two blacks, their Technicolor dashikis on fire, burst out into the street. They were screaming something in what Spurlock took to be Swahili, or Bantu, or something like that, screaming and firing wildly with one hand while they whirled and beat out the flames with their free hand. It was about as unenviable a position as Spurlock had ever seen anyone in. Those two blacks and the next three were mowed down like wheat, black and red blossoms opening up all over their colorful clothing.

The last one emerged blinking. He was shooting, too, apparently knowing better than to seek mercy from the Izods.

"Let him go! Let him go! Let him go!" Mark screamed. "I want him to tell the bastards all about it!"

The riflemen popped off two rounds before they could slow their momentum, but only one of them hit him, and that was in the fat part of the upper arm. He wasn't burning badly either. It looked as though he would make it home. He ran screaming and shooting down the street, disappearing around the corner.

Mark whirled and hugged his father. "Howdaya like that?" he crowed.

Spurlock hugged him back. Not because he was happy with what Mark had done, but because he hadn't had the chance in a long time. "I'm sorry you found that necessary," he said, "but you did it very well. Why were those guys stupid enough to come down here anyway?"

Mark looked at him, surprised. He reached out and patted the CAR-15, and said. "I told you. People in this town would sell their soul for an automatic weapon."

The next two hours passed quickly. Mako sent word for all the Izods, except for twenty to guard the perimeter of their territory, to assemble in the ground floor of the building they were in. The walls of several rooms down there had been knocked out to make enough room for the entire gang to assemble.

"The first thing I need," Mako said to Marlon, as Spurlock and Megan followed them down the stairs, "is a list of weapons, and who has them."

For the time being this was Mako's show, with Spurlock and Megan just tagging along as straphangers. Spurlock was surprised to see how quickly he fell into a dual way of thinking about the kid. When he was Spurlock's son, he was Mark. When he was president of the Izods, he was Mako.

First Mako got out a spiral notebook with a list of the subgroups of the Izods. From his conversations with Marlon and others, Spurlock deduced that there were about a hundred Izods and there were five of these groups. For this joint operation with the JDL he was leaving the girls and all but a couple of the juniors at home, which left him with these five groups of from five to twenty guys each. Some had evolved out of neighborhood basketball teams and some were mini-gangs with strong leadership of their own.

Some were very good and some were collections of losers led by weasels. Simultaneously most had their own weapons that they had bought, stolen, made, or killed somebody for. Mako had a lot of power, but he didn't have the power to give anybody's weapon to somebody else.

He and Marlon, his war counselor, had to figure out the best way to juggle this jumble of guttersnipes to hit one of the hundred best light infantry companies in the world. Admittedly the Spetznaz were already engaged by the JDL and they were fighting on turf that Izods were much more familiar with.

And we'll be launching a surprise attack from the rear, Spurlock thought—for somewhere in there, in his own mind, he had joined the Izods as an adviser—with the mission of killing as many Russians as possible, taking their weapons and as much of their gear and ammo as possible, and getting the hell out before most of the Spetznaz know we're there.

The Izods weren't going after the main body of the Russian company. They were only going to try to pick off the rear guard and any strays they could find. He figured they would come out with ten or twelve AK-74s and maybe a couple of RPGs, but those plus the twenty the JDL had promised would be plenty to make them the most powerful gang south of Harlem.

Watching his son, Spurlock was deeply thrilled and, at the same time, wryly amused at his own reaction. It was so similar to the kind of calculations he had made when he was in the army. To see his boy with furrowed brow, intently glaring at his notebook, set up jumbles of emotions in him. He wanted to cry; he thought his heart would burst for joy. He wanted to see what the kid would do, and he wanted to jump in and take over before the kid fucked it up. He also wanted to stop the whole thing before his son got hurt.

Fortunately he was wise enough to do none of those things, but to stand there with his mouth shut and watch. The kid was pretty good.

Megan watched Spurlock watching Mark, and he was quietly aware that she knew all these feelings. God, how he wished that she, not that loony bitch he had married, were the mother of his children.

CHAPTER TEN

THE MINUTE they hit the street with a hundred kids Spurlock realized what a marvel of efficiency his son had created.

He and Megan stayed behind the leaders, Mako and Marlon, and a three-man fire team. Each fire team had one kid with a real aimable, firable, serious weapon, a carbine, a shotgun, something like that. The next kid had a zip gun or two, or a Saturday night special, and the little one had whatever he could put together, zip gun, knife, or whatever.

Scattered among them were four or five molookas, and in every team the second kid had a bag filled with sticks of stolen industrial dynamite, rolled in a combination of El-mer's glue and nails, nuts, bolts, marbles, and ball bearings: crude but effective. The dynamite was rigged with three- and four-second fuses.

There were also several fairly large radios, not two-way radios, but boomboxes, slung over some shoulders. They weren't on while the Izods were moving, but apparently they liked to have them around for breaks.

The objective of this mission, as far as the Izods were

concerned, was to upgrade their ordnance so that everybody with a semi-auto weapon would have an AK, the
kids with the zip guns would get the carbines and shot-
guns, and the guys with the molookas and dynamite bombs
would have real RPGs and hand grenades.

The teams worked with practiced smoothness and efficiency when they hit the street. One group of four fire
teams went ahead, two to each side of the street, each kid
five yards apart. They moved close to the buildings, silently, in short bursts of speed. The first pair would move
ahead about thirty yards and stop, checking out the street
before them.

When they had moved a block and a half, the first group
came under fire from a second-story window across the
street. These three took cover behind a stoop and returned
fire while the groups on the same side as the sniper moved
up under the window.

That group came under fire from the roof of the building
that the first fire team was trapped under.

Quickly Mako gestured to the second group on that side
to move past his command group and send a dynamite
stick in a pipe up there. They took positions and quickly
rocketed a pipe bomb through a molooka to the roof,
followed immediately by another. As soon as the first one
exploded, the second kid in the original rescue team stepped
out away from the safety of the stoop and lobbed a dynamite grenade through the open window, then ducked back
to the stoop without looking to see the results of his work.

There was a loud explosion and bricks and smoke blew
out from the roof. There was no more fire from there.

They moved the rest of the way to their subway stop
without interference.

Mako had chosen the express stop, even though the
chance of transit cops was much higher there. He wanted
an express train for a quick run to Brooklyn. He also
wanted to go over the bridge instead of through the tunnel.

That was why they had gone to the N train stop at 60th and Park, rather than take the secure stop on Lex they held on their own turf. If they had taken the number 6 Lexington Avenue local, they stood a good chance of being trapped under the East River by Russian troops in Brooklyn and New York City policemen on the Manhattan side.

The Russians would gas the tunnel, and that would be it for the Izods, and their leader's father, and his lady.

So they went the long way, through the snipers, and approached a major express stop armed and in strength, in flagrant violation of every loose agreement the gangs had with the NYPD. This was no gang rumble; this was a commando raid. The Izods were graduating from youth gang to urban terrorists.

As their point approached the stop, Mako sent two juniors down the stairs ahead of the point to check for cops. The two twelve-year-old boys disappeared down the stairs, yoohooing and skylarking like kids from the neighborhood. Then one of them came back up, held up two fingers, and disappeared into the ground again.

Mako held up his hand and the entire column stopped. "Okay," he said to Spurlock, "me and Marlon are going down alone. Give it twenty seconds and you two follow me. Leave the rifle topside with one of my guys. You'll get it back. And hide your pistol. Me and Marlon will disarm the cops. You be ready to cover us. Then we take the train to Brooklyn. We got to take another train there. And that's really going to be a bitch."

He and Marlon positioned their weapons under their jackets and trooped casually down the stairs.

Spurlock was nervous. This operation was something entirely outside his experience, and he was scared for his kid, even though Mark seemed to be handling it like a pro. Knowing that nervousness would make the time pass more quickly, he checked off twenty seconds on his watch, rather than count it off in his head. He put his magnum in his belt like Mako had, and handed his belt and holster to the nearest gang member. Then he whipped the CAR-15 off his shoulder and handed that to the boy as well. Then he and Megan followed Mako and Marlon underground.

On the platform the two boys were buying tokens from the token Negro, in his bulletproof Plexiglas booth. The two juniors had already put their tokens in and gone to the platform. One of them turned and cast them an anxious glance and gestured toward the tunnel. There was an ominous rumble coming toward them.

They were going to have to disarm the transit cops before the train came in, and that wasn't going to be easy. The cops were plastered against the wall like cornered rats and already eyed the two gang kids nervously. They were not armed like the transit cops Spurlock remembered. They were both young guys in baseball caps. One of them had a .12-gauge riot gun in his hands and the other had a slung MP-5 submachine gun. The one with the SMG was starting to fidget with the sling on his weapon.

In fifteen seconds the train would be on the platform and armed gang members would come pouring down the stairs.

A gunfight seemed due to start just as their train pulled out of the station.

Spurlock figured that he, Mark, and Marlon plus the two transit cops would die in the first fifteen seconds, and the roar of gunfire would echo up and down the tunnel for about a minute. Clearly a diversion was called for.

He advanced on the nervous cops, trying to look like a tourist from Texas. "Skewze may, Awfsers," he said. "Duz this heanh tryne go ta Coney Allen?"

Both cops looked at him dumbfounded. This bozo had said something that sounded kind of like English, but . . . what did it mean?

"Say what?" they both asked simultaneously.

Very carefully he enunciated, "Excuse me, Officers. Does this train go to Coney Island?"

SPURLOCK: SHERIFF OF PURGATORY 221

Comprehension dawned in their eyes, and one started to reply. Then a second level of comprehension dawned as a pistol was poked in each of their ribs.

"What's happening?" said the one who was about to verify that the train did indeed go to Coney Island. Mako and Marlon quickly relieved both cops of their radios and weapons as the train came into the station with an ear-shattering roar and piercing squeal of wheels on track.

The doors slammed open and one of the juniors stepped in the doorway so it couldn't close again. The train was rigged so it couldn't move unless all doors were shut. About twenty people got off, eyed the scene with the transit cops very quickly, and hurried past with averted eyes.

The doors tried to close, repeatedly batting their rubber guards against the kid standing in the doorway. They blapped against him four or five times, giving him a slightly dazed expression, but he stood his ground. The announcement, "Please get away from the doors so the train can leave the station," came gargling from the train's public address system.

"Get that motorman," Mako yelled, and Marlon, with a wave of his arm for a fire team to follow, vaulted the turnstile and sprinted for the head of the train.

"No real problem, Officers," Mako said soothingly. "We're only going to borrow this train for a quick run to Brooklyn. And just so our visit comes as a surprise, you're coming with us.

"But unless things go very badly, there's not going to be any . . . killing or hurting. We'll even give you your gear back when we get there. We certainly don't want any permanent hard feelings with the NYPD.

"Unless you like the Russians, you're probably going to enjoy this." His brow furrowed and he looked at them sternly. "You don't happen to be Russian-lovers, do you?"

Both cops vigorously shook their heads no. "Oh, no!"

said one. "No, no!" said the other. "Not us, we hate them."

"Ah, good," said Mako, smiling, but not lowering his weapon. "Then we're all going to get on well."

As he spoke, the Izods poured past and flowed over, around, under, any way but through, the turnstiles. Mako turned the two cops and their gear over to one of the fire teams, with orders to release them when they were through with the train. Then he nodded for Megan and Spurlock to follow him. He strode through the exit gate next to the turnstiles and quickly to the front of the train, where Marlon held an old .45 on the motorman, an extremely frightened black man wearing a gray Transit Authority uniform cap that looked like something from the 1890s to Spurlock. The man's hands were straight in the air with no bend to the elbows.

"Ah, good afternoon, sir," said Mako. "Sorry for this inconvenience, but my associates and I need to get to Brighton Beach as quickly as possible." He paused for a moment. "You must be terribly uncomfortable. Please feel free to lower your arms. But *don't* let your hands stray anywhere near the controls until we tell you. We want you to make a straight-through, no stops, run to Neptune Avenue. I want you to go as fast as you can and still stay on the tracks. Got it?"

The motorman lowered his arms and nodded.

"You're going to have to disregard normal routing, and I don't want any stalling behind any other trains, so you'll have to call ahead. When you do, please emphasize that we have you and all the passengers here as hostages, and we don't want any trouble. Understand?"

The motorman nodded. "Yessir!"

"Very good," said Mako. "I like your attitude. Let's go!"

The motorman twisted his throttle and the train shot off down the tunnel with a lurch, gathering speed and roaring on through its next stop without slowing down. Passengers in the double R local across the track gaped as they blasted through.

"Lemme make an announcement to the passengers," Mako said to the motorman. "They're probably nervous."

The motorman, realizing that he was in all likelihood going to survive with no permanent damage, had relaxed a bit. He smiled cynically. "For sure," he said, and twisted the mike on its long gooseneck cable so Mako could talk on it. Then he flipped the switch for him.

"Uh, ah, attention, passengers. Please don't be alarmed. We have borrowed this train. If everybody is just patient, we'll have you back on your regular run after about an hour delay. If you will please treat the gang members courteously, they will respond in kind. We apologize for the inconvenience." He pushed the mike back toward the motorman.

"Three hundred and twenty-six," muttered Megan, standing outside in the corridor of the car.

Spurlock turned and said, "What?"

"I've been counting felonies," Megan said. "As nearly as I can figure we are now implicated in three hundred and twenty-six felonies."

Mako grinned and said, "Don't worry about it. We got pretty good relations with the cops. They don't bother us and we don't bother them. Let's take a look at the train."

He put one of his teenage gunmen on the motorman and led off through the swaying, lurching train. Abrupt turns almost knocked them off their feet several times. They swung from subway strap to subway strap, like Johnny Weissmuller in a Tarzan movie. Their roaring passage through the trapped static air in the tunnel kept a breeze going through the cars strong enough that Spurlock had to jam his hat down hard on his head to keep both hands free.

In the sickly light of the cars the regular passengers

looked like corpses packaged like sardines. Aside from the occasional flicker of fear their faces were blank.

Fortunately they hadn't taken the train during rush hour so the aisles were fairly clear. The Izods had spread out through the train so that there was a fire team at either end of each car. They were grim-faced and ready, but their guns were not directed on the passengers.

Since it wasn't rush hour, most passengers were casually dressed in jeans or the popular fake Russian peasant garb. They seemed to be about nine-tenths black or Puerto Rican, and maybe 60 to 70 percent women.

Several times they passed beggars trapped in the cars. Two of them blind, or at least billed that way, one with a cane, one with a dog. There was one "war veteran" who must have been about eight when the war ended, and a little black guy in an alien-from-outer-space costume, complete with wire antennae, tights, and a cape. He held a saxophone and a tin cup, and was pressed up against a chrome pole, blowing Coltrane riffs on the sax. Nobody paid him any attention at all.

Suddenly the train started up an incline, which slowed it considerably, and they emerged into sunlight. They were crossing the blue Art Deco Manhattan Bridge.

As the subway climbed out onto the bridge, it slowed almost to a crawl. It reminded Spurlock of a roller coaster on its long creaking climb to the top. The first thing Spurlock noticed was a cop, even before his eyes lit on the graceful spans and Gothic supports of the Brooklyn Bridge, a half mile away toward the Statue of Liberty, hazy in the distance, her poor upraised arm now blown off, the torch extinguished. He was a plainclothes cop in a plaid windbreaker and porkpie hat, trying to look like a transit worker. But he was too clean to be working on a subway crew, and wore no iridescent orange vest. He was also speaking into a handy-talkie.

"Cops," said Spurlock.

"Got it!" responded Mako, taking off at a dead run toward the motorman's compartment. Megan and Spurlock chased after him. He barged through three cars, past the zombie passengers. A few looked up in alarm, but most kept their noses buried in their Kafka or stared straight ahead even when armed people ran past them.

"The abandoned stop just before De Kalb Avenue," Mako yelled at the motorman. "Pull in there and we'll get off. They're gonna have an ambush ahead at De Kalb or Atlantic Avenue. I don't wanna get tied up with any hostage crisis. We got work to do."

The motorman nodded vigorously. "Me neither," he said. "Mama have supper on the table and I be down here hungry."

"Yeah, or dead," said Mako.

The motorman nodded. "Yeah! When you get off, I can back over the bridge. They might start shootin' if we keep goin'."

Mako nodded. "Yeah, once we're off the train, back off any way you can."

The train leveled out and then nosed down, diving into Brooklyn and the blackness of the tunnel, with an occasional blue light dancing by as the train rollicked past. But the train was slowing, not rocketing through the tunnel as it had before.

They pulled into a deserted station, the tiles on the walls covered with black soot, planks and cargo pallets piled at random, the exit boarded up. It was lit dimly by the light of their subway cars, casting weird shadows between windows. The car doors whooshed open and the Izods started bailing off the train.

"Give those two cops their weapons and radios," said Mako over the loudspeaker. "But keep their ammo and flashlights. It's gonna be dark in here when the train goes."

He jumped off the train with his father and Megan

following, and grabbed a crew to force open the subway entrance.

Behind them, already half forgotten, the train started backing slowly toward the bridge, taking their light with it. A boy carrying the cop's two lighted flashlights strode importantly past, taking them to Mako at the entrance.

Spurlock watched the train recede, noting that the majority of the passengers seemed no more moved by their release than they had been by their capture.

Five Izods started breaking up a cargo pallet to make torches, and soon the silent, abandoned platform was lit by a dozen smoking, guttering, burning boards. Upstairs he heard a rattle and a chain. "Chained," he heard his son's voice call. "Motherfucker's chained."

Marlon and Mako were both up at the entrance and nobody was in charge of the mass of the Izods down on the platform. They milled around and bitched in the absence of orders.

But down in the tunnel he heard a rustle and a squeaking sound.

He grabbed a kid with a torch and said, "What's that sound?"

The kid shrugged.

Spurlock grabbed his torch and held it out over the tunnel. Debris lay all through the tunnel, uncleaned for weeks, and through the debris ran hundreds of filthy, beady-eyed rats, rats the size of cocker spaniels, all going the same way, the way the train had gone.

"Cops coming," Spurlock muttered. "They're not using lights because they want to surprise us. But they're driving these rats in front of them. Pass the word up to Mako to get that gate open fast. And get me a couple of dynamite bombs. We're going to send these fucking rats back at them."

The kid did as he was told while Spurlock watched in horrified fascination as a seemingly endless army of the

largest rats he had ever seen scurried and bounded end-
lessly down the filthy tunnel.

"Look at that!" he said to Megan.

She looked into the tunnel and muttered, "Ooh, yuck!"

The kid was back a minute later. "Mako says ten
minutes on the gate."

Spurlock took the two dynamite bombs from him. "Tell
him he's got five if we're lucky." The kid left again, to
deliver this message.

"What are you going to do?" she asked.

"Pied Piper in reverse," he replied. "In a second all
these rats are going back up the tunnel. I don't think
there's a guy in the world who wouldn't rather take a
gunshot wound than get rat-bit, and then have to take
rabies shots. For ten days in a row they stick this needle
straight into your stomach." He lit a dynamite grenade and
threw it far enough ahead in the tunnel to deflect the blast.

"Fire in the hole!" he bellowed, and he and Megan and
the gang kids on the platform shrank back and crouched.

The explosion boomed hollowly in the tunnel. Shrapnel
and debris flew past them.

A voice down the tunnel screamed, "What da fuck was
dat?" and another bellowed, "*Rats! Yeeaacchh!*"

The migrating rats panicked and hundreds charged in the
direction of the advancing policemen, who also panicked.
The sounds of automatic-weapons fire and shotgun blasts
mingled with shouts of "Jesus, I'm hit!" and "The
muthafucka bit me!"

But at the same time that all the rats on one side of the
blast were running back up the tunnel, the ones on this
side panicked and charged the other way. Three of them
actually bounded up onto the platform. The gang kids
kicked and shot at them, screaming, "*Rats! Fuckin' rats!*"
and two were hit by ricochets.

Three more gang kids, in panic, jumped off the platform

into the tunnel, which was now magically free of rats in that spot.

"Oh, shit!" one of the kids called. The cops, having lost the element of surprise, flashed on their lights. The rats had provided only a momentary respite, even though they had thrown the cops into a state of demoralized confusion. "There they are!" one called as he spotted the three kids in the tunnel. He started firing. Fortunately they hadn't calmed down enough to hit anything, and ricochets sparked and spanged off the steel tunnel supports.

"*Hit it!*" Spurlock bellowed, and the three kids dropped into the filth and rat guts, as Spurlock lobbed another homemade grenade down the tunnel. The cops were a hundred feet back, too far for the shrapnel to do much harm, but enough to keep them demoralized and throw their aim off. There was another spate of screaming and yelling and undisciplined, unaimed fire.

"Aw right! Aw right! Settle down!" one of the cops yelled. That was the last thing Spurlock wanted. He dropped off the platform into a puddle of filthy water just as the cops stopped yelling and got their lights back on.

Spurlock ducked behind one of the steel supports before they got their lights straightened out. There were three lights, two big flashlights and one bigger. Great targets. He put the CAR-15 on single shot and put the scope on the biggest light. The light filled his entire field of vision. He was going to be night blind in one eye for an hour or so, but what a target! He squeezed off a round and the light shattered. "Jesus, my hand!" screamed the guy who had held the light. "Jesus, my ass!" yelled the guy behind him.

The two holding the other lights quickly switched them off, but another fusilade of poorly aimed fire whanged and spanged and ricocheted down the tunnel, shotgun blasts and automatic weapons. He jumped around the support and sprinted forward so he was even with the gang kids,

who were flat into the filth. Once again Spurlock had
reason to be thankful for the universal tendency to fire
high when terrified.

When the din had died down, he said in a normal tone,
"When I open up, get back on the platform quick as you
can. Then tell Mako to get that gate open *now*! I'm going
to bust up these assholes one more time. Then I'm coming
out of here and going through that gate whether it's open
or not. Got it?"

"Yeah! Yeah!" one of the kids muttered.

"Then do it!" he bellowed as he opened up full auto
down the tunnel.

By that time the cops had gotten smart and they were
spaced out against the walls and behind the columns. So
his fire was only effective as suppressive fire. But it was
enough for the three Izods to get their elbows on the
platform and haul themselves back up. Sparks and the
clanging of ricochets off steel supports made it one of the
better light shows he had ever participated in. But now he
had to get back across the tunnel and onto the platform
without getting killed. No easy task. And every time the
cops opened up they were a little bit closer. He wished he
had one of those bombs to hold them back.

From up the stairs he heard two shots and saw a dim
light from the top of the stairs. The barricade must be
open. He had a momentary vision of all the kids rushing
out and leaving him here, with Megan helpless on the
platform.

Suddenly in the dim light he saw a broad-shouldered
figure dart to the edge of the platform and lob a sputtering-
fused lump down the tunnel toward the cops. As soon as it
exploded he heard a voice yell, "Run, Dad!" and he
sprinted, slipping and splashing to the platform. As he
leaned his elbows over the platform, two of the Izods
grabbed him under his armpits and dragged him bodily
upward. "Thanks," he gasped.

"Thank you, and let's get out of here," responded his son.

Most of the gang had already clattered up the stairs. Spurlock scrambled to his feet and followed the last two past the booth and up the stairs. Mako paused to lob another dynamite bomb down the tunnel.

Light flooded Spurlock's eyes as he emerged onto Flatbush Avenue. He blinked into it.

Gang members were already shepherding passengers off a passing bus they had hijacked.

CHAPTER ELEVEN

T HE FORMER passengers of the bus were left standing beside the abandoned subway entrance to greet the SWAT team, or whatever the hell they were, when they emerged. The gang swarmed aboard and Marlon placed a pistol at the base of the driver's skull. "You don't need that, man," said the driver. "Just tell me where you want to go."

"Take us to about four blocks from Neptune Avenue at the lower end of Brighton Beach," said Mako.

"On second thought, just shoot me, man," said the driver, easing out on the almost empty street. "You don't want to go that close to Brighton Beach in no bus. That's a hot area. You can hear them Russian guns a mile away."

"Okay," said Mako. "Make it six blocks."

The driver sighed. "Eight would be better. Look, I don't argue with nobody with a gun to my head 'less I got a reason. Those motherfuckers will kill you."

Mako shrugged. "Okay, eight blocks. We'll walk the rest of the way in combat formation."

The atmosphere on the bus was a little like that on the

team bus after a successful basketball game; they hadn't
lost anybody in the firefight and they had got away clean.
There was a lot of hand-slapping and Yeah-babys and
We-made-its, and nervous adrenaline-charged laughter. Then
as the little hoods (Spurlock stumbled on the term. He
wanted to call them boys, but they were not boys, and they
were not yet exactly men either. He decided on "little
hoods") settled down, it slowly dawned on them that this
had been the practice and that they were on their way to a
game where the object was to be one of the players and not
part of the score.

The bus headed up Flatbush Avenue toward Prospect
Park. The people on the street, those that could be seen on
the other side of huge piles of trash and garbage, scuttled
alertly, like apprehensive wraiths.

The bus topped the crest of Park Slope and slewed
through the huge traffic circle around Grand Army Plaza,
with its stately arch commemorating the Civil War, into
Prospect Park. It was a jungle.

For miles they drove through the gutted and rutted city,
lined with empty buildings, and buildings too full, with
garbage stacked and piled and tumbled in the street. And
always and everywhere these pale lifeless people. He wondered who they were. The gang kids still had energy
enough, and apparently the JDL had the juice, to wage
urban guerrilla warfare, but the vast mass of the people
had stacked arms, hung up their jocks. They were like
outpatients. Maybe the difference was that they were the
ones who had lost all hope.

Just as the driver had said, they started picking up the
sounds of artillery about a mile away from their destina-
tion. It was a persistent low rumble on the horizon. Mako
stopped the bus and said to the driver, "You're right.
We're not taking the bus any farther. Good luck!"

He jumped down the steps and the Izods piled off after
him. Quickly he spread them out close to buildings with

clear and authoritative hand and arm signals, and they started down the street in their spread out, mutually supporting, formation.

Finally they pulled into a warehouse compound and were met by three armed men, wearing old green fatigues and camouflage yarmulkes. But instead of boots they wore sneakers. Their equipment was all Soviet, from their tiny ill-made ammo pouches to their crude but highly effective AK-74s.

Mako led Spurlock and Megan to the one who seemed to be in charge. "Mr. Burgos, this is my dad. His name is Frank Spurlock. He's going to knock out the FDC for us."

The kid simply left Megan out of his introduction, an omission Spurlock corrected. "All I'm going to do is be delivery boy," he said. "It's Megan's stuff that will do the work."

"Lou Burgos," he said, and shook both their hands. He was a square-built, bearded man, with a wavy Mediterranean 'fro, going gray.

"What brings you to Brighton Beach, Mr. Spurlock?" he asked amiably.

An artillery shell whistled overhead on its way deep into Brighton Beach. They had started picking up artillery sounds twenty minutes before, but from here they set up a continuous simultaneous roar, whistle, and crash that continued for ten or fifteen minutes at a time, to fall silent for a while and then begin again. The ground shook under Spurlock's feet. He had seen what this stuff could do to a mud-wattled and -daubed village, and he had seen what it had done to most of Beirut. He could imagine what it was doing to a block of brownstones, and in his imagination it was not pretty.

"Just tourists," he said in answer to Burgos's question. "Up to see the kids."

Burgos eyed Spurlock up and down, Levi's, shitkickers, ammo vest, and scoped CAR-15. "We should get more such tourists." He looked at Megan in jeans and with her hair tied back. All her flamboyance had been put away, but still her sullen beauty and brooding eyes cast their spell on all who looked into them. "How can you two knock out this FDC?"

"All we need do is professionally deliver a few pizzas," said Spurlock.

Burgos shook his head. "Poison won't work. They'll make you eat some yourself, and wait around and wait until they see if it kills you or not."

Spurlock shook his head. "We're not trying to kill them. But they'll be so fucked up for six or eight hours that they won't be able to fire their guns accurately. And if it doesn't work, you can resort to Plan A and go in with a commando raid. But if it does work, it's all gravy."

"It's very dangerous for you," said Burgos.

Spurlock shrugged. "They ain't gettin' a cherry," he said.

Burgos sent Megan with one of his men to do her cooking. "Take her to Lembo's Pizzeria," he said. "We can use his delivery vehicle.

"You come with us," he said to Spurlock. "We'll show you what these boys are taking on." They set out in a gaggle, the two JDL commandos, Mako and Marlon, and Spurlock. Behind them the Izod group leaders were putting their kids into defensive positions around the empty parking lot. Spurlock and Burgos stepped out a little ahead of the others. Burgos had an air of mature authority and he handled his weapon in a competent and familiar manner. Spurlock felt he could value his assessment of the situation. "How are these boys?" he asked Burgos. "I've seen them fight the other gangs, and the cops a little, and they did okay, but, Jesus, the Spetznaz are big time."

Burgos nodded. "It will be a revelation to them, and not a pleasant one. But they are good boys; they'll do okay."

"Yeah, but how many will they lose?"

Burgos shot him a look which was full of anger and pity. "No more than anybody else," he said. "It is a war."

Spurlock nodded sadly. Childhood is more severely rationed in war than are coffee and cigarettes.

They went into an office in one of the warehouses and Burgos rolled up a window shade which had been mounted over a map, a line drawing actually, of the blocks of apartments in Brighton Beach that were under attack.

"They're going from the south to the north. When they started, we moved all civilians north of the fighting, except we lost many in the first barrages, and some we lost later when they tried to sneak back in to get some more of their things. We put our boys into defensive positions. They pound a block into rubble with artillery, then lift it and attack with Spetznaz. Many of our boys are killed by the artillery and the rest have to keep down. The Spetznaz are upon them before they are back in good defensive positions. Usually we must pull back a block and the pounding begins again.

"But if you can knock out that artillery for six or eight hours, my boys can attack the Spetznaz from the front here." He tapped the blocks in question with a pointer. They had advanced about a mile into Brighton Beach.

"The Spetznaz have established rear security points here and here"—he tapped the map—"to detect any attack from the rear or flanks. But they are counting on artillery support to hold down the people they're attacking while they divert their attention to the rear.

"What you boys have to do is knock out the outposts and take up defensive positions behind the Spetznaz. We'll drive them into you and you kill them."

Spurlock could see that the JDL had assigned to themselves the most difficult part of the mission, a frontal assault against elite troops. The Izods would have the best of it from shielded defensive positions.

Burgos then said to Spurlock, "I will take Mako and Marlon forward for a reconnaissance of the Spetznaz rearguard positions. You rejoin your lady and pick up your pizzas for delivery."

Spurlock shook hands with Burgos again and clapped Mako on the shoulder. "You guys be careful. I don't want to lose you right after I found you."

Mako nodded. He was growing more serious by the minute. Already he looked about three years older than he had that morning.

The whistling of overhead artillery and the shattering crashes of explosions almost a mile away shook the ground at Spurlock's feet.

Burgos and the two boys turned and left, walking purposefully, weapons at the ready.

The other JDL man, a slender sharp-featured guy about thirty, who looked far less at ease with his assault rifle than Burgos had, led Spurlock to a small dark sedan and drove him in silence to a street of shops, many with the front windows boarded and taped, with few goods in the windows. The shops were shielded from random artillery barrages and short rounds by sandbagged walls or walls of fifty-five-gallon drums filled with rocks and dirt. Many sandbags had been ripped open by jagged pieces of metal thrown by artillery shells.

They pulled up in front of a barricaded restaurant. The JDL man, who had spoken not a word on the way, led him inside Lembo's Pizzeria. He walked through the maze of sandbags into the entrance.

Inside he found Megan sharing a cup of coffee with a pop-eyed smiling man, short and round, who wore a sweeping handlebar mustache and a slicked-back barbershop-quartet haircut. Megan looked up and smiled. "Oh, here's Frank," she said.

When the pizza man stood to shake hands, Spurlock saw that he was five-six or -seven and weighed easily 250 pounds. He wore a dress shirt, baker's apron, and a plaid bow tie. On him it looked dapper.

"Salvatore Lembo," he said. "So you'a d'sheriff of Poigatory, Okkinsawr. I took basic trainin' in Okkinsawr durin' d'war. Very pretty place, but I din' get to see much of it."

Spurlock smiled. He and Lembo quickly compared notes and found they had both taken basic at Fort Chaffee at about the same time. Lembo had then been assigned to a combat engineer battalion and sent to build bridges in the desert. Mostly his battalion had fought as infantry, and mostly they had died. Lembo had been lucky enough to receive a million-dollar wound. He had been shipped home none the worse for wear than a slight limp. "But I didn't expect the war to follow me here," he said.

The JDL man left them for a time. "I'll be back about three in the morning," he said. "That's when we want the pizzas delivered. They'll be sleepy then, and that's when the FDC usually orders some anyway. The timing is just right for a dawn attack."

Spurlock nodded. "Look," he said, "I'm bushed, and I gotta take these pizzas in about eight hours. You mind if I log a few Zs in one of these booths?"

Lembo smiled. "Be my guest," he said. But he and Megan and Spurlock chatted for an hour before Spurlock nodded out.

The JDL man woke him at three o'clock. "Ahem," he said to Lembo. "The pizzas."

"Five minutes," said Lembo. "You want coffee?"

They sat quietly for a few minutes, drinking coffee and waiting for the pizzas. Spurlock was already beginning to feel the little knot of anxiety building in his stomach. This mission had its humorous aspects, but it was plenty dangerous and the adrenaline was building in his system to the overload point. Good, he would function better.

Lembo put his coffee down and started taking pizzas

from the stacked long flat ovens with a pizza paddle, and expertly slipping them into their boxes. "Here you are," he said. "Eight of Lembo's best, with special mushrooms."

He stacked the pizzas and led them out back to a small three-wheel used post office vehicle that had been converted to a pizza delivery scooter. It had a sign that said Papa's Pizza, a reasonable precaution since Sal would not want them to know where the pizzas came from, and a sticker with Cyrillic letters on it.

"Meet me out front," said the JDL man. "I'll lead you to within a couple of blocks of the Russians."

Spurlock drove around to where the JDL man had parked and then followed him through a maze of streets and back alleys until he stopped. Spurlock pulled up beside his window, and the Jewish guerrilla leaned out. "The FDC is in the middle of one battery of six guns, up there a couple of blocks."

The continuous roar of falling shells had been going on so long that Spurlock had almost ceased to notice it. But they were very close now to the repeated *crack!* of 130-millimeter towed howitzers, firing.

"The other batteries are close by here, in other big parking lots, but the fire direction for all is handled here."

"Right," said Spurlock, "but I'll never find my way back after I get out of there. I don't know this city at all."

The JDL man nodded. "I'll come back in two hours. If the area is clear I'll wait twenty minutes. Otherwise you're on your own."

Spurlock nodded. Considering the degree of risk, it was more than he could expect. "I'll be here," he said. He waited a couple of minutes until the JDL man had cleared the area, then put his little green and yellow putt-putt in gear and drove off toward the enemy. At the end of the first block he saw the flat area, and rows of concertina wire came into view. He was glad his kid wouldn't have to scale that. Knock wood, he thought.

By the end of the second block he could see the old storm fence behind the concertina and begin to make out the guns firing. He drove down to the gate, past three of the guns, the crews working in light shirts or T-shirts in the forty-degree weather. Handling those heavy shells at fast speed was hard work.

The minute he entered the Russian area the color seemed to drain from everything. He could still see it but it seemed more drab somehow. It was the soul-deadening effect of rampant bureaucracy.

Two gate guards, wearing baggy uniforms, with shaven haircuts under their mushroom-shaped helmets, stopped him at the gate. *"Sobri vyechyer yah,"* said the young one, in a friendly enough manner. "Stop! Show your papers!" said the older, more authoritatively.

Spurlock's heart was pounding. If he got past these two, he'd probably be all right. But if these jokers didn't buy the bumper sticker on his scooter, he was cooked. He pointed at the sticker and said, "Pizza."

"Ah, pizza," said the young friendly one.

The older one scowled. "Pizza?" he said suspiciously. "You eat!"

Spurlock blew out his cheeks and held his arms out to pantomime getting fat, then shrugged.

The younger Russian laughed. The older one opened the pizza container on the front of the scooter. He opened the top box, pepperoni and mushroom. Under that was sausage and mushroom. The kid looked in eagerly, almost drooling.

"I got an extra," said Spurlock. "Have some."

"Shto ehtah zuahchyeet?" said the young one with a puzzled expression. Spurlock pointed to him and pantomimed eating, rubbing his belly and making chewing motions.

The older one said, "We eat! *You* eat!"

Spurlock looked around and thought, deadening fucking

atmosphere to trip in. Plus he'd sworn never to do it again. Still, for God and country. He shrugged. "Okay, let's all have some."

He ate a piece with them and left the rest of the box. He wheeled his little scooter into the artillery compound and turned left just as the gunner on the first howitzer he passed jerked the lanyard on his gun and it fired with a thunderous explosion, running back hard on its carriage, while its crew jammed their fingers in their ears and ducked under the concussion. The shell shrieked off into Brighton Beach.

The shock wave almost knocked Spurlock off his scooter. His ears rang, and he knew from experience that they would for hours.

He pulled the scooter up in front of a dun-colored trailer with a ground-searching radar dome on top. He went to the door and knocked.

A shaven-haired goon with the insignia of a Russian master sergeant opened the door and peered at Spurlock. *"Kto Tarn?"* he demanded in a surly voice.

"Pizza!" Spurlock said.

The sergeant turned and hollered into the interior of the trailer. Spurlock figured with twenty GIs in there they wouldn't know whether anybody had ordered a pizza or not. Finally the sergeant jerked his head for Spurlock to come in. He went back for his pizzas and juggled the boxes up the steps and into the trailer, setting the pizzas down on the desk.

Suddenly the grain in the wooden desk jumped out at him and it occurred to him that the intricacy of that pattern was all the proof one needed of the existence of God.

He was coming onto the psilocybin in the mushrooms. He thought he'd better get all his practical tasks out of the way right quick because in about five minutes they would elude him.

"Lessee," he said, toting up the bill, "we got pepperoni and mushroom; pepperoni, black olive, and mushroom; sausage, green pepper, and mushroom; and anchovy and mushroom. Uh, that'll be two thousand four hundred and eighty-two dollars.'' He knew he was right, but the price was hard to figure with Sal's numerals twisting and swirling on the receipt like that.

The sergeant contemptuously counted three thousand off a wad of bills in his pocket and sneered, "Kip change!''

Spurlock smiled and said, "Thank you,'' marveling at the New York prices. Those pizzas wouldn't have cost over twelve hundred in Purgatory.

The sergeant gestured toward the boxes. "We it, you it!'' he said.

It must be in their goddamn phrase book, Spurlock thought. The sergeant picked one slice from each box. He required Spurlock to eat the first one, crust and all.

Jesus, I don't know if I can get through this, he thought. He turned to the sergeant and pantomimed the same gesture he had to the gate guard, puffing out his cheeks and holding his hands out away from his sides. The sergeant laughed around broken teeth. "You it!'' he said. On the second one Spurlock disgarded his crust. And after that he just took a couple of bites out of each piece, avoiding the mushrooms where possible. He was going to be so fucked up . . . he could hardly function as it was. The sergeant watched, but didn't say anything.

Spurlock gestured toward the boxes. "We wait!'' said the sergeant.

They sat. All the details of the trailer jumped out in startling relief, and he thought, Oh! He hadn't even begun to come on to what he'd eaten there in the trailer.

The walls inside were painted a depressing institutional brown. About fifteen Russians in their late teens and early twenties worked in the trailer. Four of them sat in front of radar screens wearing headphones, the shifting green of the screens reflecting eerily on their faces. The rest operated various radios, computers, plotting boards.

Back in the back of the trailer somewhere a radio was tuned to the same rock station that had been playing at the Izod headquarters.

But the walls were starting to breathe and shift. He became fascinated by the character of these Russians. This old sergeant here in his face was an okay guy. He had just bought into all his training and blotted out with vodka everything that was not his job. These kids were not as far gone as the sarge, but they were trying. It was as though they were looking out at the world through a cylinder the size of a tin can strapped to their nose.

One of the kids spoke to the sergeant in Russian. But Spurlock knew what he said. He knew GIs and could interpret gesture and inflection as though it were a simultaneous translation.

"Hey, Sarge! Are we gonna have to wait all night for this? The pizzas getting cold."

"It might have a slow-acting poison."

"That guy don't look worried about it to me. You ever hear of an *American* suicide bomber? This ain't Damascus."

The sergeant grabbed the next pizza box and flipped it to the kid like a Frisbee. "All right, numbnuts, you be the next guinea pig."

The kid opened the box and took a couple of bites. "Tastes good to me."

The sergeant nodded and the rest joined in. Everybody got a couple of pieces. The old sarge took three.

All this time the work of the FDC was going on. The radio operators took sightings from forward observers the Russians had planted on rooftops near the fighting and from the radar operators. The plotters took the sightings and converted them into firing data, and other radio operators relayed instructions to the guns.

The sergeant, even as he munched, continued to watch Spurlock suspiciously.

Spurlock for his own protection fell to watching the shifting play of green light on the face of the nearest radio operator. He had no idea how long he did this, but finally the first kid who had agitated for the pizza said, *"Ya plakah syeebya eyust vuyu,"* I don't feel well, and the sergeant yelled back, "What's the matter?"

"Stomach."

The sergeant drew his ancient Tokarev. "This son of a bitch has killed us."

Spurlock shook his head. "It's okay, you get over it," he said reassuringly.

The sergeant, continuing to hold the pistol on Spurlock, reached for a telephone, obviously to call security. If Spurlock didn't do something quick, this place would be swarming with GRU agents in about three minutes, and Spurlock would have accomplished his mission, but he would be in for an "interrogation" that would leave him in two or more boxes. These dudes were starting to come on to the mushrooms, but they were going to feel a little queasy for a while first.

Somewhere in the background the radio was playing the Beatles' "Day Tripper" and one of the Russian kids turned it up loud enough to have kept him peeling potatoes for a month under normal circumstances. He almost had them.

The sergeant's attention was distracted for a second as he cranked the field phone and spoke into the mouthpiece. As soon as he dropped his eyes, Spurlock darted his hand into his breast pocket and withdrew a small cylindrical object and a device about three inches long, with a loop at each end. "Hang it up or I'll use this," he ordered.

"What is it, a bomb?" one of the kids asked in a mildly interested tone.

"I don't know," replied the sergeant, watching the cylinder as though it might be a snake.

The rest of the crew didn't seem much interested. They were beginning to stretch and fidget and move around to the music.

"No! No!" said the sergeant as Spurlock unscrewed the cap and stuck one of the loops into the cylinder.

"Hang it up!" Spurlock demanded.

Slowly the sergeant complied. Then he stopped, as though stunned, and turned his head to catch one of George's better guitar riffs. When he turned back, Spurlock blew a long stream of heavy soap bubbles into the air. They hung, quivering and shimmering, the lights in the room and from the computer screens reflecting off their sides.

The sergeant tracked them all the way to the floor, rapturously, and his face fell when they burst.

Spurlock loosed another stream of bubbles, to a smattering of applause from the kids at the plotting boards. The radio was on full blast now. The kid at the nearest radar had his headset draped around his neck so he wouldn't be distracted by any boring radio transmissions, and twiddled the dials on his radar, making it do bleeps and lulus and weird changing geometric shapes. "*Bojemoi!*" he muttered. Others were starting to group around to watch.

I've done my work here, Spurlock thought, and handed the bubble mix to the sergeant, who received it gratefully. "Lock the door after I leave," he told the sergeant. "Keep the party private."

"*Da! Da!*"

Spurlock stepped down the steps into the cool night air, and the stars and the moon. The air was a shock after the closeness of the trailer. Something was different. Then he realized the guns had fallen silent. At the gun nearest him the crew stood around, starting to shiver as the sweat dried on their bodies. Their radio operator held out his headset with a puzzled expression. Dimly from the headset Spurlock could make out Beatles music and the words to "Day Tripper."

He kicked the scooter into life and headed toward the gate. The sentries were firing short bursts of AK-74 fire at the moon as he went through.

The JDL guy was waiting for him at the appointed place. Spurlock nodded and he started the car. Spurlock followed him though the silent streets.

The drive back to Lembo's was sobering enough. New York had never been exactly a primo setting for the psychedelic experience anyway. But now his most crying need was to get straight for the balance of this night. He sat tensely at the handlebars of the scooter, trying to get his head together, but his thoughts kept getting away from him, jumping to the illuminated numbers on the speedometer, focusing on slices of the moon, glimpsed between passing buildings.

By the time they got to the assembly area for their attack, he was past peaking and reasonably coherent. Sad even, because he hadn't felt that those Russian kids he had just duped were any different from Mako's gang kids, and a lot of both were going to die this night.

He found Mako, Marlon, and Burgos in a vacant store a couple of blocks from the first Spetznaz outpost they were going to attack. The gang members sat around with their faces darkened, mostly with mud, their weapons draped over their knees. They were all psyched up for the fight, smoking last-minute cigarettes, alternately yawning and fidgeting. One kid was compulsively going through karate forms. They were ready, and if there was any influence that could get Spurlock's head together, it was the vibes in this room.

Just as Spurlock, Megan, and their JDL driver entered though, the first round of a series of cannon shots fired.

Burgos shrugged. "I thought you had succeeded," he said, "but they are firing again."

Marlon started beating his right fist into his left hand

compulsively. "We're gonna have to take the FDC," he said. "I knew it."

In spite of himself Spurlock had to grin. He recognized the rhythm of the guns. *"Boom! . . . Boom-boom! . . . Boom! . . . Boom-boom-boom!"*

"Look out the window," he said, a silly involuntary grin slipping all over his face. They did and saw seven flares drifting harmlessly down over the Atlantic.

"What da fuck are they doin'?" Marlon demanded.

"Turn on one of those ghetto blasters," Spurlock said just as the second series of artillery rounds boomed out.

Mako snapped on one of the radios and it was just as Spurlock had suspected. The FDC was sending out fire missions, all right. The battalion was firing illuminating rounds, in time to Warren Zevon's version of "Bo Diddly's a Gunslinger." But their timing was awful. No sense of rhythm. None.

CHAPTER TWELVE

IT WAS an hour before dawn. Spurlock stood close to a warehouse wall, CAR-15 at the ready, and watched the Izods move into a block of apartments that had been ventilated by artillery and decorated with random piles of rubble. The Russians had stormed through here a couple of days before, after they lifted their artillery barrage, and that most sickening of odors, the smell of death, hung in the air. He felt the tightness of impending combat in his gut.

He was still tripping quite heavily, if he stopped to think about it, but adrenaline had, for the most part, superseded psilocybin.

Spurlock felt like he was going into the Superbowl with the state high school champs. Not an exact analogy because although the Spetznaz were world class, they were not the world's champs. Frazier's old outfit, the 7th Ranger Battalion, was his nominee for that honor.

But Spurlock had fought Spetznaz around Damascus and they had been very good, if unnecessarily brutal.

And these kids, young as they were, had developed a

level of feral rage that was totally beyond anything he had ever seen in this country. Still they were just untrained kids.

Untrained, but very experienced. They flitted on ahead of him, slinking from shadow to shadow, moving quietly, not getting too close together or too far apart.

Spurlock's self-appointed mission was to cover Mark's ass, be a combination bodyguard and medic, but to stay far enough away from the kid that he could do his job without worrying about the old man.

Mark moved up ahead of him, crouched behind a dumpster, scanning the street and muttering into a handy-talkie. The plan was for Marlon to take thirty Izods ahead and knock out the first Spetznaz outpost and get their weapons. Then the entire gang would take up defensive positions behind the area the Spetznaz had been trying to clear. At first light the JDL would attack in overwhelming numbers, and the Spetznaz troops, unable to call in artillery, would be forced to retreat, right into the waiting arms of the Izods. That was the plan, and it might be just simple enough to work.

Having made sure that the main body of Izods was in place, Mako nodded to Spurlock to come on ahead. He was leaving one of his honchos in charge and going ahead to join Marlon for the assault. He moved out at a crouch, with two of his kids for company. Spurlock hooked on as tailgunner and they flitted like a basketball team of wraiths, moving by leaps and bounds. Mako and one of the Izods moved out and darted forward about twenty yards, while Spurlock and the other kid scanned the windows and alleys for signs of movement, listened for any voice, watched for any flash. Then Mako and the other one performed the same service while Spurlock and his buddy moved out crouching in the shadows, frequently changing speed and direction so it would be impossible to draw a bead on them.

out.'' Just since they arrived, the room had filled with the smell of sweat and fear.

They moved as close as they could by concealed routes of approach. The idea was to knock out the machine gun with molookas and storm the building. When they were in position, Mako crouched behind the molooka gunner, but the kid was nervous, so his first shot was low, into the sandbags. Immediately after the first flash the machine gunner opened up. But he hadn't seen where the molly had come from and he was firing blind. The second molly coated the crew with sticky burning gasoline, and when they stood up, screaming, the Izods cut them down.

"Let's go!" Mako screamed, and for a second Spurlock watched his long-lost only son charging alone, into auto-weapons fire plunging from the windows above. Then he and Marlon were running and firing. One molly shattered harmlessly against the wall above. But the next burst into flames inside the building.

Then Spurlock bounded over the scorched sandbags and dead Russians in the door and joined Mako and Marlon in the hallway, along with the dozen or so of their fighters who had made it with them. He looked back across the street at a half-dozen dead teenagers whose mothers proba-bly expected them home for dinner. Two more went down as he watched, but another dozen made it across.

Then a grenade rattled down the stairwell.

"Hit it!" Spurlock called.

Everybody got down, but they still picked up a couple more wounded.

"Clear the ground floor," Mako called to Marlon. "I'm going upstairs!"

Marlon grabbed a couple of fire teams and started them down the hallway, bashing in doors, throwing grenades, and hosing down rooms.

"Everybody else follow me," Mako called as another group of new arrivals barged through the door. As quickly as he could pull the pins and throw, Mako lobbed grenades up on the second landing. The first went off just as he threw the third.

Before Mako could move on the stairs Spurlock charged past him, screaming, *"Yaaaahhhhh!"* He stormed up the stairs, spraying the landing as he went. No way was he going to let Mark charge those stairs. But there were only six corpses up there by the time he arrived. Mako was right behind him. "Jesus, Dad," he said, "you coulda got killed."

"Shit!" said Spurlock.

A door opened down the hallway and a grenade came rolling toward them. Spurlock grabbed Mako and crammed him into a corner, but it caught the two kids behind them and sent them ripped, bleeding, and screaming back down the stairs.

Quicker than thought, Spurlock scooped a grenade off a dead Russian and charged the hallway, screaming the ancient battle cry of the Arkies, *"Whoooo-pig! Soooooey!"* Without hesitation he kicked in the door, lobbed in a grenade, plastered himself against the wall, and, right after it exploded, he charged inside, fanning the room with fire. It was empty.

He went to the window and saw the Russian grenadier dead on the ground below. The kid across the street had wasted him when he tried to escape. Spurlock looked up to see Mako in the door behind him. "That's kind of an embarrassing battle cry, Dad," he said.

"It's a part of my rich cultural heritage," Spurlock replied.

In twenty minutes the building was theirs. But at what cost? Of the original ninety-six they had started with that morning they had twelve dead and fifteen wounded.

Mako quickly had an aid station set up downstairs. They couldn't do much with what they had, a tourniquet and a shot of junk was about it. But if the attack went well, they'd be treated by the best Jewish doctors in New York before noon, those who lived.

Mako ordered a team to gather all the captured Soviet weapons. "What about any live Russians?" asked the kid in charge of the weapons-gathering detail. He was understandably nervous about trying to take prisoners.

Mako hesitated.

"Waste 'em," said Marlon. "We ain't got time to fuck wit' prisoners."

Mako nodded. "He's right."

The group of boys he had selected went off to loot and kill.

Quickly Mako divided his force in two, to occupy this building and the one across the street. They would be in concealed positions with good fields of fire, and the street the Spetznaz should be coming down passed right between them. Originally he had planned to occupy three buildings, but his force was now too small.

Once his people were deployed in doors and windows he signaled the JDL to begin their attack.

There was a wait then, and Spurlock's adrenaline level subsided. The walls started moving again, and his gaze became fixated on the faces of the Izods. They were so young, peach fuzz on their chins; but their faces were, for the most part, pinched and mean. He was filled with a terrible sadness for the lives they should have had, and would never have in this world. But they weren't afraid anymore. They were so wired they were running on autopilot, and they were grateful for even this short break in the carnage. Glad to be alive and savoring every precious second granted to them.

Marlon rolled a cigarette into the corner of his mouth. Several others did likewise.

Shortly thereafter they heard the intense rattle of automatic-weapons fire up ahead along with the *whoom!* and *blam!* of rockets and mortars.

"Steady!" called Mako. His kids had already been through hell today, and this was supposed to be the hard part coming now.

The sounds of combat grew louder, and the first Spetznaz appeared. They retreated in two columns, in good order, split down each side of the street. But they were moving fairly quickly. They wanted to get out of there.

Now was the test of discipline. If the Izods held their fire until Mako fired, then they could obliterate a good portion of the Spetznaz and drive off the rest. If they opened fire too soon, the Spetznaz could deploy against them and inflict heavy casualties without taking many and get away clean.

They held.

Mako held his fire until there were fifteen Spetznaz in the intersection. Apparently they had no idea their rear had been infiltrated. Mako fired and brought one down, and both buildings of Izods opened up on them. Spurlock held his fire and simply watched his son.

They dropped the first fifteen quickly, and the Spetznaz column stopped and took cover. They returned fire, but not many of them were in position to fire effectively. To do so they would have to occupy the buildings across the street and they didn't have time for that. They had left behind only a small force to hold off the advancing JDL. To escape they would have to go back a block and over two, either that or cross the street into withering fire and run a gauntlet a block long between two buildings occupied by the Izods.

They chose the latter, because the JDL was closing fast, and they had to collect their dead. Like most good units, they'd rather lose men than leave their dead to the enemy. They charged into the intersection, firing everything they had, including rockets.

The room dissolved into chaos. The Izods were firing. Incoming rocket-propelled grenades blasted in bricks, glass, and smoke. Some of the boys were blown back into the room, mangled and screaming.

One boy sat in the middle of the floor with jagged chunks of glass stuck in his face. One, half bloody, fell out on the floor. "My eyes!" he screamed. "My eyes!"

Marlon Donadio sat against the wall. One side of his face was a bloody pulp, and he sat trying to fit the gray greasy coils of his intestinal tract back into his stomach. They kept escaping from his fingers like some crazed Slinky toy.

Then it stopped.

The Spetznaz were gone, leaving behind more dead than were originally in the intersection. The Izods had killed more of what were supposed to be the best than they had lost. When they cleaned up, they would have more automatic weapons than they had people left. It was a great victory.

"My eyes! My eyes!"

Marlon gave up on the guts and started screaming, piercing, gut-wrenching screams. He was in great pain and was obviously going to die. Not the best surgeon in the best hospital in the world could save him. And there would be no surgeon and no hospital until long after he was gone.

Without missing a beat Mako went over and blew his brains out with a single shot from his AK. He turned and said to one of the group leaders, "Chuck. You're number two now. Get the wounded downstairs. Send somebody to hook up with the JDL and get us a doctor. Better yet, several doctors. Send a group to get the weapons and ammo off those dead Russians. And send Bernie to check security. We're gonna have to fill in for the dead guys."

Chuck looked at him blankly, blinking.

"*Move!*"

Chuck moved.

Mako cocked his head at Spurlock and led him down the

hall to an empty room, where he promptly threw up in the corner.

When he was through, he looked up and there was vomit on his shirt and tears streaming from his eyes.

Sobbing, he came and put his head on his father's shoulders. Frank put his arms around his boy.

"Dad," he cried. "Me and Marlon been best friends since the second grade. And the other guys. Oh, God, the other guys."

Spurlock hugged him. "Be still, son, be still. It's just life. Nobody could have run this better than you did."

The kid had made a couple of mistakes, but Spurlock had seen West Pointers do worse. He was simply learning the awful lesson that grief is the unavoidable by-product of combat.

Frank was glad he was here to help his son through this moment. He had missed so many others.

CHAPTER THIRTEEN

THREE FLIGHTS up, through the rotting stink of garbage and the accumulated filth of generations, the smell of rotting vegetables hung in the hall. Spurlock wondered whether they had to pay rent on this pesthole, or whether it had long since been abandoned and occupied by scavengers. And were Linda and the kids the scavengers?

They moved down the hall and stopped in front of a door. The door was a flimsy affair, although Spurlock saw bolts on the outside where many strong locks had been installed. But he could hear voices coming under the door quite easily.

"But, darling, I'm your mo-thirr," came the first voice, and at first he didn't recognize it. Then when he finally did he had a hard time believing it. Linda's soft musical lilt had acquired a raspy edge to it, a tinge of steel, desperation, and lunacy.

The voice that answered back was all salty, feminine, but young and hoarse. "I don't care what you say, I'm not balling that spic."

The implication of that hit Spurlock with numbing force. His daughter was fifteen years old.

"Sweetheart, nobody said you have to make love to Mr. Nestor. He only wants you to have dinner with him and spend some time. He's lonely."

It gave Spurlock a certain sour amusement that she still used the term "making love" as a synonym for sexual intercourse. It had made a certain finicky sense when she used it in connection with herself and him because they had genuinely and truly been in love. At least he had been. But later, when she started to screw around on him, she had used the same terminology to describe copulation between two people who wouldn't know love if it flew by and bit them on the ass.

"Maybe not," came back the tough-tender little girl's voice. "He's a goddamn junkie faggot. I doubt if the shmuck can get it up anymore."

"Darling, this is a difficult town to live in for a lone woman with children. We need a protector. You see how bad things have gotten since your Uncle Jack left. Let's be honest . . ." He wasn't sure, but he thought he heard a snort of derision at that. "Since I've been ill, the men don't flock around anymore. But you're a fine, big girl with a lovely figure. I'm afraid you're going to have to assume more than your fair share of the responsibility for holding our little family together."

Angrily the little girl's voice came back. "You just want me to ball that pusher to feed your habit. What about Mark? Why don't he assume *his* fair share of the responsibility instead of running around with those goons all the time?"

There was a considerable pause. "Doesn't, darling, not don't. Girls mature faster. I'm afraid Mark's still a baby."

Mark, who was standing beside Spurlock, grinned lopsidedly at his father when she said that. "Shit!" he said, and pounded on the door.

"Mom! Mom! It's me, Mark. There's somebody here to see you!" There was a strange excitement around the kid.

"Who is it, Mark?"

"Mom! Dammit, open the door!"

There were further whispers, and several locks and latches were thrown and the door opened quickly.

A young girl stood inside the door and Spurlock's eyes went first to her. She was a cocky-looking little girl, with a slim waist and big breasts. They'd have been big on anybody, but she was only fifteen and that made her probably the girl with the biggest tits in the sophomore class, if she went to school. Some girls would have been embarrassed and some would have grown cocky. This one had grown cocky. It was hard to relate to her as his darling baby girl.

Then he looked past her to the woman framed in the door. It was she. There was no question of not recognizing her. She had changed. She did not look healthy. She stood awkwardly where before her stance had been full of grace. She wore an idiot satiated smile and yet she did not look well fed or healthy, but it was unquestionably she. She had the same legs, long thin numbers, made to teeter on extravagant heels, the same thin body. Her face was more lined, her complexion more sallow, and the fire in her eyes had banked. Her hair, which had once floated in the vicinity of her head like a white-gold cloud, was now merely frazzled.

"Hello, Spurlock," she said, and there was great caution in her voice. She looked at him with a wariness in her eyes. He wondered why that was, and then realized that she'd had a few complaints, too.

"Hi!" he said. "I thought you might not recognize me." He said it somewhat awkwardly, still feeling the weight of what they had been and the pain of how they had got.

She shook her head and laughed nervously. "I would recognize your shadow. Come on in."

Nervously he crowded into the room, with Megan beside him. Linda's eyes went to Megan with an unspoken question.

"This is Megan Carney," Spurlock said. "She's with me."

Linda's lips pursed slightly. "So I see," she said.

They entered the apartment and Linda indicated several ratty chairs for them to sit on. Spurlock sat on an overstuffed chair with a broken spring in the seat and filthy doilies on the worm-grimy arms.

"Leslie, darling, please make some tea for our guests."

The girl glared resentfully at her mother for a second, and then said, "Are you really my dad?"

Spurlock nodded, and advanced, shyly, to give her a hug. She backed away a step and he stopped. Then she ran and threw her arms around his neck. He scooped her a foot off the floor and twirled her around the room. He felt as though there were sandpaper on the backs of his eyelids, but he wasn't tired now.

"I'll get the tea," she said when he put her down. She started toward the kitchen.

Megan sat in a chair near him and Linda sat facing. Mako sat on the floor near his mother, since all the chairs were taken. Linda wore an old flowered muumuu and she regarded them with some tension and hostility, frail body all wrapped in her muumuu. She smiled a smile which seemed to intend to be her old-time merry grin, but which came out hard and twisty. "What brings you so far from Arkansas?" she asked. "The Gray Line tour's closed down and none of the shows are any good." She smiled that smile again.

Spurlock shook his head. He sat awkwardly, with his boot crossed over his right knee, his hat hanging on the left, CAR-15 lying on the floor beside him. She was tense and he was tense. Megan looked alert, and God only knew how the kids felt.

Spurlock laughed to break the tension, but it reverberated hollowly in the room, like a fun-house laugh machine. "No," he said, "we didn't bull our way across half a continent to see Grant's tomb or a revival of *Little Mary Sunshine*. I came to see if the kids are all right and to offer help if it's needed."

Linda appraised him coolly. "The children are as you see them," she said, "healthy and happy."

As far as Spurlock could see, they were healthy enough, but neither looked exactly happy. "As for the help," Linda went on, "it seems only your duty to financially assist your children, and we are very poor."

Leslie reentered the room with a plastic tray on which sat a cracked teapot and several mismatched cups. She served them carefully and properly around the room. Spurlock wondered why Linda had worked so long and hard to make Leslie, to whom she was openly hostile, properly ladylike, and let the boy run wild. It could be that she just didn't know what to do to raise a man.

He suspected the latter. Leslie handed Megan her cup first, then Spurlock, then her mother. Mako refused his and Leslie started to sit down on a pillow on the floor. Her butt had descended to a point six inches above the pillow when her mother spat out the word "Darling!" Leslie's hand shot out and she caught herself before she fell on her behind.

"While you're up," Linda went on, coolly ignoring the fact that Leslie was not really up at all, "would you get Blossom for me, please?"

Leslie leveled a glance at her mother that would have melted steel; then, pushing with one hand while she precariously balanced the tray with the other, she rose to go get Blossom, whatever that was.

Spurlock smiled at his former wife and said, "I don't

know how I could be of help financially. My total paycheck wouldn't support one of you for a week in this town, and there's no assurance I could even get the money to you. No, what I can offer is safe haven for you and/or the kids, in Purgatory. Food and shelter won't be a problem there. We have an excellent school and a lot of good country to move around in. Another thing we have there that you don't here is a reasonable level of personal safety."

Leslie came from the other room with a small wire cage and handed it to her mother. Linda opened the cage and reached inside, withdrawing a small bit of snub-nosed squirming fur. "Hello, little baby," Linda said, and gently stroked the animal. She looked up brightly, and for a moment Spurlock saw the pretty girl he had loved so. It gave him a horrible pang because he had not thought in a long time about the sweet and wonderful spirit she'd once had. Somehow all that had turned to bitterness and back-biting before she left.

"This is Blossom, my hamster," she said. "We found her in the apartment in her cage when we moved in, poor thing. I think she was nearly on the verge of death, but I nursed her back to life." She patted the animal again and held it against her cheek, where it squirmed frantically.

Leslie opened her mouth to say something and then closed it again.

Then Linda turned her attention back to Spurlock. She regarded him disdainfully. "Moving to Arkansas is out of the question," she said. "One can scarcely compare the cultural advantages of a place like Purgatory with those of New York City."

Spurlock was having difficulty believing his ears. She lived in this suffering pesthole with rapists and dope pushers in every alleyway and talked about cultural advantages. When they were married, he let her do that, twist facts to suit herself. He let her do that because he wanted to believe they were on the same side, when, in fact, she always acted as though they were in an adversary relationship. He always gave her everything he could, but she left when she discovered that she wanted more than he could ever give her. More than life itself could give, in his opinion. But those days were gone. He hadn't pandered to other people's illusions for a long time, "Listen," he said, as gently as he could, but it still came out grating, "when we arrived in this neighborhood a teenage punk tried to stick us up, and I just stood outside the door and heard you try to get my daughter to peddle her ass to a junkie with a big stash."

Even now he left out the battle in Brooklyn. He didn't think there was any way she could relate to it. "The question isn't whether the kids are coming with me. The question is, are you coming with us?"

She grew tense at the harsh sound of his voice and stroked the little hamster harder than the beast wanted her to.

It bit her.

"Gawd fucking dammit!" Linda shrieked, and dashed the little creature to the floor. Immediately she realized she had lapsed out of her public character. She softened her features and picked up the dazed little animal, stroking it again. "Aw, diddums hurtums widdle self?" she asked, all anxiety and concern.

She was lost in stroking the little animal's body and paid no attention to anybody else in the room.

Spurlock and Megan exchanged a glance.

Linda looked up. She regarded them distantly. "I will not permit the children to leave," she said. "They have their friends here, and the quality of the schools is much better." She carefully put the hamster back in its cage.

Spurlock, as always, was completely nonplussed when trying to deal with someone who will not face reality. "You have no choice," he said. "The thing is done. They are going. Do you want to go, too?"

Linda had grown more and more nervous when he started to lean on her. He knew that her character had never been too strong, but she was becoming nervous out of all proportion to the situation. Her nose began to run, too. Spurlock had dealt with junkies enough to know that it wouldn't be too much longer before she excused herself, and if he ever wanted to make sense to her it was either going to be now or wait several hours. He glanced at Megan again. He was depending on her now, because he didn't trust his judgment completely in this situation.

"What do the children want?" Megan asked. It seemed a sensible enough question. Spurlock hoped they would want to come, because that would make it a lot easier, but he didn't care, they were coming anyway.

He looked at the children and tried to smile, making a horrible botch of it, he was sure. "How about it, kids? You want to go to Arkansas?"

Leslie looked up from the position she had finally chosen, sitting cross-legged on the floor. "What's in Arkansas?" she inquired cynically.

Spurlock was unprepared to go into a sales pitch. "Trees, hills, horses, and hard work," he said.

Leslie brightened slightly at the mention of trees, hills, and horses, but her face fell at the hard work part. It made no difference to Spurlock. He was tired of messing around and he wanted to get this show on the road. He would drag them back, herd them back at gunpoint if necessary, or knock them out and carry them if he had to. He had been under a big strain for a long time and he was turning into the old Frank Spurlock. He was nobody to mess with.

"You'll like it, honey," Megan put in. "It's much freer and safer than here. You'll probably have your own horse to ride, and yes, we do have to work hard, but I bet you'll find it a lot more fun that scuffling in the city. I came there from Miami, Florida, and that's a better place than here. My son, Jon, and I like Purgatory much better."

Leslie gave a little shrug. "Sure, I got nothing to lose."

"Leslie!" her mother exclaimed," but she said nothing more.

"How about you, kid?" Spurlock asked Mako. Even he thought of him as Mako now.

The boy looked at Spurlock with something akin to longing in his face. Then he looked at his mother, who was looking at Spurlock with undisguised loathing and hatred. It hurt Spurlock to see it.

Mako looked back at Spurlock sadly. "I gotta stay here with Mom," he said. "She needs me, and the Izods need me."

Linda seemed to gather strength from the boy's reply. She pressed her mouth into a prim line and said, "That's right, Mark, and Leslie's staying, too. Let's hear no more about it." She sighed and looked at Spurlock in a kindly fashion. "Will you have more tea?" she inquired.

"Linda," Spurlock insisted, "the children are leaving here with me in ten minutes, with or without your consent. Are you coming?" These words had a hard, bitter edge.

Wordlessly Linda rose and left the room. There was the sound of a drawer opening and closing, and a second later she returned with a .32-caliber automatic pistol in her hand. Gripping it in both hands, she leveled it in Spurlock's direction and fired five shots in rapid succession into the wall over his left shoulder.

He watched her do it with a curious sense of detachment. He heard the rounds snap in his left ear and got an incredible adrenaline rush from that. He turned and looked at the holes over his left shoulder.

Linda gasped at him, apparently unable to believe that he had not crumpled into a neat ball at her feet. Megan got up and removed the pistol from her hand.

"I hope you feel better now," Spurlock said. "Would you like to go pack?"

An utterly baffled look came over Linda's face and she crumpled to the floor in a faint.

Mako immediately went to her side. He knelt, then turned to Spurlock and said, "Do something!"

"Get her a glass of water," Spurlock said, and the kid headed for the kitchen.

Leslie regarded him with equanimity. She was a tough little cookie. Spurlock rose and went to Linda's side. She had little color in her cheeks, but her pulse was okay. He grabbed the cushion off the chair she had been seated on and elevated her feet. A couple of seconds later her eyelids fluttered open.

"Frank," she said weakly, "I can't leave, Frank. I can't go back to Purgatory. I'll die there. I hate that place." She reached up and grabbed his shirt, pleading. "Oh, Frank," she was crying, "don't take my babies. I love them and I need them so. Frank, can't you just go away?"

Spurlock sat down cross-legged beside her and took her hand. "Honey," he said, and then caught himself and said nothing for a while, because it was all wrong. "I can't leave them here," he said finally. "Jesus, do you want this place to do to them what it did to you?"

Mako knelt and took his mother's other hand. "I won't leave you, Mom."

Linda brightened at this. "I know you won't, darling," she said, and squeezed his hand.

Spurlock was nonplussed. It would be pointless and cruel to drag Linda back to Purgatory. She would be utterly miserable there and would simply die. And God help him, he still loved her. But if he took the kids and went, she would die a lot sooner. It was obvious by now that she couldn't make it without them. But to have traveled all this distance and go home without them and to leave them in this miserable place was equally repugnant. No, he would have to stand by his original decision.

He shook his head. "Linda, I've got to take the kids. I just can't let them grow up here."

She sat up wretchedly and started to cry again.

Megan came and gripped his shoulder. "Spurlock, I want to talk to you for a moment."

He nodded and got up.

They walked over by the window. "That poor woman can't handle herself in this city alone and she won't make it in Purgatory either," she said.

Spurlock set his features into a hard mask. "All you're saying is she's done for anyway. I can't consider her. I have to think of the kids and only the kids."

Megan gripped his forearm in her right hand. "The only way you're going to get that boy to Arkansas is to tie him up, and I'll bet you a pretty he'll take off for New York ten minutes after you let him loose."

Spurlock's jaw muscles tightened. Waves of frustration worked through his body, and somewhere back down in his head he was thinking, I don't have to take this shit. I can make it be my way. "I'll just go get him again," he grated.

She gripped his arm harder. "Don't be an asshole," she said. "This is something you can't do anything about. You will have to give them up."

It almost broke him to hear that. The feeling came from deep down in his pride. For years he had carried a nagging feeling of guilt somewhere down in the back of his head. He'd never be rid of it if he left the kids here. There would be a feeling of failure he'd have to carry forever. Almost his total contribution to his children's existence was to screw their mother. It wasn't enough. He cried too much for that to be enough.

And also this was going to be another time that Linda had beat him. She'd beaten him too many times when they were married, she'd beaten him when she left, and now she was beating him again.

He broke away from Megan's grasp and went to the window. He leaned his forehead against the cool glass, heard a staccato rattle of small-arms fire from down in the street. "No deal! They come with me," he said. A funny thing started to happen to him then. He started to cry. He managed to sniffle and cover up the two tears that got started, under the guise of rubbing tired eyes. He was pretty sure he got away with it, too.

He had made the least lousy of two lousy choices, but it still hurt him. He thought of Linda alone here, scuffling, trying to survive, and wondered why he didn't just take the CAR-15 and blow her shit away right then. It would probably be more kind. He got another quick glimpse of how she had been . . . then. He stopped and turned and looked out the window again, then turned and his voice choked as he grinned a twisted grin and said, "It's not as though you'll never see them again. We'll probably look you up every time we come to New York." He laughed and it sounded like machinery stopping.

Linda picked herself up off the floor slowly. She looked like she was starting a cold and getting a nervous breakdown at the same time. "I have to excuse myself for a few minutes," she almost whispered. "Mark, could you help me, please?"

The boy started to get up, but Spurlock shot out, "Nothing doing. You and the kid want to stay, and you might cook up some kind of trouble."

Linda looked at him like he was roaches in her kitchen, then let out a kind of exasperated sigh. "All right, then, sweetlips," she said, "you do it."

He was surprised. He had been so sure that she was going somewhere to plot against him that he wasn't prepared for the possibility that she really had a chore for the kid.

"Mom!" the boy said.

"Don't worry about it," she shot back.

The kid nodded and shrugged.

Spurlock followed her into the back bedroom, alert for another gun or knife, or a surprise blunt instrument. The bedroom had been originally furnished with taste, although with very little money, from a grab bag of thrift shop items, scrounged stuff and leftovers. It gave Spurlock a heavy wrench to see a rug they used to have, and an old red rocking chair with one rocker flattened. He hadn't thought about that chair in years and suddenly the discomfort of it, and the clunk-*clunk*-clunk, clunk-*clunk*-clunk, of trying to rock on that crummy rocker came back to him. Where did it go? he wondered. It was all so beautiful. Where did it go?

Linda did not pause for sentiment. She went directly to the desk by the window and sat down in an old swivel chair with no rollers. She pulled the center drawer open briskly and began to lay out her instruments: a spoon, two small squares of glassine containing what appeared to be a brown powder, cotton, alcohol, and a glass hypodermic syringe with red calibrations on it. She turned and looked at him with hate-filled eyes.

"Take me just a minute to cook," she said matter-of-factly. She turned back to the equipment. Emptying the contents of the bags into the spoon, she added some water from a glass on the table. She stirred the mixture with the plastic cap from her needle. Then she lit a candle and propped the spoon over it, laying it on some books beside the candle. While it cooked she fitted a small ball of cotton over the point of her syringe and carefully drew the mixture into it. She held it up to the light and flicked the glass a couple of times to shake loose any final bubbles, then pressed the air out of the rig.

Holding the syringe in her left hand, she leaned forward in the chair and let her arm dangle down between her legs. She shook her arm vigorously. "Come over here," she commanded.

Numbly he did as he was told. She laid the needle down for a second and grabbed her right arm above the biceps. "You do that!" she said, and let go. He did as she directed, but she wasn't pleased and had to show him twice more before he got it right. "Okay," she nodded, like a surgeon. She took the syringe and carefully put the needle against the purple vein he could barely see showing through her arm. She'd have to be good to hit it.

Her hands made one quick motion and she nodded. She shifted her grip on the rig and drew her blood into it. Spurlock watched closely as the first red swirls mixed with the transparent khaki mixture in the syringe. It occurred to him that this mechanical contrivance was now part of his former beloved's circulatory system. Slowly, and with infinite care, she depressed the plunger, then withdrew the needle.

She laid it down, soaked some cotton in alcohol, and wiped down her arm. Then she drew some water into the needle and shot it straight into Spurlock's face. "Gotcha!" she cried. "You always were a sucker, Franklin." She seemed considerably cheered.

For a second he laughed in spite of himself. "You always were a smartass," he replied.

She drew some more water into the syringe and shot that into a potted plant. "Like to keep m'points clean," she muttered.

Spurlock was impressed. He had never seen a doctor or a nurse give a better injection.

Linda rose, somewhat unsteadily, and stood, a lackadaisical smile spreading over her face. "Well, Frank, old buddy," she said, imitating his Arkie act. He wondered how she could remember it after all this time. "Let's get this show on the road."

She walked unsteadily toward the door. Megan was still seated in her chair, and now Mako stood at the window, watching out with an expression of concern on his face.

But Leslie stood by the door in her Russian peasant outfit, a peasant cap on the back of her head, and a cardboard box with a string around it at her feet. Her mouth was drawn into a very determined line.

Linda smiled, and there was not a trace of sarcasm in it. "Well, darling," she said. "Are you all ready to go?"

Leslie shook her head up and down vigorously, but she blushed at the same time. She forced herself to look straight at her mother.

Linda gathered herself together and managed to glide across the floor. She kissed her daughter on the cheek. "Take care of yourself, darling," she said. "And don't forget to write."

"I won't," Leslie said, suppressing a sniffle. It was a big step for a little girl to take, after all. Spurlock wondered if they knew how hard it would be for a letter to get through, or were they just playing a role?

"I think we'd best be going," Spurlock said.

Mako looked at him warily.

Mako went into the hall, followed by Leslie and Megan. Spurlock turned to leave, then stopped and looked at Linda, and the whole of their marriage flashed in his head again. It came out a lot of sex, screaming, and psychedelics, but he had liked it and she had not, and even though he understood it now, comparing the lives they had each chosen, it still ate his lunch. He thought about kissing her on the cheek for a second, and then realized it had gone too far even for that. Then she did a curious thing. She put her cheek to his, like a plastic celebrity on a TV talk show, and said, "Ciao!" Then she turned to Leslie and in her best Dame Edith Sitwell manner, said, "Good-bye, darling, and God bless."

Spurlock laughed inside. He had always been more amused by her affectations than anything else.

She looked at him and smiled, a slight sardonic smile. He had finally figured out that she was concealing her true emotions, but he didn't know what those emotions were, never had and never would. She had an operative definition of the word "love" that was alien to him.

She closed the door and they stood in the darkened hallway alone.

They clattered down the stairs. A couple of Izods in jeans and sneaks, carrying their new AKs, stood at the door. It suddenly occurred to Spurlock that he really wasn't in any position to dictate terms. Uh-oh, he thought.

"Uh, dad," said Mako.

"Yes, my boy," said his father apprehensively.

"Having you along in Brighton Beach was the greatest thrill of my life, and Ms. Carney probably saved the lives of half the Izods with her pizza scheme, but it's time for you to go, and Les and I aren't going with you." Mako reached out and put his hand on his father's shoulder. "Nobody comes in here or leaves without my say-so, and I say no."

"Speak for yourself, Fuckface," said Leslie, leaning forward with her hands on her hips. "I want out of here, and I want that horse."

Spurlock smiled. String him along till the last minute, he thought, then we'll see how it goes. "Let's discuss this at the van, shall we? I want to see how it survived your young men's guardianship."

Mako smiled back. "It'll be like new," he said, "or there'll be big trouble. I'm glad to see you taking it so well."

"I'm not taking it well at all," Spurlock said. "I just don't see that there's anything I can do about it. I wish to God you'd come with me. I can understand why you don't want to though." He remembered when he'd been wounded in '88 and how he'd talked the doc into letting him go back to his outfit instead of sending him home. Men you've fought with are closer than family, and leaving them feels like treason. "I wish you'd reconsider about

Leslie, though. She doesn't have to stay, and she'd like it out west.''

Mako shrugged. "Mom says no.''

Spurlock grabbed him by the shoulders. '' 'Mom says no!' Goddammit, boy. Your mother is a junkie. She doesn't know what's good for Les any more than she knows what's good for herself.''

He felt the skin crawl on the back of his neck and turned to see two AKs down on him. Their selectors were on full auto and their fingers were on the triggers. Grabbing the president was serious business.

Mako waved them off. "Mom says no," he repeated. "Look, if you and Ms. Carney want to get out of here tonight, we'd better get started. Those fuckers will still have a couple of snipers down the street, and we're gonna have to run, because, let me tell you, Dad, they are gonna be *waitin'* for us.''

"I wanna get out of this neighborhood and start finding some way off this island,'' Spurlock said. It suddenly occurred to him that he was with one of the city's foremost authorities on stuff like that. "Mark, you got any idea how we can get us and the van into Jersey tonight?''

"What's today?'' Mako snapped.

"Thursday, Mako,'' one of his kids answered.

Mako pulled a black plastic notebook out of his hip pocket and leafed through until he found what he was looking for. "You go to the Holland Tunnel tonight about ten, eleven o'clock. It's closed, but still usable, and there's a lot of illicit traffic at night. It's Maf guys that hold it open, and they'll let anybody through for forty thousand.''

Spurlock thought for a moment. "I ain't got any forty thousand.''

Mako grinned. "I'll give you that for a quarter pound of that weed you got in your van. I can move it for twice that.''

Spurlock nodded. "It's a deal," he said. "Let's get to

the van. I'd rather discuss this in the open air, if you don't mind.''

Spurlock and Mako nodded. Leslie grabbed her cardboard box and pouted.

Spurlock paused and looked out the broken window in the door. They couldn't see anybody out there in the street, but that didn't tell them much. The only thing to do was run like hell and hope they made it. All the kids with the automatic weapons were either home asleep or at the hospital in Brighton Beach. The kids in charge of the neighborhood were still armed with their old weapons, and it was no more secure than it had been.

But there were ten Izods standing at the foot of the stoop, younger kids. Mako checked the street, turned to the boys, and said, "Clear the street!"

They rose, exited through the door, paused a moment, and then ran loosely down the street, prepared to fire at anything that moved. Nothing did.

Mark jabbed his thumb at Spurlock. "Me first, women in the middle, you bring up the rear. Zigzag a little and run like the wind." And he was out the door and gone.

The two women hesitated a second. "Do it!" Spurlock commanded, and they were pell-mell out the door, running pretty fast, but Spurlock had to hold back to keep from passing them, which, considering the reason they were running, made him very uptight. He kept looking over his shoulder for snipers, ready to fire a suppressive burst from his CAR-15. But there were no snipers. Instead, looking over his left shoulder, Spurlock ran into a pile of garbage.

He fell down in the fragrant mess, muttered unintelligible curses, picked himself up and ran on, brushing coffee grounds off his knees, running like a bull ape and cursing the weight of his gun and ammo.

Eventually, though, they rounded the corner to the van, which, surprisingly enough, sat exactly as they had left it, with two teenage boys with carbines guarding it. The other kids, the ones who had run interference for them, were lounging in doorways, exactly as they had been before. Spurlock and party stopped to breathe for a few seconds. Mako, however, resumed his air of authority and walked to the two boys guarding the van. "Any trouble?" he demanded.

The kid who seemed to be in charge said, "No problems, Mako."

The van was intact. That took a lot more discipline than Spurlock would have expected from a street gang, even after yesterday. They had shown themselves to be brave, but not particularly honest.

Spurlock wanted time to formulate his pitch to Mako, to see if he could get him to change his mind and let Leslie go. He felt like an idiot after all that bluster back in the apartment, just assuming he had authority, when he had never established authority with the kid. "I'm going to clean the van out and get it ready to go," he said.

"I'll help." Megan climbed into the back of the van and Spurlock followed. They'd cleaned up before they left the medicine show, but it was a mess again.

Spurlock found a cardboard box that he started putting trash into. "I'm about half glad we're not taking that little son of a bitch back to Purgatory," he said with a strong note of pride. "Did you see the way he handled those punks out there? He'd be giving either me or Frazier a run for our jobs a month after we got home."

Megan was shaking out the sleeping bags and piling them in the corner, folded neatly into squares and stacked. Spurlock put the box with the weed in it next to the door. Next to that he put the box of grenades and .223 ammo.

It set him to thinking, seeing all that stuff stacked up there. He'd used his gun on the way up, but for some reason he didn't have the same feeling about the trip back that he'd had coming up. He'd made the trip so far without personally killing anybody, and he expected to make it back without killing anybody. He had earned the right to travel without guns.

He still felt bad about not being able to contribute anything more to Mako's upbringing. But Spurlock had learned that you frequently didn't have to be there every day to get the job done. The important thing was to be there at the right time with the right stuff.

And while Spurlock had apparently worked off his killing karma, Mako obviously had not. He hopped out of the van and unloaded the ammo and grenades and stood there with his prized scope-sighted CAR-15 slung at his side. He carefully unbuckled the .357 magnum at his hip and threw it on the pile at his feet. Then, on impulse, he got two pounds of marijuana and threw that on top, too.

"Hey, kid!" he called to Mako, who was standing there, jawing to Leslie.

"Yeah!" Mako called, and started over. He stood cockily in front of his father. Spurlock swung the assault rifle off his shoulder and holding it by the barrel, handed it stock-first to his son. "Here, kid," he said, and kicked the pile of stuff with his toe. "Build yourself an empire."

Mako grinned. The CAR-15 didn't have the value it had yesterday, but it was still rare; it had class. It was American. And it had belonged to his father.

Maybe that fact would temper his use of it.

Spurlock smiled gently. He wasn't at all sure he was doing the right thing, but his son was fighting a perpetual war in the streets, and if he was going to do it anyway, he might as well have the stuff to do it right. "If you're smart," he said carefully to the kid, "you'll use this very sparingly. If you don't, I predict an early demise for you. No shit, kid, be careful with it."

Mako nodded quickly, but his eyes were elsewhere. "Yeah, right!" he said in a tone that made Spurlock question his own judgment.

In the background of his thoughts there was the thrumming of an internal combustion engine, but he paid no attention to it—until he heard a familiar voice say, "Y'all want a ride?"

He looked up to see a long black Mercedes limousine, driven by a uniformed guard, with another beside him in the shotgun seat. They were dressed in the same outfits that good old Clarence had worn in Purgatory. But the thing that held his attention was the sight of his old friend Captain Frazier in the back seat.

His hair and beard were neatly trimmed, though still long. Spurlock had never seen him look that way before—almost didn't recognize him, as a matter of fact. He also wore a gray Maf uniform. All in all he looked very little like the Captain Frazier of old. Of course, the AK-47 he had pointed at them was the same, and that was a dead giveaway.

CHAPTER FOURTEEN

"HI THERE, Frazier," Spurlock said. "How'd you happen to come to the big town?"

"All y'all climb in this Mercedes here," Frazier said, "and nobody'll get hurt."

The gunsel in the Mercedes had the drop on everybody visible in the street. Spurlock shrugged. "Okay, children," he said resignedly. "I don't see that we've got a whole lot of choice but to do what he says."

Mako looked at his little pile of empire-building material, seeing his dreams of glory going down the drain. He looked at Spurlock and grinned a show-off grin. "No fucking way!" he said.

Frazier favored the kid with exasperated condescension. "Anybody not in the car in one minute gets his ass blowed off, kid. You better do like old Spurlock says."

Mako grinned in Frazier's face. "If you fire one round, you'll be dead two seconds later," he said tonelessly. "I've got this place covered with six snipers."

Frazier opened the door and climbed out. "Your minute's about up," he said menacingly.

"Take out his headlights," Mako called. Six shots rang out from six different directions and three of Frazier's four headlights disappeared in explosions of sharded glass. The little captain jumped about a foot. "Jesus!" he said.

"Maybe we better talk this one over," Spurlock put in.

Recovering his composure, Frazier shrugged. "It don't matter that much. I can bottle this area up and keep you here forever."

Mako laughed. "Oh, Brer Bear, don't throw me in the briar patch."

Frazier jerked his thumb at Spurlock. "It's not you I want, kid. It's him. My boss needs to talk to him."

Spurlock nodded. "And I need to talk to your boss, at least eventually, and I can't afford to be stuck here forever. Lay off these people and I'll go with you. The rest stay here, and I'll come back for them later."

Privately he put his chances of living to come for them at least three to one against, but he didn't want to say that. But with him gone Megan might have a chance to make it back to Purgatory. He turned to her. "If I'm not back in five days, you take the van and start back for Purgatory, okay?"

Megan pursed her lips and shook her head. "Where you go, I go," she said. "What's the matter with you, Spurlock? You've been trying to shake me ever since we started this trip."

Spurlock shrugged. "I just keep trying to save your life and you insist on trying to lose it."

"I'm going, too," Leslie insisted. "I don't care what anybody says. I'm not staying here another day!"

"No!" Mark exploded.

"Shuddup, kid," Spurlock snapped. "Nobody gets it all." He turned to Frazier. "You reckon Senigliero will let them go if he has me done in?"

Frazier favored him with an elaborate shrug. "Beats me," he replied.

Spurlock grimaced. "Thanks a lot, Frazier. You're a big help." Logic would indicate that the best thing would be to stay here, bide his time, and try to fight his way out, but that was a dead end. He couldn't make it back to Purgatory with the Maf after him, and he'd just have to fight another war if he did. But he might bluff and sweet-talk his way out if he went to Senigliero. Probably not, but maybe. But he didn't want Megan and Leslie killed.

Once again logic wasn't going to tell him what to do. He tried to clear his mind and fish for an answer beyond himself. He turned and grabbed his son and hugged him. The kid looked surprised and then hugged him back. "Keep your ass down, kid," Spurlock said.

Mako's eyes were wet, but no tears escaped them, and he wore a grin. "I'd say the same to you, but *your* ass is out a mile."

Spurlock nodded. "It always seems to be," he said. "But I make out okay."

The kid nodded. "I hope it's hereditary," he said.

Mako and Leslie hugged each other one last time. Megan started to give the boy an honorary family-type buss on the cheek, but instead planted a big wet smack full on his lips. Her eyes flicked to the weapons Spurlock had left the boy. "You will have to learn the quality of mercy," she said.

The kid looked surprised for a second, then nodded seriously, then grinned, but didn't say anything. Once again Spurlock felt that in one stroke Megan had justified her coming on this trip.

Spurlock ushered his daughter and his lady into the back of the limo. Frazier kept his AK on them as they climbed in. Then he handed it to one of the goons in the front seat and piled in with them. He unsnapped a fold-down seat across the spacious passenger compartment and settled in comfortably.

As they drove off, Spurlock waved to his son, who

stood with the CAR-15 slung over his shoulder, a proprietary foot on his ammo, waving.

"So you took Senigliero's offer," Spurlock said to Frazier. He was disappointed in him. Bad as he was, Spurlock had always thought his first loyalty was to his dream of restoring the United States of America to its former glory, whatever it was that Frazier conceived of that having been.

Spurlock had always thought of Frazier's mind as being full of psychedelic red, white, and blue bunting, and weird eagles flying around with arrows in both claws and a banner in the beak that said "Don't Mess with Me!" Frazier knew less about history, economics, and political science than Spurlock knew about the ballet.

All he knew was to follow the flag and kill people, but he had taken incredible pride in an army that had never been defeated in the field, debatable as that claim might be, and when the United States surrendered in the Middle East he had just totally freaked out, could not accept it, and decided that he and the other guerrillas were the "true" representatives of the United States, and the government in Washington was a bunch of quisling traitors. He might be a bandit to the rest of the world, but to himself he was George Fucking Washington, with a Russian assault rifle.

The last thing Spurlock had expected of him was to hire on as a gunsel for the mob. Spurlock was really disappointed. "I never expected you to do that," he said.

Frazier grinned, shrugged, and winked. "All part of the long-range plan," he said, but it didn't look like Frazier's old plan to Spurlock. The whole thing was so incongruous that Spurlock simply didn't accept it. There was more going on in this arrangement than met the eye.

"I been sleepin' on the ground for ten years, babe. An army cot woulda been luxury. Now me and my boys are sleepin' on silk sheets and eatin' off bone china. If you can't lick 'em join 'em . . . right?"

Spurlock shrugged.

Frazier looked at Spurlock very seriously. "That would be my advice to you, compadre. You'll never keep those guys out of Purgatory. You might as well hang it up and save what you can for yourself. Nobody'll blame you. Shoot! You might go and get elected to Congress." This last was said with such a cynical, lopsided smile that Spurlock laughed in spite of himself.

"What do you think my chances are?" he asked.

Frazier leaned back in the seat. "Well, let's try to define your options, as they used to say at the Pentagon. Option A is you tell Senigliero to go shit in his hat. You do that and he'll probably kill you on the spot, and these two charming ladies too, I imagine." He said this with a sweeping gesture to Megan and Leslie.

"That has a rather limited appeal," Spurlock said with a wry quirk to his mouth.

Frazier nodded as the limo dozed its way through the vacant streets of late afternoon Manhattan. "Wait'll you hear the other one. That is that you fall all over yourself to kiss Senigliero's ass, promise absolute cooperation, beg his forgiveness, and promise to give him everything he wants if he'll just let you live."

Spurlock felt as though he were about to throw up. "What happens then?" he demanded.

Frazier shrugged. "Oh, probably the same as if you go the other way. But who knows? He might just keep you around as an exhibit. After all, you embarrassed him in public, and he's such a sensitive little nerd that his nerves are just raw all the time. On top of that you waxed his two best hit men out there in Illinois, and he don't like that very much either. So he may have decided that killin's too easy for you. He may want to keep you around for a while, just to watch you crawl. He may even let you stay on as sheriff of Purgatory, just so you can see how he fucks the place up. The man doesn't like you, Spurlock.

You're not going to like it very much no matter how it ends up.'' There was a suggestion of a bitter smile playing around Frazier's mouth.

The limo pulled onto a private ferry dock and drove onto the boat without stopping. Immediately the ramp was pulled aboard and all lines were cast off for the sail to Jersey.

Spurlock sat lost in thought halfway across the foul and fetid water. Then he looked up, frowned, and ran his tongue around the inside of his mouth nervously. ''Well, old buddy,'' he said. ''I hate to impose on a friendship of long standing, but why don't you just let us hop out on the other side and hitch back to Purgatory?''

Frazier laughed out loud. ''Whether I wanted to or not, them two goons up there''—he nodded toward the two guards in the front, on the other side of the glass partition—''would blow the whistle on me in a minute. You'll notice that Senigliero didn't send me to get you with two of my own people. If I let you off, we'd have to kill them and I'd have to go with you, and I'm not about to blow this deal to save your ass, so you can forget it.''

Spurlock nodded. ''So your recommendation is Option B,'' he said.

''Looks to me like the onliest chance you got.''

''Yeah,'' Spurlock muttered. ''Well, if you really think that's all the chance I got, then that explains why I whipped your ass in the guerrilla wars.'' He scrunched down in the seat as far as he could and attempted to clear his mind.

No one spoke after that. Leslie said nothing at all. She merely gave him a look of mingled confidence, admiration, and doubt. Ambiguous was the word for it. But she had high hopes, having read a number of romantic novels, and knowing full well that the good guys always win.

''Road seems unusually well maintained,'' Spurlock said.

''All the big shots live up here,'' Frazier replied.

They bored along on an almost deserted eight-lane divided highway, and the countryside around them was quite beautiful in most places. They passed a couple of small cities that were the same kind of garbage heaps New York was, only smaller, and finally drove off into a little town that seemed to be a carefully preserved replica of an old New England fishing village. It looked rich and quaint.

Then they were through the town and back out in open country. Beautiful country, full of old stately trees, stone fences, and fine old mansions. The roads were still well maintained and wound around through the trees to make a very pleasant drive. It would, of course, have been more pleasant if they had not been prisoners on their way to execution, but, Spurlock reflected, you have to take the bad with the good.

The house, when they finally turned into it, was an old villa of the Bauhaus School. The boxiness of the architecture was mitigated by the free use of stone, and the total effect was very pleasant. He was fairly sure that the execution would not be consummated here. Surely Senigliero wouldn't want bloodstains on these fine old flagstones.

Frazier reclaimed his AK from the goon in the right front seat and led them up the flagstone walk to the house. Spurlock had never been much of an admirer of Bauhaus, because it was so blatantly geometric, but this home had been softened by stone construction and well-laid-out shrubs and trees. It was quite graceful.

The goons from the limo disappeared somewhere, probably into the servants' entrance. Senigliero was the sort of clown who would have a servants' entrance. Frazier rang; the door was quickly opened by a short black man wearing a white jacket and a fake smile. Frazier and the black conferred briefly in low voices. Then Frazier turned to Spurlock and his two ladies.

"Mr. Senigliero says that you all are to have the freedom of the house and grounds, but if you attempt to leave, you will be, uh, detained." Frazier allowed a grin at that.

"We're having guests for dinner tonight, and you are all invited.

"C'mon," Frazier continued, "I'll show you to your room."

Spurlock shook his head. He had expected they would be thrown into a dungeon, clapped in irons, with the torture to begin immediately. He wasn't sure, but there was some possibility that before it was all over he would wish they had been. At the very head of all things he distrusted was kindness from the Mafia.

Frazier handed his AK to the butler, or whatever the hell he was, turned and led them down a hall, up some stairs and to a small suite of two bedrooms and a sitting room, all furnished in a style that offended Spurlock with its opulence.

He was in no mood to stand on ceremony at that time, however. He spun around on his toes while flying across the room, and sank down on the bed, meanwhile sighing, "Lord!"

Megan looked at him with some irritation, then turned to Frazier and said, "We can't go to dinner like this. We've been in these clothes for three days. We need a bath. This has all been rather a strain."

Frazier grinned at her. "Well, ma'am," he said, "we've laid on some clothes for you and old Spurlock because you were expected. You got an hour or so for a bath. We don't have fresh clothes for the young lady, but then she hasn't been on the road, either."

Spurlock, lying on the bed, heard all this as though it were a buzzing in the background. He had never been so tired. He had a headache. Every muscle in his body felt like a too-tight piano wire. "Hey, Frazier," he moaned, "I don't want to sound crabby or nothin', but I sure don't want to go to any dinner party. I don't even want to move."

Frazier, leaning against the door, yawned and said,

"Me neither, old buddy, but it's been my experience that when Senigliero issues an invitation, the best thing is to accept. Otherwise the next one is apt to be to your own beheading."

Spurlock nodded. "Yeah, I can see where that might be. Okay, we'll go."

Frazier smiled. "I'll come get you when it's time." He disappeared.

"Anybody wants to bathe first," Spurlock moaned from the bed, "go on ahead. I just wanna lie here for a minute." He supposed Megan and Leslie reached some sort of arrangement about bathing, but he paid it no mind. His original plan was to rest, or meditate, or to plan his next move, but none of that happened. What happened is that he went fast asleep, flat on his back with his feet still on the floor, still in his boots, still in his clothes, hat beside him on the bed.

He was awakened a little later when Megan shook his shoulder. "You've got twenty minutes to get ready," she said. "Wait'll you see the bathroom. It's a sybarite's dream."

"It's just gorgeous," Leslie agreed. "I've never seen anything like it."

The sheriff opened one eye to see his daughter in her Russian clothes, but scrubbed and glowing. She was quite a fetching young lady. Unless he missed his guess, she was also what they used to call a hot little number. He thought of her living in the same house as Jon and grinned. He and Megan might have to do a little counseling. Funny, he was thinking as though they were going to make it back, and no odds maker would even consider such a proposition. Ah, well.

Without moving from that wonderful, soft bed, he kicked his boots off and eased his socks off with his toes, immediately becoming aware that his feet could use some soap and water. He unbuttoned his shirt and only then stood up to start dragging his clothes off. He was down to just his pants when he lurched and staggered into the bathroom.

He was completely unable to assimilate that bathroom. He was assaulted by an impression of glossy green flatness and shiny chrome. The bathroom was about the size of the living room at the farm, and he had a feeling he had stumbled onto the set of a Busby Berkeley, or Berkeley Busby, or whatever, musical. "Lord, will you look at this mother!" he exclaimed. It made his body seem twice as grimy to look at all that gleaming tile. He immediately shucked out of his pants and sat down to take a luxurious crap, finding, as always, that his bowels had moved better squatting in the woods.

The shower that followed was a sort of gleaming dream. He hadn't seen Crane plumbing in eight years. Now that he thought about it, he hadn't seen any sort of commercial plumbing in about five. He laughed out loud as soap and hot, hot water cut through the greasy crud on his body. He practically sanded himself with a fluffy green washcloth, the like of which he hadn't seen since he ran away from home at fifteen.

His body was still tense and nervous when he got out of the shower. He would have given anything to be able to do a full hour-and-a-half yoga set. Megan sat at a lady's vanity table, putting on makeup from a stock she had found in a drawer. "I never saw you do that before," he said.

She shook her hair at him. "When in Rome . . ." she said. "Look in the closet."

Spurlock did so, his eyes opening wide. "Oh, mother . . . !" he cried. "Oh, shit! I'm not gonna wear that." There was one complete costume in the closet: dress trousers, a black velvet dinner jacket with red piping at the cuffs and lapel, and black patent-leather pumps with red velvet bows. A white linen ruffled shirt hung beside the jacket, with a black bow tie—a regular tie, not the clip-on kind—draped around it. The studs and links were on a dresser top beside the closet.

He shook his head. "I ain't believin' this."

"You better believe it," said Frazier's voice from the door. "You also better get in it. You're gonna be late, and believe me that's not going to go over very well."

"I'll wear my regular clothes then," Spurlock muttered.

Megan frowned at him over her shoulder. "You better smell them first."

He knew when he was licked. "Okay, okay!" he muttered, and started to get dressed.

As soon as Spurlock was ready, they got Leslie from her room and the three of them swept down the stairs at the head of their escort.

There was a cocktail party going on in the living room, the guests being dressed very much like Megan and Spurlock, except that most of them, both men and women, had their hair cut modishly short. The horrible zoolike roar of cocktail party conversation rushed out to meet them.

Spurlock's eyes quickly noted a discrepancy between this and the average office Christmas party. There was a uniformed goon at every means of entrance and egress from the room: hallway, doors, and windows. Each guard carried a slung M-16 and an ammo belt with two pouches, enough for eighty or a hundred rounds each, and each man also carried two grenades, which Spurlock thought indicated an unprofessional disdain for the welfare of one's guests.

Surely that's not so Megan and I won't escape, he thought. These assholes must be terrified of each other.

He made another quick sweep of the room and noted two things. None of the guests were packed, their dinner jackets being worn snug that season, and there were no bulges at the waist or under anybody's armpit. Then he picked out two exceptions, hard-faced young men in identical rent-a-tuxes with no expression on their faces and the bulges of large-caliber automatics conspicuous under their coats. There was one each of these guys at Senigliero's right and left rear. Senigliero spotted them at the head of the staircase and surged through the crowd, guards in his wake, making every person in the room readjust his position to accommodate their passage. There were five or six big-screen TVs in the room, all simultaneously showing *La Traviata* so Senigliero could follow it no matter where he looked.

Senigliero emerged from the crowd with his hand extended. He grabbed Spurlock's paw and pumped up and down with a great show of friendliness. "Ah, Spurlock, good to s-see you again at long l-last. You certainly gave my p-people a merry chase . . . and disposed of my two b-best assassins. Naughty! Naughty!" Senigliero clucked nervously. "Well, enjoy yourselves tonight, and we-we'll talk about it t-tomorrow." He favored Spurlock with a shark's grin and disappeared into the mob. Everybody shifted position again.

Megan looked at Spurlock. "So that's him. What is that man doing? I don't know what to think. I don't even know how to feel."

Spurlock had felt awkward, tired, and scared until the meeting with the Maf don, but his metabolism was a strange one, and things that were supposed to frighten him often had the opposite effect, a jolt of adrenaline both energizing and calming his thought processes, so that he functioned better than normally. He grinned at her, his old confident grin that he had not worn in many days, not since Illinois.

Certainly he had not grinned like that in New York. The place was alien to him, and the situation had not been one with which he was prepared by temperament or training to deal. But this—hell, people had been attempting to terrify him with threats for years. Not that he was making light of the situation. This was the tightest scrape he had ever been in.

Megan looked at him as though she were about to cry, as though she were saying good-bye, as though it were all over.

"Look happy!" he snapped. "I don't want that shithead to think he's got us buffaloed. First off, if you get out of here knowing I only crawled to get you and Leslie out, I already beat him at *that* game. Second, I haven't decided to do it yet. That's the only advantage I have. I don't know what's going to happen, and he thinks he does. That means he can be surprised and I can't." He smiled and put his hand on her arm.

A jacketed waiter came by with a tray of drinks. He paused in front of Spurlock and Megan. She reached up and quickly snatched a martini off the tray. "Drink, sir?" the waiter inquired.

"Yeah," Spurlock replied. "You got any ginger ale?"

The waiter gave him a shocked look. "I'll see, sir," he said, and disappeared into the crowd again.

"So what you want to do," he said, smiling and gripping Megan's arm, "is drift into this crowd and make pleasant cocktail party chatter and smile. Don't let that bastard think you're scared."

She managed a brave grin. "I'll try," she replied. Then she smiled bigger. "And later tonight I'll cast a spell to stop him."

Somewhere in the back of Spurlock's mind he caught a thought before it became words. He was about to tell Megan to drop it, to butt out of his showdown. The old macho demon dies hard. He just grinned. After all, they were both using different techniques to marshal the same cosmic forces. And indeed it was not his showdown, nor hers. They had both been brought here by the same agency, as Senigliero had been brought here by that to which he gave his ultimate allegiance, and the real showdown was between those forces. He had no right to keep her out. Keeping her out was an ego maneuver, and therefore a loser's maneuver.

And what of Frazier? What force had brought him here? Frazier, he decided, was a wild card.

"Atta girl," he replied.

She shook her head. "If I can get something of his, a cut of his hair or a fingernail clipping, anything. That'll be a start."

"Good luck," he said, pleased that she had found something to occupy her thoughts. She disappeared into the crowd, smiling radiantly all around.

There was something a little odd about the way this crowd moved. And it had to do with the atmosphere of the gathering. He made a serious effort to close off his thoughts and soak up the atmosphere of the place. This crowd had an aura of fear. No question about it. You could almost smell it. These people were smiling and milling and talking, but they were all talking too fast and nobody was listening to anybody.

Almost anytime Senigliero moved, the entire room readjusted itself, not just in the wake of three people moving in unison, but instantaneously everybody shifted so they could keep their eyes on him. Spurlock remembered Clarence and realized why. It was because Senigliero was apt to execute anybody at any time. He shuddered slightly. How could a guy like that keep people working for him?

Ah, he thought, big payoff. This guy pays people more money than they ever dreamed of before. So much that they don't even realize that they aren't happy.

Looking at them, that's what he saw, a lot of really ugly, unhappy pugs. If Senigliero was famous for instantaneous total retribution, though, he must have attracted a lot of attempted hits. That was the reason for the heavy security. Senigliero had no reason to trust these people and no regard for them. He was a surfer on a wave of terror, betting his skill in manipulating people's weaknesses against the almost universal loathing he inspired. He must be some smart son of a bitch, Spurlock thought, and that's the reason for this vendetta. This man perceives anything less than total control of anything or anybody he meets as a threat. .

It was then he realized that Senigliero had him outclassed. He was smarter, stronger, and in total control of the situation. The only thing Spurlock had going for him was that he was a nicer person, and, really, he failed to see how that was relevant.

It was at that moment that Senigliero really got to him. Senigliero was the master of terror, and the first real wave of it that Spurlock had felt in many years rolled over him, chilling him; his knees went weak, an icicle grew in his belly. He was so scared . . . he wanted something to hold on to. He wanted his mama.

It almost got him. Senigliero's party almost served its purpose, but Spurlock knew how to handle it. Be here now, he thought. It's not happening now except in your mind. Be here now. This fear has no utility. Be here now. The most he can do to you is pain and death, and what is life but pain ending in death? So it does. Be here now; enjoy the party. Be here now.

He suddenly found himself face-to-face with a little old lady who was the only other person in the room who wasn't scared besides him and Megan. He had been scared, but he had decided not to be, and this lady appeared and she wasn't. Even Senigliero was scared, all right, else why all the guards, and with good reason. That's two points of advantage, he thought. We're nice and we're not afraid. Us and this little old lady here.

She was an elderly lady in a pale blue dress with hair to match. But she held herself proudly, like a much younger woman, and her smile was genuine, unafraid, and refresh-

ing. "Good evening," she said pleasantly. "Are you related to the Seniglieros?"

"No, ma'am," he replied in his best shitkicker accent.
"Do Ah look like it?"

She smiled. "You remind me of old Amadeo. You look
aggressive enough"—she paused—"and intense enough,
but I judge from your accent that you're from out west."

"Yes, ma'am," he replied. "I'm Frank Spurlock from
Purgatory, Arkansas."

"How do you do?" she replied, and extended a small
hand with a spray of liver spots on it. She was a pleasant,
kindly-looking lady, the type he automatically typed as the
protected wife of the successful businessman. She seemed
disdainful of her surroundings.

"I'm Madelaine Carstairs. My husband is in gambling
in Michigan." She spoke as though Spurlock were expected to know the name.

"I'm the sheriff back home," Spurlock replied pleasantly.

One of her eyebrows shot up at this information. "Oh,"
she said, equally pleasantly, with no trace of condescension. "Are you here to accept a bribe?"

The waiter arrived at this point with his tray. "Your
ginger ale, sir," he said, the slightest hint of a sneer in his
voice. Spurlock smiled at that and accepted his drink.

"Would madame care for a drink?" the waiter asked.

"Martini, very dry," she said, without looking directly
at the waiter. He handed her one and disappeared.

"No, ma'am," Spurlock replied to her question. "Me
and my lady and my daughter, we're prisoners here." He
sipped his ginger ale.

She sniffed and examined his outfit. "Rather better than
your jail, I should imagine."

Spurlock smiled. He liked Mrs. Carstairs. "No question
about that, ma'am. I don't much like being a prisoner, but
this is definitely a gilded cage."

She tapped out a cigarette and looked at Spurlock as
though expecting him to light it for her.

He shrugged and said, "Sorry, no fire."

She sighed. A hand attached to a lighter shot out of the mob and lit it for her. It was attached to Senigliero's arm. "Good eve-evening, Madelaine," he said. "Are you entertaining Mr. Spur-spurlock?"

Mrs. Carstairs returned Senigliero's smile with one of her own, a purely social one that did not reach the eyes. "I should say rather that he's entertaining me. I never met a sheriff from Arkansas before, except John Wayne in *True Grit*."

Senigliero's smile broadened as his eyes narrowed into little snake eyes. "How p-pleasant for you."

"He played a U.S. marshal, ma'am," Spurlock corrected. "Different service."

Senigliero turned his attention to Spurlock. "Have you any i-idea why your woman wants to get cl-close to me? She's been circling like Indians around a w-w-w-w-wagon train. My b-bodyguard keeps sort of heading her off, b-because she's got this terribly d-determined look about her."

Spurlock laughed. "Beats me. Maybe she wants your autograph."

Senigliero grinned and shrugged. "I d-doubt it," he sneered. "Well, maybe she'll get it tomorrow, whatever it is."

Spurlock grinned and shrugged. "Tomorrow is always a surprise," he snapped.

"Tomorrow," Senigliero said, "I th-think the s-surprise will be yours."

Spurlock laughed again. "If that were true it wouldn't be much of a surprise now, would it?"

Senigliero looked away quickly. "I s-see someone across the room," he said, and disappeared.

"What do you expect to happen to you tomorrow?" Mrs. Carstairs interjected.

Spurlock shrugged. "I'll probably be tortured and killed."

Mrs. Carstairs looked concerned. "Oh, that's terrible," she said. "Isn't there anything you can do?"

"Crawl," he said. "But I won't because I think he'd enjoy it, and then kill me anyway and enjoy that."

She took a sip of her drink. "You're not just teasing me, are you? You don't look terribly concerned."

He smiled. "I'm concerned, all right, but it wouldn't do me any good to get scared."

She smiled wanly. "I suppose not, if you have that kind of control over your emotions. Will your wife and daughter be tortured and killed, too?"

Spurlock shook his head. "Not if I control my emotions."

"So you have an incentive."

"Yes, ma'am. I have all the incentive in the world."

She took his hand and looked squarely into his eyes. "I have faith in you, young Mr. Sheriff."

Out of the corner of his eye, Spurlock caught a glimpse of Megan chatting with Frazier. He grinned, never having seen them close together before. Megan was half a head taller than Frazier.

They walked over to where Spurlock and Mrs. Carstairs stood. As they approached he heard Megan say, "If we're good, tomorrow's the best chance you're ever going to get."

"Best chance to what?" Spurlock asked, although in truth he knew. Frazier would never be content to be Senigliero's flunky for long.

Megan smiled beguilingly at Spurlock. "Best chance to see some high-grade witchcraft. I got what I wanted from Senigliero."

"That's great," Spurlock replied as Frazier spun off into the crowd, not wanting to be seen talking too long with the pariahs. Mrs. Carstairs seemed to be the only one with guts to do that. He introduced her to Megan.

"Senigliero was here a minute ago," Spurlock went on,

"and asked me what you were stalking him for. He said you couldn't get close to him."

She laughed a silvery, confident laugh and put her hand on his wrist. "I got something better than hair or fingernails," she said. "I got his number."

Mrs. Carstairs smiled as though she knew everything.

Spurlock started to ask Megan what she meant, then decided he was better off not knowing. So he joined her in her laughter.

Senigliero's terrorized courtiers looked at them in amazement. Even Senigliero looked, with the first glimmering of doubt in his eyes.

At that point the majordomo, or butler, or whatever the hell he was, came out and tinkled a little silver bell. "Dinner is served," he announced.

Spurlock held out both his arms. "May I escort both you ladies to dinner?"

"Why, thank you, Sheriff," said Mrs. Carstairs. "I'd be delighted."

CHAPTER FIFTEEN

THE DINNER made Spurlock reflect on the banality of evil. The clowns were killers, all right, but for the most part they were dullards, uninteresting except for Senigliero and Mrs. Carstairs. If the truth were told, he'd almost rather Purgatory be overrun by junkies, whores, and gamblers than these klutzes. It was a complete mystery to him how Frazier could endure even a week in Senigliero's employ.

He managed to get through dinner by chatting amiably with Megan, Mrs. Carstairs, and the clown at the end of the table who was a Mafia accountant obsessed with the notion that his life had been ruined by attendance at parochial schools.

As soon as the dessert course was completed, Senigliero stood up and dinged his glass with his knife. "Ladies and g-gentlemen, I'd like to introduce our g-guest of honor this evening. Frank S-spurlock, the sheriff of Purgatory County, Arkansas, one-one of the last p-places in the country we don't control, and the n-next to f-fall. A few days ago I m-made Sheriff Spurlock a m-most generous offer, which

297

he ch-chose to reject. He is our guest here tonight to s-see how it could have been had he ch-chosen to accept.

"A-all the gentlemen here present are invited to see his f-farewell appearance tomorrow, when he l-learns wh-what happens to those who oppose us. The ladies, except his, of course, are excused." He shifted his gaze to Spurlock. "Stand-stand up, Spurlock. Let us see you."

Spurlock rose and nodded to the assemblage.

"S-speech!" Senigliero demanded.

"Hear, hear!" said the accountant. The rest applauded.

So Spurlock laid it out for them. "Yeah!" he said. He swept the room with his hand. "At least this way I get to keep liking myself."

Mrs. Carstairs and Megan applauded warmly. Several others started to join in, rather hesitantly, only to be silenced by a sweep of Senigliero's eyes.

They sat down, Spurlock feeling he might have shot his mouth off too much this time, and Senigliero looked murderous.

As soon as the dinner was over, Senigliero, still furious that Spurlock had lipped off during his speech, came and grabbed him by the arm. He smiled his shark's smile. "Come w-with me for a m-m-minute," he said.

Megan fell in behind them.

Senigliero started to warn her away, then thought the better of it. "Y-yes, m-maybe you should s-s-see this, too. Come along." He led them out of the dining room, through the large room where the party had been, down a long hall, and threw open a double door leading down into darkness.

It was pitch-black down there, but a dark and musty smell, like a tangible presence from some continent of the damned, rolled out to meet them, and a strange mixture of sounds, soft tapping, gentle squeaks, gigantic creaking noises, and the soft croak of geckos.

Spurlock recognized it at once. Senigliero had opened

the door to a jungle. What kind of time-warp magic was this?

Senigliero flipped a switch, lighting a single spot which focused down on a strange apparatus, a chair rigged with straps like an electric chair, but mounted on a long pole which stuck straight out the back like a stiff tail. It was impossible to tell how far the pole went, since it went out of the light from the spotlight, but before it disappeared it passed over a swivel.

And just to the left of the chair Spurlock could see water lapping on the edge of a pool. He saw nothing that looked like jungle, but those sounds and smells continued to assault him.

"D-do you know what tha-that is?" Senigliero demanded.

Spurlock shook his head. "Looks like nothing I ever saw before."

Megan shivered, a shiver that seemed to come from her bones out. "It's a ducking stool," she said.

Senigliero grinned. "D-d-do you know how it w-w-works?"

She nodded. "Very well," she said. "It's a device they used to use around here in the seventeenth century to test for witches. You strap the suspected witch in the chair, swing him or her out over the water, and let the chair down. If the suspect drowns, she is then judged not to have been a witch and given a Christian burial. If the suspect does not drown, she is then burned at the stake."

Senigliero exploded in a guffaw. "R-right!" he laughed. "O-only I do it a little d-differently. I al-almost drown 'em for hours and ow-ow-hours. They can't even in-inhale drown, because I have a p-pulmotor standing by. Tha-that's one of my little sur-surprises. I thought I'd sh-show it t-to you, so-so you'd have s-something to sleep on."

He flipped the switch and shut the door, then strode off down the hall, not looking to see if they followed him or not.

Shortly after, he and Megan managed to slip away from downstairs.

"Where's Leslie?" he inquired as they entered the door of their suite, and he immediately kicked off his patent-leather pumps and began clawing at his bow tie.

Megan was back at the vanity, carefully doing whatever it is that women do to remove their makeup. "She cut the dinner, thank God, and made friends with a teenager who works in the kitchen. The last I saw of her they were sitting on the back steps chugging Mumm's champagne from a bottle."

Spurlock laughed. "Jesus!" he said. "Well, with all those guards around she's safe enough. We might as well let her go ahead and have a good time."

Megan looked at him over her shoulder. "I guess you're not going to be an overly protective father."

He shrugged as he carefully got out of his jacket, hanging the borrowed tux on the rack from which it came. "Hard to say," he replied. "I haven't hardly got into the role yet. I got just about no idea what the father of a teenage girl is supposed to do."

As soon as he was stripped, Spurlock turned and ran at the bed, doing an over-the-shoulder judo fall on it so that he ended up flat on his back with his head at the foot of the bed.

He swung up off the bed and went into the shower, taking his time to be thorough. He spent almost an hour in the shower, shampooing crud out of his hair that ran down over his shoulders in rivulets.

When he got out of the shower, he dried himself carefully, folded the towel carefully. He was doing everything necessary and being careful to do it all right.

Megan was in her robe at the far end of the cavernous room, drawing diagrams in the rug and muttering to herself.

He went into his yoga routine, the first time he'd even tried since they were stalled at the ferry, which, come to think of it, was only day before yesterday. But that hadn't been any good and he hadn't done it for a couple of days before that either. So he was really stiff. He took his time and did almost twice as many exercises as he normally did, and by the time he came out of it he was loose as a goose.

Except for his head, of course. He was still frazzled in his head, worried that he was living out his last evening on earth. He snapped his legs into the full lotus and went into a breathing exercise called the breath of fire, which was sort of like panting through the nose. He did that for about ten minutes. Then he turned his body into a fountain of light, letting the energy flow up through his body, like fine gold dust.

A dozen of those and he was left alone in a world of swirling gold lights and the thoughts that kept coming . . . Senigliero . . . death . . . Purgatory . . . Leslie . . . Linda . . . Mako . . . Megan . . . death . . . Mako . . .

He let them come and they came and went and suddenly he had the feeling of falling backward through a trapdoor, and there were no more thoughts. Then slowly they came swimming back ....
...........Megan ....
...............Leslie..................Death ....
.........................Senigliero ....
..................death ....
....
He fell through another trapdoor..............................
....
.........................Purgatory.....................
....
....
....
....
....

He was keeping his consciousness right up at the top of

his head, and a clear gold light poured down through him from there, clear gold light that was more powerful than any he'd experienced before. It wasn't complete, though. All words were banished but there was still the thought which was more a frown than anything else, a thought of dissatisfaction with himself, a sort of cosmic frown in his head. He kept pouring his consciousness up into the top of his head, kept pushing until it rose over his head like a cartoon light bulb simulating ''idea'' like a cosmic *a-ha*, and even further, higher and higher and higher and higher and then he was filled with a feeling of joy and peace that flooded the whole of him which was no longer connected to any body. That was long lost, left behind, back down there, oh, hell, the thought of it brought it back and he shoved himself back into the light and started climbing again, stuff that looked like heat lightning radiating from the center of some thing, the center of at.

Then there was no at and no nothing, but a blinding white that was all and it was light and it was love and it was peace.

He had never been there before and his self freaked and grabbed hold again. His eyes opened and he sat there on the floor, tears streaming down his cheeks in a torrent that wouldn't stop. Tears of joy and sorrow, tears of love and hate, tears of peace and war, tears of everything, tears of more horsepower than he had developed the capacity to handle, but he was complete and he would prevail.

He sighed twice and toppled over in a dead faint.

Spurlock awoke the next morning lying in bed beside Megan. He stopped and remembered the light and the tears. He didn't remember anything after that, although he supposed Megan had dragged him into bed.

He still had some of that feeling of peace and love that he'd felt the night before, and he wanted to hold on to that for as long as he could before the world came and took it away.

In fact, he seemed to remember that there was something he had to do today. Oh, yeah, he had to deal with Senigliero. A bolt of fear went through him when he thought of Senigliero.

Fear, for Spurlock, was not exactly like fear to an average man, for whom fear was a stranger. For Spurlock fear was not panic. Fear was a tool. It packed his mind and body with leashed energy.

He lay on the bed beside Megan's sleeping form and felt a cold chill ripple up his back, the old chill of impending death. When the chill reached the top of his spinal column, he began to gasp for air, great racking gasps of air, jammed into his lungs with great force.

Then he was attacked by waves of sleepiness. One would hit him, then go away, leaving him wide awake. Then he would start to nod out again.

Finally that passed and his body decided to clear itself out. He was familiar with all these symptoms, from combat, from police work, but usually when they came, he was unable to take the time to actually take a crap, so he slipped from the bed and strode to the bathroom to rid his body of all waste products in one instantaneous rush.

When he emerged from the bathroom, he felt strong and clean and ready for anything. He had no assurance that he would win, and logic told him otherwise, but he was damn sure he would be bringing into this contest the very best Spurlock there was.

His only real problem was patience. He was bouncing on the balls of his feet, feeling like he would start beating his fists into his palms at any moment.

"Well, look at you," Megan said from the bed. She was smiling, but she looked at him with something very near to awe. "You look like William the Conqueror."

"William the Bastard," he said.

"Huh?"

"Before the Conquest he was known as William the Bastard. That's probably why he did it; he got tired of being called William the Bastard."

He strode to the closet and threw open the door. If he'd been just a little more wired, he'd have jerked it off its hinges. His cruddy old jeans and jacket hung next to the tux, washed and ironed. *Ironed*. Jesus! They'd never been ironed before, with creases yet. "Old Senigliero treats his victims first-class," he said, stepping into the newly spiffy jeans.

"Yeah," Megan said. She said nothing else. He knew why. She was afraid anything she said would be wrong. It probably would be, too. He was too wired.

"Probably a first-class funeral."

"That's what I was thinking," she said, "in those exact words."

He nodded. Their fear had synched them in like a psychedelic.

The door to their room opened and Spurlock jerked like he'd been plugged into an electric light socket.

"Breakfast, sir," said the white-jacketed Jamaican, who pushed a covered cart.

Spurlock shook his head in wonderment. It was one thing to be wired up to one's best, and quite another to leap in fear at the arrival of breakfast. "Thanks, just leave the cart," he said, and the words gushed out of him like a speed freak riding a heavy rush of crystal meth. It was very like that, and for that matter it felt that good, but it was not appropriate.

"Thank you, sir," the man said, and disappeared.

Megan went over to the cart and lifted the cover. "Bacon and eggs, paper-thin crepes, chilled orange juice. This may be the best breakfast you ever had."

He shook his head, whipped it back and forth, actually. "Not going to eat it," he said. "Senigliero just wants to make me heavy and slow me down. He's trying to lull me so the shock will be greater when he jumps in my stuff. You go ahead. I'm going to breathe."

"Okay," she said, and started making herself a plate.

The heavy smells of food drifted to Spurlock's nostrils. Any other time he would have been ravenous, but in his present frame of mind the food smelled heavy and greasy, totally indigestible. He sat down on the floor cross-legged, with his head against the foot of the bed. He went into a deep-breathing exercise, closed his eyes, and tried to clear his mind again. Surprisingly enough, it worked. He was out there again, almost immediately.

"Aw right, Spurlock! Off your ass."

Spurlock opened his eyes to see a gnome towering over him. He realigned his eyes and it was Frazier, although that fact did not seem particularly important then. None of this seemed particularly important. His own life, for instance, seemed no more important than Frazier's or Megan's or that of the fern in the pot by the window. Just for the form, though, he said, "Oh, hi, Frazier."

Frazier grabbed him by the collar and jerked him to his feet. "I said, off your ass."

Spurlock felt the first twinge of anger, but he didn't want to feel anger, so he sent it back and held on to the unimportance of it all. As he did so he realized that Frazier was playing a role, that he wasn't angry either, that in fact he was very sad. Frazier liked him and was sad that he was about to die, although he was willing to sacrifice Spurlock for the sake of some game of his own. The power game. Spurlock saw that Frazier was playing for Senigliero's power. It was in his eyes, in his thoughts, whatever it was. With his own wants and grabbings cleared out, Spurlock could observe everyone else's with ease, and Frazier's were written all over him.

Frazier wanted Senigliero's power so he could put the United States back like it was. If it had been important,

Spurlock would have laughed. "Well, I'm off my ass. Now what?"

"We go downstairs, all of us. Megan and the girl, too."

Spurlock nodded. "Get Leslie," he told Megan.

When she had done so, they started down the stairs, Spurlock in the lead, Frazier and his AK bringing up the rear.

Frazier directed them out the back door of the house and into the garden. He realized that had he been in another mood he would have been impressed. The garden was covered with curved glass, so that it was actually a greenhouse that would grow tropical plants all year round. The garden was ringed with them: frangipani, orchids, banana trees, bamboo clumps, rubber trees. The trees were packed with monkeys, toucans, parrots, and he wasn't sure, but he thought he saw a boa gliding through the branches. That explained the smells and sounds from the night before.

There were also rocks up to the size of boulders, two large ones flanking the stairs they descended. All in all it was a collection of jungle lore from three continents. His eyes went to the ducking stool, but it had no importance either.

The heat was junglelike as well. It must have been ninety-five or a hundred and the humidity was sweltering. None of this was any bother to Senigliero, however. He sat at his ease beside the large free-form swimming pool that served as the centerpiece for this Tarzan set. Spurlock noted that the atmosphere of realism had not carried over to the pool. The water was clear, with a faint smell of chlorine emanating from it.

Senigliero sat in a deck chair in a black lightweight jumpsuit, idly smoking a cigar and watching his omnipresent videocassette rig. As they came down the stairs, he turned it off with a remote control, which shut down the image and the sound, but not the power to the set. Spurlock had a quick glimpse of it before the set went dark—*The Barber of Seville*.

If Senigliero appeared to be comfortable, the same could not be said of the audience. They were in their gray high-necked uniforms, and the sweat poured off them freely.

There must have been fifty hoods in the garden. Senigliero had packed in an audience, apparently to demonstrate, once and for all, what a tough guy he was. Some of them looked familiar, but with the beards gone he couldn't tell for sure who were Frazier's and who weren't.

Spurlock looked at his host closely and saw that his appearance of being at ease was a complete sham. Senigliero's brow was furrowed, although his mouth was carefully composed into an easy smile. From the set of his shoulders and the angle of his back it was clear that tension ran all along his spine.

Clearly Senigliero viewed this as some sort of major battle. Spurlock couldn't tell exactly why.

That tension was written on every face in the garden. All those people, Megan and Leslie included, were girded up to witness some sort of final battle between good and evil for the control of the world. That was the way everybody acted. Spurlock was the only person there with anything to lose by it, and he was the least affected.

It was obvious that the world had no meaning, that the only meaning it had was what one gave it. And he himself gave this incident no more meaning than any other. He might be killed. No matter, he would have died sometime anyway. He might be hurt—big deal. Linda had hurt him far more than Senigliero could, and that was so long ago as to be forgotten. This was no big deal, because there were no big deals.

The tense Senigliero rose as they entered and said, "Ah, Spurlock, good of you to come." This got a low chuckle from the crowd, considering that Spurlock was being herded down at gunpoint.

Senigliero held out his hand to shake. Spurlock walked to him, but did not take his hand.

Senigliero's smile turned into a sneer. "You reject my friendship," he said.

Spurlock smiled, but not so much in humor as in appreciation of Senigliero's embarrassment. "I have never refused friendship," he said. "But you don't mean it."

Senigliero colored slightly. "We have business," he said. "I have decided to take Purgatory. Do you want a piece or not?"

Spurlock smiled a little. "Cut it out, Senigliero. I'm not going to give in. I'm not going to crack and I'm not going to crawl. Whatever you're going to do, get started."

Senigliero smiled. "Ah!" he said. "Another example of your hard-won mystical objectivity. I've researched you, mister."

Spurlock nodded. "Call it what you want."

Senigliero rose and addressed the company. "You see, our friend here is a fake. He carries a gun and talks tough, but he hasn't used his gun in years. He's all hung up on Jesus, or Buddha, or some other mystical bullshit. He has no balls."

He turned to Spurlock. "Oh, I've done my research on you, my friend. You used to be a tough guy, but you've lost what you had. You've lost it all now."

He turned back to the assembled hoods. "This man is chickenshit," he said. "He doesn't have the nerve to kill anymore." Senigliero grinned broadly. "Really," he said. "Here, I'll prove it to you. Gimme a pistol."

Senigliero held out his hand, and his chief guard, who was not the same one he had appointed in Purgatory to replace Clarence, handed him a pistol. Senigliero took it and sneered. He jacked a round into the chamber and handed it, butt first, to Spurlock.

Spurlock smiled and looked at it disinterestedly. It was a Walther PPK.

"Take it, my friend. You take this weapon and kill me and you can go free. Take it and kill me or none of you will last out the day. You will all go slowly, my friend, and you will go the slowest of all.''

Spurlock never really considered taking it. Senigliero may have done his homework, but even so he must realize that there was a very large chance that Spurlock would shoot first and ask forgiveness later.

"Go on! Take it!" Senigliero grinned. "It's the last chance you'll ever get to live."

Spurlock looked at the humor of it and laughed. His laughter flowed free and clear across the garden, and fifty cheap hoods marveled that he was unafraid. Senigliero was one of them. "Tell ya what, old buddy," Spurlock said. "If you think I won't fire, what say I do it with Frazier's AK?" Spurlock held his hand behind him for Frazier's assault rifle.

There were little beads of sweat on Senigliero's upper lip. "Don't get cute, Sp-spurlock. I didn't say any g-gun in the room, just the p-pistol."

Spurlock shook his head. "Well, I don't want to. How's about you kill me with it, or Megan, or Leslie. You can kill anybody you want to with it as long as you get them to pull the trigger. Go ahead, pull the trigger. It'll blow you halfway across the pool."

He turned to the assembled hoods. "Any you guys wanna pull the trigger?"

No one answered.

Spurlock had the initiative now. This was his moment. Senigliero's fear was out fully. In a second Senigliero would recover and it would be his moment again. He would not have proved his point, though, and he would be angry and hungry for revenge. But in that one single instant Senigliero's fear, which he had fought all his life and never truly conquered, was written plainly on his face. And for Senigliero all fear related back to one source, his father.

Last night Senigliero had given Spurlock his moment of

terror, but it had been poorly timed and had not taken hold in Spurlock. He possessed the mental discipline to throw it off.

Now this was Senigliero's moment of terror. It was his own fault really. He was so sure that a man facing the worst imaginable would crack that he was unprepared for being wrong. He was thrown off guard, and the terror that was his central force was upon him.

As for Spurlock, he was thoroughly into the moment.

The universe is a thought, which may be deduced from the fact that it has no dimensions. Its nature is such that when one is able to enter totally into any moment, one is able to mount that moment and ride it into eternity.

People who learn to live in the moment always and forever are properly worshiped as gods and sons of gods, and some who are given godlike skills, but not so grand a role, are frequently revered as saints or burned as witches.

Such moments can come to any man, but are much more likely to come to one who believes in them and actively seeks them, and they are much more likely to come to such a person at a time of need. When such a moment comes, that person perceives the entire moment whole. He sees it as one, and is one with it and everything and everybody in it. In making himself one with the One he becomes the whole of it. He has made himself and his will one with the order of the universe.

In those moments sometimes the sick are cured and the dead raised. Sometimes people walk on water, others on fire. Sometimes the moment calls for great personal sacrifice and one can be crucified or burned as a witch, but sometimes the moment calls for the exercise of some of the powers that witches get burned for.

Spurlock perceived that at this moment he had the power to reject the cluster of ugly feelings that had come together in the form of Senigliero, and to return them to the void. This power has appeared many times in many moments in history, and it scares people to death. In this culture it is sometimes called the evil eye. Spurlock did it by turning Senigliero's own feelings back on him, full force.

At a time when Senigliero was prepared only to receive capitulation, he saw in Spurlock the features of his own adored and hated father, set in an expression of total rejection, with the clear white light of judgment shining in the left eye.

The bone structure was there, his own resemblance to Senigliero's fear already close. That's why Senigliero hated him so. All it took was a cant of the head, a slope of the shoulders, a narrowing of the eyes, a quirk of the mouth. Spurlock didn't think about it. He didn't even know what he was doing, except to feel Senigliero's fear and show it back to him.

Megan gasped. "Amadeo Senigliero!"

That did it. Senigliero turned ash white. Spurlock took a half step toward him, and as he did so DeWitt and Kathy's crucifix tumbled out of his shirt, hanging on the chain around his neck, caught the light, and flashed across Senigliero's face.

"Oh God! . . . Father!" Senigliero gasped, and fainted, tumbling back against the table with the TV on it. He, the table, the TV, all crashed into the pool at the same time, the power to the TV going through the water for an instant, before the flash, sputter, and smoke, the explosion of the picture tube, and the odor of burning electricity. Then that was over and Senigliero's body floated face-down in the water.

"Jesus!" somebody said.

There was the heavy sound of the bolt on an automatic weapon being drawn back behind him, and Spurlock thought, at least it's going to be quick.

But there was only the sound of Frazier's voice, commanding, "Aw right! Don't nobody move!"

Frazier moved to the right so he could cover everybody

with his AK. Senigliero had blown his moment, then Spurlock had had his, and now it was Frazier's.

"Top!" he bellowed. "Take five men and take over the comm center."

One of the hoods in gray started moving. Then Spurlock recognized Frazier's old first sergeant. The topkicker grabbed five of Frazier's men and took off up the stairs.

Next Frazier directed that all Senigliero's men be disarmed and locked up. In an instant the garden was transformed as pistols came out from under uniform tunics and dropped to the floor.

As soon as that was started Frazier turned to Spurlock and said, "Frank, I'm takin' this outfit over. You want a piece of it?"

Spurlock shook his head no.

"Okay, listen. I'm going to be busy for a while. Take your ladies back upstairs and I'll be along in a couple of hours." He glanced at his watch. "Yeah, it'll take at least that long to get things started."

Spurlock nodded. Suddenly he was very tired. He started up the stairs with Megan at his side and Leslie a little bit behind.

CHAPTER SIXTEEN

FORTUNATELY THE breakfast was still upstairs, not quite cold, and Spurlock ate all of it, every last morsel, standing beside the cart and shoving food into his mouth.

A couple of times Leslie started to ask him what he had done, but it was so weird to her that she had a hard time phrasing the question. Finally she said, "What did you do to that man?"

Spurlock shrugged. He didn't know how to explain it either. He reached out and scooped her to him with one arm and scooped Megan to him with the other, trying not to get his greasy hands on their clothes. "Honey," he said, "I didn't do anything to him. He did it all himself."

She squeezed him around the waist. "I saw it," she said. "You scared him to death."

He shook his head. "Nope, he was a bad man, and God struck him dead. You mustn't confuse the light with the bulb."

That seemed to satisfy them, and he kicked off his boots and collapsed on the bed to sleep for five solid hours.

* * *

As it happened, it was three days before Frazier got back to them. Spurlock didn't mind. He and Megan made love on the big bed. He spent hours getting to know his daughter. She disappeared for long hours with her friend in the kitchen. Spurlock browsed around in Senigliero's excellent library, which was light on mysticism and law enforcement, Spurlock's major interests, but heavy on history and political science. He found plenty to amuse himself with.

There was, of course, some danger that Frazier would take the first opportunity to settle old scores, but their best chance was to wait, not run, so he waited. He didn't think it ever occurred to Megan or Leslie to worry that they might still be in danger, so he didn't bring it up, but it was definitely a consideration.

Finally, some eighty hours after Frazier had said he would come to see them, the Jamaican majordomo came up and said, "Sheriff, General Frazier wishes to see you in his office."

Spurlock looked up from *The Rise and Fall of the Third Reich*, grinning at Frazier's assumption of rank. It looked like the Maf was about to undergo a massive reorganization. He put down the book and followed the majordomo downstairs and into a back section of the house that he had never been in before. Glancing in the doors as he walked down the hall, he saw men in uniforms, some gray Maf jobs, but others in clean, bleached-out army fatigues, poring over papers or looking at arcane symbols superimposed over acetate maps.

Apparently Frazier's guerrillas were the new head honchos of organized crime in the United States.

Frazier's office was the last on the left. The majordomo knocked.

"Yeah?" Frazier snarled.

Spurlock walked in unannounced. He took the room in at a glance. Frazier sat at his desk, a huge mahogany number, back in his almost-bleached-white fatigues, no insignia on the collar, a ranger beret down low over his nose. The flag of the United States stood on a staff behind him, but there was no red general's flag with white stars on it.

"Hey, General," Spurlock said with a grin as he entered the room, "where's your flag?"

Frazier returned the grin sheepishly. "I can't figure how many stars to put on it," he said. "Five might be a little presumptuous, do you think?"

Spurlock laughed. "Yeah, you probably oughta wait a little while for five stars. I mean, George Washington never had more than two."

That took Frazier aback for a moment. He had obviously been planning on at least four, and George Washington was his hero. He shook his head. "Got to have at least four," he said. "I can't let some quisling dickhead in Washington outrank me."

Still grinning sardonically, Spurlock flopped into a chair in front of the desk and propped his old shitkickers up on the brand-new general's desk. "I'll have to leave those kinds of high-level decisions to you, General. But how about gettin' me and my family back to Arkansas?"

Frazier shook his head. "Look, I need your help. I got all the power in the world, and nobody to help me run it but a bunch of trigger-happy old rangers and Senigliero's goons. You're the only man here I can trust who has enough brains to pour piss out of a boot."

Frazier got up and strode to a red curtain that ran along one wall of his office. "Looka here," he said. "This ain't no jive undertaking we're involved in here." He snatched the curtain back to reveal a map of the United States that covered almost the entire wall.

"Now this overlay here," he said, pulling down a sheet of acetate with various boundaries marked off in colored tape and grease pencil, "shows the regional organization for the Mafia in the United States. There are eleven regions with headquarters in Boston, New York, Washington, Miami . . .'' He went on clicking off the regional headquarters. "Now, what I've pulled off here amounts to a *coup d'état* in a feudal empire. And that means the barons and dukes don't just necessarily want to get in line.'' He paced in front of his map, tapping it with his swagger stick to emphasize points.

"Okay, my first order of business has been to consolidate my control on this headquarters here. I got one of my Gs paired up with every one of Senigliero's top hoods. He don't eat, he don't sleep, he don't shit without one of my Gs is right there with an automatic weapon. Now, obviously we can't keep that up forever, but once I get my control consolidated, I won't have to. In the meantime they've been real cooperative. So far, with their help, we've been able to consolidate control pretty solid up and down the eastern seaboard by buying a few people and arranging untimely accidents for a few others. Only places we're not in charge on the eastern seaboard is the Bronx and northern New England.''

Spurlock shook his head. "That won't get it,'' he said. "The rest of the Mafia will combine against you and throw your ass out.''

Frazier nodded. "You ain't just a-whistlin' Dixie they will,'' he replied. "But''—he whipped down another overlay, superimposed over the first—"this overlay here shows the location of most of the guerrilla bands in the U.S.''

The overlay was a riot of green grease pencil, mostly in the mountains and rough terrain areas, but a surprising amount in the cities as well. Spurlock noted an entry for the Izods.

"Now, the Gs are hungry. They been living off the land for years. Most of them are hot to get in on my deal, for some radios, a lot of ammo, and a few discreet promotions. With these guys we can completely disrupt any dissident Maf operations in about half the places where the

Maf guys don't want to play. That way we got two thirds
of the country either with us or off guard. So we got a
chance, babe, but it's gonna be nip and tuck, and I need
help.''

Spurlock shook his head. "Not me, pal. For one thing
the best you can hope for is to become a military dictator,
and I don't see any advantage to the country in that. For
another I figure that by about next Thursday we'd have
disagreed on something and you'd have to have me killed,
and for thirds, all I want is to go back to Arkansas and be
left alone. You reckon you can arrange that?''

Frazier thought a minute. "Yeah!" he said. "You're
probably right, and after what I saw you do to Senigliero I
wouldn't screw around with your act for love nor money.
Go back to Purgatory. Run the county any way you like.
I'll see that nobody gets in your way.''

Spurlock nodded. "Okay," he said. "If you can loan
me a car or something, I'll be on my way first thing in the
morning.''

Frazier looked up startled. "Car or something, my ass!
I'll have y'all flown back in Senigliero's—uh, my—jet.
You'll take off from Newark Airport tomorrow morning
and land in Fayetteville four hours later. An' I'll have a
convoy waitin' to take you home from there. This is a
first-class operation.''

Spurlock nodded. "It don't get no better than that," he
said.

The next morning found Spurlock dressed in his freshly
washed and ironed, but at his request, creaseless, blue
jeans, rolling a fresh toothpick into the corner of his
mouth, hat on the back of his head, feet steppin' right out
in his old shitkickers. Frazier offered to lay some Colom-
bian on him, but he figured if he could control his own
mood when somebody was about to kill him, he ought to
be able to do it for a trip to the airport. Maybe he'd smoke
again and maybe he wouldn't, but he didn't want to now.

Megan and Leslie were right beside him. Leslie was solemn-faced, starry-eyed, only ten minutes before having been torn from the embrace of the kitchen boy, whom Spurlock disliked at first sight. He couldn't say precisely why. He didn't like his lousy crew cut, but they all had that. He had a sneaky look. Ah, well, they were leaving him behind now.

They trooped downstairs and into the main hallway. The majordomo, in his white jacket, came bustling out from the dining room as they came downstairs. "Are you ready, sir?" he asked.

"Yeah!" Spurlock said, "except that I'd like to say good-bye to Frazier." He was quite sure that Frazier would be too tied up. Embarking on a course of world conquest seemed to be eating up his free time.

"General Frazier will be up in a minute, sir."

Indeed, Spurlock could hear his voice coming up the stairs now, with his old first sergeant beside him. As they topped the stairs, Frazier jabbed his finger into the belly of the man, who had taken off his stripes and now wore the eagles of a full colonel. "Colonel!" Frazier said, jabbing with his finger. "You tell that fucking comm officer that if I don't have a radio in the hands of, and commo established with, every guerrilla band in New England by the first of next month that his ass is grass. You understand? He'll be in the fucking Bronx with a full field pack and a steel hat. Y'understand!"

"Yessir!" the colonel said, and all but clicked his heels. He clattered down the stairs again.

Spurlock stood taking all this in with his hands on his hips. It looked like a lot of fun, and if Spurlock didn't think the whole enterprise was doomed to failure and disappointment, at the cost of a lot of lives, he'd have jumped right in the middle of it.

"You about ready to hit the road, Spurlock?" Frazier asked, stepping forward. He kind of reminded Spurlock of

Raúl Castro, with the long hair and beard and the black beret with four stars and master parachutist badge pinned to it. Sort of a cross between Raúl Castro and Leon Russell.

"Yeah, we just wanted to say good-bye."

"Yeah, yeah! Right, right, right!" Frazier said, snapping his fingers a little and jiggling on the balls of his feet. "Listen, my car's right outside. Take you right to Newark Airport. Jet'll fly your ass right home. How's that, eh?"

Spurlock grinned. He thought it was funny that Frazier was trying to impress him. "That's really impressive," Spurlock said.

Frazier blinked. He led the way to the door and down the handsome flagstone steps to the waiting Mercedes. A guard in guerrilla uniform with an AK slung on his shoulder jerked open the door.

They both stuck out their hands and shook. "Keep your ass down," they both said simultaneously, and laughed.

Spurlock shepherded his ladies into the back of the limousine and got in after them. The guard slammed the door and got into the front seat, propping his AK up between him and the driver. Spurlock waved to Frazier, already bustling back up the stairs.

The drive was uneventful, the forested countryside broken up with slag-heap cities. Spurlock rustled in the record box. "Lord!" he exclaimed. "John Mayall! *Blues from Laurel Canyon!*" he crowed, holding up a compact disc.

"Who's John Mayall?" Leslie inquired.

"Plays blues," Spurlock explained.

"Is he good?"

Spurlock reached back and scratched his head, looking for a way to explain John Mayall's music.

It occurred to him that he didn't need to describe it and he put the CD into the machine, filling the car with raunchy blues.

He leaned back and watched the odd foliage drift by outside, mind soothed by Mayall's harp. He felt almost embarrassingly luxurious.

As the New York skyline loomed on the horizon, a persistent low whistling whine in the background turned into a full-throated roar that shook the car and almost shattered their eardrums. They were just across the river from the Bronx, and Spurlock looked up to see a flight of four ancient F-4Ds flying in such perfect formation that they all seemed to be models suspended along the same wire. Their insignia was a white circle with a black hand on it.

Spurlock tapped on the glass. The guard pressed a button and it hummed down. "What was that?" Spurlock inquired.

The jets banked over the horizon, keeping their perfect formation, and turned. "The Maf guy in the Bronx don't wanna join," the guard said.

At that point the F-4s released two big black bombs each, which tumbled end over end like eight toys and hit into the slag-heap city, bursting into huge orange and black balls that smoked up a third of the horizon. The explosions shook the car.

Spurlock shut the window of the limo and leaned back in his seat. Then he reached forward and turned the music back up, muttering.

"What?" demanded Megan.

"Yeah, what?" echoed Leslie.

"I said, 'We live in interesting times.' "